The Rooted and the Winged

SAMANTHA CURRAN

Windweaver Press

Book Cover: Samantha Curran

Interior Artwork and Illustrations: Samantha Curran

Editor: Rachelle from R. A. Wright Editing

Formatter: Cassie Weaver of Weaver Way Author Services

Published by Windweaver Press

samantha@windweaverpress.com

ISBN: 979-8-9924249-0-4

For all the trees of the earth.
And us humans who live beneath their branches.

Pool of Divination

Esen & Tristans'
Homeland

Queen's dam

River Fae

Rath Siaorí

River If rath

Fafnir's Home

Isolde's Home

Mountain Fae

Sea Fae

N
W   E
S

The Land of
**The Rooted
and
the Winged**

⊞ Esen and fafnir's Journey

Around the circular emblem:

AT AGE ONE HUNDRED, A FAERIE SHALL UNITE WITH A DRYAD, AND SO GIVE THEIR IMMORTALITY

AT AGE THREE HUNDRED, A DRYAD SHALL ROOT INTO THE EARTH, AND SO GIVE THEIR WALK

Center:

FOR THE

FOREST

TO

SURVIVE,

WE MUST

UNITE

The Ancient Law

written on the third day of Creation

CHAPTER 1: THE FLOOD

Fafnir bolted forward, his breath ragged. The world flashed white. A terrible crack of thunder followed, like the sky splitting in two.

Like the world ending.

The wind screamed in his ears. He ducked as it hurled a twig as large as himself over his head. The grasses writhed like snakes, striking the breath from his chest, stinging his hands. Rain drops crashed over his head.

Ahead, the body of a fallen hawthorn towered above him. Dragans clustered around it, devouring the trunk, their shifting eyes black wells of sorrow. Gritting his teeth, Fafnir leaped and caught hold of the fissures in the bark. The wet, rotting wood—wood that had once held a body pulsing with life—crumbled beneath his fingers. He climbed hurriedly, swung onto the top of the trunk, and dropped down on the other side.

Cold mud splashed in his face. Up to his chest in it, he pushed on, holding his chin high, until he stumbled out onto a crest just above the bank of the river.

His ears drew back.

It was as he'd feared.

The River Ifrati was white with froth, roaring like a stampede of deer. It had burst its banks by fourteen and a half martens and counting. Almost double its usual width. He had never seen it so—

A frenzy of sound intensified to his right. Turning, he paled.

A massive wave crashed down the bank, headed straight for him.

Breath hitching, Fafnir scrambled up the crest, grasping at blades of grass. His feet slipped and slid in the mud.

Rot.

He toppled. Water struck his back, and he fell into its depths.

Noise. All was noise, frenzied and chaotic. He clawed at the depths, but they beat back against him. His arms jerked over his head, a fire of agony seizing his joints as the water pulled and pulled.

He bit the inside of his mouth, the taste of copper competing with muddy water.

Then he was falling, sinking. The waters folded softly around him, cradling his form as they pulled him down into their depths.

No.

He couldn't die. Not now; not like this. He was a faerie, with immortal blood surging in his veins.

He *must* live.

He tried to move his limbs, but they were heavy, as though the entire ocean pressed upon them. The roar of the tides sounded from above...he had sunk far, far down. The waters churned around his ears, whispering. Spots of black fogged his vision.

His back collided with a hard surface, and water rushed by him, but now, he was going *up*, not down. The pressure in his chest lightened, the blackness fading.

It was a miracle. It was—

Light dazzled his eyes as he burst out of the water. A large brown face looked back at him, eclipsed by the sun.

A dryad.

He was in her hands, draped across her cupped palms, her long, slender fingers forming a wall between him and the river.

His stomach flipped. Turning over, he crawled forward and retched up a lungful of water over the side of her hands.

"You are alive." Her voice lilted like the murmuring of a stream, saturated with relief. "Hold on. I will put you down."

Her palms tilted inwards, encasing him within as she lowered him to the ground. As her fingers flowered open, he stepped out.

"*Aeonida*, good faerie. My name is Esen. What is yours?"

Eyes the color of the summer sun looked back at him. Her face was round, the distance from her chin to her forehead the same as his entire height. The forest must look so different to her, from so high up.

Her acorn-brown bark was smooth with youth. Shiny green hazel leaves curled around her head, sprouting from her branches and in shoots off her shoulders. Likely, she had only just recently left the roots of her parents and begun to Walk the earth. Behind the kindness in her eyes, a deep sorrow looked back at him.

Fafnir stepped back, his chest constricting.

He had been rescued from death by a being who would soon die, all because he had dared to change the Ancient Law...

He had dared to try to be free.

He bowed slightly to the dryad. "I-I thank you, Esen."

She frowned at him, tilting her head.

His fault.

This was all his fault.

Spinning on his heels, he walked away. He soon found himself running, splashing through puddles of mud.

The rain had stopped. Suckling sounds surrounded him—the sounds of the soil pulling the water into itself.

It had been a thousand years since he changed the law. All that time spent trying to perfect himself, to mend the pain, to reach new heights of discipline...

It had all been a lie.

The forest had been dying around him all that time.

A bramble snagged him in the chest, and he tumbled headlong into a clump of ferns. Cursing, he struggled upright; his head pounded and pounded.

This time, the forest had survived, but only because enough Rooted Ones remained to pull the water up through their roots. But if the faeries continued to refuse the dryads and leave them to die off entirely...

When another flood came, the entire forest would be destroyed.

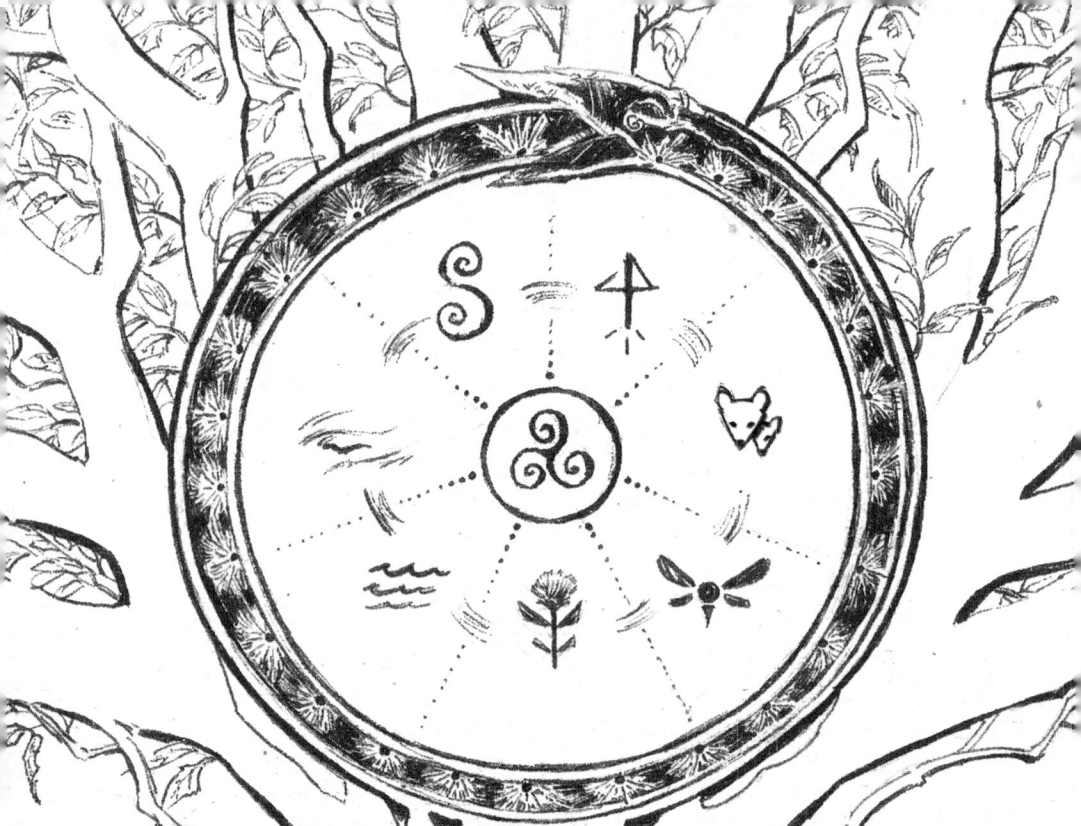

Cycle of Giving

The beating heart of the forest, designed by the Mother herself. When each creature gives beyond itself in the way it is called to, the cycle continues.

The Land of the Mother Wind

and the forest lives on. The cycle begins with the faeries Uniting, continues when the dryads Root, a mother marten shelters her kits, and on...

3

CHAPTER 2: THE SORROW OF THE FOREST

"That branch is caught," Tristan called. "Move the alder aside."

Esen nodded and bent back the tender young branch of the alder. The leaves at the tips of the branches sprouting from Esen's head and shoulders rustled with the movement. Tristan pulled at the broken frame of the hawthorn, his leaves rustling too, until it untangled from the alder's branches, then Esen helped him heave the body aside with a crash. The limbs of the alder lifted at once, relieved of the burden.

Esen lay a hand on the alder's thin frame and murmured the ancient word of blessing: "*Aeonida*. May the Wind guide and keep you."

The round, serrated leaves of the alder rustled, forming a medley of speech in Wind-Speak—the language the Rooted Ones used to communicate with Walkers and fae. "*Aeonida. Thank you both. You have saved my life.*"

Esen bowed to the alder. "I am glad," she said.

A magpie chirped a merry tune. Gold light flickered upon the fresh spring leaves of the Rooted Ones around them. She dropped her gaze to the fallen hawthorn they had lifted. His full green crown was already wilting, the edges of the leaves turning brown. Serpent-like forms with open mouths wove within the grooves of his broken trunk.

Dragans. The mediators of death. Along with the fungi and insects, dragans ate away at lifeless bodies. No one knew where the dragans came from, or where they went after the body decayed. Esen's mother and father believed they were the visible sign of the Mother Wind taking back her spirit from the dead. They must be right, for the dragans appeared most visibly in the lifeless forms of the dryads and faeries, the beings who received the most of the Mother Wind's spirit. Only faint glimpses of dragans could be seen on fallen animals, insects, and plants.

Already, the dragans were consuming the hawthorn's trunk. Soon it would decay into the earth below, with no trace that he had ever lived. Terror writhed in the dragans' hollow eyes, reflecting the last emotion the hawthorn had felt before he died. Esen wiped away her tears.

She thought of the strange faerie she had rescued from death just that morning. If she had not saved him, his body would be lying somewhere, broken like this hawthorn, with dragans feeding on his flesh.

There had been a terrible fear in his eyes as he'd looked at her...as though something about her made him afraid. Why had he fled so quickly, without even giving her his name?

A gnarled hand rested on her shoulder, the fingernails extending into black, dagger-like thorns. A trait unique to Tristan, as a blackthorn dryad. He stood beside her, a somber look in his storm-gray eyes. A cut marked his cheek, jutting across the smooth dark-gray bark.

A branch must have scraped him.

"Tristan, you need to be careful."

He pressed his lips. "That's nothing. We need to keep looking, Esen. There are many Rooted Ones in need of our aid."

"Yes," said Esen. "I am sorry. I... I never knew how truly beautiful the forest was before. I also had no idea how many of our kind are perishing; how much the lives of the forest are suffering. This flood has only made it worse."

A black look flashed in Tristan's eyes. "Yes," he snapped. "It would be shocking for a new Walker. You've been sheltered all your life."

He strode away from her. She hurried after him, struggling to match his long, forceful strides.

"Tristan, I did not mean to upset you."

"I know," he said, without looking at her.

"Where are you going?"

"To the next dryad in need of help. I cannot stand your idle talk."

Esen flinched, then rubbed at a hazelnut ripening near her ear. She followed him until he halted in front of a juniper. A large oak branch had fallen on top of the juniper, bending her frame. Esen rushed to help Tristan lift the branch. They let it drop in the grass.

"Tristan." She knew he was angry, but she yearned to understand. "Why are the faeries neglecting us and allowing this to happen? Can't they see the forest falling around them? Why don't they care?"

Tristan ran a hand over his face. "Did Ian and your parents tell you nothing?"

"I know the faeries aren't Uniting with us because they want to keep their immortality, but I don't understand. What can they do with an eternity that they can't do in a thousand or so years with a dryad?"

Tristan moved to the next Rooted One, untangling branches with a grunt. Esen stepped in to help him.

At last, Tristan said, "They don't think of it like that. If they don't Unite, they remain at the height of their youth forever, and infertile, like us before we Unite. So they can sleep around and live until the end of time unless physically killed. Sounds like a pretty good life, right?"

Esen paused, flinching as the branch she held scratched against the soft bark on her face. "I never knew that."

"They only United with us before because the Ancient Law forced them to. They never cared for us."

"That can't be true. I heard that the faeries used to Unite with us out of the gladness of their hearts. Our cultures were one, entwined. And what of Ian and Niamh? They came here of their own desire."

Tristan pried the last of the branches free and stared at Esen, his jaw working. "Don't speak of Niamh. You know nothing."

"What do you mean?"

Silence stretched between them.

Esen's shoulders tightened, her leaves stirring. "I am trying to understand what's going on. I am afraid the forest will collapse around us and we will all die. I am trying to have faith. To believe the Mother Wind will help us, somehow."

She lifted a hand and tilted her fingers as a small breath of wind ghosted through them. "I can feel the wind at her back, the tendrils of her hair in flight. But I don't feel her presence."

Tristan began to stride forward again. Esen matched his pace once

7

more. "Go talk to Ian and your parents about the Mother. They will tell you what you want to hear."

"They say what is true." When he didn't speak, she added, "What do you say, then?"

"The Mother will do nothing. She does not care for the land she created."

"How can you say that? Do you know nothing about her? All the tales say she is true and kind, always roaming the land, breathing upon it."

Tristan ground his heels into the earth. "You said you cannot feel her. I don't either."

"No. I have been fraught with fear. I am not seeking her as I should."

He reeled back. "Then go look for her, and leave me alone."

"Tristan…"

Pain burned beneath the anger in his eyes—the same pain in her. "You say talk is foolish," she said. "But what can we do to stop this?"

Tristan drew close to her, a storm raging in his eyes. She stepped back, her pulse quickening.

"I don't know," he said, swallowing heavy. "Something other than sitting around, waiting to die."

Spinning on his heel, he stormed off, then called back over his shoulder. "I'm going to keep helping. Follow me if you wish to be useful."

Esen faltered, swaying the crown of leaves upon her head as hurt and shame burned in her chest. He disappeared within the shadows of the Rooted Ones. She stepped forward, thinking to go after him, but stopped.

She was afraid of him. Her best friend.

Before the flood, just last moon, they had gone out on an adventure. He had come running to her as soon as he heard she had broken free of her Root Tie to her parents. She remembered the firmness of his hand as he'd clasped it in her own, delight gleaming in his eyes.

Grinning, he had said, "One day, we will make change together. For now, let me show you the world."

He had brought her to a place where white foaming waters crashed down into the river below. The Ifrati Falls. How the water sparkled in the light. It had made her laugh, the most amazing thing she had ever seen. But as they were heading to the next place, which Tristan kept

8

secret despite her begging, the storm had begun. Rain pounded upon them until the river broke its banks and tore through the forest.

The Rooted Ones issued desperate pleas for help, and Esen found herself toiling with Tristan to save them, all the joy sucked from his eyes.

Later, he might soften and show her his next secret wonder. But how could she hope for such happy things when all the forest was dying?

Esen turned and began walking in the other direction.

She would help as many more Rooted Ones as she could, alone.

ESEN WALKED through the dappled light of the summer forest, her weary limbs tingling with the heat of the sun's rays. The birds trilled overhead, and a fat bee followed her for a time, buzzing a melody. Glimpsing a deer treading on silent hooves through the blue shade, she nodded to him. He nodded back, white antlers bowing, then darted off into the thickets.

Over a moon had passed since the flood. At last, she had tended to her and Tristan's section of the forest and was circling back homewards. Her spirit ached to be with her family.

Amid the birdsong, a river flowed, the sound like laughter to her ears.

She emerged from the cover of the Rooted Ones. It was the River Ifrati—the same river from whence she had rescued the faerie farther downstream. It stretched even wider here, the other bank over a league or so away. White sunlight danced off the waters in flickering shimmers like stars.

A series of crashes and the tear of splitting wood sounded upriver. Her breath quickening, she looked to see the long, dragging limb of a fallen oak dryad emerge from the cover of the Rooted Ones. A vast network of ropes was tied around it, and following it appeared many faeries mounted on pine martens. The faeries pulled on the cords, dragging the limb toward the water. Already, a pile of limbs lay over the top of the falls, where several more faeries worked with clever hands to arrange them in a tight networking pattern up against the rocks.

They were clogging up the flow of the river.

With the bodies of her kind.

She ground her teeth, the wood scraping. It was normal for the fae to use lifeless wood for their own needs, but to use freshly slain dryads — who had died because of the faeries' selfishness — to try to save their own lives…

Then they knew the dangers of their actions. They knew that without the dryads, the forest would not go on. But instead of changing their ways to restore the forest, they were covering up the problem with a spiderweb solution — thin, bound to snap.

And the poor river. Its laughter, its bubbling glee, would be silenced.

She almost stepped out but pulled herself back at the last moment.

What could she do? They wouldn't listen to her.

She walked on, following the river in the direction of her home. For a time, she buried her fears in the water's gentle melody, hearing only its song and the calls of the birds above.

Up ahead, the river dropped down, and fell laughing among a bed of stones. Walls surrounded the gully, sheltering the river within its own private space. As Esen approached the stone, she began to make out strange fissures, trailing lines carved over the surface…

Her eyes widened.

They were dryadic symbols.

She hurried forward and stood before the stone, her brow furrowed. Like the structure of a Rooted One, the sequence always began at the bottom and rose up. Stooping, she peered through the blue shade at the base of the rock, tracing her fingers along the form of the carving.

At the very bottom was the symbol for *faerie*, enveloped within a larger symbol representing *dryad*. The Union of Stór.

The stone was cool beneath her fingers. She dropped her hand, rubbing the opening in her chest where the wood gaped open. Inside was a tiny faerie-sized chamber — her heart chamber — where one day, a faerie might lie down atop the decaying leaf matter and sleep, then wake United with her, with wings of hazel, as a Winged One.

She wiped a tear from her eye, then traced higher. *Walker*. The symbol signified a Walker in the act of Rooting forever to the earth…

She traced on, rising to her feet, the imagery shimmering in her mind.

Marten—a pine marten sheltering her kits.

Bee—a worker bee dying for her queen.

Seeds falling from goldenrod in autumn.

The river pouring into the ocean.

And last of all…

She wobbled on the arches of her feet and felt above her.

The Mother Wind, her face shrouded in sorrow as she left her father—the Wind of Worlds—to breathe life into the land.

Esen lowered her heels. "The Cycle of Giving," she murmured.

Shutting her eyes, she pressed herself against the cool stone, breathing slow.

"But now… it is broken…"

A soft wind drifted by her, caressing the leaves growing near her cheek. "Oh Mother. I do not know if you can hear me, but…" She wiped at her eyes and sank to her knees. "I am so afraid. My parents say the forest was once an unbroken canopy across the land, as far as eyes can see. They say the air had sung with rustling leaves and green dappled light. But now, there are so many gaps, and fallen ones, their bodies lying broken on the ground. And I can do nothing to stop it. I feel so useless…"

A shudder broke over her. The scent of rosemary ghosted on the wind as it murmured around her. She stilled, trying to make out words, but could discern nothing. Soon, the breeze passed, leaving her in stillness.

Tristan's parting words echoed in her mind.

"I don't want to wait around to die," she whispered.

Once, when the Ancient Law was first revoked, all the Walkers of the land had come to the Rath Síoraí—the palace of the fae—to speak against the injustice. There had been thousands of Walkers then, a sea of swaying faces and leaves by the door. The Faerie Queen sent them all away without a hearing—denied without ever having spoken.

Now they had grown quiet once more, their voices stilled. What if they tried again? The danger of revoking the law had not been evident then. It was now.

But what if the queen simply sent them away again? What if, like Tristan said, she and the rest of the fae didn't care?

She pressed her lips tight, thinking of the dam. Her leaves rustled together in a moan. The blue shadows softened to a dull gray, the yellow sunlight fading. She looked up to see a haze had gathered over the blue sky.

She ached for her home.

Esen picked herself off the ground, shook her stiff limbs and, with a final lingering glance at the carvings, turned and walked on.

IN HALF A MOON'S CYCLE, she made it home at last. The sun was setting, draining the land of its color, as she rounded the hill to her home. She glimpsed the forms of her parents, Rooted together at the top of the hill. The lithe, winding trunk of her mother wrapped around the smooth green trunk of her father. His trunk pressed the slightest bit closer to her mother than when she had seen them last. Every summer, he used the strength of the sun to grow a little closer to her, and her to him.

Their leaves glinted with the last golden rays before nightfall.

"Mother," Esen said, darting forward. "Father."

She slowed. A figure the size of a faerie swayed in the shade of her parents' crown of leaves. It wasn't Ian, or Niamh…

She gasped, her breath in her throat.

"Aisling."

Her little sister. She had come up from the earth.

Her sister's body was made of smooth, pale-green bark. Her trunk extended up from the ground, twisting toward the base into roots that dove below the soil. Only a few shoots sprouted from above her head and along her fingertips. Her blue-green leaves had a faint sheen, with yellow veins and spikes along the edges. Their tips were brown and frayed.

She was a holly dryad, like their father. And terribly weak.

Aisling turned as she approached. Tiny eyes the bright blue of a robin's egg opened and gleamed at her, like little stars in a clouded sky.

"Sister, what happened?" Esen said. "You've sprouted very early."

"I was starving." A smile glowed over her face. "*Aeonida*, sister."

Her parents stirred their boughs. The music of their voices, tinged with pain, filled the space around her.

"*For three days after the flood, the water lingered in the earth. Aisling dear has scarcely formed her roots. The water choked the soil, nearly suffocating her. We poured all the strength we could spare into her —*"

"Why didn't you tell me?" Esen cried. "I would have run home on wings."

She could have come home and found her sister dead without ever having seen her.

"*Esen.*" A sternness came into her mother's leaves.

"How could you let her come up like this?" Esen asked, her voice cracking. "It is late in the Mead Moon. Winter's breath is already approaching. You didn't give her enough strength. And what about Ian —"

Esen faltered, blowing out air. She was sounding like Tristan. She knew they had all done everything they could for her. Her shoulders shook. The pressure that had been building in her since the flood broke, and she wept.

"Esen," Aisling whispered.

Her father's voice washed over her. "*Esen, you were far away for two moons, tending to the lives of many. We have done everything we can for her. We didn't wish you to worry.*"

Esen's tears stilled, but the heat of them remained. "I know."

Aisling was smiling up at her, her mouth twitching. Esen laid herself flat on the ground, face to face with her. She wrapped her arms around her.

"*Aeonida*, sister," Esen said. "I am so glad you are here."

A soft flapping reached her ears. Esen pulled back from Aisling to see Ian drifting down toward them, flapping the hazel leaves on his back. An armful of earthworms wriggled against his chest, staining his dark-green leather tunic brown. His daughter, Niamh, landed beside him, folding in her round, spiny blackthorn wings. She carried an armful of worms too, her white face pinched with discomfort. Bits of leaf and bur poked out of her rose-gold hair, which was braided all the way down to her ankles. Her flaxen blouse and skirts looked even more ragged than usual.

"Esen," Ian said, struggling to keep the worms from escaping. "You have returned."

He staggered up to Aisling and let the worms drop. Their pink bodies tangled into each other, snaking along the dirt until they burrowed within. Niamh followed, scowling as a worm slapped her in the face. She hurled her worms down.

Aisling giggled, stooping to watch the last of the worms disappear. "They're tickling me."

"It will help her soil," Ian said, turning to Esen. His spring-green skin looked almost gray in the fading light, and his blue eyes were clouded. "They will help drain the last of the floodwater and create tunnels for her roots to grow and breathe. She was just beneath the surface when that storm happened. She was immersed in water for three days, losing her breath, and starving…"

He choked and wiped tears from his face.

Esen knitted her brow, swallowing a surge of anger. Aisling was innocent, yet already, she had suffered so much.

It must have been terrifying for her.

Esen turned back to Ian. "What will we do when winter comes?"

"We will do all we can," Ian said. "She is not alone; your parents told me this has happened to other Rootlings in the land. They are speaking with all the Rooted Ones in the Root Web, gathering wisdom. I know already we must keep her warm, above all else."

Esen nodded, looking at her sister, whose head was tilted up toward the sky, her jaw hanging open. She was in awe of the world. Despite everything.

Her sister was finally here, above the earth. She had spent the past year since Aisling's birth dreaming of this day, eager to play with her, laugh together, and plan all the wonderful places they would go when Aisling finally Walked beside her.

Naively, Esen had thought the forest would look as it had in the days

14

of the Ancient Law, like in the stories her parents told. She knew better now. She had Walked, and seen the pain of the forest firsthand. Unless something changed, Aisling would only ever know a world of suffering.

It was so unfair.

"Ian," she said, turning to him. "Do any fairies still Unite with us? Tristan said they do not care for us."

Ian's brow furrowed. "I wouldn't take everything Tristan says for truth. There are some faeries who still Unite and become Winged Ones —about a hundred a year—and the Winged Ones give their children to the dryads when they turn of age. But it is not enough. Most dryads are still without a faerie."

A leaf caught on Aisling's face. She puffed her cheeks and blew it off, laughing.

"Is there any hope?" Esen whispered.

Ian's face softened. He lay a hand on her knee. "I don't know. But the Mother Wind is always with us. She severed her tie to her father to create this land for us. She still breathes upon the land, giving life to her creatures. I can't imagine she would let it be destroyed."

A wind brushed in her ear—no words, but a feeling of warmth and assurance.

She wanted to believe that, with all her spirit. It had to be true.

It *had* to be.

So Aisling could live a long, happy life.

"Let us hope," she murmured.

BY THE FAERIE QUEEN

THE NEW LAW

From this day hence, all fae are free to choose whether they wish to Unite with the dryads. Those who wish to Unite may, but those who do not wish to, are free to live as the wind takes them, for all of eternity.

So we may know the birthright that was always ours.

Queen Maeve Finvarra

Stewart Angus Madoc

Palace Diviner Eama Atus

Declared at the Rath Siaori,
the seventh of the Blood Moon,
by Queen Maeve Finvarra

CHAPTER 3: FOR MY BELOVED SON

Fafnir staggered back from his writing desk as the memory seized him by the throat.

He could still hear the maddening roars of the crowd, see the delight in the queen's black eyes as she stood on the steps of the Rath, the final words of the speech hanging triumphant in the air.

His speech.

And that feeling, surging up from his toes, electrifying his veins as his mind soared high above the world.

He'd thought he had finally found his freedom.

But then he'd glimpsed the king, standing beside Niamh, with infinite sorrows in his gaze.

In the blink of an eye, the king had seized Niamh, leaped on a pine marten, and sprung off the platform.

Chaos ensued. Fafnir stepped back as faeries swarmed, jostling him. Confusion writhed in his chest. The queen's hoarse cries echoed in his ears as she screamed for guards to follow the king.

Something struck him from behind. With a ragged cry, Fafnir whipped around and lashed his arms out; his hand slammed against a hard object, sending it flying to the floor with a crash.

Fafnir blinked, heaving short, ragged breaths. His ceramic inkpot lay broken by his writing desk, oozing sticky black ink over a mess of papers strewn across the floor.

His desk. He had backed into his desk. He had let the memory carry him away.

A dry, wheezing sound hitched from his throat—a lingering symptom from his near-drowning two moons and five suns ago. He collapsed into his oaken chair and leaned forward, running a hand through his tangled hair, then slugged a long draft of water from his wooden mug.

One thousand and seven years had passed since the day the Ancient Law was revoked by his design—the law that had stood unquestioned since the dawn of time. It had demanded each faerie at age one hundred Unite by sleeping within a dryad's heart chamber. In the morning, the fae would emerge as a Winged One, with wings made of the leaves of their dryad unfurling from their backs and all immortality drained from their blood.

He had dared to question it. Uniting was a good thing for most other faeries. Through the act of Uniting, both the dryad and the faerie became fertile. The faeries had their children, and the dryads their Rootlings, and they acted as one family unit, caring for each other.

But that wasn't for him. He had no need for families or communities. He needed to keep his immortality and live forever in freedom, bound to no one but himself, in a regimented world of his own design.

Before the flood, he'd had a taste—a thousand years of blissful solitude. He'd woken with the dawn and structured each day in units calculated with the shadow on his sundial. He'd lost himself in endless rhythms of violin playing, wood carving, meditating by candlelight, and exploring the depths of the land. His life was an endless cavern of wonders to uncover, both within his own mind and the world without.

His plan to revoke the Ancient Law could have worked. If only a handful of faeries had chosen not to Unite with the dryads—including himself, of course—then the dryads could have carried on reproducing at about their normal rate. Only a few lives would have never been born. A minimal loss. He could have lived like that forever.

But his words were too convincing. He'd made sure of that, obsessing over them for a year, knowing it would be blasphemy to question the law. He'd discovered a yearning among the fae that had lived quietly for a long, long time, perhaps since the birth of the land—a desire to escape the clutches of death. Death took children from their parents, lover from lover, friend from friend, but the faeries were born immortal. Why should they have to take on the mortality of the dryads? Wasn't eternal life their *birthright*?

He'd seized onto that word—*birthright*—and exalted it in his speech. He'd used other tactics too — faeries were called Wingless Ones before they United, a term that implied a sense of lack. As though a faerie was not whole before the act of Uniting. All of it had a bile taste; something that was easy to call out. And then the New Law was born, abolishing the old. His words had spread like a fever. After the speech, as the years flitted by, he saw fewer and fewer Rootlings and Winged Ones, until he would pass a hundred dryads without a single faerie among them.

Now, over a thousand years later, nearly every faerie refused to Unite.

And the forest was dying.

He glanced beneath his elbow at papers crammed with feverish scribbles. He had to tell the queen of the danger, to ally with her again and get the faeries to Unite. Rambling about the flood to her would be senseless. She was too intelligent for that, and too possessive of the new freedom he had helped her win. He had to construct a clear, fact-based narrative, with enough evidence to pile it on her head like the thunderous death sentence he knew it to be.

He bolted up from the seat and staggered, just catching himself. His streak of working all night for the past three suns was catching up to him. He'd give himself a few hours of sleep. He could afford nothing more.

With stiff limbs, he rose and shut each window, before pulling the lever to close the skylight overhead. A dimness settled over the interior.

He clattered up the ladder into his loft bed, wrinkling his nose. The moss layer over his blankets was stiff, more brown than green. It smelled faintly of pond scum. He likely didn't smell much better; he'd been wearing the same linen shirt and brown cotton pants for... how long again? It didn't matter.

He loosened the bands around his ears, and took the strip of bark he wore for a hat off his head. He picked up his timekeeper, a little wooden device he'd invented to rattle a terrible sound to wake him along the phases of the day, and set it to high sun. No, three-quarters to high sun.

19

After snapping on a blindfold, he threw himself down on his bed, aligning his body perfectly straight, and glared at the black fabric over his eyes.

It was no use. His mind whirred like the wings of a hummingbird in flight, chewing over countless fears, his limbs tingling with adrenaline.

Wasting time, again. He would take care of himself later. When his plan was finished.

He pulled off the blindfold and, with a tap of his finger, stopped the timekeeper. After stumbling down the ladder, he opened the skylight and blinked as a dazzling beam poured in, illuminating the interior of his home with a golden glow. The medley of subtle color shifts in the inner bark of his walls—pale rose gold, red-brown ocher, blue-gray—all glowed together as though streaked with fire.

Passing a hand over his face, he walked toward the hearth, cursing as he slipped on a paper. He lit a fire within, and as he set the water boiling for tea, he noticed his knees were shaking. He was wheezing with every breath now, a nasty headache pressing at his temples.

He couldn't remember the last time he had eaten.

From his larder, he piled into a bowl a helping of sliced dried slugs, and frog legs spiced with ground mustard. Between mouthfuls, grease covering his fingers, he poured the water in a mug and set in sprigs of lemongrass. The fragrance wafted up to him, sharp and sweet, and a steadiness returned.

He could do this. He had to do this.

Hurriedly, he drained the tea and washed his hands in a basin before crouching by his writing desk to gather the papers on the floor. His hand brushed a cold, hard surface, and he froze. Lifting the piece of paper over it, he glimpsed beneath a little flute made of bone, snapped in two.

"Rot," he cursed.

Hurrying to his wood-carving station, he snatched a jar of plant gum and darted back to the flute, then knelt, cradling the two jagged pieces in his hands. After smearing the gum on either end, he held them together. It wasn't a perfect fit; small shards had broken off, impossible to find in all the mess on the floor.

He brought the flute closer to his eyes. Still drying. Maybe it needed another coat—

A crack shattered the silence and pain lanced through his left hand. He unclenched his fist. Countless little white shards pierced his flesh.

The last piece of the flute slipped from his right hand with a clatter. Closing his eyes, he rose and breathed as deep as his chest allowed.

In his mind, he clawed desperately to find the first strings of the numerical sequence of life—the sequence connecting all in one regiment of order, predication, and stability, traceable from the pattern in a dragonfly's wing, the petals of the rose, the spiral of a spiderweb, down to the smallest forms of life.

0 and 1 is 1. 1 and 1 is 2. 1 and 2 is 3.

He drew his breath out slow. His heart thumped in his chest. Quiet. Quiet.

2 and 3 is 5. 3 and 5 is 8.

He tilted his head side to side to the beat of the numbers, drawing another deep breath. His heartbeat returned to normal. At last, he opened his eyes to see a small, crumpled paper lying beneath the flute. He crouched down to fold it over in his hand. Small, graceful letters inked the other side: *For my beloved son.*

His stomach clenched. He scooped up the broken remains of the flute and squeezed his fist tight, fighting the urge to hurl them on the floor.

He still remembered his mother's face before he left her. Her long, white hair draped over her in tangles, her eyes pleading, love etched in her every feature, despite everything.

His shoulders drooped, his limbs suddenly heavy. He loosened his fist and laid the remains of the flute back on his writing desk as though it were a bird with a broken wing.

It was the only thing he'd still had of hers.

A cutting pain burned in his left hand. With gritted teeth, he grabbed a pair of wooden pliers and, one by one, pulled out the little pieces of bone from his flesh. The golden sunlight shifted across the room, lingering on his hand, flushing the gray skin in warmth. At last, he wrapped his bleeding hand in a thick gauze of cobwebs. The last of the papers on the floor called to him. He scooped them up and once again lost himself in his work.

Red light flickered across his page. He glanced up through heavy lids, his mind full of soil sediments and their effects on flooding. Small motes of dust, made visible by the light, drifted onto the white fragments of the flute. Splotches of crimson stained the shards where he'd bled on them.

What kind of notes would the flute have sung? Would there have been something of his mother's spirit in its sound? Something of her song, of her laughter?

After a thousand years, he could scarcely remember her voice...

And now, he would never know.

He rose, gathering the pieces into his hand, and set them on top of the bookshelf.

Then he bent over his work once more.

Dryad Life Cycle

Dryads are the pillars of the forest. They are born as seedlings (fig.1) in the earth. Their parents bind their roots to them and nourish them. The child gradually pushes up and up (fig.2-3) until they sprout out of the earth as a Rootling (fig.4). For an average of twenty-five years the Rootling grows, fed by their parents with stories and nourishment. Finally when they are strong enough, they break their tie to their parents' roots and spring free. Now they are named a Walker. (fig.5)

called by the Ancient Law to Root (fig.6). In this final stage of life, they bind their roots into the earth, losing all their senses as we understand them, and joining their roots to their kin. They will never move again.

fig.1   fig.2   fig.3   fig.4   fig.5   fig.6

CHAPTER 4: INNOCENCE

Esen furrowed her brow. Aisling wiggled opposite her, swaying her closed fists in the air. She seemed to put more grip into her right hand. Maybe the *Aeonida* bone was in that hand. But the way she fluttered her other hand as though it were a butterfly, grinning slyly, made her second-guess herself.

The sporadic, lethargic beat of Niamh's drum kept slicing through her thoughts. Finally, she gestured with her thumb toward the left.

Laughing, Aisling twirled both hands open. A plain bone rested in the left hand, and a bone carved with the spiral shape of *Aeonida* in her right.

Esen groaned and slammed her hands together. "You got me!" she cried.

Aisling's laughter was infectious.

"Great job, Aisling," Ian said, laughing too. He leaned forward from where he sat cross-legged in the grass beside Esen. On the straw mat in front of them, he moved a bone from their pile onto Aisling and Niamh's. They had five points now, while Esen and Ian had three. It was five to three now.

Niamh handed the bones to Ian. As he shuffled them behind his back, he dropped his mouth in a mock frown, cocking his eyebrows up. Esen couldn't help but laugh. He always got her with that face.

When Ian was ready, Niamh began to guess, crossing her arms. Esen lifted her flute from where it hung over her neck and played. The wind stirred the crowns of the Rooted Ones above them. Heat shimmered in the air, moisture clinging to her like wet moss. The feathery fluff of a milkweed seed flitted by, twirling like a faerie. It was a day just like this when Esen had first played Cnámha, back when she was a Rootling like Aisling.

Though she had been Walking for a little more than two moons, it felt like she had always been Walking; as though her life as a Rootling had happened to another.

She was not that child anymore.

Before Aisling, Tristan had always been the fourth player in Cnámha. He would holler, pull wild stunts, and beat on his drum in a frenzy. She had not seen him since he left her.

Ian nudged her. "I got your bone back." The bone she had lost to Aisling sat back on their pile. Esen lowered her flute and let out a victory whoop.

Ian gave the bones back to Niamh, who flopped to the ground with a roll of her eyes. Her shoulders wobbled as she placed the bones in her hands.

Aisling began to beat on her drum, giggling. "You won't have it for long!" she cried. "You can do this, Niamh."

Niamh began to dance from her seat, her arms winding round each other like snakes. Her eyebrows were lifted, a smirk on her face. Ian leaned forward, stroking his scraggly red beard. At last, he gestured to the left.

Quick as an adder, Niamh's hands met in the air. A blur of white slipped between them, then she lowered them. The *Aeonida* bone lay in her right hand, the plain bone in the other.

Esen frowned. Had she cheated?

They adjusted the score and went for the next round. When it was Esen's turn to guess, and Niamh hid, she made the same motion with her hands before presenting them. This time, Esen could see a glimpse of the *Aeonida* symbol on the bone as it slipped between her hands.

Ian hesitated beside her. He must have seen it too.

"Niamh," Esen said. Someone had to say it. "I saw you swap the bones in your hands. Please play fairly. This is Aisling's first time, and I don't want to confuse her experience."

Scowling, Niamh dropped the bones with a clatter. "I didn't want to play anyway."

Niamh began to rise, but Ian leaped forward and gently grabbed her wrist. "Niamh, please. Can we talk about this?"

Niamh jerked her hand back. "No. I want to be alone."

She stalked off. Ian stared after her. He looked like a shrunken leaf with the color seeped out of it.

"What happened?" asked Aisling. "Why doesn't she want to play?"

"She's not feeling well," Ian told Aisling. "You'll have to play with just Esen." He turned to Esen, his face grave. "I'm sorry, Esen. I know you love Cnámha too—"

"It's not your fault, Ian." Quieter, she added, "Do you think the flood is worrying her?"

"I don't know. She used to be so happy, but lately, she's getting more impatient with me. I feel like I'm losing my little Nia." Tears welled in his eyes, and he wiped them with the back of his hand. "I'm going to try to talk with her. Tell Aisling I'll be back soon."

Springing into the air, he flapped his wings until he caught a drift, and flew off.

Esen turned. Aisling stood still, holding her drum limp in her hands. Grabbing the playing bones Niamh had dropped, Esen hurried forward.

"I'm sorry, Aisling," she said. "We can keep playing together if you like."

"Just the two of us?" She sniffed and clutched her drum tighter. "Then we won't get to play music."

"Let's play some songs, then," said Esen. "Would you like that?"

Aisling gave a small nod. Smiling, Esen grasped her flute in one hand and twirled in a circle. The first goldenrod blossoms grew beneath her, vibrant yellow like the sun. Her spirit swelled. She knew how she could make Aisling happy.

"Did you know that flowers can sing?" Esen asked.

Aisling's eyes widened like two moons. "Mother and Father told me, but I've never heard them."

"Let me show you," said Esen. "They love music and love to echo back variations of the sounds they hear. They say it is the Mother's spirit that speaks within them."

Esen began to play her flute. A gentle breeze stirred through the grasses, lifting the heads of the goldenrods so they seemed to nod to the rhythm of her song.

"I sing unto the earth," she sang. "I sing unto the sea."

"*We sing unto the sun, we sing unto the rain,*" the goldenrods sang in turn.

Esen grinned. "I sing unto the sky, I sing unto the soil."

"*We sing unto the ash and we sing unto the dew.*"

Esen swayed her body, flowing her free hand toward the sun. The wind swirled around her, caressing her, almost as though tendrils of hair flowed against her bark.

A gasp broke from her. Mother Wind? Was she here?

"I sing unto the water!" Esen cried. "I sing unto the fire!"

"*We sing unto the ash and the sun and the rain.*"

"I sing unto the spirit, I sing to her above."

"*As the cool wind blows, on this fair summer morn.*"

The last voice echoed in the air as Esen slowed her melody.

The wind had stilled. She strained her ears for a whisper, a breath in her ear, but she only heard the last few echoes of the flowers repeating their cry.

"*As the cool wind blows, on this fair summer morn.*"

The clapping of hands brought her back to herself. Aisling was dancing as well as her limited mobility allowed her, humming the melody.

"I want to try, I want to try!" she said.

"Of course," said Esen, shivering. She had never felt the Mother's hair upon her before. She must have imagined it. But she had never felt anything like it…

Little hands pressed on her calf. Aisling was pushing at her, eyes pleading. "I want to sing to the flowers," she said.

Esen laid herself on the ground, flat on her belly. Aisling stood just above her eye level now, giggling with her hand over her mouth. Nose to nose with her, it was difficult to look past the signs of weakness she still bore. Though she was growing some leaves, they were sprouting terribly slow, and several were yellow already, browning at the tips.

"You're so big," Aisling said.

"You will be big like me before long." Esen managed a smile. "Do you know how to sing, Aisling?"

"I think so." She opened her little mouth in an O. "Ooohhh!"

The flowers swayed in silence.

With a laugh, Esen said, "You have to do a bit more to catch their attention. I'll help you make a song."

They tossed ideas between each other. Aisling kept focusing on birds. "Ian put seeds in my hand yesterday," she said, "and told me to stand super still. So I stood like a rock. No, stiller than a rock. Then, finally, a bird flew down over my hands. It tickled me with its wings as it snatched all the seeds up and flew away again. I named it Needle because it had a tall crest on its head, like a bunch of pine needles sticking up."

"You saw a crested tit, then. I wish I had been there! Ian did the same thing with me when I was your age. But I got impatient, so I never saw a bird."

As the sun began to slip below the horizon, bathing the forest in a rosy glow, they finally had their song.

Aisling cleared her throat. "Okay. Flowers, listen up."

Closing her eyes, she began to sing. If white fluffy clouds could sing, they would sing like her—light and airy, high above the world.

"Fly happy bird, fly happy bird. Fly up so high in the sky."

The echoes of the flowers flowed like a stream beneath Aisling's voice as she continued, complimenting her. "*Fly happy bird, fly happy bird.*"

"Once you did lie, now you do fly."

"*Fly happy bird, to the sky.*"

"Keep your head high, soaring so high."

"*Keeping your smile so wide.*"

"May your wings kiss the sun above."

"*Let the sun shine so bright above.*"

"And may your wings never touch the ground."

A deep, sonorous voice rang out the last line—one they hadn't made.

"That's a really loud flower," Aisling said.

Esen turned in the direction of the voice. It sounded familiar…

Round the crest of the hill appeared the sturdy form of a rowan Walker. It was Cillian, the last of the Storykeepers. She had not seen him since he had come to visit her when she was a Rootling.

His earthen lips were parted still, though he had ceased singing, and a smile lit up the features of his face. All across his young green bark ran banners of marks depicting fantastic symbols and shapes. Among them were the forms of faeries and dryads, intermingled with animals, insects, and plants. It almost seemed to her that more marks were upon him than when she had seen him last.

Esen darted forward. "*Aeonida*, Cillian!"

"*Aeonida*, Esen!" He embraced her before stepping back and forming the sacred sign of Saol over her with his fingers. "Wind guide you, Esen. How have you been?"

"I am okay," she said. "It's been hard, as you know, but we can speak of that another time. You are here to teach Aisling?"

"Of course." His eyes—the deep hue of the forest—lowered as a cloud passed over them. He laid a hand on her shoulder. "Let us talk later."

He walked over to Aisling, who had not taken her eyes off him. "Are you a Storykeeper?" she whispered.

"Yes!" Cillian said. "You have found me out."

He bowed low before Esen's parents. "*Aeonida*, Niall Holly and Rowena Hazel. I am here to teach your daughter Aisling. Do I have your permission?"

Esen's mother stirred, her leaves lilting with excitement. "*Aeonida, Cillian. Of course. Stay as long as you are able.*"

Cillian bowed again. "I will stay for three suns. There is another Rootling down the river I must visit after."

"What is a Storykeeper?" Aisling asked.

Cillian turned to her, a playfulness gleaming in his eyes. "Since you recognized me, I thought you knew."

Aisling pinched her face. "I only remember Storykeepers have carvings."

"That's right," Cillian said. "In the times of plenty, three Storykeepers were appointed to roam the land and share the ancient stories carved upon them. We are a living memory of the truths and tales of the land. But now, I am the only one left."

"Did the other Walkers carve you?" Aisling asked. "Did it hurt?"

"Yes, but not as much as you might think. They were careful to only carve the outer layer of bark, where less pain can be felt. It hurt only in

30

the act of carving, and for a little while after. I've never felt any pain since."

He spun in a circle, smiling, so Aisling could see glimpses of the marks all round him. "Would you like to hear one of the stories? I have looked at them so many times that they are carved upon my spirit as well as my body."

Aisling's gaze traveled in wonder before fixing on an image upon his inner arm—the Mother weaving forms that looked like faeries from the tendrils of her flowing hair. Cillian followed her gaze to the carving and held it out for her to see.

"Ah, you have chosen the best of the best. This tells the story of the creation of the land. You would like to hear it?" In an extended mosaic of imagery, the faerie forms flitted from the Mother's hands like seedpods, spinning to land upon a depiction of a vast dotted mass representing the forest.

Esen leaned closer. It seemed so long ago that he'd sung this tale to her. It had stayed in her head ever since.

Aisling nodded, and he began. His voice took on the full, sonorous tone once more, lifting the words high in song.

"Through the mists of the world breathes the Wind of Worlds,
And His daughter, the Wind, once flew amid His pull.
But on a lonely morn, she spied a land adrift at sea,
And her heart, oh it ached, to see life there within.

With a final word to her Father so dear,
She sundered her tie to His great loving winds.
Around the lone land she wrapped her care,
And it was here that she became our Mother.

On the first day, she breathed round the land;
The grass flushed with green, the flowers did bloom.
Oh the animals pranced and danced with glee,
As the waters rushed full, down into the sea.

31

The next day, she breathed her spirit in the trees;
They would Walk for a time, keeping peace on the earth.
'Then each of you shall Root,' she said unto them,
'And hold up the earth as one binded family.'

On the third day, she wove from strands of her hair
Faeries, born small, with her immortality.
'Each of you shall Unite,' she said unto them,
'To give to the land and grow your hearts in love.'

And so formed the law, as sanctioned as the sun,
And from dawn to dusk, the Mother haunts her land.
A land that is pillared on love and sacrifice,
Just as she once gave to form this land anew."

AISLING'S MOUTH HUNG OPEN. "How did she create so many faeries from her hair? She must have had so much hair. Is that why she made them so small?"

Cillian laughed. "Maybe so. Some say she has infinite volumes of hair, and so, it was no trouble for her. Others say she gave away every hair on her head that day and it took thousands of years to grow it back again. I think it is some mysterious combination of both."

"How can two things be true at once?" Aisling pressed.

Cillian knelt before her and pointed toward the moon. It was a perfect silver disk, illuminating the black veil of the night.

"Have you seen the moon in the water at night?" he asked.

"Yes," Aisling said. "In a great big puddle at my roots."

"How can the moon be both at your roots and in the sky?"

Aisling pinched her brow. "I don't know."

"Ah, just so," said Cillian. "I think the truest truths are beyond our understanding."

Esen thought of the breath that had ghosted over her as she'd danced. There was so little that she knew.

Aisling began to wiggle, her eyes gleaming. "I like you. Can you tell me another story?"

Cillian rose and twirled. "Pick one."

Aisling pointed to a spiral on his shoulder resembling the curve of a butterfly's wing. "That's pretty."

"It is a pretty story too," said Cillian, "though a profound one. You found the symbol of Cerridwen Willow. Every Walker is given a symbol upon their forehead when they Root, representing their life story as a Walker. In the last thousand years since the Ancient Law was revoked, I have dedicated myself to filling the last of the space on my body with the life symbols of Walkers who Root during these dark times." He put two fingers to the smooth bark above his eyes. It was unadorned, an island amid a sea of carvings. "My story is still being written." Lowering his fingers, he winked at Esen. "As is yours."

Esen's fingers drifted to her forehead, feeling the bare bark. She still had three hundred years to Walk before she would be called to Root into the earth.

What symbol would be carved there, at the end of those years?

What story would she live?

Cillian knelt before Aisling once more. "I will tell you the story of Cerridwen Willow, daughter of willow and ash. Cerridwen grew up, as all dryads do, knowing she must one day Root. But she was afraid."

"Why?" Aisling asked. "I am rooted, and it is not scary."

Cillian laughed. "Allow me to explain. You are rooted now, Aisling, but it is temporary. You are joined only with your parents, no other. Soon, you will break free of their bind and Walk upon the earth. Then, when your time to Walk is over, you will Root again, binding yourself to the earth forever."

"I have to be Rooted forever? But the faeries get to move all their lives."

"Ah," said Cillian. "It is all part of the Cycle of Giving, which the Ancient Law kept in motion. It called for the faeries to Unite at age one hundred, and for Walkers to Root at age three hundred. Thus, faeries give their immortality to the dryads. The dryads give their Walk to the care of the forest, and finally Root so they may be the pillars of the forest itself. And all the animals, insects, and plants in turn give in their own ways. Thus, it is a cycle of giving and receiving, designed by our Mother."

Aisling stared at him with wide eyes. "And the faeries are breaking it."

"Yes," said Cillian. He gathered his breath. "But let us return to Cerridwen. She began to Walk, like your sister. She Walked and Walked through the mighty mountains of the south, by the salty sea, and among the sloping hills of the north. She was happy. But then, she came near her appointed time to Root. 'I don't want to Root,' she said. 'I want to Walk forever.'"

"But she must!" Aisling interjected. "To preserve the Cycle of Giving."

"You're a fast learner. But behold!" Cillian wound his fingers together and made a flapping motion with his palms. Aisling giggled. "A butterfly flitted onto her finger. It whispered to Cerridwen, 'I wanted to be a caterpillar forever because I was afraid to molt. When I finally gathered my courage, I turned my skin inside out. It felt like I was dying. But, as I waited, shivering in my chrysalis, I grew wings, then I soared out into the unknown. I think it will be like that for you also.'"

"Butterflies can't speak," said Aisling.

"Not in a way we can understand, but Cerridwen knew it was the Mother speaking to her through the butterfly. Cerridwen believed, and she Rooted when her time came. She stretched and strained, growing taller and taller, and dug her Roots deep beneath the earth. Then she discovered she could hear the voices of all the Rooted Ones! Her roots twined with the roots of her neighbors, whose roots entwined with their neighbors, and on and on, beneath the whole land. Their voices hummed to Cerridwen as one, welcoming her. She had joined the Root Web. It was like finding her wings."

Aisling made a little noise of wonder.

Cillian continued. "I believe Cerridwen's story is the truth the faeries have forgotten. They have forgotten how to turn themselves inside out and let suffering grow them into who they were created to be."

AFTER SEVERAL MORE STORIES, Aisling grew sleepy. A wind blew, carrying a faint chill—a warning of the cold to come. Putting off the rest of the lesson for the morning, Cillian took Esen's hand, his fawn-colored bark pale against her red-brown. Spiraling carvings wove even to the ends of his tapered fingers.

"Let us walk together," he said. "I want to hear how you have been."

As they walked down the hill, Esen told him of her experiences as a Walker so far, and what the flood had done to Aisling. He listened in silence, his face grave.

"I am sorry, Esen. I can tell your parents and your faerie are doing all they can for her. She is happy despite her frailty. She is far better off than some other Rootlings I have seen."

Esen nodded. With his hand in hers, she felt tethered to the ancient ways, as though they weren't slipping away beneath her feet. His stories swirled in her head.

"Cillian," she said, "I want to keep the spirit of our culture close to me, as you do. Before you go, could you carve the spiral of *Aeonida* on my right wrist? I'd like to look at it whenever I am afraid and trust it will guide my spirit home."

Cillian pressed her hand. She could see the glimmer of his smile in the faint moonlight. "I will gladly do that for you."

Uniting

.Not much is known of the physical nature of Uniting. Only that somehow, our immortal life force seeps out of our skin - invisible, yet moving through the air like a scent, and the dryad absorbs it into their bark.

Both dryad and faerie must be asleep for the transformation to occur.

The faerie Unites in the dryad's heart chamber. This structure is built into the "bones" of the dryad

As the faerie sleeps.

As the wings made of the leaf type of the dryad unfurl from the faerie's back.

The Land of the Mother Wind

CHAPTER 5: THE LOST PRINCESS

Niamh twirled her fingers through her hair, frowning at the star-shaped patterns of light flickering on her green sheets. They ghosted in and out of view as the flame in her ceramic vessel burned lower, almost to the end of the wick.

Everyone was so happy about Aisling, and Aisling didn't need to do anything—she could just smile and sing and dance. While everyone would soon look at Niamh, already white and weak, and demand she give even more of her energy to Tristan's parents for the coming winter.

But she didn't want to.

She wanted to say no. No. *No.*

The dandelion puffs dangling above her bed looked like little pale moons. The real moon breathed a silver light through the window. Black shadows snaked across her bed, crisscrossing over her like the braided pattern of a firefly cage. She'd been here almost a thousand years now…

Was this home? It wasn't a home she'd chosen.

Her father was a dark shape at the other end of the room, buried in blankets in his bed. That thought rose up inside her… the one that had come on suddenly a few hundred years ago, when the blurred memories of her childhood finally clicked into place.

He'd done this to her.

She could still see her mother's face, white as a moon, as her father had swept Niamh onto the pine marten, off the platform, and away, away. The panic that had torn at her stomach. Her father's hand on her wrist so tight it hurt as he forced a liquid down her throat. And then, that gray morning, waking with tiny, folded wings. The air moaning with her dryads' distress as she stepped out, wobbling.

She had been so young then... just a child.

She wrapped her arms tight around her middle, her skin scratching against the coarse cotton of her dress. She hadn't understood the full reason for the dryads' horror then. Over time, she learned. As her father aged over the long blur of years, acquiring wrinkles like a tortoise, she only grew a few spans in height, and her skin stayed smooth. Like her body was frozen in an eternal winter, scarcely daring to grow. And she was always weak.

Tall, white pillars rose like ghosts from her memory, with ivy curling down the sides, and endless corridors with doors, doors, doors...

Somewhere in that palace of long, long ago, her mother, the Queen of the Fae, waited for her—the lost princess torn from her loving arms.

But the memory was like a dream. Was it true?

Her life with her father was the only life she knew for sure.

A loneliness pulled at her chest. Her river fae, Rowan, would be sleeping in his village now, his breath going out in little puffs.

She slid off the bed, slipped on her shoes, and gathered her long, long hair behind her back. She would visit him. Her father didn't like it, but it was a little spark of freedom.

The wind whispered along her skin as she opened the door and stepped out into the warm night. She folded out her wings and leaped into the air, flapping for balance. She caught a southern wind, and coasting along it, she let her mind wander, dreaming of pillars and ivy and Rowan's brown eyes, soft as a doe's as he looked at her.

She had met him the first and only time her father had taken her to the World Market. She'd begged her father for years and years to let her go, to let her see the rare and wonderful fruits and pots and bows and cloths that faeries brought from all corners of the land to trade.

Secretly, she had hoped she would see her mother.

Her father always denied her request. She sensed he felt her secret wish and feared it. Finally, to celebrate her one thousandth birthday, he consented, and took her.

She'd flitted through the stalls by her father's side, drinking in the rich scents of the steaming meat, sage incense, and cedar woodsmoke. Rows of elaborate stalls packed with colorful goods and eager faces hollering their wares blurred into one tapestry of sound and color, wonder and delight.

Then a young green faerie with oak wings had fluttered out from the crowd with a basket of hand-sized fruits in orange and green hanging from his arm. He paused before her, hovering just above the ground.

"Care for a squash, miss?"

She shook her head. "I've nothing to trade."

He tilted his head as he looked at her, his moss-green curls bouncing. His eyes were warm and sincere, glistening amber like honey in the sun. "How about a song?"

Her cheeks burned. "That's not worth a squash," she muttered. Whatever a squash was.

The faerie landed, tucking his wings behind his back, and frowned at her. "Sure it is. Anything from the heart is worth a thousand squashes."

Her father tensed beside her. He wore that pinched look, his shaggy red brows almost obscuring his eyes. He sifted a squirrel hide from his armful of pelts and held it out to the faerie. "Take this for a dozen squashes, and leave my daughter alone."

The faerie was still looking at her, a hopeful smile on his face. She loved the way his eyes crinkled with it. So she did something she'd never done before—she disobeyed her father.

"Father, I would like just one squash, and I want to earn it myself. I don't want to sing in the middle of a crowd, so I'm going to sit with him by that oak dryad"—she pointed to one at the edge of the crowd, still in plain sight—"and sing for him, right where you can see me. And then I'll come back."

Now she *really* couldn't see her father's eyes; he was all wrinkled brow, with a heavy frown. "All right," he said finally.

It was her first victory. She'd beckoned to the faerie, blushing with the rush of her own daring, and sang for him beneath the oak. She fell in love with him then, and he with her.

She never found her mother.

As she continued south, a crooked black shape huddled on a rock emerged before Niamh. She drew short, faltering in the air. It was

39

Tristan. Away from his parents. He raised his head, his branches creaking. A pinch formed in his brow. He looked heavy and tired, like he was nearly stone himself.

"How are you doing, Niamh?"

The question startled her. She'd expected him to accuse her, ask her where she was going in the middle of the night.

"I, um," she stammered. "I'm okay. I have to go."

Tristan was the son of her dryads. She'd grown up with him, played games with him. But as time went on, something had begun to fester in Tristan's core—a scary sort of anger.

She'd quickly learned to keep her distance.

She surged back into the current and flew away without looking back.

main beams

Curved

hull

rudder

Seat

Lock

43 piece

made

CHAPTER 6: A DELICATE SYSTEM

Pushing through tall reeds and cattails, Fafnir picked his way along the riverbank. A cloud drifted over the sun, casting a dark, close shade about him, the musk of the river filling his lungs. As he made his rounds, checking on the major sites of soil erosion where the levees of the bank had caved in from the flood, his mind churned over the clamor of the rushing waters.

A dragonfly flitted by, and for a moment, his vision was filled with its glassy gray orbs and flashing wings, then it flew off, a flash of brilliant blue against the sun. He slipped his journal out from under his arm and noted the sight. A king dragonfly; the third king he'd seen this year. A notable decrease—he'd seen eight by this time last year.

He chewed at his lower lip. If he was correct, and not imagining things, the system that served as the foundation of the forest was beginning to shift at the base level. Other insect populations, including mosquitoes and bark beetles, were thriving, overproducing in the slightly warmer climate. More notable was the increase in temperature shifts and sudden weather events…

A thin stream of water before him scurried away from the main body of the river. He frowned. It was still broken after the flood. He crouched and slipped a hand in the soil, crumbling it in his fingers. Fairly dense still, the soil healthy.

After wiping his hand on his pant leg, he reached inside the leather bag on his hip until his fingers brushed the soft fur of a rabbit pelt. He pulled it out carefully with both hands and unfolded the pelt to expose Floaty—or, as he more seriously called it, the buoyant temperature indicator. The sunlight glistened off its green-obsidian surface, the same color as the river.

It was a device he'd made as a child, back when measuring the world around him had been a game, not a matter of life and death.

He lifted Floaty. Eight vibrant bulbs, also obsidian, hung suspended in water within—three at the top by the waterline, and five toward the base. Good. None of them had broken.

A bulb with bright-blue liquid was the lowest among the three bulbs at the top. Fafnir read the tag hanging off it. Eighty units. About the same as last moon. Now to measure the water…

He approached the waterline and laid Floaty in the water so that over half of it was submerged. Crouching, he kept one hand on the pointed tip of the device and watched the bulbs inside with a furrowed brow. A bulb with green liquid disentangled itself from the others at the bottom and floated up to tap the base of the blue bulb. Seventy-six units.

Fafnir scratched the number into his journal, frowning. Also about the same as last year. Likely a fraction of a unit warmer. Over a thousand years ago, when he had first invented Floaty, he had measured this river during the Mead Moon—this same moon—at seventy-two units.

It could be a coincidence. He had only made two readings since the flood, one last moon and one now. But both times, the reading was the same.

And if his fears were correct, it would continue to increase.

Lifting Floaty back out of the water, he shook the streaming water off it and wrapped it back in the pelt before putting it in his bag. As he rose to his feet, a dark shape leaped out from behind him, jolting him.

A muddy brown frog crouched in front of him, facing the water, rumbling low like a wood saw. Fafnir stared with wide eyes as the frog hopped its way toward the water, finally vanishing with a plop into the trickling stream.

If the insects were diminishing in population, could one of their main predators—the frogs—be diminishing too?

He jumped to his feet and darted to the edge of the riverbank before stumbling to a halt. He held his breath, listening. He could still remember it. The rumbling of frogs would echo all across the river during the summer, their steady hum the backdrop of laughter as he and his sister built little wooden ships and pushed them into the currents...

Shaking his head of the memory, he listened once more to the sounds around him. He heard only the rushing of the water, and the occasional low croak, with much time in between. Too much time.

He skidded down the river, sliding on the gritty sand under his feet, and crept along the rocks, looking for the breeding pools. By a small, stagnant pool of water, he crouched and observed the tadpoles as they swarmed in an aggregate mass, writhing against each other. They were large, nearing the end of their metamorphosis. Most had wriggling back legs, and some had already sprouted their front legs and were beginning to hop about the rocks.

"Ten... ten..." he muttered, grouping them in his head as he counted.

A gray-green frogling leaped just a few spans from him, its throat expanding and contracting, its beady eye staring.

Fafnir started, then stared down the frog until it hopped back toward the others. He wiped at his brow.

Six... twenty-six altogether.

He recorded the few other schools nearby and hurried down the river. Although he searched until late sun, scouring the banks, he found roughly eight hundred tadpoles and froglings, and twenty-two adult frogs.

His hands began to shake. There had to be more of them. Maybe he'd just missed the right places...No. He'd done his best. The numbers were correlative.

He sunk down on a rock and wrapped his arms around his knees. The dramatic shifts in weather must be affecting their young. Last winter the temperature had dropped too early in the year. It must have killed many tadpoles on the cusp of growing their limbs and leaving their pools.

If this was true, what animals depended on the frog to survive? How far down the line was the system already shattering? He didn't think it could have gotten this far, this soon.

There were too many variables and not enough time. He had to trace the line through the system, but he was groping in the dark. This wasn't his area of expertise.

But it was his sister's.

He bit at the inside of his mouth. He had avoided her for over a thousand years, ever since the day his father left. She despised him. He could still hear the sound of the door slamming…

Fafnir slid his hands from his knees. He could scarcely see them. Looking up, he glimpsed the sun slipping behind a thick veil of clouds, casting him in a haze of shadows. Thunder rumbled in the distance.

A dull patter sounded above him. A water droplet pooled over the end of the strip of bark he wore over his head, filling his vision. He knocked it off, frowning.

He was sick of nature's taunts. No doubt this would be a passing summer shower, but there was always the chance. Tomorrow, or the next day, could be his last day alive.

He could still feel the pressure of the floodwater on his chest, pushing him down, down…

He needed time.

Isolde had been an avid researcher of the creatures of the forest since she was very little. If he could get her to help him, he'd likely finish his studies before the end of the moon. But how would he get her to listen?

He did not want to be back in her life, or anyone's. He doubted she would want him back anyway. He'd hurt her too deeply.

He rubbed his temples with his fingertips. At last, he straightened. He'd appeal to her love for the forest. She would want change too, desperately. Perhaps she was already working on creating change. He could prove an asset to her, with his knowledge in other spheres of study.

He rose and slipped off the rock, just catching himself from falling.

It would be approximately a three-day journey. He would take his boat, Serenity, as far as the river allowed and then run the rest of the way.

Sliding in the rain, he darted toward his home.

the pool of Divination

CHAPTER 7: ATHAS

Cillian spent the next three days with Aisling, until they had gone through the story of every carving upon him. Ian joined along, but Niamh was scarcely around. On the last day, Cillian sat with Esen and carved her wrist. It hurt less than she had feared, and he made quick but elegant work of it.

He left Aisling a thin slab of stone and a carving tool. "To practice the dryadic symbols I taught you," he said, "and to let your creativity run where it takes you."

The day after he departed, the morning dawned cool and clear. Esen told Aisling she would return, then went for a walk to gather her thoughts.

In time, she found herself heading toward a small waterfall that flowed near her home. As she approached the break in the Rooted Ones, a wind blew past her, stirring the tall blades of grass to nod their heads and sigh. She glimpsed the brown flowing waters of the river and the white foam of the falls.

Growing by the bank was a cluster of blackberry bushes. The berries were dark purple, ripe for harvesting. Excitement fluttered through her. She'd been staring at every blackberry bush as she cleaned up after the flood, but they hadn't been ready to eat yet.

She plucked a handful and crouched down to crush the berries in her hands, spattering the juice on the ground at her feet. A soft, mellowed sweetness coursed up from her feet as the root-like tips of her toes drew up the nutrients.

They tasted like a sunset in late summer.

She'd have to come back and gather some for Aisling, like Ian had done when Esen was a Rootling.

Stepping out from the canopy of the Rooted Ones, Esen walked carefully among the mossy rocks and waded through the shallow waters. The water lapped cool on her bark. She sat on a familiar ledge protruding out from the rock by the falls. Water sprayed against her back, soothing the stiffness. Folding her hands in her lap, she called to her mind the words of a traditional prayer.

"Oh Mother. Thank you for the warmth and strength of summer. May it nourish all life, and linger in our bark, a shield against the coming cold of winter."

A brilliant blue dragonfly flitted over, landing on the empty space on the rock beside her before flitting away again. The sunlight flickered, casting gleams of gold onto the dark-green moss on the rocks. She brushed her hand over the moss; it looked like it was composed of countless little green stars. A bird twittered above, and cicadas chattered, forming a melody with the rushing of the water. Pink clouds wove through the blue sky.

It was all so beautiful, every detail its own wonder. She could almost believe all was well.

Bracken snapped. Tristan stepped out from the shadows of the Rooted Ones. His eyes were dark, sunken in their sockets.

Esen leaped up, that strange fear seizing her again.

"Esen," Tristan said. "I'm sorry for how I treated you. I let the flood get to my head."

Esen lowered her shoulders, but the fear remained curled in her limbs. He had not come here only to apologize. She could see that in his eyes.

But why was she afraid? This was her friend, and he had been in a lot of pain.

"You can sit down," Tristan said. "I'm not a wild animal."

He sat on the ledge adjacent to where she sat, leaning back into the spray of the water. Foam frothed on his dark-gray shoulders. Esen lowered herself beside him.

"Again, Esen, I'm sorry. I want to make it up to you for being so rude. How have you been? I heard your sister was born."

"Yes." A smile broke her face at the thought of her. "Cillian came and taught her. She soaked it all in. She's writing her first letters already. She's really good. And I am okay, thank you for asking."

"I'm happy for you," he said, though he didn't sound happy.

"You disappeared for some time. How have you been?"

Tristan pulled back from the water and, with his teeth, tore at a cord binding a smooth white bone to his arm. He twirled it and held it in his palm for her to see.

"I promised you when you were a Rootling that I would help you make your first Walker flute for Athas," he said. "I never lie."

Esen's eyes widened. She had forgotten that Athas—the late summer festival—was only a quarter moon away. All the Walkers would gather at the heart of the forest to thank the Mother for the gift of summer, and she would fill their spirits with strength before the coming winter.

Tristan placed the bone in her hand. It was cool to the touch. From a pouch on his wrist, he pulled out a carving tool. The handle was the mandible of a fox, tied to a chiseled stone tip.

"Thank you," she said, "but you didn't answer my question. I've been worried for you, Tristan."

"What do you want me to say? That I've been fine as a dandelion?" He held the carving tool out toward her. "I snagged this bone from a deer, cut it, and cleaned it already for you. Now you have to carve it into shape."

Esen took the tool from him and held it to the bone, frowning. "How do I…"

Tristan leaned toward her and placed his hand over hers. "Like this," he said, guiding her hand in the motion. "Slower. Use your whole arm. That's better."

His breath stirred the leaves by her head. She bent over the flute, continuing the motion to carve the end piece. She *was* excited. The flute Ian had made for her as a Rootling was awkward in her large hands, and it had only three holes, instead of the five of the Walker flutes.

Tristan pulled back, tapping his hand in an erratic pattern on the rock as though it were a drum. "I heard what happened to Aisling. It's not right."

Esen pressed her lips tight. "No."

"I am glad she is well, though," Tristan said quickly. "I'll come see her soon."

"She would like that." Esen chipped at the bone, forming the notch where she would put her lips. Silence formed between them.

"In two springs, I will be three hundred," Tristan said.

A shock of pain rent through Esen. White sap oozed from a slice in her finger.

Tristan held her finger and wrapped an oak leaf tight around it, then bound it with a stem of ivy. "Sorry," he mumbled. "I'll take over if you like."

"No, I'm alright," Esen said. With the help of the pressure of the leaf, the pain was already subdued. "I can keep going."

She had always known he was older than her, but she hadn't realized...

He would soon be due to Root.

"Is that why you are angry?" she asked.

Tristan rose and paced in front of her. "The forest is dying, and I'm expected to plant myself in the ground and watch it die around me."

Esen bit her lip. "It's not like that. When you Root, you will help uphold the forest —"

Tristan whipped round. "Don't give me that Cycle of Giving talk. The faeries broke that."

Esen flinched. The anger slipped off Tristan's shoulders like steam from a lake. He lowered himself back on the ledge.

"I'm sorry," he muttered.

A cicada shrilled amid the song of the birds. The news settled in her, along with something like grief. She had only just begun to Walk with him.

"Esen." Tristan rested his hand on hers. It twitched over hers, restless. "We always said we were going to make a change together. Will you promise me something?"

Her mouth opened and closed. When she'd asked him what could be done, right before he left her before, she didn't like the raw, wild emotion that had consumed his face.

"You saw the bodies yourself," Tristan said. "Do you want Aisling to end up like one of them? Strewn on the ground, broken?"

"No." The image of Aisling dead, her little body broken in two, made her feel sick. "Of course not."

"Then promise you will help me."

His gray eyes burned with intensity. He was right. Something needed to change. They couldn't go on like this. But what could they do?

"What is your idea?" she asked. "You said you didn't know before."

"I'm working on something good," Tristan said. "I'll get back to you with it."

Something in his eyes made her feel cold amid the heat of the sun. He was her friend; she wanted to trust him. But she couldn't agree to something without knowing what it was. "Tell me your idea when you have it, and I will tell you if I will help you."

Tristan's brows quirked. "That's fair. I'll let you know soon."

He plucked the bone from her hands and turned it to the light, poking at it with the knife. "It looks good. I'd chip just a little more to the left of the opening to give it the right pitch. Then you can add the holes."

"Thank you, Tristan."

THE NEXT FEW days passed in a golden haze. The summer heat thickened, as though it sought to burn its warmth into the earth before winter crept in. Without a breath of wind to relieve it, the air swam with heat, the chirping of grasshoppers and the shrill drone of cicadas the only sound. Tristan came and visited Aisling. He helped Esen finish her flute and joined in their games and stories. He acted like his old self again. Esen could almost forget her fears.

The night before they were to leave for Athas, a light rain fell. By morning's light, a white mist curled above the grasses. Esen stirred, lifting herself up on one elbow. Aisling stood beside her, her head tucked into her chest, her eyes closed. Dew gathered in bright beads on the tips of her branches and meager leaves.

"Aisling," Esen whispered.

"Mm?"

"I must leave for Athas this morn. I will be back in a quarter of a moon, okay?"

Aisling stirred, scattering the drops of dew. "Okay. I will miss you."

"I will miss you too," Esen said, smiling. She heard a snicker behind her. Tristan. His arm hooked around hers, and he twirled her in a circle.

"Stop having so much fun," Tristan said. He released her, and she spun to a halt, laughing.

"Okay, okay, you made me laugh," Esen said, catching her breath.

Tristan had already knelt by Aisling and was playing a hand game with her. He messed up on purpose and groaned. As she giggled with delight, he faced his palm to the earth and circled his other hand in a fist around it, flowering it open in a sun circle—the gesture of Saol, for peace.

"Stay warm, Esen's sister," he said.

They walked down the hill. At its base, carved into the side, was a green door rising to half the height of Esen's calf. Rose bushes flowered around the door, their sweet perfume filling her senses. She knelt and knocked gently. Muffled rustling sounded within, followed by the padding of feet.

The door opened. Ian stood in the entryway, wearing a moss-green tunic with flowers embroidered on the sleeves, and a circlet of ivy on his head. His blue eyes were clouded, but the moment he glimpsed Esen, a smile lit up his face.

"Happy Athas," he said. "I am ready to go."

As Ian stepped out, Esen asked, "Will Niamh be joining us?"

Ian looked away. "No. She's with some river faerie."

"Oh. Why is that?"

Tristan huffed. "Isn't it obvious?"

Ian shook his head and jumped into the air, flapping his wings. "Let's go," he said, motioning for them to follow.

For seven days, they walked toward the heart of the forest. The trunks of the Rooted Ones grew wider and denser. Among them, she glimpsed dryads she had never seen before. Their trunks were red as clay, the bark layered in long, weaving strips like flowing water. Their yellow-green canopies towered high above them, the tops of the branches grasping at the sun. The sweet scent of pine and sap permeated the air.

Esen's spirit fluttered in wonder. "Ian, who are these dryads?"

He flew alongside her and Tristan, drifting in the warm currents. "These are the mighty sequoia. It is said the Mother breathed her fullest breath in the first sequoia, causing him to stand tallest of all the dryads."

A wind murmured by her ear. One day, she would stand like them— not as tall, but still high above the ground, a pillar for the earth and sky, with the wind in her crown and her feet in the stones of the earth. A thrill surged within her.

Before then, she had three hundred years ahead of her to Walk. The land was still rare and beautiful, with a thousand secrets for her to discover. She had to save it before it was too late. So she could Walk with Aisling and see the world with her.

At last, they grew near the heart of the forest. A clearing yawned ahead, a bright beacon amid the thick canopy of leaves. At the center of the clearing, a still lake shone, glittering gold in the sunlight. Four sequoias, an oak, and a hazel were Rooted round the lake, their trunks pointing straight toward the sky. They had Rooted alone. They were the Elders of the forest; the wisest of the Walkers who Rooted to counsel the Sage.

At the head of the pool, two sequoias wound round each other in an intimate embrace. Together, the width of their trunk stretched the length of three wolves. Esen tilted her head back, looking up and up, her mouth agape. The leaves at the tips of their branches seemed like stars dancing among the heavens.

"The Sage," she breathed.

Rooted together, they had become one as the Sage—the leader of the dryads, their guiding star. The faeries had their king and queen, but the Sage was one entity made of two. Two parts forming a whole, bound in service to the Mother. It represented Aoradh, union with the Mother; the highest symbol of the Trinity of Unity. The other two pieces of the Trinity—Grá for love bonds, and Stór for friendships—were the branches that held up Aoradh, the shimmering crown.

The air vibrated with the deep thrumming of the sequoias as they rustled their mighty crowns as one. A hand folded in her own. Tristan stood beside her, sunlight lighting up his eyes. "Come on!"

Looking for Ian, Esen found him among a group of fae and Walkers already beginning to dance in pairs by the pool. She let Tristan lead her toward them. There were hundreds of Walkers. Their bark ranged from pale white to the black hue of saturated soil, with many shades and colors in between. The branches of the youngest were just sprouting from their heads, like hers. The eldests' branches towered almost twice the height of their bodies.

Cillian stepped out from among them as she approached.

"*Aeonida*, Esen!" he said. "Happy Athas."

"Happy Athas!" she cried, yelping as Tristan began to twirl her round.

As they spun, Tristan whispered in her ear, "I know this will be the best Athas I've ever had, because I have hope."

Confusion surged within her. She didn't know if she had hope, but she couldn't think of that here. The music was thrumming in her bark, excitement surging through her.

As they danced, more Walkers entered the clearing, accompanied by a few families of faeries. The rhythm of the sequoias deepened, as though the very earth were crying out in song. The Walkers and fae began to file along the edges of the pool; Esen hurried forward with Tristan to join them. As the faeries joined an inner circle, she joined hands with Tristan and an oak Walker in an outer circle behind them.

The great dance began. The air sang with music and the pounding of feet, and all was golden.

A wind wove round their dancing forms, breathing soft in her ear. She shivered. This time, she could not mistake the soft brush of hair upon her bark.

Words slipped within her, whispering in syllables that could not be named. The tones echoed of promise. Of strength in dark times.

"Keep us, Mother," she whispered. "Do not let us die."

Our New Home

Designed by

Isolde · Mom

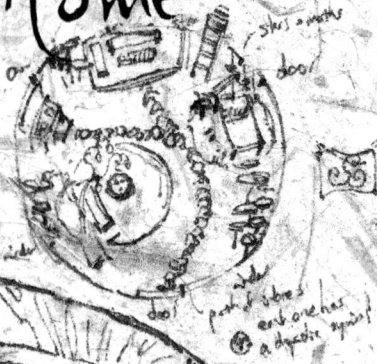

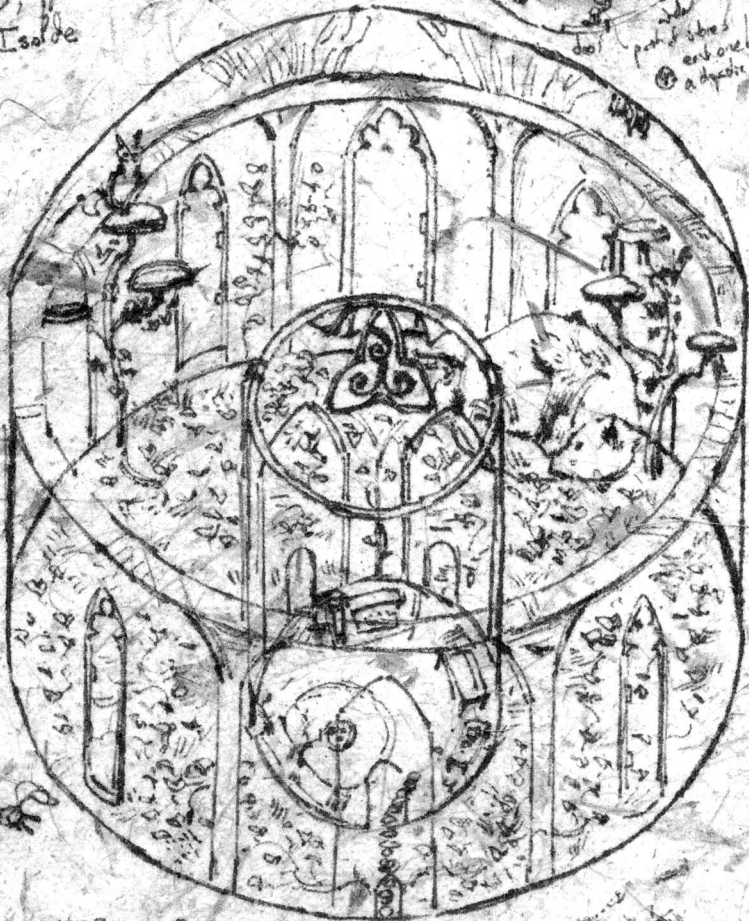

pretty
decor!

the mother's old one

door for
big guests.
fae door

CHAPTER 8: SISTER

Fafnir balanced the wheel of Serenity with one hand, staring at the calm waters as they flowed about him. His other hand rested on the shaft of the crown. The last rays of the pale autumn sun glistened over the water, sending little white flashes about the surface, dancing like fireflies.

A smile flickered on his lips. He hadn't allowed himself to touch his boat since the flood, two moons and seven suns ago.

The pummeling of the wooden mechanisms driving Serenity upstream churned amid the flowing melody of the water—a song of order, a remnant of his studies during his thousand years of solitude.

He could almost believe he was headed toward his secret cave, where his violin would echo off the great walls. Just himself and his instrument, immersed in an abyss of reverberations, flowing over the murmur of water below. Shrouded in absolute darkness, a place where time lost all meaning. The past and future revealed themselves for the phantoms they were, and the freeing present reigned.

It was something like the state between dreaming and consciousness. His dreams, when he had them, were wild things, strange and chaotic. But right before he fell asleep, his mind soared above the body, but still within the tether of perception. There, all the freedom and the vibrancy of a dream could be had. And the control.

59

He could go anywhere in the world, soar on wings, taste the sky.

Music was like that.

The whirring of the propeller on the back of the boat began to stutter, the gears slowing. With wide strokes of his right arm, Fafnir rotated the crown.

"Ten," he muttered, counting the rotations. "Twenty… Thirty."

He released the crown and caught hold of the wheel with both hands to steady his course. The gears sprung to life, the propeller whirring in suit. The water rushed white beneath him.

Isolde's home had been the talk of the land when it was first finished, six hundred and thirty-two years ago. So much so that it even managed to reach Fafnir's ears. It was said to be so tall even a young Walker could fit inside it. A place where all creatures of the land could enter within and be cared for.

He squinted ahead at the grassy knoll emerging from the cover of the Rooted Ones on the bank. It was about half the size of the Rath Síoraí—the great palace of the fae. Ivy climbed up and down the mound in an interwoven pattern resembling the weave of a basket. A pleasant little lane, gleaming white in the moonlight, led to a massive oaken door carved within the face of the hill. Cut into this door, like one bright shell on the shore, was a faerie-sized door painted the deep blue of a summer sky.

Like the color of that dryad's eyes.

He stiffened. He docked his boat on a sandy shore and stepped out cradling a wooden beam. He jammed the beam into the sand and tethered his boat to it with a rope, then climbed up the bank and onto the several stone stairs built into the earth leading up to the blue door.

A single light flickered, illuminating his way. He stepped beneath it. Its source was a flame within a vase-shaped ceramic vessel. An arrangement of holes carved upon it caused the positive space to look like a Rooted One with spiraling branches. The arrangement was repeated on the front and both sides. He cupped the edge of a hole with his finger.

It was very patient work, beautifully articulated. An inventive design.

He blinked, his eyes straining. He was distracting himself.

Pulling back, he breathed deep, recounting a few numeric sequences, before stepping up to the door.

Over one thousand years…

He tapped his knuckles on the door.

Silence. He shifted his weight from side to side, counting more sequences under his breath. Biting his lip, he raised his fist to knock again, when he heard footsteps padding toward him from the other side of the door.

The click of a lock sounded, and Isolde's coal-black face emerged, her usual white painted swirls dancing along her features.

Her brows pinched. Her golden catlike eyes met his, and her face twisted in fury.

"You!" she cried, the door screeching as she flung it wide. "Mother died because of you!"

She swung her fist—

And struck him in the jaw.

Fafnir cried out, stumbling. He hunched over, one hand covering his mouth. Blood dripped onto his palm.

What? Mother? She had *died*?

Isolde's jaws gnashed, clattering the trinkets dangling from her ears. "Why are you here? Get out!"

Like a rabbit caught in a thicket, every muscle in his body burned to flee. He breathed heavily.

He was cold. He felt nothing.

With all his will, he forced himself to stand straight. He gathered up the blood in his mouth, spat, and met her gaze.

Her pupils contracted. She clenched her fists, her lips trembling, as they always did before she cried. Jagged alder leaves tensed behind her back. She was a Winged One, but she had United recently. Only a few wrinkles marked her face.

"Isolde, please," he said. "I need your help."

"I'm not helping you with anything. Get out!" she snarled, her voice piercing his ears.

"The forest is dying, Isolde. I know you see it."

Isolde worked her jaw as her eyes flitted across him. She released a small huff of air. "What's it to you?"

"I've been tracing the banks of the rivers, and in many places, the levees are eroded, broken in. Soil density is diminishing, the weather increasing in severity. Soon, we will reach a point where, if it rains again

61

like it did two moons ago, there will be mass flooding, far, far worse than last time. We may all die."

He risked a glance to see her frowning at him, her brow furrowed. He continued, speaking rapid-fire, stumbling over his words. "Therefore, I am forming a cohesive narrative of data illustrating our doom to try to win the faeries back to Uniting with the dryads. To stop this change before we reach the point of no return. I need your help. I've realized insect populations are diminishing, and today, I saw it is affecting up the line, impacting the frogs. I fear it is disturbing species across the system, so I—"

"It is," said Isolde, crossing her arms. "It's been going on for hundreds of years."

Fafnir's mouth twitched. "I don't know how much longer we have before everything collapses. Please, lend me your wisdom so we can restore the forest as soon as possible."

Isolde stared at him in silence, her arms tight across her chest.

Rot it all. She was like a rock.

Hurriedly, he added, "You must be seeking change already. What are you—"

"Why do you care about the forest?" She narrowed her eyes at his shoulders, where the wings would extend if he had them. "I see. You only care so you can live forever."

Fafnir flinched. "No, that's not—"

"Let me help you understand something." Isolde closed the gap between them in one step, her head right beneath his chin. In another lifetime, he used to tease her about their height difference, about being a whole head taller than her despite being a year and a half younger. Now, he felt strangely ashamed of it. "Mother and I began this house together, after Father left, and then you. Our old home was haunted with memories. We were going to live here together. She helped me design it, to plan out the space to shelter animals and take care of them. We would live a new life here, giving ourselves in service to the forest. But after a few years, she became ill…"

Fafnir's ears flattened against his head. He looked at the ground, dissolving her words as she spoke them into mere sound, abstract rises and undulations in tone.

"She talked about you often." The words sliced through him. "More than Father."

Fafnir looked up, his stomach twisting. He had broken her flute...

Tears welled in Isolde's eyes, her fists clenched tight. He should have tuned her out again. But each word drove in like a nail, answering questions he had rolled in his mind for centuries.

Isolde snarled. "She took every fault of yours and bore it on her back. It slowly killed her. She wasted away, getting sicker and sicker, until one morning, she didn't wake up."

Fafnir swallowed. He felt nothing. He felt nothing...

Isolde raked in a breath, shaking her head of the tears. "And *now*, over a thousand years later, you dare show your face."

She strode to the door and held it open with one hand, looking over her shoulder at him with tight lips. "So, no, I will not help you."

The words hit him like a shock of cold water. He stumbled forward. "Wait, can you at least tell me..."

She paused. One chance.

"...what creatures eat frogs? So I can study the next ones in line."

Her lips pulled, trembling, in a small smile. She arched both hands and pranced her arms, flexing her long nails as though they were claws. Tears sprang to her eyes. She pressed a hand to her mouth and darted behind the door, slamming it shut.

Fafnir stared at the closed door.

Of course. Pine martens, the close companions of the fae. That was good; he could appeal to them that way. They were also one of the creatures Isolde and Fafnir would mimic as children, prancing about among their mother's garden on all fours, growling and scuffling. He rubbed at his aching jaw and frowned. Those times were long gone. He was not that child anymore. He felt like a lone moth fluttering about the light only to be cast out. He turned and walked back down the lane, kicking at loose stones, his head spinning in frustration. So much wasted time, and... and...

It couldn't have been his fault. Mother must have taken an illness and died; nothing more.

He would have to finish without Isolde. The queen would be his only ally.

Design Plan
Of the Rath Skaori

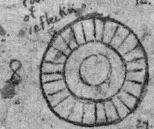

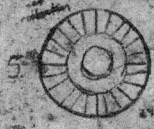

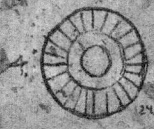

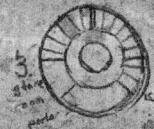

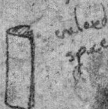

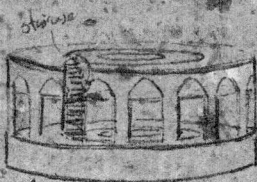

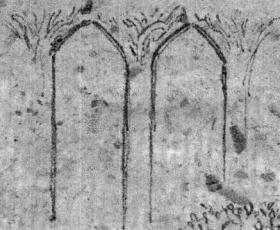

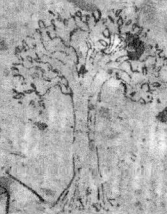

CHAPTER 9: WINTER DRAWS NEAR

After Esen returned from Athas, the warmth soon stole away. Chilling gusts of autumn crept in, lining her bark with white frost at night. The few leaves Aisling had managed to grow during the summer began to grow dull.

"Esen," Aisling said to her. "Why does the Mother blow so cruelly? I'm so tired and cold."

A fist tightened inside Esen. She knelt before Aisling and folded Aisling's hands in her own. They were only a little bigger than when she had first sprung up. "It is the way of the forest. Hard times must follow the good," she said, her voice thick. Aisling had known too little of the good. "The dark days of winter are approaching, but do not be afraid. As the cold deepens, you must pull your care from your leaves. You will not have the energy to maintain them. Just curl into yourself and sleep awhile. When you wake in the spring, you will be stronger for having endured winter's chill."

A leaf broke free of one of Esen's branches and fluttered to land at Aisling's roots.

"Okay," Aisling whispered.

Esen's breath choked. She pressed her sister's hands. "We are all going to do everything we can for you, Aisling. All you need to do is sleep. Winter will be over before you know it."

Aisling nodded slowly, her eyelids fluttering. "I'm tired."

"Sleep, then. I'll sing you a lullaby."

As Esen swayed, singing a soft lullaby about birds, Ian appeared with a jar of water twice the size of his head. His wings were brown, the edges beginning to fray. Niamh walked behind him, carrying another jar. Shadows bruised under her eyes, her knotted hair a tangled mess.

Esen grew quiet. Aisling was asleep. Ian and Niamh laid the jars by Aisling.

"It's more important than ever that we do this," Ian said. "We're going to gather a good number of jars by her. She must be kept hydrated, for her own safety."

She could protect herself better, with water flowing within her. Otherwise the cold could cause her bark to tear.

"Thank you, Ian," Esen said. She smiled at Niamh. "How are you?" she asked.

Niamh kept her eyes on the ground. Her thin fingers curled and uncurled. She looked so very young beside her father—perhaps only two hundred years old—while Ian's aged skin marked him as closer to a thousand, at least.

Ian had never told Esen who Niamh's mother was and why she did not live with them. Did Niamh know her mother?

Ian's brows creased. "We'll be back," he said.

"I'll come and help you," Esen replied.

That night, Ian climbed with the nimbleness of a squirrel up the trunks of Esen's parents, finding handholds in their fissured bark. He slipped within the darkness of their joined heart chamber.

"I thought he already United."

Esen started. Aisling was looking where Ian had disappeared, wide awake.

"He did," Esen said. "The faeries lose their immortality when they Unite with a dryad, but something of the Mother's sacred energy lingers in them. Before every winter, the faeries give again, just a little more of their energy, to help their dryads get through to the spring."

Aisling's eyes widened. "Do they ever run out of energy?"

"They would die if they did," Esen said. "We would never come near to taking that much from them."

ESEN'S EYES FLEW OPEN. Someone was shaking her hard.

"Esen," a voice hissed. Tristan. "Where is Niamh?"

"I don't, I…" The cold weighed her down, making her sluggish. She forced herself to rise to a seat. "I don't know. The last I saw, she was with Ian."

Tristan tore down the hill.

"Wait!" Esen cried. She stumbled to her feet, shaking her head. Leaves fluttered off her. She hurried after him.

What happened? Why was he so upset?

She stopped at the base of the hill. Tristan towered over the little green door, his fists clenched. The door cracked open, and Ian appeared. His face was pale, haggard.

"I've been talking with her," he said. "She's—"

"Stop letting her hide," Tristan snapped. "Let her speak for herself."

Esen stepped forward. "Tristan. What are you doing?"

Tristan's head whipped to glare at her. "You stay out of this!"

Esen shrunk back, her hand flitting over her chest. She watched as Ian stepped aside and disappeared within. Muffled voices sounded, then Niamh stepped out with Ian. She kept her gaze fixed on the ground, her hair partly obscuring her face. She looked whiter than the previous day —ghost white.

"What do you have to say for yourself?" Tristan demanded. When she didn't speak, he added, "Do I need remind you? My parents are already weak from the pathetic bits of energy you've given them all these years. Go give your energy to them. Now."

"Tristan—" Ian said.

Niamh put up a hand, silencing him. She lifted her head and tilted it back to meet Tristan's thunderous gaze. Defiance gleamed in her eyes. "No."

Tristan's limbs jerked, his eyes a smoldering fire. "You're a rot-brained spoiled brat. You get to do nothing all day—*nothing!*—and when one thing is asked of you, you can't rotting do it."

Niamh shivered, and Ian wrapped her in his arms. Fury trembling in his voice, he said, "Leave my daughter alone. I know you're angry, Tristan. Let me talk with her. I'll—"

"I'm going home," Niamh cried, shoving herself out from Ian and darting away.

Ian drew in a sharp breath. "Nia!" He hurried after her.

Tristan stared, his chest heaving.

Esen hesitated. Wasn't *this* Niamh's home?

She approached Tristan. He whirled round and gripped her wrist with startling force. His hand shook. "I want to tell you something."

Her spirit knocked against her chest. She let him lead her through the Rooted Ones. At last, they came to the waterfall where they had spoken before. He sat her down on the ledge, still gripping her hand with a terrible fierceness, as though he were cast over a cliff and she was his last tether to life.

"Tell me the things Ian did for you as you grew up," he hissed through clenched teeth.

Esen drew her shoulders back. "Why?"

"I'll tell you," Tristan growled, "after you answer me."

She turned her face to the ground, gathering her thoughts. "Before I even came up as a Rootling, he nourished the soil I grew in with worms and decaying matter. Cillian taught me to read and write, but Ian continued the teaching until I perfected it. He gave me water when I was thirsty, and in the winter, he covered me in skins to keep me warm. He played countless games with me and helped me carve my first flute. And when I first began to Walk, he told me where the brambles grew, and where all the fox dens were so I wouldn't fall into them." A laugh broke out from her. She had still tripped over a mole den dug that morning.

When she looked up at Tristan, she wished she could draw back her laugh. His mouth was twitching, pain echoing in his eyes behind the anger.

"Niamh did none of that for me."

Esen's mouth hung open. "None of it?"

"She played some games with me when I was little, but she had no idea how to care for me. When I started to Walk, I learned where the ditches were by falling over them. I learned everything the hard way. I raised myself."

"What about your mother and father? Did they not help?"

"They did what they could, but you just told me yourself how much your faerie does for you that they can't."

Esen's brows pinched. "I don't understand. How did she not know how to care for you? Didn't Ian teach her before she United?"

Tristan grated his teeth and drew closer to her. "Did he tell you anything? Of how they came here?"

She pulled back. "No."

"He's been sheltering you, but I won't let him keep you a child. Niamh just left to go back to the Rath Síoraí."

"Why? How do you know?"

"She's a *princess*." He spat the word like it was venomous. "The adopted daughter of the King and Queen of the Fae."

The queen was still ruling, but the king had stepped down to Unite years ago...

She reeled. *Ian.*

Ian was the king.

"I... I remember," she stammered. "I heard the king took his daughter with him to protect her from the queen. But I never thought that Ian and Niamh..."

"Here's the part they don't talk about," Tristan said. "Ian fled from the queen, deep into the forest. In a panic, he promised two joined dryads he would Unite with them. There was no ceremony. He climbed in their heart chamber, waited until they fell asleep, and came back out."

"What?"

"He put Niamh in there instead, after drugging her with a sleep potion. Then he went and United with your parents that same night. Niamh was ten years old. Uniting is only ever done with grown fae. The dryads—my parents—took nearly all the energy Niamh had. It almost killed her. That's why she's a thousand years old but still a child. She's messed up."

"H-how..." Everything Esen knew was shattering before her eyes.

69

"How do you know this? It can't be true. Ian wouldn't do something like that."

"Ian would never disobey the Ancient Law. The queen was pursuing him. If she had found them and taken Niamh back, she would have never let her Unite."

The sky tilted before her, the leaves smears of green. All those happy years of her youth… Had they really been happy?

Tristan put out a hand to steady her. "Niamh told me, once. She was nice sometimes… when she was younger."

"But I thought… I thought my family was happy, apart from the breaking of the law."

"You are still right," Tristan said. "If the law hadn't been broken, this would have never happened."

Esen looked up at Tristan. She felt small, fragile. "I am sorry, Tristan. You are angry with her because she cannot give enough in the winter?"

"She gives less than she can. I know it because my parents are always weak. And now that she's abandoned us, I don't know if… My parents might…" Shuddering, he seized a rock and hurled it in the water. "They might die this winter. And she would too, since she is bonded to them."

Esen laid a hand on his arm. "I'm sorry. Maybe Ian will be able to get her to come back?"

Tristan snorted. "That's a lost cause. He'll try anyway though."

He leaped up to pace once more. A frantic, almost nervous energy came over him, like the first eager winds before a storm. "Listen, Esen. We need to make our plan. We need to do something quick and efficient to end this suffering as soon as possible. And I thought of an idea."

That strange fear crept back into her. Something crouched behind his words, restless and desperate. But he was right. The suffering needed to end.

"Okay," she said. "What is it?"

Tristan stopped in front of her. "I need you to hear me out. I haven't told this to anyone yet—you are the very first." Sliding back on the ledge, he took her hand once more. "Picture the Rath Síoraí, the faerie palace. Close your eyes and picture it. It has pillars upon pillars; long, circular hallways that pile up like the coils of a snake; columns and buttresses and walls and floors, all built with marble. How do you think the faeries did that?"

"We helped them," she said, remembering a warm summer day when Cillian had told her. "They asked for a safe gathering home—a place to center their entire culture around, keep them safe from predators and storms, and host their festivals, so we built it with them. But what does this have to do with—"

"Right," Tristan interrupted. "*We* built it. We hewed the marble from the mountains, shaped it into a palace, and laid a mound of green over it. We were generous. We labored for centuries, creating the finest of architecture for them. They only did the detail work, the furnishing, and now, they are squatting in that palace like fattened drones and laughing as we die around them." He drew a hasty breath and stared her full in the eye. "Let's destroy it."

With a gasp, Esen drew back. "But there are always faeries inside of it. You're not suggesting—"

"I am not suggesting we kill them, no. We can order them to exit the palace first. Esen, listen. We destroy the Rath to destroy the symbol of our bond with them, just as they have destroyed their bond with us. We will cast out the queen and her royals to feel the cold on their skin, as we do. We will shatter their lies, force them to see the truth and Unite."

On the rock face of the River Ifrati, those carvings of the Cycle of Giving remained, worn by moss and lichen. Forgotten.

She drew her free hand, looking at the *Aeonida* carving on her wrist. She put her fingers to her heart chamber and fingered the lip of the opening. How could she force a faerie to lie there, against their will?

"That would only bring more pain and anger," she said. "If we shun the ancient ways like them, how will that make them want to return to us?"

"Forget the ancient ways, Esen. Peace makes change at a snail's pace. We are dying now. We need the speed and cunning of the fox. We will command their attention when we destroy the Rath. We can say to the queen, 'If you do not give us fae willingly now, we will take one hundred faeries from you every year—'"

Wrenching her hand free, Esen rose to her feet.

"You want to capture them?" she cried. "Force them to Unite against their will?"

"Do you see them Uniting willingly? We are the guardians of the forest. We must keep it alive if they will not."

"No," she said thickly. "We will find another way. I cannot do such a thing."

Tristan made as if to speak but swallowed hard. Hurt writhed in his eyes. "I was counting on you," he said, his voice low.

"I'm sorry," Esen whispered, then she turned and hurried away.

It is said that when the Mother first created the land, pine martens preyed upon us like other flesh-eating creatures. Until one marten saved the son of Finvarra, the first faerie father, from drowning, and the two formed a bond of life. Over time, martens became our close companions.

When our wings are unusable, martens are useful for quick travel.

To tame a wild marten, a bonding ritual must be performed, in which the marten senses the heart of the fae. If they judge the fae to be good, they bond with them for life.

Pine martens have become central to our customs, including festival rades.

Martens are dressed in fashion unique to the paticular festival, and mounted by palace officials including the Faerie King and Queen, in solemn procession.

Pine Martens - Friends of the Fae   3

CHAPTER 10: RUNAWAY

Thickets tore at Niamh, slicing her dress and scraping her arms like the whole forest hated her, wanted her blood. She kept leaping, gliding a little, before her ragged, paper-thin wings gave in and she rolled to the ground.

Her father's voice cried out. She kept running, running, her heart in her throat, but a hand grabbed her elbow.

She gasped. Her father looked at her, a world of hurt in his face.

She tore her arm out from him. "Get back!" she cried. "I'm going home."

"Nia, please." Tears stood in his eyes like little drops of dew. "Don't go."

She snarled. "No. You'll make me give my energy. I don't want to. I never wanted to!" Her voice rose to a shriek, like a fox in the night.

"Nia, I know. We can work this out —"

"You always say that. It means nothing!" Before he could speak again, she turned, and she ran and ran until at last, she slowed, throwing a glance over her shoulder.

He was still there. Small and green, as ragged as the brown grass enshrouding him.

"Go away!" she screamed, her voice hoarse. She ran again, stumbling, gasping for breath. Hot tears spilled from her eyes. She smeared them with the back of her hand and clamped her jaws on the wet skin. Her chest was full of fire, raw and burning. She screamed into her hand.

A hard surface slammed into her knees. She fell back on the ground, gasping. An oak root jutted up from the ground in front of her. All those dryads did was hurt her. "Curse you!" she cried. She threw a feeble kick at it. A jolt of pain coursed through her as her foot bounced off the wood.

She struggled to her feet, tearing off bits of dried leaves, and stalked on.

She had finally freed herself. So why did her heart feel so hollow?

Those marble columns would be white as pearls, the ivy green and glistening... and her mother a regal tower, her arms stretched wide to welcome her.

BEFORE LONG, Niamh befriended a marten and rode on his back. The sun rose and fell, and rose and fell... She found rosehips a few times, bright red against the scraggly rose thorns, and ate them greedily. Otherwise, she found herself chewing on flaky birch bark, her stomach a gnawing chasm. She couldn't quite get herself to swallow the bark. It tasted like ash.

The sun was setting when she rode into the village of the river fae. When she slid off her marten, her knees wobbled beneath her, fragile little things. She crumpled to the earth and breathed, just breathed...

"Niamh!" Rowan's voice pierced through her fog like the sun. He came darting toward her, a slender white bow in his hands. Dappled light played across his deep-forest skin, his tufty hair. His wings were withered like hers. He crouched by her and put a hand around her shoulder.

"Niamh, what happened? You look ill."

"I fled." He smelled so nice... like the warm musk of the river. She licked her dry lips. "I'm... I'm going home."

Rowan's brow knitted. "You're not going anywhere until I feed you."

He lifted her into his arms like she weighed a feather and carried her into the center of the village. Faces swam past her, eyes wide with concern. She'd come here to ask Rowan for directions and get him to come with her, not to sprawl at their feet, half-dead. But Rowan's warm smell enveloped her like a blanket, softening her thoughts into a haze.

The next she knew, she was sitting up, blinking as a wooden spoon pressed against her lips. She opened her mouth. A hot, chunky liquid slid down her throat, swirling into her stomach. Frog stew. She gaped her jaws open for more.

At last, the haze cleared. Rowan looked back at her, his mouth parted. He held the spoon in one hand and an empty bowl in another. The inner yellow walls of a gourd house curved behind them.

"Are you okay?" Rowan asked.

Niamh propped herself up on her elbows, reeling with a wave of nausea. Her vision swam. Soft furs and moss pressed against her palms.

She blushed. She was in his bed. He let her sleep there when she came to visit while he slept on the floor, but she had never gotten used to it. She ran her hand along a light-brown fur—rabbit, maybe—still rumpled with the memory of his body sleeping beneath it.

"I think so," she said.

Rowan sat on the edge of the bed, grasping her hand. "What do you mean by 'going home?'"

A fresh wave of determination coursed through her. "I'm a princess. I'm going home to my palace." He flushed, his ears reddening as she lifted his hand and kissed it. "Come be my prince!"

"Do you mean you are going to live with the queen?" he asked.

She nodded.

His brow furrowed. "The queen is colder than frost on the river. I wouldn't trust her. And what of your father?"

Her father's face, twisted with pain, flashed in her mind. Niamh jerked her hand out from Rowan's. "You don't understand. Don't pretend like you do."

Rowan frowned, his ears drooping. She bit at her lip. She was right.

He didn't have to look so hurt. She reached for his hand again. It folded in her own, willing.

"Rowan, please. Won't you be my prince?"

He shook his head gently. "I like my quiet life here, and I can't leave my family."

Niamh's lips trembled. He was supposed to say yes. She had dreamt of it so many times—of him playing his reed flute while she danced in the garden, and the sticky honey coating their mouths as they ate candied desserts and laughed and did only what they wanted to.

It wouldn't be the same without him.

"But, please," she said. "You can wear fine clothes and flit beneath marble columns all day. We won't have to work or know any hardship."

"I like working," he said, his face irritatingly calm.

She huffed. "I don't understand you."

"You can come visit me." Rowan frowned again, grasping her hand tighter. "Please do."

No. She didn't want to keep visiting him. She wanted to be with him. Her breath hitching, she shot out her arms and embraced him. He relaxed into her like water, enveloping her in his warmth.

When she finally pulled away, the last of the light had faded. "I promise," she whispered.

His finger touched her face, then pulled away. A tear clung to his fingertip like a bead of dew. He looked at her, his mouth parted.

"Could you at least show me the way there?" she asked.

"Of course. I will be your guide."

"Okay. Thank you."

Niamh wiped at her face. She was still getting to live with her mother, after all these years. She didn't need to cry. "How are you? How has the village been?"

"I'm fine..." Rowan said, his voice quiet. He put his finger to his mouth, squishing the tear. It trickled down his lower lip. "...now that you are here."

Her cheeks heated. "Answer me really."

Rowan lowered his gaze, tracing a line in the springy moss at the edge of his bed. "The river is still spilling from its banks. Two more houses were flooded. Four more are expected to be. The owners are already moving out."

Niamh's ears flattened. "I'm sorry. That flood was really bad. I haven't seen anything like it before."

"None of us have," Rowan said. "Not even the immortal fae among us."

Although Rowan's family were the only fae who still United in his village, he always spoke of the others as though they were a separate species from him. Perhaps they were. They would live forever and ever, while he and his family… would not.

"Do you know why it happened?" Niamh asked. "Was it just a coincidence?"

Rowan stared hard at the moss as though the answer lay somewhere within it. "I don't know."

That night, she lay in Rowan's bed, his scent washing over her like an embrace. Dry straw crinkled beneath her. She could glimpse his form in the dark, rolled on his side on a straw pallet. The soft sighs of his siblings sleeping in their beds filled the space like music.

Even with all his blankets, she was cold. Terribly cold.

"Rowan?" she whispered.

"Niamh?" His voice caressed her like a cool breeze in summer.

"I'm cold. Can you hold me?"

Straw rustled, and then his face appeared, pale against the blackness. He folded himself out beside her and held her close. He was so warm. She pressed her ear to his chest.

Thump, thump, thump, went her lover's heart. Was it faster than usual?

"How long will you be with your mother?" he whispered.

Somehow, she hadn't thought of that. "I don't know. A long time. Maybe forever. Why do you ask?"

His hand curled around her braid—the one that fell down to her ankles; that she'd braided and re-braided again and again on long nights at her father's when she couldn't sleep.

"I want to marry you," he said.

Her hand flew to her mouth. "Oh."

Her, married to Rowan, a Losgann Bank river faerie. She had dreamt of it before, but it would mean so many responsibilities. Bearing children, working on the land, keeping a home, holding votes with the council. And, as a member of Rowan's family, she'd be expected to give her children to the dryads. She could never escape them that way. They'd drain her and her children to death.

"I... don't think I can," she murmured.

He fell silent. Eventually, his breathing grew even, his limbs unmoving, but still, sleep wouldn't touch her. The blackness pressed against her, squeezing her chest.

Her father had looked so small against the dead bracken.

Where was he now? Was he crying somewhere, alone? A shudder coursed through her. What was she doing? Had she been cruel?

Tristan's eyes flashed in her mind like daggers.

No. She'd had no choice. She'd had to leave.

Heat rushed to her head, and her stomach clenched. She bolted up, clutching at her middle. A thousand daggers writhed inside her.

Gentle fingers brushed her arm. "Niamh?"

His touch was like the soft brush of a butterfly's wing. She needed him to take her away from this pain.

She fell back onto the bed and wrapped her arms around him. "Kiss me."

Although she couldn't see his face, she could feel him looking at her with concern. Her stomach still writhed.

"Are you sure about this?" he whispered. "About going to the queen?"

"Kiss me, please," she begged.

His mouth met hers, closing softly over her lower lip. She kissed him back, deep and full. Her hands clung to him, weaving spirals in the tangles of his hair, and then, before she could stop herself, she was feeling the skin beneath his shirt. She traced the line of his spine, his shoulder blades, imagining she was looking for a door that led to a land where she could fold into him, and him into her, and lose herself utterly.

At last, she urged him out into the night. She needed to be made whole, to forget everything... In the black woods, they tangled and wound together like snakes. She had never known him this way before.

It was like breathing after being underwater all her life.

When they returned to the bed, she stared at the ceiling as he slept, still feeling the ghosts of his hands, his mouth over hers.

But as she thought of her father, the writhing pain seized her again.

She ran out, hurled a frothy mess in the woods, and then she wept and wept.

Faerie Wings

Just like the dryad's leaves, our leaf wings bloom and fade again, following the wheel of the seasons. In the spring (fig. 1), the leaves bud from the back and begin to grow. Gliding becomes possilbe as the wings grow larger. In the summer (fig. 2), the wings are fully mature, and we have full flying ability. In the fall (fig. 3), the leaves wither until finally in the winter (fig. 4), they fall off altogether. We walk until the wings bud anew in the spring.

[1] Spring
some gliding ability

[2] Summer
full flying ability

[3] fall
gliding ability
until leaves
wither

[4] Winter
cannot fly

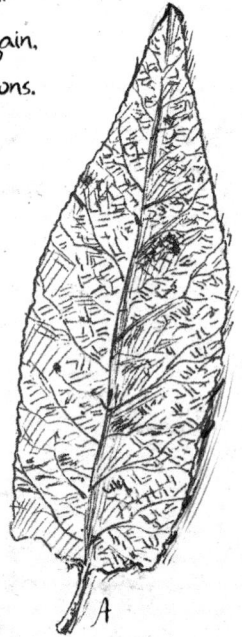

A pressed piece of a willow wing

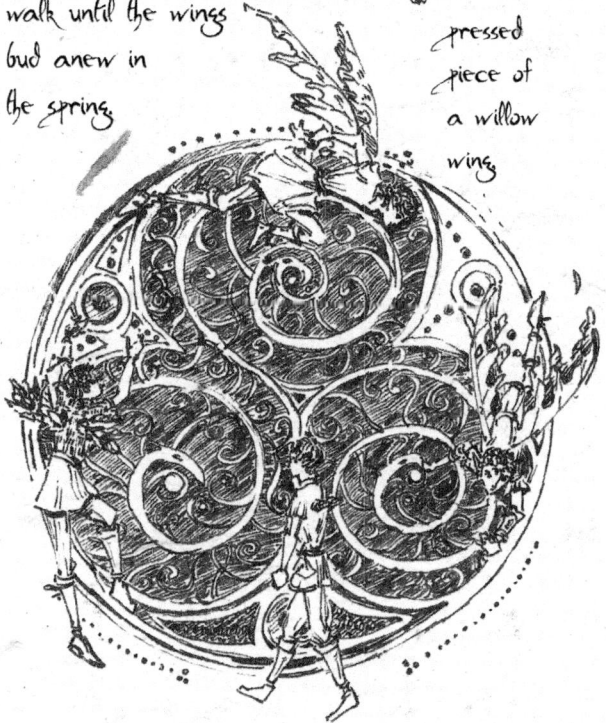

CHAPTER II: A LIGHT IN THE DARK

Esen awoke to the soft crunching of dry leaves. Blinking the heavy sleep from her eyes, she glimpsed a pine marten leaping out from the bracken toward her. Ian rode on the marten's back, his face drawn. His wings hung shriveled behind him—just the veins of where leaves would grow again in the spring. A thick pile of skins lay beneath him.

He had come back. Without Niamh.

Esen pushed herself to a seat.

Ian drew up to her and gathered the skins in his arms. *"Aeonida,* Esen," he said. Despite his age, she had always known Ian to have a brightness to him. Now, he was a flame extinguished, all the light gone from his eyes.

"Aeonida," she returned.

She thought of the things Tristan had told her. Words jumbled inside her, confused.

"Ian!" Aisling was wriggling with excitement, her eyes beaming. Frost from the cold night coated her bare branches.

"Hold still," Esen murmured, and wiped at the frost with her forefinger and thumb.

While she worked, Ian laid the skins at Aisling's roots and began to wrap them around her. "This winter is already very cold," Ian said, "and it will get even colder; I can feel it in my bones. I want to be sure you are as warm as can be. I made these for you. I don't know if it will help much, but it is something."

Aisling pulled a skin up to her nose and breathed it in. "It smells like you. And a squirrel."

"A few squirrels helped make it too," said Ian, managing a light laugh. "I thanked the Mother for their lives, for they fed me with nourishment and will now feed you with warmth."

"Thank you," said Aisling. She wriggled underneath the skins and popped her head out to smile. Esen couldn't help but smile back.

"I have one more idea," Ian said to her. "I must check it with your sister first."

He walked some distance away and knelt on the hard earth. Esen followed.

"I am thinking of creating a firepit near Aisling," Ian said. "I know fire is the bane of the dryads, so I would lay it very carefully with stones to keep the fire in, and I will light it only when I am awake and can keep an eye on it. How would you feel about this?"

Esen hesitated. It could be the very thing that would keep Aisling alive… or the thing that would kill her.

Finally, she said, "I think that would be wise. I trust you, Ian, but please keep a careful eye on the fire. I will watch too as I am able."

Ian nodded. "Of course. I will not let anything happen to her."

He rose and started to move back to Aisling.

"Ian—"

He turned, not quite meeting her eyes. Thousands of questions spiraled within her. Did she really want the answers? What good would it do to know? The damage had already been done.

"Did you speak with Niamh?" she finally asked.

"Yes," he said, his face contorting. "I'm sorry, Esen. I spoke with her the day she fled. I just couldn't—I couldn't come home, at first… without her."

Crouching by him, Esen held out her hand. He pressed himself against her palm, trembling. "You've grown so big," he said at last, his face tilted up at her. "It seems only the other day you were a little

Rootling like your sister. You are my daughter too, Esen, and Aisling my third. The only reason I am still standing is to care for the both of you."

Warmth flooded within her. *"Aeonida*, Ian," she said. *"Aeonida."*

fig.2 - Trilogy

fig.3 - Leaflets

fig.4 - Bird/Starling

fig.9 - Hoot

fig.1 - Oak

fig.5 - Dryads

fig.6 - Owl

fig.8 - Aeorida

fig.7 - Swirl

Taibshe Masks

CHAPTER 12: PETITION TO THE QUEEN

Through a gap in the foliage of the Rooted Ones ahead, Fafnir glimpsed the mound of the Rath Síoraí. It towered higher than the youngest of the Rooted Ones, backlit by a pale-yellow gleam on the horizon. It looked like an old, rounded tooth, jutting high above the ground.

Most likely, the queen would be in there. He was not bringing her news that she wanted to hear, but he was armed with evidence to back his claims. She would have to believe him, and then she could help him restore the forest, so he could return to his solitude with no shadow of guilt.

Fafnir wound the mainspring again, angling Serenity toward the docking station by the bank. Several firefly lanterns dangled from the posts, guiding his way. Squinting through the low light, he made out forty-three boats, simple things with oars, already resting by the docks. More than usual, especially at this hour...

The light faded, casting the river in shadow. As Fafnir approached, he wound Serenity less and less, until she nudged the edge of the landing. He scooped up the rope and leaped out, then tied her to a post. The connector piece had to be taken out of the propellers to disable them, the motor bound with a cord sealed with a lock, and more cords and locks around the body of the boat. Tedious, but necessary in this public space. He'd invented the thing, after all.

At last, he strode forward, following the lighted path. The flapping of firefly wings within the woven baskets whispered behind the shrill cricket song. It wasn't long before voices and laughter pierced the silence. The rich, savory scent of boar wafted in the air. Oh, yes. That explained the boats. It must be—

Jagged teeth leaped out from the dark. Fafnir jumped back, whipping out his knife.

A second, smaller pair of teeth grinned beneath. "Calm yourself," it said. *He* said. A faerie. "It's Taibhse Eve."

Fafnir blew air out his nose and sheathed his knife. Right. The masks. The first teeth he had seen were fox teeth, adhered to the faerie's forehead, obscuring his eyes. Hideous amalgamations of fur from various animals covered the rest of the mask, leaving only his mocking smile on display. Another masked faerie hooked the first one by the elbow, and they vanished back into the gloom.

Fafnir frowned. It was an abhorrent modification to the traditions. He'd forgotten this eve was the night before Taibhse, the festival of the spirit. Traditionally, the faeries wore wooden masks for the festival, carved with dryadic symbols to represent the union of wood and flesh when fae and dryad United. But over the course of the thousand years since the Ancient Law was revoked, the queen had begun to alter the rituals. She stripped them of their sacred rites reflecting the Trinity of Unity, the Cycle of Giving, and the Mother Wind, instead substituting carnal, material delights to please the senses.

A clever tactic to keep them in her power, but terribly foolish—it contributed to the number of fae who turned from Uniting. The Ancient Law was fading even quicker because of it, causing the dryads to die. While tonight, the fae of the Rath were parading in their hideous masks, taunting death. Laughing at it.

Soon, the clamor of the fae ahead drowned out the night noises. Fafnir stepped out into the clearing. A crowd had already amassed, setting up market stalls, apple-bobbing bins, and instruments. Masks obscured nearly every face. Putting up his arms in front of him as a shield, Fafnir ducked through the gaps in the crowd. A myriad of smells and sensations assailed him, but at last, he leaped out onto the steps leading to the entrance of the Rath.

A blast sounded to his left, and he turned to see a faerie shooting up into the sky with shoddy wings attached to her back, a rope flying out behind her that hooked under her shoulders. A wild grin lit up her face. The rope connected back to a simple wooden contraption resembling a giant crossbow. The faerie floated back down and danced with glee.

Fafnir grimaced. A petty game of pretend.

The Rath loomed high above him. The door was wide open as faeries streamed in and out in a bustling aggregate mass. Fafnir brushed his way through them, wincing with discomfort as bodies brushed against him.

Within the lavishly furnished entrance hall, he scanned faces until he glimpsed a faerie who had been an attendant of the Rath back when he had allied with the queen to revoke the law. He had a round, childish face... What was his name again? Oh, yes. Caden.

Beside an ivy-adorned white marble pillar stood Caden, dressed in the signature gossamer robes worn by the attendants of the Rath. He laughed with two other faeries wearing masks of rat fur.

"—marvelous, I know!" cried Caden. "They say it took a dozen shots to bring her down."

Fafnir slipped out from the crowd and stood before them.

"But she's a meaty one. They're trying out a new recipe. Garlic, cloves, and—"

Such shallow, senseless talk. How long would he prattle on for? Fafnir interrupted them.

"I wish to speak to the queen."

Caden started and turned to look at Fafnir. His smile faltered. "You look vaguely familiar. Who are you?"

"I am Fafnir Fiachra. You once welcomed me as the queen's personal musician. I retired for a time, but I am working on a marvelous piece I know she will enjoy. I would like to demonstrate it for her, to see if she will permit me to play it at Taibhse tomorrow."

Caden laughed. "Oh, that does strike a bell in the brain. What, did it take you a thousand years to write one song?"

The two rat-masked faeries snickered. One nudged Fafnir. "Let's hear it, then. Play your ditty."

Fafnir jerked back. "You'd scarcely hear it in this ruckus. And the queen would be aggrieved if her ears were not the first to hear it."

Caden's eyebrows perked up, and he rolled his jaw. His eyes fell on the violin strapped to Fafnir's back.

"Is that a violin? It looks funny."

Fafnir smiled thinly. A stump had more brains than this faerie. "I've improved the design."

"If you say so," Caden said. He silenced the laughter of the other two fae with a wave of his hand. "Wait here. I will ask if she wishes to see you."

Muttering under his breath, Caden turned and vanished within the crowd. The other two faeries glanced at Fafnir for a moment before slinking away to joke with the other fae.

Fafnir rubbed at his face. The bustle of the crowd about him kept his nerves on edge. At the end of the room, a black shimmer caught his eye —the Mirror of Divination.

He shouldered his way toward it, the crowd thinning as he moved closer. Faeries came from all regions of the land to gaze into its black obsidian surface. It was said that it showed visions of all kinds, from one's past, future, or an image of the essence of their heart.

He had never bothered to look in it before, but now, curiosity surged within him, drawing him forward. It was currently unused, forgotten in the preparations. Maybe it would show him if he would be successful in saving the forest, what his life of freedom would look like.

Or maybe…

He bit his lip.

His mother had passed. But he didn't know whether his father still lived. Maybe it could show him if he was still alive. If he was wandering out there, somewhere…

Seating himself in front of it, Fafnir clasped both hands together and leaned forward, gazing into its glassy depths. Only his own reflection looked back at him, his face a black, indiscernible shadow. Was this the vision? But it was behaving like common obsidian.

"Fafnir?"

Fafnir jumped to standing, and the legs of his chair scraped against the marble floor. Caden stood above him, his arms crossed.

90

"The queen has accepted your request for an audience. You can find her in the Room of Reflection."

Fafnir nodded and strode past Caden, back through the crowd toward the inner hall of the Rath.

"You're welcome!" Caden called after him.

The crowd thinned out as Fafnir passed under the archway. The white marble hall was cast in gray shadow, lit by rows of firefly lanterns along the walls. In the garden at the center, he glimpsed the carved roots of the marble tree, the trunk shooting up past his view. He sped down the hall as it wound in a circle. Soon he came to the spiral staircase leading up to the next floor, then came out to the second hall and rounded the circle again.

A cold sweat formed on his brow. He had not walked these halls in over a thousand years.

Approaching the railing that looked down into the garden below, he glimpsed in the flickering yellow light the tall ferns and bloodred lilies, lit by lanterns hanging from the low branches of the marble tree. There was the white ornate bench carved with dancing forms of faeries and dryads, where he and the queen had once sat. Dining together, laughing as though they were not crafting a plan in secret that would forever change the forest.

Windchimes echoed faintly from the branches of the tree. Faint moonlight glinted off them from the opening in the skylight above.

They had been close then. Too close for comfort.

He pulled at his collar. She knew his desires, and hers were much the same. The longing for immortal freedom, anyway. He only needed to remind her of this, to show her how it was still true.

He walked on. The clamor of the faeries faded to a distant hum, like the chattering of cicadas. Soon he found himself mounting the steps to the ninth floor, just below the top surface of the mound. The air here was clearer. A gentle gust lifted a few strands of his hair beneath his hat. Through the opening in the skylight, he glimpsed a sliver of the moon.

Before the door, he paused. He was cold. Calm. Controlled.

He opened the door —

And jolted.

The king's daughter sat facing the queen.

Niamh. The little child he had glimpsed on the platform of the Rath over a thousand years ago. She was taller now, her limbs fuller. Her rose-gold hair draped down the back of the chair, coiling at her feet. Her blackthorn wings were folded behind her.

Her skin was still as smooth as his own, as though death had been afraid to touch her. Her eyes were the same as he remembered them — large and round, the hue of the shadows of the deep woods.

And fearful.

A hideous mess of animal parts lay strewn about the marble table. The queen spoke in a low, feverish tone, pressing a mask in her daughter's white hands. A needle flashed in her other hand as she sewed a wolf tooth to the fabric. The shape of the tooth was not unlike the sharp points of the crown of yew on the queen's snow-colored hair. Her long, sweeping gossamer dress looked ghostly in the light, falling in folds about her shoes, the heels sharp as her needle. A thick albino rabbit cloak engulfed her shoulders, clasped at her sternum by two brooches, each carved in the ray-like pattern of the symbol for everlasting.

The door moaned as Fafnir opened it wider and stepped inside.

"There is an urgent matter I must discuss with you," he said, his gaze locking with the queen's.

Her eyes gleamed cold, her brow furrowing. The next moment, she straightened tall in her seat and set the needle on the table, a smile curling up the corners of her mouth.

"Ah, you lied to me," she said. "I was looking forward to a song."

He forced a stiff bow. "I would be honored to play for you again. But I must discuss something with you first."

Her smile wavered. "I see you haven't changed. Very well." The queen gestured to a seat beside them. "Please, sit."

Fafnir walked across the room and seated himself, leaning back with one leg resting on top of the other. The strategy of an animal in battle — take up as much space as possible.

"Fafnir, you look surprised," said the queen, her smile twisting wider. "I am so delighted my daughter has returned to me! I sent notice all through the Rath, but I presume you were too engaged in your own affairs to hear."

"Yes," said Fafnir.

He turned toward Niamh, meaning to greet her, and stiffened. She stared at him with narrowed eyes, with an intensity that startled him. He fought the temptation to drop his gaze to the floor.

"Welcome back, Niamh," he said, forcing a smile.

Niamh lowered her head, twisting her fingers in her lap. She looked uncomfortable.

The rustling of fabric sounded beside him. The queen had risen from her seat and stood by her daughter. She stooped over her, giving her a kiss on the forehead before grasping her hands to lift her from her seat.

Wait. Niamh's dress pulled over her stomach in a sloping curve.

She looked almost... pregnant.

"Nia, dear, I will speak to Fafnir alone now. You may go to your chambers. I will come by to say goodnight after we are finished."

The queen walked her to the door before shutting it, engulfing them both in the thick darkness of the room, the only light a flickering candle on the table casting weaving shadows on the walls. The queen turned and walked toward him, the echo of her heels piercing the silence.

"I am simply overwhelmed with delight." She spun in a childish circle, her gown swishing at her heels. "I cannot tell you how joyous I am. All I have wanted all these long years was to see her again."

At last, she seated herself, and reached for a bottle on the table by her. "However urgent this matter of yours is, I am sure it can wait a moment longer. I have not seen you in a millennium. How have you fared in your precious solitude?"

Fafnir pulled at the pointed tip of his ear. He wasn't here for idle chitchat.

"It has been well," he said—a partial truth. "And I am happy for you that your daughter has come home." He sifted through the options of things safe to say. "You are making masks with her for Taibhse?"

"Oh, yes," she said. With a twirl of her wrist, she popped the cork of the bottle. "Are you still afraid of a bit of liquor?"

Fafnir frowned. "As before, I will refrain."

The queen pouted. "What a bore." The mead glimmered bloodred as the queen poured it in her cup. Fafnir dropped his gaze to the floor.

"Come, Fafnir, don't be so stiff. You make me think you have forgotten how to hold a simple conversation. Can you count on one hand how many words you have spoken to another soul all this time?"

93

Fafnir quirked his mouth. What did it matter? She had never understood his need for solitude.

A smile played over the queen's lips. "I suppose so. Talk to me now. You have had years heaped upon years all to yourself. How have you spent the time so far? What are your plans for the next five thousand years, ten thousand, one hundred thousand? Is it everything you always imagined it would be?"

In the seclusion of his own home, he had often dwelt on these questions. The answers were knotted, the initial thrill confused by the shadow of death that had begun to suggest itself to him. But on those late nights, when he thought too long, slipping into the dredges of sleeplessness… he would question his own sanity. He would question whether, by regular discipline and routine, he could keep the suns from sliding away from him; keep his life from feeling like one fever dream, an elegant symphony repeated again and again and again until each note, in truth so perfect and pleasing, at last meant nothing to his ears.

But he could not speak of that. Not to her, nor to anyone. And it was only late-night delusions that brought on those thoughts anyway.

The queen clicked her tongue, her eyes glittering.

Fafnir ran a hand over his face. He would direct her to his point. He couldn't bear to step around it anymore.

"My plans going forward are dependent upon our present discussion," he said. "Over a thousand and seven years ago, we came together to make a change for the better. Today, I have come to propose a new change."

"Our minds meeting at last." Sipping at her cup, the queen leaned toward him. "What is this change you propose?"

Did she mean she wanted to work with him again? Likely not in this way. Fafnir clasped his hands together, forcing himself to meet her eyes.

"As I started to say earlier, I can't be silent any longer. When we formed our plan all those years ago, we did not anticipate nearly all faeries would turn from Uniting with the dryads. Now we are coming to the end of the generation of Rooted Ones who received faeries by law in the old days. They are perishing at an alarming rate. Within a few hundred years, they will all fall from old age. And though their children are growing, there are not enough to take their place."

The queen's face might as well have been carved of stone. He pulled at his collar. He had hoped she would at least be partially moved by this. Regardless, he continued.

"Without the dryads to pull up water from the earth with their roots, the soil is eroding during heavy storms, weakening the levees of the banks. The earth is still weakened from the flood of four moons ago, and it grows worse every day. The climate is shifting, with erratic spikes in temperatures and dangerous weather events. The systems of life are falling out of balance. Cold-blooded creatures, including many insects and frogs, cannot regulate the internal temperatures of their body enough to adapt to the changing climate and are perishing. The populations of our valued pine martens are already on the decline with the decrease in their dependent food source."

The queen's lips twitched in a frown, betraying her. He leaned forward, seizing the seed of hope.

"Maeve, we cannot survive without the dryads. We will soon perish without them, whether it is by flood or starvation or drought. Let me speak to the faeries under your approving presence. We must inspire fear in their hearts and encourage them to Unite once more. We do not need to restore the Ancient Law; we can determine how many are needed based on the number of existing dryads, and ask it of those who would most wish to Unite."

The queen arched her brows, a crooked smile twisting her face. If there had been any friendliness in her the moment they began, it was now gone.

A coldness settled through him. He had bet everything on his words winning her over.

This wasn't good.

The queen's voice split the silence like a frozen dagger. "Let us assume you are correct and we are in danger. Who exactly are these faeries that are allowed to be free from Uniting in your proposed plan?"

Fafnir's fingers tapped out an erratic rhythm on the arm of the chair, and he willed them to still.

She was forcing him to make a move on her terms, not his.

"I am correct," he said. "Ask me questions about anything I have said. I will explain it further. I can show you the banks of the River Ifrati, place your hand on the eroded soil."

The silence returned, heavy and oppressive. She would not speak, then, until he answered her.

Finally, he said, "As you know, now that the dryads are dwindling, there are more faeries than dryads. Not all faeries would need to Unite. Those who are most ill-favored to Uniting can withhold."

The queen leaned forward in her chair, her obsidian eyes glittering in the yellow light. "You mean to say enlightened, *useful* faeries such as you and me should live forever, and watch the rest perish for the world's benefit?"

Fafnir grimaced. "No. You are twisting my words in an effort to disconcert me. I said nothing of usefulness; only desire."

"And what is it you desire, Fiachra? I see no wings on your back."

The queen knew how it stung when he was called by his surname alone—his father's name. Heat rushed through his veins. He hadn't thought of that. How would he turn the tide back to Uniting if he had not United himself?

The queen stared at him, her eyes predatory. Already dismissing, denying, sweeping him aside. Sweat pooled at his collar.

"I will lead the change myself," he blurted out, speaking quickly. Too quickly. "I will be the spokesperson this time. I will only need your backing. I will turn the tide, restore the forest, and Unite along with those I inspire to provide a model for all. You needn't worry about yourself. You can keep your queendom and your life. I will make them leap to Unite so you do not have to."

Revulsion shuddered through him. He wanted to cut his tongue out and throw it away. He had lied. Like a cornered snake, with nothing but its mouth to defend its own skin.

Lies were his father's language. The language of animals, of serpents that slithered on the ground, entirely separate from the rational self-consistency he sought.

Now he had promised to lie for the rest of his life.

The queen was still staring. "And when will you tell your dryad that you are the one who caused their kind to die?"

Fafnir flinched. "They won't need to know."

"Ah," she said, sipping at her mead. "Evasive."

Wrong answer. He had to get himself together. He couldn't lose to her.

96

The queen turned to him. "Over a thousand years ago, you came to me, begging to be free of Uniting so you could enjoy your solitude. If your heart is so changed now, why have you not United already?"

Anger tightened his stomach like a fist. She'd pushed him into a corner, far away from the point of his argument. He had one card left, and he had to use it. He rose to his feet and held her gaze.

"Because death is encroaching, Maeve. Any day now, a flood could strike again and kill thousands. If I United today, I could die before I made change happen. And if we do nothing, your loving daughter—who returned to you after a thousand years—could die under your very roof at any moment."

The queen's face passed from white to red to white again. She rose from her seat, trembling, and stepped toward him, her face shrouded in gloom. Only a small stub of the candle remained, withering among a bed of oil.

"Sit." Her voice cut like ice.

He sat slowly, his fingers writhing on the armrest. Stupid things. They revealed him.

0 and 1 is—

Cold, thin fingers slipped under his jaw and gripped, forcing his head upward. A chill shivered up his spine. Her black eyes filled his vision, boring holes through his skull.

It felt as though if she kept looking, she would see all, know all.

Panic flooded his veins. He had to flee. He had to—

"I will let you live," she hissed, "because I liked you once. Now listen to me. It is *you* who is asking for death. If my daughter had never been forced to Unite, she could have been with me always. I am protecting my people from her fate. All your talk of floods and climate and animals dying is a delusion from your fevered brain. You are ill, distorted from too much isolation."

She gripped tighter, forcing his teeth to gnash. "Starting tomorrow, you will attend every festival. You will laugh with us, drink, dance the night away. Enjoy the fruits of your labor. You have everything you always wanted in life, do you not?"

He knew nothing but the racing of his heart, the violence of his breath. At last, her fingers released him. His head fell forward, his limbs like gelatin.

"If I hear of you sharing your delusions to others, know that I *will* take action against you. My rangers will be watching."

At once, Fafnir rose and stumbled, just catching himself on the armrest. His thoughts clattered together, a pounding pressure on his brain. He staggered toward the door. The queen's voice rang out behind him.

"And don't insult me again. You and I both know you will never Unite."

As Fafnir retreated out into the dim hall, he felt a gaze burning his back and looked to see Niamh standing in the shadows by the door, ghost white, her eyes wide.

"I am sorry," she stammered. "For my mother."

She stepped back and fled down the hall. A door slammed shut soon after.

The Trinity of Union

The Trinity of Unity summarizes the three Unions we form in our lives. Stór is the bond between friends, most deeply represented by the act of Uniting. Grá is romantic in nature, and is culminated in the marriage of two lovers.

Although beautiful in themselves, these two loves serve as mere reflections of the highest love, Aoradh. In learning to love in both Stór and Grá, the heart is made ready to reach toward the Mother and unite the soul to her.

Aoradh
Self-Mother

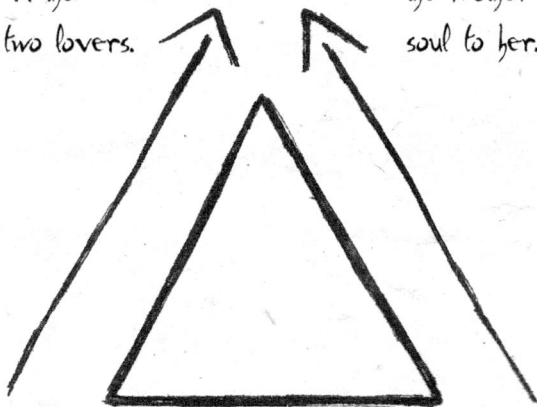

Stór
Dryad-faerie

Grá
Dryad-dryad
Faerie-faerie

CHAPTER 13: MOTHER

Niamh leaned against the door, her knees shaking. She slid down and folded her arms around her knees. Fafnir's words churned through her brain like the thrumming of heavy rain.

If what he said was true, then the forest was dying…

Any moment, Tristan's parents could crack and splinter, and splinter her along with them.

And what of her father, and Esen, and Aisling? They were in danger too.

The gentle rustling of fireflies whispered to her. Their yellow light flickered from baskets hung over the ceiling, illuminating her tiny bed heaped with pillows and the plush mouse on the floor with a crown sewed onto its head. Echoes of her childhood. All of this had been here, exactly the same, when she had lived here as a child. There was no trace of a single cobweb.

She placed a hand over her round stomach. She wasn't a child, though. She was a mother now. Her love had born a seed, and she was its vessel. A faint movement stirred from beneath her hand.

In about a moon, she would give birth. It would take her energy, like her dryads. Would it kill her? Would it kill her dryads in turn?

Hot tears pooled from her eyes, sliding down her face. Or… would she survive, only to die soon after when a flood strikes the forest, like Fafnir said? How long would her child live?

She clutched at her hair, braiding a section and unbraiding it again. She imagined her hair was Rowan's skin...

The echo of heels on marble reverberated outside her door. With a gasp, she scurried to her bed and threw herself in it, curling in a ball to fit inside, and drew the sheets over herself.

A slash of light pierced the room. Her mother's imposing form cut against the glare, her face masked in shadow. She bent, grabbed the mouse off the floor, and approached Niamh.

"Why are you crying?" her mother asked.

No. She wasn't supposed to be crying. Niamh wiped at her face, drawing the blankets over her mouth.

Her mother leaned over the woven railing of the bed and grasped her hand. Her touch was cold as ice. She placed the mouse in her palm. "It's King Squeak. Haven't you missed him?"

Niamh's breath hitched.

Don't cry. Don't cry.

Small sobs broke out from her. Fabric swished, and then her mother was beside her in the bed, pulling her into an embrace. Her hand ran through Niamh's hair, petting her like she was a marten, like she used to do when Niamh was little.

"Sssh," her mother whispered. "I know, sweetie. I can't believe your father did this to you. And you were so young. But you're here with me now. You're safe."

She didn't feel safe. She felt cold, so cold.

"When can I visit Rowan?" she sputtered.

"Tomorrow is Taibhse, dear. We'll have to finish our masks in the morning. And you'll be riding in the parade beside me. I'll give you your own marten. If Rowan happens to be there, of course you may see him, if there is time —"

"There is never time," Niamh cried. She straightened up, out of her mother's embrace. "I've been asking and asking. Why won't you let me see him?"

Her mother straightened too, her mouth pinching in a frown as she looked at Niamh's stomach.

Oh no. The blanket had rolled off her.

"I know you were a thin little stem when you came here," her mother said. "And I've lavished you with many delicacies, but…Nia dear, you're not pregnant, are you?"

Niamh blushed, hesitating.

Her mother went sheet white. "Was Rowan the father?"

"Yes," Niamh whispered. Tears started fresh in her eyes. "I love him."

The corners of her mother's mouth twitched in distaste. "You will be in labor within a moon, Nia, by the look of it. You can still go to Taibhse and see Rowan, if he is there, but I will not have you traveling anywhere. You must relax. I will do everything I can to see that your delivery is safe."

Niamh's ears flattened. "I'm not made of glass, Mom. I want to see him. Please."

"My answer is no." Her mother's words hurt. Would her father have let her go? But he was overly protective of her too. Her lungs felt tight, like she couldn't breathe.

"Can he visit, at least?" she pressed.

Her mother frowned, tossing her eyes to the ceiling. "I can send messengers to bring him. Why are you so insistent though, dear? You need to rest."

Because she could die… At her next breath, the next hour, the next sun…

She wiped her eyes. She would try to speak of her fears. "Mom, I… I didn't give my energy to my dryads yet. I am scared I won't have enough to give them. I can feel myself growing weaker every day. I am afraid that they, or I, might… might…"

Her mother seized her hands and pressed them tight. "Don't worry about them, Nia, dear. They have taken your energy plenty of times already. They should have enough. I will make sure you are okay. I won't let anything happen to you."

Niamh sniffed. Maybe her mother was right. They had taken her energy every year before, for almost a thousand years.

"Would you like me to sing you a song to help you sleep?" her mother asked. "Maybe 'The Grasshopper,' one of your old favorites?"

She wasn't a child. Niamh held her head high, pulling her hands back to fold them in her lap. "No thank you. Please go."

"Only if you are okay, darling," her mother said.

"I am okay."

Please go away.

Her mother sighed. "I will be down the hall, in my chamber. Wake me if you need me."

She helped Niamh lie down and folded the blankets over her. Placing King Squeak in her arms, she petted her hair, and bent down to kiss her on the forehead.

"Sweet dreams, Nia, dear."

Her mother rose and grasped a vial on the nightstand. She walked down the length of the room, tapping the powder into the baskets holding the fireflies. One by one, the fireflies fell asleep, their light dimming until the room was black as night. Black as death. A coldness seized Niamh's bones, shivering through her.

"Mom?" she breathed.

Her mother turned.

The question burst from Niamh before she could stop it. "Is the forest really in danger?"

Her mother stiffened. "Why are you asking that?"

"I am afraid I might die any moment anyway, like that faerie—"

Niamh clamped her hands over her mouth. *No.* She'd revealed herself.

Footsteps rang toward her, each one piercing.

"You are forbidden to listen to my private discussions," her mother's voice hissed, terribly close. "I am your mother and your queen. Would you take his word above mine?"

Niamh glanced to see her mother's face beside her, a pale apparition in the dark. "I'm sorry."

A cold hand cupped her cheek. "He was lying, dear. That faerie is mad. Come, be of good cheer. We'll finish up your mask in the morning for Taibhse, then there will be games and music and as much delicious food as you can eat. You'd like that, wouldn't you?"

What was true? Who could she trust?

"Okay," she muttered.

A smile brightened her mother's face. "You are safe, Niamh. You needn't fear. Go to sleep now."

She gave her one last kiss, then lingered in the doorway. At last, she left. *Good.*

Niamh wriggled beneath the sheets, but she couldn't get warm. She was here, in her marble palace, with fineries, comfort, and a mother doting over her, ensuring she had her every need.

Why did she still feel hollow? Was she selfish, like her mother?

She had been thinking only of what she wanted. Whether Tristan's parents would die or not, they were out there in the cold, while she lay here among warm pillows.

What kind of life would her child live? Would she lie amid warm pillows too, and not give to help her dryad through the winter?

It all felt wrong... So wrong...

You are cordially invited to
attend the wedding ceremony of

The Good Queen of the Fae Maeve Finvarra

and

The Good King of the Fae Ian Finvarra

At the Rath Sioari
from the first to the third
of the Flower Moon

An answer is requested to the steward Angus.
or through the Messenger dryad.

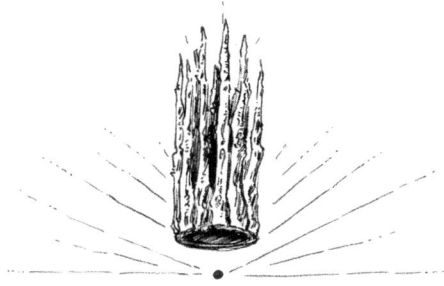

CHAPTER 14: THE QUEEN DECIDES

Maeve walked down the length of the hall, her footfalls ringing hollow. The shadows snaked long across the marble floor.

Niamh's face had looked like a ghost in the dark, with those shriveled, terrible wings folded behind her.

For over a thousand years, Niamh's room had remained empty. Maeve had chased away every cobweb and speck of dust with her own hand, fraught with longing. On her throne, she had counseled mothers who had lost their daughters to death. Her own grief had been a kind of death too, except there was no respite with time. Not when she was always inclining an ear in the night, in her rides about the land, for the voice she sometimes feared she had forgotten.

Now her daughter was finally home, but death had a claim on her.

And she was pregnant…

Very soon, Maeve would be a grandmother. There would be a little one in the palace once more, filling the marble halls with laughter. Running through the gardens with childish delight, just like Niamh had done when she was little.

But what if Niamh died, just like her birth mother had? Struck down because her dryads died moments after she gave birth?

A shiver coursed through her.

She came to the end of the hall and opened the old wooden door to the royal bedchamber. Shutting the door behind her, she began to pace the length of the room between the bed and the dresser.

Fafnir was mad. He must be mad. But if there was any truth in what he had said, then death was very, very near Niamh. Lurking just behind her, one hand poised to steal her away into some shadow realm and out from her love altogether.

She kept hearing his final words. He had spoken with such intensity, with the surety of a fae who had scaled a mountaintop to plant a flag of truth and could only be cast down from it by force. He had spoken with the same intensity when he had first come to her all those years ago. He had stood by a different truth then. It would take nothing short of the death blight of which he spoke to change his mind so thoroughly.

She could still remember how he had come to her then, a year before the day of her last hundred years of reign, when she and Ian were expected to Unite with dryads. All her life she had worked feverishly to earn her crown. She was the twenty-fifth child of her parents, born fifty-three years after the last. An unwanted accident, thrown to a surrogate mother the very night of her birth. She'd climbed her way up to queendom by the skin of her teeth.

And then, she was expected to take the first step that would eventually lead to her relinquishing her crown after five hundred years of reign, and going to live quietly, just her and the king who had disappointed her, doing nothing of any importance, only to die in time, torn suddenly from life, like Niamh's mother.

What was death? To what end were her feet taking her? The ancient ways of the forest promised that when you die, your spirit—the part of you that the Mother breathed—flies out of the body and soars over the world, reunited with the Wind of Worlds. But she had never felt the Mother's breath upon her, nor heard her voice. She was supposed to have, at her coronation, but she'd felt nothing.

How could she trust that this was really true? Wasn't it equally possible that there was nothing at all after death? Perhaps she would vanish like a puff of smoke. Or worst of all, couldn't it be even worse than life, in ways she couldn't begin to conceive?

There was surety in immortality. In living forever, on her own terms. She'd had Niamh already. She had her immortality then, and her daughter hers. Who was the Mother to demand they give it away?

Death was an option. And she wanted to live.

Then Fafnir had come to her with his brilliant strategy. He had wanted only to preserve himself. But by her prompting, they had worked to save all the fae. Disguised as her musician, he came to her secretly, working many nights into the late hours. He shared her desires, her questions about the ancient ways.

He was so much sharper than her drivel of a king; sharper than anyone she had met. If he had just accepted her offer, he could have ruled alongside her as her new king. They would have been an unstoppable force.

She stopped her pacing and rubbed at her eyes.

Never mind that. She had to weigh this matter before her. If there was any chance Fafnir was right — that in time all life in the forest would end without the dryads — then she was not her people's savior.

She was their demise.

And her daughter's…

With a sweep of her cloak, she began to pace once more. She pressed two fingers hard to her temple. The firefly chandelier flickered low, casting shadows across the room.

The dryads *were* dying. Sometimes it seemed they were dying faster than usual. The flood did affect that, of course. But they could be dying simply from their age. As Fafnir said himself, the generation of Rooted Ones alive during the Ancient Law was fading.

All the while, Fafnir had been holed up in some secluded place, watching the dryads dying around him. Knowing it was him who had caused their deaths.

Maeve halted. It must have been the guilt, on top of the isolation, that drove him mad. So he'd invented a slew of fantasies — temperature shifts, animals dying and the like — to try to get the other fae to Unite. So the dryads could stop dying, and he could be freed of his guilt.

Adrenaline rushed through her veins.

Yes. That must be it. The dryads were simply dying. It was a shame; they were naturally peaceful creatures. Slow to anger, and even slower to take action. But without having to share in their curse of death, the fae would live on in a world where no one has to die. Where daughters live alongside their mothers and all the fae of the land, laughing and dancing for all eternity.

She *was* her people's savior.

And she would fight to keep them alive to her very last breath.

Nollaig

Nollaig is our eighth festival of the year, on the sun of the Winter Solstice. It is a celebration of the birth of the new solar year, as the sun begins to grow stronger than the night.

The Spiral of the Moon is decorated with evergreen needles and bayberry candles, and dancers twirl in and out of the spiral, as they coax the sun back from sleep.

Traditional garb consists of evergreen needles, heavy furs, holly and yew berries, and crowns of lit candles

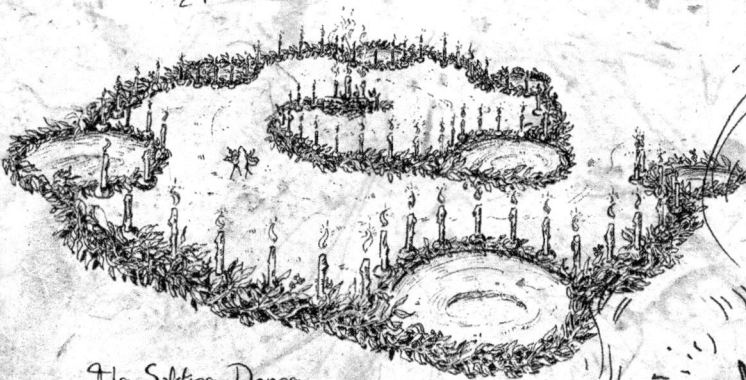

The Solstice Dance

The Saol Log is placed at the center. It is lit by the Faerie King and Queen, and blessed by the Palace Diviner. The burning brand it becomes represents the sun itself.

Saol Log

CHAPTER 15: NOLLAIG

Fafnir brought the cup of tea to his lips, his hand shaking. The liquid splashed onto his chin, scalding hot. He started, and the cup slipped from his hand and shattered on the floor.

Rot it. Rot it all. He kicked at the pieces, sending them flying, then paced the room, running his hands through his hair.

Maybe he was delusional, like the queen said. He'd scarcely slept since the flood, fixated on finishing his plan as soon as possible. And now it was shattered, like that broken cup.

He drew up to the basin of water on the larder counter. His reflection shimmered on the surface, gray as cold stone, his eyes dark with heavy bags.

Taibhse had gone long into the night. He'd joined the festival bards to have something to do with his hands. He'd donned the mask they gave him, mute. The only sound he made was with his violin, sighing among the clattering ruckus of the other musicians. He hated their riotous jigs, their empty laughter as they swarmed about him like a sea of leaping shadows.

He would not dance in ignorance with them. He would not be *normal* like she wanted.

A chaffinch trilled outside. It was morning now that he'd finally returned home. He should sleep. But how could he sleep when there was no plan between him and the death of the forest?

He rubbed at his temples, breathing shallow.

Without the queen's support, he would have to move the faeries to change on his own. Under her nose too; she would put all his efforts to a swift end if she found out. How could he do that? He was no one. He knew no one. There was next to nothing he could do alone, except try to convince the faeries one by one. At any moment, one of them could betray him and put an end to him.

His brain was hot, like it had been left out in the sun to bake. He needed sleep.

He sighed, a rattle in his throat, and trudged toward his meditation space. From separate clay pots he gathered handfuls of sage, pine needles, and cedar twigs, and wove them together into one bundle before placing it in the wall sconce in front of him. He lit the end, watching the flame linger a moment as it ate away at the herbs. Then he blew out the flame into a puff of smoke.

Crossing his legs, he closed his eyes. His body felt faint, like a flame clinging to the stub of a wick. He pulled in his breath as far as his stomach would let him.

0 and 1 is 1. 1 and 1 is 2.

The soft smoke curled around him, saturating the room in its fragrance. He let the breath release from his lungs.

2 and 3 is 5. 3 and 5 is 8.

The moss soft beneath him; flames licking cedar. He was the mist off the hills in the early dawn… He drew in a new breath.

5 and 8 is 13. 8 and 13 is 21…

Niamh's face, merging with the shadows in the hall, flashed in his mind. "I am sorry, for my mother," she had said.

13 and… and 21 is…

His head dropped to his chest, his mind blurring with weariness. Images of the queen leering at him and Niamh running down the hall assailed him.

Niamh… would she really want to bear her child under the queen's smothering gaze? Or would she come to miss her home beside King Ian, and—

He jolted up, his eyes snapping open.

King Ian. He was on the side of the dryads. Though the king had sparked a great controversy when he had stolen Niamh away at the ceremony, there were many that still respected him and remembered his reign with reverence. If he could get the king on his side, many fae would listen. Well, if he could get Ian Finvarra on his side. He wasn't the king anymore.

Fafnir had caused Ian's ruin. He had changed the law, had driven him out from his role and into the panic that led him to have Niamh United so young.

Fafnir's hands trembled. He clasped them together until they steadied. Ian might remember his face, like a shadow from another life, but he wouldn't know...

A pile of ash lay where the incense had burned. Fafnir swept it up and stood. Niamh was his key to get to Ian. The queen had kept her by her side for the entirety of Taibhse, never letting her out of sight. He doubted she would let Niamh leave the Rath at all until she bore her child. How would he get a chance to speak with her?

He rubbed at his temple.

Niamh had looked to be in her first moon of pregnancy. She would give birth by the middle of Oak Moon, most likely. She would hopefully have more freedom then. But then there was the child for the queen to obsess over.

He couldn't count on finding her alone. He could count on her being at the next festival, though—Nollaig, on the twenty-first of the Oak Moon. The safest place to hide was a crowd anyway. He could slip in, disguised, and try to get a moment to talk with her somewhere the queen couldn't overhear.

His chance of success was as thin as spider silk.

But it was a chance.

FAFNIR LEANED toward the small mirror of quartz propped up on the table, applying the last of the flour to his face with a scruff of cotton. He pinched powdered epsomite from a bowl and crusted it over his cheeks, his eyebrows, his jaw. He pushed out his lower lip and nodded at his reflection. It looked good, like a dusting of snow. He added more to the shoulders of his wool cloak, the hem of his pants, and his boots. They were all new articles he'd sewn for the occasion—dark gray with a few simple frills. He crusted his hair until it was nearly white. When he was satisfied, he gently took the mask of quartz. The crystals glittered with the sunlight streaming in.

He put it over his face, the cloth on the back resting comfortably on his skin, and strapped it behind his ears.

The faerie reflected back to him looked like a sea faerie, with skin the cold blue of the ocean. The queen would only recognize him if she stood right before him, but he would be sure to avoid her.

Hesitating, he turned to look at his violins. He couldn't bear to go on a journey without one. There would be plenty of other musicians there; it should be fine as long as he kept it covered behind him.

He grabbed his second-favorite violin and swung it over his shoulder. Just in case something happened to it—he'd still have his favorite. Munching on cricket legs, he packed his bag with dried food. When he opened the door at last, a deathly chill swept into him.

Winter had only recently begun, and it was already terribly cold.

He stiffened his jaw. Was this another temperature abnormality?

Either way, he had a plan to finally fix this.

Ian was out there somewhere. He wondered how he looked now, all these thousand years or so later. Without the immortal energy in his veins, age would have scored his face with lines, sagged his flesh, and perhaps bent his frame.

Those same years had passed for himself, and yet…

Fafnir put a hand to his cheek, feeling the smooth firmness of the skin. He often forgot that he was escaping the clutch of aging. How strange it must be to feel the body decay over time, the hand of death growing ever nearer, calling you to your fateful hour…

The darkness felt suddenly oppressive.

He stepped out into the night.

FAFNIR LINGERED at the edge of the cover of the Rooted Ones with his cloak pressed close to his chest. His breath fogged in white crystalline vapor, clouding his vision. Faeries streamed past him in the hundreds, jostling him.

The Rath Síoraí towered ahead, a huge, dark mass against the twilight sky. Countless candles and holly wreaths adorned the entrance and stairway. Twenty thousand or more faeries were jammed about the Rath like tadpoles, filling out the clearing and spilling over into the edges of the forest. Some of them wore the traditional thick garments of fur and wool, with holly crowns over their heads. A few bore lit candles mounted to the shoulders of their capes and crowns. They walked regally among the rest, keeping their heads high to prevent the candles from slipping. But most of the fae were dressed like him, with salt coating their faces and clothes to pass for snow. It was a relatively new fashion, quickly increasing in popularity.

So many fae... and all of them without wings.

Fafnir narrowed his eyes, scanning the crowd. No sign of the queen or Niamh about the Rath. At the center of the clearing, the Spiral of the Moon had been decorated in traditional Nollaig fashion. The spiral pattern of the eight pits dug into the ground—each representing a phase of the moon—was accentuated with woven holly and ivy, and rows and rows of candles leading inwards. At the center, resting in the largest pit, representing the full moon, was the Saol Log—a log of yew wood adorned with sprigs of fir, pine cones, and holly berries. Soon the Solstice Dance would be held along the Spiral. The Spiral was large enough for a thousand fae to dance within and out again. It was empty of fae now; the dance had not yet begun.

Fafnir studied the banquet table beside it, heaped high with meats, steaming broths, plates of diced and candied nuts, and meads of all colors. Above the sea of faces he caught the sharp point of the queen's crown of yew. He leaned forward. As bodies shuffled about, he glimpsed the queen, her face tight with an emotion he couldn't name. Niamh was beside her, pointing at a plate of frosted hickory-nut slivers. Within a wool bundle across Niamh's chest, a tiny face the soft green of a dandelion stem poked out.

Her child.

She looked no older than a few suns.

The crowd shifted and blocked his view. Fafnir started forward, brushing against countless bodies. Music flitted above the cacophony of voices, quick and wild. The thick aroma of the meats mingled with the smoke smell of candles, along with the scent of each body he passed. His spine straight, he forced himself to keep his nose from wrinkling.

The banquet table appeared ahead. He drew up to the end and grabbed a wooden bowl, then slid his eyes down the table. Niamh was piling her plate high with one hand and laughing, while covering her mouth with the other. But there was something in her eyes… a kind of somberness. The queen was stiff beside her.

Someone bustled into Fafnir, nearly knocking him over. Straightening, he moved to the center of the table and began to pick at a severed rabbit head, its glassy eyes staring. He swiveled his ears, straining them.

"When will the dance begin?" he heard Niamh ask.

"At dusk," the queen replied. "But you may not —"

"Please, I haven't danced the Spiral of the Moon since I was a little child."

The queen's white brow pinched. Eventually, she said, "Very well."

Fafnir stepped back from the table. That would be his chance. The Solstice Dance was a dance of flashing movements and weaving in and out of partners. He would try to get a turn with her.

He bided his time, wading through the crowd and eating the spiced meat in his bowl. At last, as the sky turned the color of smoke, the queen, Niamh, and her attendants began to walk within the Spiral of the Moon. A faerie with white-frosted fur about her shoulders ran ahead of them, lighting the candles dotting the way. Small at the edge of the ring and thicker and brighter toward the center, they illuminated the night.

A hush fell over the clearing as the queen paused at the center of the Spiral, before the Saol Log, and threw her hands up toward the waning crescent moon. Now a thin sliver of white against the dark, the white would swell over the next nights until the moon shone full, bright and whole. Like he hoped to be very soon... if he could do this.

"Let us dance to coax the sun back from sleep, to bring brighter days ahead," the queen cried. "May warmth and blessings come upon us soon. Three cheers!"

"Three cheers!" roared the crowd.

An attendant handed the queen a staff with the end lit. She raised it high above her head before sweeping it down to light the Saol Log. A flame blazed forth, burning away the fir and pine cones before licking along the log.

The sharp taste of sap perfumed the air. Fafnir's eyes watered with the smoke. The last time he had attended Nollaig was the year before he had run from home. A Diviner, the meditators between the Mother Wind and fae, had stepped forward amid the smoke and uttered a prayer in a language akin to Wind-Speak, sounding of wind and leaves.

But that was another lifetime ago. Now, the faeries simply hooked arms with their partners and began to spiral within. Niamh swayed in to join them, keeping one hand on her baby. The queen stepped out from the spiral and stood at the edge, watching.

Fafnir followed after Niamh. The musicians played with a new fury, setting a rush through his veins. He let his limbs flow to the rhythm, twirling up to the start of the spiral. A tall blue faerie grabbed his hand, and he spun with him. Hands grasped and unclasped his own, faces blurring before him in a flurry of movement. Closer, and closer...

A pale face flashed ahead of him. He twirled out from his partner and grasped Niamh's free hand. Her hair flowed in tangles about her face, her eyes wide. She was breathing heavy, a falter in her step. He frowned. The dance had just begun. Had the pregnancy weakened her?

"Do you remember me?" he asked, speaking low. "The night before Taibhse, I spoke of the forest dying."

A little gasp escaped Niamh. "Fafnir?"

He hushed her, sliding his eyes about them. The faeries danced on, heedless.

He hadn't been able to get the queen's warning out of his ears. *"My rangers will be watching."*

"Others may hear," he whispered.

She gave a small nod. She flitted with him in and out of the other dancers. Her baby looked on with wide eyes, her mouth open in a little circle.

"Your life is in danger, Niamh," he said.

Niamh's eyes widened, though her words came out steady. "Why should I believe you?"

A good question. "I have done very diligent research."

She pinched her mouth. Of course she would. Anyone could say such a thing. He racked his brain. He had met her with the queen on the thirtieth of the Blood Moon, over a moon before winter.

Was it possible that...

"Have you given your energy to your dryads yet?" he asked.

A lump formed in her throat. He'd gotten her. They twirled, and the second he released her hand, another hand grabbed Niamh's and pulled her away.

Rot.

He partnered with another faerie, twisting and reeling, pushing closer and closer, until at last, he joined back with Niamh. Her palm was sweaty, a tightness in her face.

"I haven't," she whispered.

Her eyes reflected a deep well of pain.

He knew that pain. He swallowed. He didn't want to pry at it like an open sore, but it was his best chance.

"You must give it to them. The life of the forest is hanging by a thread. There will be more floods like the one we experienced already, but worse. If your dryads don't receive your energy, they may not be strong enough to survive. You will lose your life and leave your daughter without a mother."

Niamh paled, then her brows furrowed. "What about you? You don't have any wings."

He stumbled and readjusted his rhythm. Who was he to ask such a thing of her? He would never give to the dryads himself.

A chill coursed through him. The queen had said to him, *"You and I both know you will never Unite,"* but did it matter? He would get every other fae to Unite. That would be more than enough to save the forest.

Revulsion lingered in his stomach. Whenever asked, he would have to promise to Unite later. Likely he would be asked often.

His father had promised his mother so often that he would better himself for her. It had been a vile lie.

"I do care," he said at last. "I came to ask if you could take me to your father. I have a plan to save the forest, and I need his help."

As he twirled her, she released her hand to caress her daughter's soft, green hair. Her daughter giggled. She had at least a thousand years of potential ahead of her. If he failed, she would not live to see those years.

Fafnir pressed on. "What kind of future do you want for her?"

Niamh glanced at the dark shapes of the Rooted Ones pressing close to the clearing. A determination flashed in her eyes. She caught his hand again and danced with new vigor.

"I will go with you," she said. "When we are blocked from her view, we can slip out. There are martens at the edge of the forest we can ride."

Adrenaline shot through him. He glanced to the far left to see pine martens saddled for the parade. He looked back at her and nodded. They danced together to the edge of the ring on the opposite side of the queen, shrugging off the hands that reached for them. At last, they leaped out into the thick of the crowd and darted through the fae.

Niamh ran ahead of him, pulling him along until they slipped into the shroud of the Rooted Ones beside the martens. Several rangers stood by, watching the dance with crossed arms, their backs facing them.

Niamh pulled a piece of venison out from her pocket and held it out, clicking her tongue. The marten nearest them turned, swiveling its round ears. By its elongated cheekbones, smaller teeth from what he could see, and its size overall, he guessed it to be a female. Glimpsing the meat, the marten lunged forward and licked it off Niamh's hand. Niamh took the marten's reins and guided her into the shadows, then mounted carefully and held out a hand to Fafnir. He hoisted himself onto the marten behind her, careful to use his own strength. With nothing else to hold onto, he was forced to wrap his arms around her middle.

The marten leaped into the forest. The brittle air stung his eyes, the Rooted Ones around them a blur.

He glanced back. No one was following them. Yet.

"Do you think they noticed—"

Niamh's child began to wail. *Rot.* She'd been so quiet before.

Niamh urged the marten faster. As the marten leaped over fallen trunks and across thick branches, Niamh drew her face against her daughter's, humming a melody deep in her throat. A nursery rhyme—one his mother had sung to him when he was little, though he had forgotten the name. Her daughter grew still, her eyes wide with wonder.

He had not seen a faerie child in hundreds of years. Her ears were so small, with the slightest point. Every one of the Rath fae had been like her once. Small and vulnerable, cradled in their mother's arms. But now, they were hundreds or a thousand years away from their child selves, and they would never bear children if they never United. Did they ever think of that? That they were creating a world devoid of children? Where everything under the sun was known and taken for granted?

"I don't know," Niamh said finally.

He'd forgotten his question.

"My mother will notice soon," Niamh continued. "We must ride all night. If there is time, I want to quickly stop at a river village to leave my daughter there with her father. It is on the way."

"Very well," Fafnir said. "I will keep a close eye behind us. And I thank you, Niamh. For trusting me."

Those words felt wrong, somehow. Only a suspicious person assures that they are not so. Niamh looked straight ahead of her, silent.

"I want my daughter to live how I should have lived," she said. Cold wind whipped by them, the marten panting as she ran. "To care for others beyond herself, and live in a world where others do the same."

Fafnir pressed his lips. It was a lovely vision.

"I commend you."

The Sage

The heart of the dryads, as both their leader and the guiding symbol of the land itself. The Sage is composed of two sequoia dryads joined in the act of Rooting, and represents all three unions of the Trinity of Unity. Together with their circle of six Elders, they commune with the Mother and guide the Rooted Ones in their reflections and judgements.

CHAPTER 16: STOLEN IN THE NIGHT

Nervousness raced through Maeve's veins. The dancers spiraled like winged seedpods, flowing toward the center of the Spiral of the Moon and back out again.

Niamh had grown so terribly weak since she had given birth. It wasn't good for her to be exerting herself like this. But there had been such a shine in her eyes when she had asked. She could never deny her daughter's happiness.

As the dance wore on, she lost sight of Niamh for a long stretch of time. She must be hidden within the dancers. But she scanned up and down the line, over and over, without seeing her.

She turned to her most trusted ranger, Tiernan, standing by her side. The moonlight turned his white tunic silver and glinted along the sheath of the blade at his hip. "Find Niamh," she said, "and bring her back out to me."

Tiernan's eyebrows lifted. "Yes, my queen. She looked to be having a good time. Do you mean —"

"Go find her," Maeve urged.

With a nod, Tiernan started toward the circle and shouldered through the crowd. He stopped the dancers at the edge of the spiral, questioning them, but they shook their heads.

A cold sweat formed on her brow. She hurried forward, faeries parting to let her pass. The dancers stilled before her. Several fae shoved themselves out from their ranks.

"We saw her ducking out from the dance," one of them said.

"She was with another faerie," another said.

"Where is she now?" Maeve demanded.

The faeries talked amongst themselves, then shook their heads. "We don't know."

Maeve paled. It couldn't be true. Niamh couldn't have left her, after all Maeve had done for her. Heat rushed to her head. She stifled the tears, holding her head high. "Describe this faerie she was with."

"He was dressed up in the snow style, wearing a dark-gray cloak. He had a violin case on his back."

She stiffened. Was it Fafnir?

Whoever it was, she would kill him. She would hang him by the thumbs over a fire.

She whipped to Tiernan. "Gather my rangers. We will ride after her."

As Tiernan darted off, she turned back to the dancers. "Which way did she go?"

They pointed. She nodded and spun around. It had grown eerily silent, every face fixed on her.

The anger coiled in her stomach. She wanted to send them all away. There could be no dancing when her daughter had been stolen. But this was the largest festival of the year, and she had to keep them happy.

"Continue as you were," she said, her voice ringing out. "I will find my daughter."

She swept through them toward the martens.

A giddy sort of relief flooded through her. Niamh did not hate her. She had only been taken from her; perhaps deceived by Fafnir. It must be part of some new plan of his.

But she would save her daughter.

She would bring her home.

Life Expectancy

Dryads live anywhere from five hundred to fifteen-hundred years, depending on their place of Rooting and their health. Past age one thousand, we faeries do not appear to age any further. When United, if one perishes, so does the other.

It is believed that the faerie Igraine of the Spéir Driofaires, and her dryad Rowina Oak were the oldest faerie and dryad to have ever lived. They lived for a total of three thousand one hundred and forty-two years, until a storm severed the largest limb of the dryad. They died shortly thereafter.

Stages of Faerie Development

Ages 1: Infancy
Ages 2-11: Early to late childhood
Ages 12-21: Adolescence
Ages 22-100: Early adulthood
Ages 101-599: Middle to late adulthood
Ages 600-1000+: Elder

CHAPTER 17: AMBUSH

A crash pulled Esen from sleep. She struggled up, her frozen limbs stiff. Tristan was darting toward her, panic in his face. Ian ran behind him.

"There's a fleet of mounted faeries coming," Tristan said breathlessly.

Esen furrowed her brow. "How do you—"

"I saw only a flicker of fur, but I know a marten when I hear one, and I heard many. And they were headed this—"

Two cloaked faeries on a marten burst out from the thicket. One lowered his hood to reveal a moon-white face veiled behind a mask of crystal. His skin and hair glittered like snow. He removed his mask, his eyes riveted on her. They were green like new leaves in spring, and strangely familiar.

And the other… She gasped. *Niamh.* Her hair like a long train of dandelion wisps behind her, frayed and hopelessly tangled. With a quiet strength, she held her spine straight.

She had returned.

Niamh slid off the marten and darted toward Ian, stumbling. Ian rushed forward and locked his arms tight around her, as though he couldn't believe she was really there.

"Nia," he gasped, tears rolling down his cheeks. "I—I thought I had lost you."

"I should have never gone to my mother," Niamh said, embracing him back. "I know I hurt you. I'm sorry, Father." She held him for a moment longer before drawing back. "Soon I will have to leave you again, but differently. I am a mother now."

Esen started, her leaves swishing together.

Niamh? A mother?

Ian's eyes widened. "What? You have a child? Where is it?"

"I left her at the river village with Rowan," Niamh said.

Ian's brows knitted. "Rowan? Is he—"

"Yes, Rowan is the father. I'll be going back there after I give my energy to Tristan's parents."

Ian stared, his brows nearly obscuring his eyes.

"Listen," Niamh said. Though she had spoken evenly before, a desperation tinged her voice. "You took me at such a young age. My whole life, I have felt trapped here, held back. That's how you felt with my mother, wasn't it?"

Ian's face twisted with pain. Niamh folded his old, weathered hands in her own.

"You started new here," she said. "Now I need to start new also."

Ian's hands shook. He had already lost Niamh once; now he was losing his daughter all over again.

"Nia, I never wanted to do that to you. I panicked. I wanted to make sure you United in case she took you from me, so you could know how beautiful life is when you live the ancient way. That was something your mother never understood."

"I see that now," Niamh said. "I want to live that life, on my own terms. Did you mean to keep me here forever so you could hold onto some shred from your past? Whatever you had with my mother is gone, but you've given so much to Esen and Aisling. More than you know, I think."

Ian embraced her, quivering against her. "I'm sorry. I'm so sorry." He finally stilled and stepped back from her with a ghost of a smile. "You've grown so strong, Nia."

Niamh looked up at Tristan. He was staring at her with a strange, intense expression, his hands twitching.

"Tristan, I'm so sorry," Niamh said. "I know I hurt you also. I'm going to—"

She drew short, whipping her head round.

Movement flitted within the darkness of the bracken. Yellow eyes flashed, and an arrow glinted as it slotted into a bow.

It was aimed toward the snow faerie.

"Watch out!" Esen cried.

The snow faerie leaped off the marten and rolled to the ground as arrows whirred through the space he had just been. Over two dozen faeries on martens broke out into the open. Half of them rode toward Niamh and Ian, while the other half restrung their bows, pointing them where the snow faerie crouched on the ground, frozen with fear.

What was happening? Why?

Quick as lightning, Tristan swung his arm, knocking the approaching faeries off their mounts. The rest of the faeries dipped the tips of their arrows into brightly burning lanterns and shot at Tristan.

Twelve shafts buried in his left knee. The flames leaped onto his bark, and Tristan screamed. He rolled to the ground, extinguishing the flames, and lunged toward the archer faeries.

"Aon Mharú!" The deep, guttural cry—the cry of peace—broke out from Esen's throat. She threw herself in front of Tristan. His weight barreled into her. Digging her feet into the ground, she wrapped her arms around him. He writhed against her with terrible force.

"Tristan, please. Be still," she begged.

The archers waited with dark faces, every arrow pointed at her and Tristan.

Finally, Tristan stilled.

"He's going to cool his wound in the river," Esen said to the archers.

A snarl sputtered from Tristan.

"Go," Esen hissed to him. "It will relieve your pain."

Tristan's lips curved down, his chin trembling. His knee was black where the flames had been. He would bear that scar forever.

He turned and took off toward the river.

The archers' bows were still drawn, their shoulders tense.

Esen gathered Ian, Niamh, and the snow faerie into her arms, then pressed them back so they crouched on the slope of her chest, her crossed arms a barricade to shelter them. Her spirit leaped into her throat. Aisling was out of reach behind her.

"Don't hurt us," she said. "We mean you no harm."

One faerie put out a hand to the others. They lowered their bows. The faerie urged her marten forward. Thick fox fur adorned her coat, her skin the silvery white of gossamer. A crown of yew rested on her head.

The Faerie Queen.

"I am here to bring my daughter home," the queen said, her voice like ice. "Release her."

Niamh looked up at Esen. "Let me talk to her." Though her body shook, a steadiness was in her gaze. Esen dropped to her knees to let her down.

Ian reached for her. "Niamh, please —"

Niamh hushed him and dropped down onto the leaves below. She straightened, looking as firm as a Rooted One, and faced the queen.

"Where is your child, dear?" the queen asked. "Go get her so we can take her home."

"Your palace is not her home," Niamh said. "Nor mine."

The queen halted, flinching as though she'd been struck. "Niamh, come here. Don't make me force you." One of her fingers twitched. Her faeries drew closer.

Niamh held her spine straight. "I have lived all my life between what you wanted for me and what my father wanted. Now, I want to carve my own way. My daughter is with Rowan. I'm going to give my energy to my dryads and then dedicate my life to raising a family and giving to the forest so my daughter can live a long, happy life."

"The Ancient Law leads to death, Niamh," the queen said. "Do you want your daughter to die?"

"She will die either way, in time. I want her to live well most of all."

"You don't know what you're talking about. Whatever Fafnir told you is —"

"I made this decision on my own. He has nothing to do with it."

The queen stared, paling. "Nia." All the ice in her voice had melted. "Did you ever love me?"

Niamh shook her head gently. "Please leave."

Tears obscured the queen's eyes. She turned her face, but finally, she spurred her marten and leaped back into the thicket. At once, her faeries followed her.

Esen helped Ian and the snow faerie down. She could still see the bright flash of flame, smell the smoke coloring the air.

Her eyes grew wet. She had nearly lost Tristan. She had nearly lost everyone she loved.

She glimpsed the snow faerie frowning at the ground. He didn't seem to have any wings. Why was he here?

"That is Fafnir," Niamh said, following her gaze.

Fafnir looked up, as though remembering where he was. Turning to Ian, he gave a low bow. "It is an honor to meet you. I have traveled here for your aid. I seek to restore the forest."

Ian stared at him, his brows furrowed. "Fafnir Fiachra? I remember you, from another life. You visited the queen often in that last year."

A slight emotion ghosted over Fafnir, but she couldn't discern what was in it. "I served as one of her musicians, yes," Fafnir replied, his face stony again. "I left the role when she abolished the Ancient Law. But that was another lifetime, as you said."

He was over a thousand years old, then, though his skin retained the firmness of youth. Even Niamh had begun to show faint lines in her face. With his cloak, she couldn't tell for sure if he had wings. Maybe they were hidden beneath his cloak... but not with a face like that.

He must be immortal.

"She hid it from us all," Ian murmured, "until it was too late." His face clearer, he shook Fafnir's hand. "We are glad to have you with us. Let us speak more in the morning. We must rest now."

"I am going to give my energy to my dryads," Niamh said, her hands shaking at her sides. Ian embraced her.

"Be careful, Niamh," Esen said. "You are very brave."

Niamh pulled back from Ian and gave Esen a small nod.

"Come with us, Fafnir," Ian said. "I will be with Niamh, but you can stay the night in my home."

They walked down the hill. Esen turned to Aisling. Her sister's little eyes were wide. "I am so glad you are okay," Esen said. "Wait one moment. I need to check on Tristan."

She hurried down the hill toward the river.

In his fury, Tristan's eyes had burned like two coals. Desperate. Vengeful.

When he was rational, he had spoken of stealing the faeries. Of

133

forcing them to Unite, treating them like the fireflies the fae trap in their lanterns. If she had not stopped him earlier, would he have killed the queen and her faeries? Broken their bodies on the soft grass, their blood pooling into the earth like water?

But hadn't the queen done that to the dryads? All across the land, bodies fell beside bodies, writhing with dragans, decaying as one...

Esen shook her head, scraping her branches together. She reached the river at last. But Tristan was nowhere to be seen.

After looking for some time, worry churning her spirit, she came home and approached the trunk of her parents. Aisling stooped beneath them, her head bowed in slumber.

"Mother," she said softly. "Father."

No answer. They must be asleep.

She rapped on their bark until at last, their bare branches stirred, scraping together in speech.

"*Yes, Esen dear?*" said her mother. By the lightness of her voice, she knew both of them had slept through the terrible encounter.

Esen bit her lip. She didn't want to do this to Tristan, but he was dangerous.

"I am scared of Tristan," she admitted. "He was just injured trying to attack a group of fae to defend Niamh. There was violence in his eyes. I do not think he will try anything else this winter, and soon the cold will force us all into deep sleep. Just in case, can you ask among the Rooted Ones to appoint a few Walkers to watch him at first thaw?"

"*This news grieves us,*" said her mother and father in unison. "*We will send word at once. Come spring, he will be watched carefully.*"

SUNLIGHT SLASHED against Fafnir's eyes. *Rot.* He'd overslept. Why hadn't his timekeeper gone off? He felt about for it, but his hand touched a soft woven cloth. That wasn't his. He sat up quickly, blinking as the room came into focus.

It was a narrow, cramped space. Wooden beams held the sloping walls in place, and a circular window on either side let in the sunlight that had woken him. A rugged cypress table, simple but thoughtfully built, filled the center of the room, with two chairs positioned by it. Across the table, on another bed, Niamh lay. A heap of cloth and squirrel skins were stretched over her, revealing only her face. She was deathly white.

The events of the day before rushed upon him all at once. He was a stranger, in a stranger's home. By necessity, he'd given up his complete control to seek help from others. He'd almost been killed. The hazel dryad had saved him. Esen.

The same one who saved him from the flood.

Heavy stone scraped in the corner of the room. Ian was stooped over an open box oven, pulling out a large pot. The savory smell of meat and herbs saturated Fafnir's senses. Ian set the pot on the larder counter and drew out several ladlefuls into a bowl. He blew on it, tested it with his finger, and carried it over to Niamh.

As he approached, Niamh stirred, a small smile on her face. She let him lift her head with a gentle hand and feed her the broth. When he had finished, she dropped her head back heavily.

Ian rose and turned to face Fafnir.

Ian was not the hunched crone Fafnir had expected him to be. He had lived as an ordinary faerie for thirty-eight years, reigned for another four hundred, and been a Winged One for over one thousand. Those years lived along the wrinkles and grooves of his skin, like cracks in barren earth, but his stature was lively, his back straight. A spark of something like youth radiated from his eyes.

How was that possible? The oldest faerie in legend was a Winged One, who lived to be just over three thousand years old. It was said she was a shriveled thing by the end, scarcely able to walk.

What made the heart finally stop beating? Was it the wearing down of the organs after time had pressed its weight too long? Or was it the wearing of the spirit?

To think he had once worked under Ian's very nose to bring about his ruin...

"Are you alright?"

Fafnir started. Ian stood in front of him, his eyes narrowed. "You've been staring intensely."

Fafnir rubbed at the back of his head. It was still crusted with salt.

"I'm fine," he croaked. His right cheek flared with pain as he spoke, as though a thousand little thorns pierced it. He put a hand to his cheek and felt a sliver of dried blood crusted over the flour and salt.

He'd hit the ground hard to evade those arrows.

Ian stepped away and returned with a wooden bowl of water, a bar of solid fat, and a rag. "Here," he said. "Wipe that salt off. It burns wounds."

Fafnir took the bowl and placed it in his lap. He wet the bar in the bowl and rubbed it until the fat pasted white on his fingers, then wiped at his cheek, wincing at the sting, and dried his skin with the rag.

He worked his jaw. His cheek still stung, but he could speak better now.

Ian had turned to look at Niamh, his brow knitted.

"How is she?" Fafnir asked.

"She survived, thank the Mother," Ian said quietly. "Tristan's parents are much strengthened and grateful, but she is terribly weak. I think she gave within a span of her life."

Fafnir pressed his lips. Questions spiraled within him, but he did not want the answers. The mysteries of Uniting was a dark, stifling realm.

Ian continued. "I'm worried for her, with the winter coming on. She can't make the journey to get to her daughter now—she can scarcely lift her head—and it will only get harder as it gets colder."

No wonder she had run from giving her energy.

"I hope she recovers soon," Fafnir murmured. He straightened his spine. "Ian, I know I do not need to tell you of the sufferings of the forest. I came here to work with you—to perfect and execute a strategy to raise awareness of our dire straits and return the fae to the dryads."

Ian's eyes widened. "You cut straight to the point," he said. "Let us talk outside. I know Esen will want to hear of this."

Fafnir nodded. "Are you her faerie?"

"I United with her parents."

Right. He'd forgotten how it worked for a moment. Ian had United with a Rooted couple to allow Esen to be born.

"A hazel and a holly," Ian was saying, "and Esen has a young sister now, named Aisling. I can introduce them to you after."

"Very well," said Fafnir. Holding the water bowl with one hand, he pulled back the quilts that covered him with the other. Why had he sat there like that the whole time, as though he were a child tucked in bed? He rose.

"Have some stew first," Ian said. "You can join me at the table."

Ian gave a bowl of steaming stew to Fafnir, then filled one for himself, and they sat at the table, eating in silence. Ian's home was extraordinarily simple, yet comfortable. It was well known that Ian had come from a simple river faerie village before the queen invited him to rule as her king. Did he ever miss the royal beauty, the ease and comfort of the palace? Or did he feel like he'd created a new home here?

It was odd that he hadn't returned to his village after leaving the queen. Did he live here, in isolation, out of shame? He'd created a scandal, after all, when he'd stolen Niamh.

When they had finished eating, Ian stepped into the larder to clean the dishes. Fafnir placed the water bowl on the table and wet his face, wiping off the flour and salt until his reflection shone gray once more. He brought his two ashwood earrings out from his pocket. They had survived with no damage. Good.

He could still smell the sweet summer grass as he'd carved them alongside Isolde all those years ago. He fitted them back into his left ear.

When he finished beating the salt out of his hair, he frowned at the floor. He'd left a white dusting over the boards. He rose and looked around the room until he found a dark brush made of yew and marten hair, and a tray, and used it to clean up his mess.

At last, Ian was ready, and they walked toward the door. Ian bent by Niamh, who had been lying completely still, and kissed her on her forehead. "I'll be back," he said.

Niamh gave a small nod, her white lips pulling in a smile.

They stepped outside. Though the sun shone in the sky, the air was cold.

"Wait here," Ian said. "I will get Esen."

He was back shortly. Though Fafnir had met Esen before and seen many Walkers in passing, their height never failed to impress him.

He tilted his head back as far as he could. Her face towered twelve times above his height, and her branches, though she was young, added above her face another five times his height again. Aside from the yellow stamens of catkins beginning to sprout, her branches were bare. The vibrant yellow-green canopy that had shaded her body when he had met her had fallen without a trace.

Her deep blue eyes looked down at him, narrowed with concentration.

She had saved his life twice now, and he had scarcely spoken to her.

"I remember you now," she breathed. "You nearly drowned in the river."

"Yes. I thank you…" He grasped for more words, but none came. He would be cold as a stone right now, a pile of white bones picked apart by carrion insects—if it was not for her.

How did you thank someone for giving you a second chance at life?

"Um… deeply," he said finally.

Esen tilted her head, fiddling with a branch near her ear. "Did I scare you then? You never gave me your name."

He hadn't realized that. He had been so consumed with fear.

"The flood is the key to what I am about to tell you," he said.

She lowered herself to a seat, cutting her height in half. "Please, go on."

ime is a strange, illusionary thing. We feel it in the passage of great heavenly bodies of light above us, and the amount of light that shines around us. We seek to capture a sense of time for the sake of keeping our festivals, rituals, and work timely with the changing flow of the seasons.

Sun: Passage of the sun in its orbit across the sky, from sunrise to sunrise anew

Moon: Passage of time as the moon undergoes one complete cycle of phases

Year: A complete round of the seasonal cycle

Seasonal Cycle

First moon: Wolf moon
Second moon: Chaste moon
Third moon: Seed moon
Fourth moon: Marten moon
Fifth moon: Flower moon
Sixth moon: Root moon
Seventh moon: Wort moon
Eighth moon: Mead moon
Ninth moon: Leaf moon
Tenth moon: Blood moon
Eleventh: Snow moon
Twelfth: Oak moon
Thirteenth (when cycle is longer): Cloud moon

The dryads honor these time passages as well, although they hold looser definitions of these terms. They name them by the following symbols:

 Sun

 Moon

 Year

CHAPTER 18: THE QUEST IS FORMED

As Fafnir spoke, his small hands moved as though he were drawing a picture. Ian sat near him and listened carefully. At first, Esen was afraid. The need for change burned inside her, a desperate flame. But the memory of Tristan's violent, angry words still roiled inside her, confusing her.

Fafnir did not speak of attack, or even the injustices of the fae. He spoke of the suffering of the forest in intricate detail, beginning with the flood. He had been tracing the pain points of the forest, categorizing what he saw. Proving the Cycle of Giving, though without saying so. He concluded with his studies on weather.

"That is why we must act quickly. Though the temperatures are rising overall by slight degrees, I have noted an increase in erratic weather events as well. If we are not killed by another flood, we could also have a shortage of rain that lasts too long, resulting in a drought that kills us. Or it could be by extremes of temperature. Already, this winter has been approaching rapidly, quicker than most years. With the dryads still weak from the flood, I fear it may prove deadly."

It was true, then. She had suspected it since the flood. It was not only the dryads that were dying. With their deaths, the lives of the forest were dying with them.

Soon, the forest would be no more…

She gripped at the earth, crumbling the dry leaves. "How can the faeries not see this? Wouldn't they have noticed these things too?"

"I can speak best for the faeries of the Rath Síoraí," Fafnir said. "Unfortunately, they encompass about sixty percent of the faerie population. The queen has numbed them well. They see the fallen dryads, but it means nothing to them. Dryads have always died. They are not counting the numbers, because they are too busy counting their pleasures. The queen has removed every aspect of the ancient ways from the culture. They have forgotten them."

The sunlight threw dappled patches across this strange faerie seated before her. Though he was immortal, with over a thousand summers behind him, he was ignited with the same passion as her—to save the forest.

"I see," Esen said. "Are you one of them, then? But you are not like them."

"I live just past the border that marks the region," Fafnir said. "Close enough to keep an eye on them, but far enough that I am assured of my solitude."

Fafnir straightened, crossing one leg over the other. "The question remains: what of the other faeries? That brings me to my plan. I had a revelation. When Niamh stopped at her river-fae's village by the River Ifrati, only a handful of them had wings. But their faces were weary with hardship. The river was swelling its banks, flooding their homes. I would have to test my theory, but I am quite certain it is the queen's dam that is causing their misery, coupled with the damage from the flood. We could go there, help them to see this, and recruit them to our side. And if we can do this with these fae, how many more could we bring to our cause?"

He leaned forward, clasping his hands. "Here is my idea. We befriend fae from three distinct regions of the land. I am thinking of the mountains and the coast as well as the river. Each region will be experiencing the effects of the dying land in unique ways. If they are not Winged Ones already, we encourage them to Unite—that creates an immediate relief, however small—and we bid them to spread the word and recruit more as they can. In the end, we come together and surprise the faeries of the Rath with an organized rally. We will speak, and bring what things we can to make the word real to them. A member of each region will share their story, and I will connect all the threads together in one cohesive narrative that will make the truth plain as day."

"Fafnir," Esen breathed. She pressed her palms together, swaying side to side. "That is wondrous. I think that really may work."

"You could be our emissary," Fafnir said, looking at her. "You could serve as the voice of your people."

She would get to see the world, and make real change.

Fafnir frowned. "Of course, we will need to determine the best place and time to stage our gathering. I haven't thought that out yet. The festivals would not be ideal. The fae would hate us for interrupting their festivities, and most of them would be roaring drunk."

He spat the last word with an evident disgust, scowling at the ground.

Esen tilted her head. "What do you mean by 'drunk'?"

Fafnir cocked an eyebrow at her.

Ian explained. "There are certain substances that can affect the mind in questionable ways. Fafnir is right; that would not be ideal."

"Why would they do such a thing to themselves?" Esen asked. "And at a time of celebration too?"

A darkness shadowed Fafnir's eyes. "There is a brief respite in the alteration of the mind. From the suffering that can come with reality."

Esen shifted. There was an emotion in his voice that had not been there before.

"What of the World Market?" Ian said. "The queen did not usually —" Ian stopped, looking askance at Esen. "Did you piece it together, perhaps? That I was... the king?"

"Yes," Esen said softly.

Ian reddened and turned away. "I'm sorry, Esen. I didn't tell you, because I didn't think it mattered." He fumbled with his fingers. "But, of the World Market... it's a day for fae to gather from all corners of the land and exchange goods. Fae far out from the Rath typically hold their own festivals, so it would be unusual for many to join at a Rath festival, but there will be many different fae at the World Market."

"Yes, that is good," Fafnir said. His face cleared, a calculating expression resumed. "And with no seas of liquor, they will be practically minded. That is perfect."

Leaning forward, Fafnir began to trace a pathway through the snow.

"World Market is on the twenty-eighth sun of the Mead Moon, which gives us two hundred and forty-two suns to work with…" He lifted his head. "Will we be working this winter?"

"No," Esen said. "We must stay to protect Aisling. We can leave at first thaw."

Fafnir dropped his head and continued his line. "First thaw is typically on the Seed Moon. We could reach the river fae by the end of that moon." He circled a spot and walked his finger down a long length. "The mountains are at the southern tip of the land; we will reach them at about the Flower Moon. Then, the coast is just beneath."

The mountains were a series of sloping peaks some unnamable distance away. She had stared at them often as a young Rootling. In the day, they gleamed green and blue, at one with the clouds. In the night, they jutted black against the starry sky.

A thrill surged within her.

In one moon, she would stand amid those heights.

Fafnir made two circles and swooped his finger back to the top of his line before pausing. "Will we tell everyone to meet at the market? Or should we meet elsewhere, then go to the market together?"

"Meeting elsewhere is likely to attract unwanted attention," Esen said.

Fafnir bobbed his head up and down. "We will meet at the market, then. We can pick a specific vendor to gather round, maybe set up one of our own to blend in. Our travel time will take us one hundred eighty-seven suns at minimum, which gives us a moon and twenty-five suns of extra time for our visits with each fae, and to allow for any delays. As the World Market is just before next winter, we can hope to be done so you can be by your sister's side for the winter once more—"

"With the forest on the mend," Esen breathed. She leaped up and twirled round. "You have given us hope, Fafnir," she said, catching her breath. "You are a gift sent from the Mother."

A strange expression flickered over Fafnir's face, something like grief. "The support of you and Ian has given me hope as well."

Esen looked over at Ian. His face was turned toward the door of his home. "If Niamh is still sickly in the spring, I would want to escort her to her village first," he said. "And Aisling will be here alone without us."

A stone sunk in Esen's core. She would have to leave her sister behind for almost a year.

"I was thinking too, what of the other Walkers?" Ian asked. "And there are many Winged Ones who attend the dryad celebrations. We could see if some of them would wish to join us."

"I am sure they have families and duties to attend to," Fafnir said. "And the more we bring with us, the more intimidating we may appear to the fae we visit. We will also be more noticeable as a group." Tapping a finger on his chin, he added, "That is the main fear I have. A stone dropped in a still lake creates a chain of ripples. The more influence we manage to have on the fae we visit, and the more they spread our plan, the more likely it is that wrong ears may hear of it. If our intentions are ever leaked to the queen, we are doomed."

"Is there any way we can avoid that?" Esen asked.

Fafnir stared at the ground. "I don't think so," he said finally. "Just that we must be careful with whom we speak. The specific details of our meeting must only be told to those whom we are certain we can trust."

A cold wind slipped among them.

"Yes," said Esen.

Ian rose and lifted his hands toward the sky. "May the Mother bless our mission." He was still for a moment before dropping his hands. "I'll be with Niamh. Later today, I will begin work on the stone firepit for Aisling. Fafnir, would you help me?"

"Of course," Fafnir said, rising also.

After thanking him, Ian stepped within his home and shut the door behind him. A cardinal flashed among the bare branches of an oak. Fafnir rose and adjusted his cloak, tilting his head up at the sky.

A grief settled in Esen's limbs, weighing her down. She had to save the forest so Aisling could have a real future, but in order to do that, she had to leave her...

"I am sorry our first meeting was so strained," Esen said to Fafnir. "I'm going to talk with my sister. You can come with if you'd like to meet her."

Fafnir nodded.

They walked up the hill. Aisling's eyes grew wide as moons as they approached. Her parents clattered their branches wordlessly.

"Aisling, Mother, Father," she said.

She'd always known, deep in her wood, that she would leave her home in time, but she hadn't known it would be so soon. She had been sure that her first long adventure away from home would be with Aisling by her side.

"This is Fafnir. He has a plan to save the forest. Ian and I are going to go with him and gather as many faeries as we can to make one big stand against the Faerie queen. We will create a legend, a tale sung in the forest for all generations to come."

"Ooohhh," Aisling breathed.

Fafnir frowned at Aisling—observing her frailty, perhaps?

Esen knelt by her sister. "But to do that… we're going to have to leave come first thaw. I promise we will be back before next winter. I will never let you endure a winter alone."

Aisling closed her mouth, a somber look coming over her—a look too old for a child to bear. Finally, she said, "You are brave, and Fafnir is too."

Tears wet Esen's eyes. She bent and wrapped her arms around her. "I don't want to leave you, Aisling. Please know that. If I could save the forest from this hilltop, I would do it without blinking. But I must go. It is the only way."

When she pulled back from her sister, there were tears in Aisling's eyes. "Save the forest," Aisling whispered. "Be the change that shakes the mountains."

Esen wiped at her eyes. "I will try."

Hiccuping, Aisling turned her gaze to Fafnir. He stood stiffly, his mouth a straight line. "Do you live far from here?" she asked. "Do you have any brothers, sisters? What's your favorite animal? Is it a pine marten?"

Fafnir's brow pinched. "I would prefer not to answer."

"It's a pine marten," Aisling said. "I know it is."

Laughing, Esen patted her on the head. "Too many questions can freeze someone right up. Leave him be."

"*Esen,*" clattered her mother. "*We would like to speak with you alone for a moment.*"

Esen's laughter died away. They had been silent until now. That worried her. "Okay."

Fafnir's eyes were fixed on Esen, confusion in his face. "You can go where you please," she said to him. "My parents wish to speak with me privately."

Fafnir nodded. "I could not overhear, if they are worried of that."

"You never learned Wind-Speak?" she asked.

"No."

During the Ancient Law, every fae was taught Wind-Speak to be able to speak with their Rooted dryad. But with the loss of the law, the teaching of Wind-Speak had largely been abandoned. If he'd been old enough to be the queen's musician in the days of the Ancient Law, why hadn't he learned it?

Fafnir stepped away. Esen drew up to her parents.

"Yes?" she said.

"*This is good news,*" her mother murmured. "*If this faerie is honest. But who is he, really? Why won't he speak about himself?*"

"Perhaps it is painful for him," Esen said. "Does it matter? I have been distraught all my life, and he has brought me hope."

"*He stands heavily. Does he have wings?*" her father asked.

"No," Esen said.

A breathy gasp sounded from their branches.

"*Why has he not given?*" her mother asked.

Esen faltered. "I don't know," she said. "Perhaps he is saving himself for a dryad."

That didn't make sense though. Why would he delay?

Her parents hummed deep and low.

"*We say this only because we care for you, Esen. Go, do what you will. Just be careful not to place your trust in those who may deceive you.*"

A dryad and their faerie
are always buried together.
Across the land, burials often
take on certain customs
unique to the region, but the
fundamentals always remain.
The faerie's body is carried
on a rose leaf in a solemn
procession, adorned with a
circlet of rose petals on their
head. The mourners lament
with songs celebrating their
life, and scatter pieces of
rose petals in their wake. At
the same time, dryads stand
by the body of the dryad, and
sing and scatter roses on
their fallen. They carve the
symbol for Aoradh,
"One with Mother", on
the dryad.

CHAPTER 19: SHATTERING

Esen had lived through many winters, but that winter was the coldest she had ever known. The wind grew teeth and ate at her bark, burrowing deep beneath her. Her body soon coated with crystalline frost.

Before the first snow, all was gray and bare, even the sky. The sun barely shone, and when it did, it was a pale shadow of its brilliant summer splendor. Then the snow came—first in short flurries, then in heavy, suffocating blankets. Once, the clefted hoofprints of deer appeared in the snow, going to where she knew not. When she woke next, the prints had entirely vanished, as though they had never been.

In and out of a deep, deep sleep, Esen had visions of Ian or Fafnir, dressed in a thick cloak, slipping through the squirrel skin that hung over the doorway of the shelter they had built for Aisling. The shelter was triangular in shape, with wooden posts that fanned out from a center point just above Aisling's head and dug deep into the ground. They had draped layers of squirrel skins over the structure, and inside, they had built the firepit into the ground with a thick outer wall. They were trading places watching the fire while the other slept in Ian's warm home. With eyes heavy with sleep, she would glimpse Aisling before the flap closed as one of them went inside.

Each time, Aisling had a dreamy, contented look on her face, like she was dreaming of spring. Her holly leaves glistened, still green with her evergreen energy, with only the slightest hint of frost on the edges.

Once, Esen had thought fire could only bring pain to her kind. Now, fire was shielding Aisling from harm, like a bubble of air at the deepest depths of the sea.

Every time Esen slipped up from consciousness, she murmured fervent prayers.

"Keep her strong, Mother. Keep her strong…"

She listened for the Mother's voice in the wind. She heard only shrill, wordless sighs, as though even the Mother was too cold to speak.

Sometimes, the crackling fire brought memories of Tristan. Fear sucked the sleep from her limbs when she thought of his wounds, and how cold cracks weakened wood…

She had to know if he was okay.

She opened her eyes. Or she thought she had. All was black. It must be a moonless night, but then why weren't her limbs moving? She tried to blink, but her eyelids ignored her. They must be frozen shut.

She tried to jerk her limbs, to scream, to cry, but she was trapped in a black void. She couldn't move—she was frozen all over.

"Esen?" a familiar voice said. Fafnir. "Hold still."

Heat breathed on her face. Pain roared to life, piercing like a thousand needles from her forehead down to her chin, but then the pain passed, and she opened her mouth, flexing her jaw.

Fafnir stood before her, shrouded in a dark wool cloak. He held a torch in one hand, the flames flickering like wraiths. Here, with her head on the ground, she had to lift her eyes to meet his gaze. How strange when he was usually a small figure beneath her.

His spring-green eyes were clouded with heaviness.

"Thank you," she managed to croak. She tried to lift herself, but her body was still frozen.

Fafnir darted out of her line of sight. Heat bloomed at her hands, her elbows. The pain tore through, then subsided. He did the same to her knees and feet.

She flexed her fingers, joints cracking, planted her palms in the hard snow, and forced her stiff knees to bend. At last, she rose to her feet.

"Is Aisling okay?" she asked.

Fafnir nodded.

She stumbled toward the trunks of her parents. "Mother," she said. "Father."

A fresh wind cracked their bare branches together like dry bones. There were no words in it.

Panic seized her. They must be sleeping. But they looked so frail, hunched against the bitter white sky. What if they were frozen solid, so cold they would never wake again?

"Mother! Father!" She beat her fists upon their brittle bark. "Please wake."

Nothing. They were deep, deep in sleep, far away from her.

Her spirit beat against her chest like a caged moth. She kept pounding. And what of Tristan? What if his leg shattered beneath him and he fell somewhere, where no one was awake to see him, as the snow buried him alive?

A gash rent through her hand. With a cry, she jerked it back. A piece of bark hung loose, attached by thin sinews. Tears sprung to her eyes, freezing as they formed. She hurried to the Rooted One near, and then another.

"Please," she cried. "Can anyone answer me?"

The wind gusted by, the only sound.

Snowflakes flurried; her eyelashes bowed with their weight. Heaviness seized her, creeping along her limbs, pulling her to the earth.

She couldn't go to Tristan. Already, she could scarcely stand—

A splitting crack rent the silence. The thick, mighty branch of a neighboring ash crashed into the snow. Where the branch had been, there was a ragged wound, the soft inner wood exposed to winter's merciless teeth.

She forced herself to step up to the ash and lay a gentle hand on the edge of his wound. *Aeonida*," she whispered. "Hold on."

The branches of the ash trembled, clattering faintly together. A faint, scarcely audible voice breathed within the sound.

"Aeonida, Esen. I hear your cries. I cannot speak to the others for you. I woke only with the pain. But remember… winter's breath is always fiercest right before she surrenders to spring."

Her mother and father had once said the same to her, when she was a little Rootling. But if the cold was this fierce now, how would she survive winter's final breath?

"Thank you."

It took all her strength to walk the few steps back to Aisling and the flickering fire. She fell back to the ground, her limbs dead weights, and knew nothing more.

"ESEN."

Someone was calling to her...

Heat whispered along her face, biting back the frost.

"Esen! Esen, please."

Ian. It was Ian, his voice wild with desperation.

Clumps of half-melted snow slid into her eyes as she forced them open. She blinked furiously.

Through a white haze, she made out Ian standing in front of her. He held a torch in one hand, the flames as pale as a winter sunset. His ice-blue eyes looked out from the shadow of his deeply knitted brow, his teeth gnashing together.

He hurled the torch in the snow and stamped on it. The snow swallowed it, leaving no trace; not even a wisp of smoke.

"Ian?" she breathed. "What is wrong?"

"It is your parents." His voice cracked as he spoke, like he'd swallowed shards of ice. The ground groaned beneath her, shuddering. "They are splitting. And so am—" He doubled over, clutching at his stomach. "So am I."

Esen gasped. She jerked both arms and found she could move them. Ian must have melted off the snow. "What can I do? What can I—"

A strangled cry burst from Ian. He crumpled to his knees and slammed both hands deep into the snow, his body heaving.

A crack sounded below, like the splinter of a spine, and the ground writhed, slamming into Esen's torso. She tore herself upright, screaming as shreds of bark tore from her back. Roots shot up through the cracks in the ground, huge and gnarled. She reached for Ian—

He lifted his head, his face ghost white. "P-protect Aisling," he gasped. Scarlet blood spilled from his mouth. "It's... it's up to you now."

He toppled into the snow as the massive trunk of her parents hurtled toward her.

Aisling.

Esen slammed into the shelter, reaching through the splintering logs and fluttering skins to feel her sister's small form. She threw herself around her.

A boom shook the earth.

Esen lifted her head, tears pooling in her eyes.

The thick, massive mass of her parents' entwined roots—roots that had communed with hundreds of thousands of Rooted Ones; that had nourished her and lifted her up from the dark soil—now formed a wall in front of her, frozen dirt clinging to them like cobwebs. Their trunk stretched out beyond, splitting into a tangle of splayed branches.

The black eyes of a dragan formed toward the base of a root, a section of bark splitting to form its gaping jaw. The dragan slithered through the gnarled wood.

No. No, no.

Her parents weren't dead. She was imagining this. They were high, high above her, dreaming of sunlight and the violet poppies that would unfurl their petals amid the sweet spring grass.

Leaves brushed her arm. Aisling stirred beneath her, her eyes fluttering open.

"Esen?"

She didn't want her to see. She didn't want her to—

A scream tore from Aisling's throat, the sound breaking Esen's spirit in two. She tightened her arms around Aisling. Her sister shook beneath her, sobbing, screaming.

Snowflakes covered Ian's body.

Esen trembled, tears spilling from her eyes and freezing on her cheeks. She had thought Ian and her parents were the sun. Bright and mighty, always watching over her. Eternal.

She had to be the sun now. She had to sing; to stop Aisling from screaming, screaming, screaming...

A sob burst from Esen.

Ian and her parents were dead, and everything she had ever known torn up with them, upside-down like their roots, gasping —

She lifted her head. The whisper of a lullaby murmured in the frigid air.

The voice of the wounded ash.

Another Rooted One rattled her skeleton limbs, and then another, until the air hummed with their mournful melody. Like a warm embrace, the music enfolded her. There was a beauty in it she had never known. The very tones of sorrow embodied. Aisling grew still and sobbed quietly while fresh tears fell from Esen's eyes.

She relaxed into the music, letting her head droop. As the song faded, she glanced up at her parents' roots.

Her breath stopped.

Their Root Tie to Aisling was severed. She would die without them.

Aisling was hunched over, her eyes squeezed shut in sleep.

Gasping, Esen gripped at her head.

"*Esen.*"

Esen started. The ash clattered his branches, beckoning to her. Esen rose and stumbled toward him.

"*I am so sorry for your loss,*" murmured the ash. "*I'm sharing the message to all the Rooted Ones who can hear, asking for help. To find a Walker who will Root with her, to create a new —*"

"I will do it." The words burst from her. She bit her lip, confused.

What of the plan to save the forest? If she Rooted now, she would be a defenseless witness to the fate of the forest, and she would never see the mountains, or the shining sea...

"*Esen, you have only just begun to Walk. You have many more years upon the land to roam. We would not wish that for you.*"

Esen looked down, picking at the bark on her fingers.

"*Wait. The Rooted Ones are speaking.*"

Shaking, Esen pressed herself against the ash's coarse gray trunk. She slid down to her knees. Snowflakes gathered on her shoulders, the tip of her nose.

"I will do it for her," she said, though her voice broke. "If no other can, I will —"

"*A Walker from the central forest has offered to Root for Aisling. Her name is*

154

Fiona Elder. It will not be as strong a tie as your parents gave, but it is the most we can offer. It will buy time for the Rooted Ones near Aisling to reach their roots toward her and strengthen the tie."

Esen laid her forehead against the ash. She remembered Fiona. She had met her briefly at Athas. "Fiona would do that?" she breathed. "She has never met Aisling."

"*Yes,*" the ash murmured.

But Fiona was scarcely over two hundred. She was giving up her last hundred years of Walking…

A stone sat in Esen's core. She wavered. Should she deny Fiona's offer? Was this her burden to bear?

Her spirit writhed in her chest. She didn't want to Root.

"*Fiona is hurrying over now. She hopes to arrive within five days. She begs you to accept her offer.*"

Esen loosened her breath. "I accept," she said at last. "Please thank her for me."

Fiona was so kind… Esen scarcely even knew her.

All at once, the image of Tristan burning flashed in her mind. "How is Tristan? Is he okay?"

The ash was silent for a moment. "*He is lying some distance from here, dry beneath an alcove. He has not moved since the first snow. He appears to be sleeping.*"

Esen nodded. Good. He had found a safe place. The weight slipped from her shoulders. "*Aeonida,*" she said. "We will wait for Fiona."

"*Aeonida, Esen. May the Wind shelter you and bring you and your sister warmth very soon.*"

As Esen turned back to Aisling, the first glimmer of dawn shone on the horizon. The light glistened on the tears frozen on Aisling's face, her eyes still closed in sleep. Stepping carefully around the splintered remains of the shelter, Esen knelt by the place where Ian had fallen. The snow had almost swallowed him completely. She bent and gathered him in her hands. He was ice cold, the green flush gone from his face.

A shudder broke over her. How would she tell Niamh? She had just returned to her father. They were finally happy, and now…

She shook her head, rattling her branches faintly. The last she heard, Niamh was still bedridden. Recovering, but pale as a ghost. If she told her now, the news could kill her.

Brushing the snow from Ian's face and cloak, she laid him down. She found a stone and hacked at the brittle earth until she had dug a suitable hole, then cupped Ian in her hands.

There should be tens of thousands of Walkers and fae to witness his burial. To sing the proper songs and speak of how he had blessed them. He should be laid with a crown of rose petals on his pale head, and a sea of petals beneath him.

But there was only herself to witness—herself and the snow.

A tear wet Ian's cloak. She laid him gently down and piled the earth back over him. Immediately, the snow worked to claim back the space.

She broke off the tip of one of her branches, the bud at the end black and hardened. She placed it upright, above where his head lay—something to mark the space and honor him.

Heaviness stole over her limbs. She rose unsteadily and faced the fallen trunk of her parents.

"Oh Mother," she murmured. "Take these lives unto you, but don't take Aisling. Keep her safe until Fiona comes."

A breath of wind brushed by, warmth ghosting her cheek. There was a sensation in it... almost the feeling of fingertips against her bark. The touch burned her like fire, but there was no pain.

The sensation faded, the wind quieting. Esen drifted a hand to her cheek, butterflies in her core.

Had the Mother... touched her?

She folded herself down by Aisling and let the weariness consume her.

CHAPTER 20: DEAD OF WINTER

The wind whipped through Fafnir's hair. He tore through the forest at the speed of a marten, his feet flying beneath him. A white fog veiled the path ahead. Faces, hard and grim, emerged from the fog—the faces of the river fae.

He tugged on the reins to urge his marten around them. Wait... had he always been on a marten?

Niamh stepped out from the fog, her dark-green eyes penetrating. The mists wreathed about her, the same color as her skin. "Who are you?" she asked him.

He flicked the reins. The marten leaped over her.

A cold sweat slicked his brow. He leaned into the marten's neck, urging her to hurry. Ian appeared next, his face unusually pale. He dodged him to see Esen's towering form emerge. Behind her stood the queen, her obsidian eyes glittering.

Their voices congealed into one.

"Who are you?"

Fafnir shot up, breathing heavy. A thin streak of white light filtered in from windows almost entirely obscured by walls of snow. The angle of the light was steep. Late sun, then. Why hadn't Ian woken him—

Who are you?

The voices again. He pressed both hands to his ears, shaking his head, willing the dream to vanish.

He threw back the covers and stood, tightening his belt. Ian wasn't there, just Niamh. In the past moon, the color had begun to return to her face. She had even risen a few times to help around the house. She was sleeping now.

Fafnir donned his cloak and then the bark hat, looping the leather straps about his ears. His fingers slipped in his haste. A chill haunted the air, even here. He placed a few new sticks in the slow-burning fire in the hearth.

He could eat later. He had to check on Ian; he must've fallen asleep at the fire. If the fire had gone out overnight, he and Aisling could be freezing.

He filled a sack of dry wood, slung it over his shoulder, and darted out the door. Flurries of snow assailed him as the sack banged against his shoulder blade. The hilltop rounded overhead. Why were there roots jutting out of the snow? A Rooted One must have —

The sack slipped from his hands.

Esen's parents. They had fallen.

Esen lay huddled around her sister, the splintered poles of the shelter sticking out of the snow like brown ribs. Most of the skins had flown away, the firepit vanished.

He was dreaming. He must be.

He slapped his cheek hard. The skin burned, a hot flame in the bitter cold. But nothing changed.

Esen shifted, grasping her sister tighter.

Her parents were dead. Then that meant Ian...

His muscles tensed, panic shooting up from his stomach.

He had lived for over one thousand one hundred years, and he had never known a winter like this. He had never seen his skin turn from gray to crimson to sea blue within moments of exposure, every breath turned to ice in his throat.

He had changed the very weather itself with his mistake.

And now it had killed them. Ian and Esen's parents.

White fog billowed from his nostrils. Squeezing his eyes shut, he paced in a tight line.

0 and 1 is 1. 1 and 1 is 2.

His heart rammed against his ribcage.

1 and 2 is 3. 2 and 3 is 5.

He drew his mind to his heart, quieting it.

3 and 5 is 8. 5 and 8 is 13.

As long as the numbers flowed, there was order in the world, and thus inside him. Plummet down… seek the stillness. The cool, dark space. The space he would be when all this was over.

8 and 13 is 21. 13 and 21 is 34.

Good. He was breathing even. Coming to a halt, he stared at the ground.

He could flee this family he had ruined and do the plan on his own. He had come here for Ian, and Ian was gone. But Esen would bring a valuable perspective to the faeries—a side of the situation that he could not fathom. And he had promised he would go with her…

A gust of wind blasted against him. Snowflakes pierced his face. He squinted his eyes open, blinking against the haze.

Dryads have survived winters since the dawn of the land. Their bodies freeze the water within them around their internal mechanisms, safeguarding them. But this was no ordinary winter, and Esen's sister was not born under ordinary circumstances. He'd spent enough long nights gazing at her, putting the pieces together in his mind. It was clear enough from her underdeveloped form—she'd been pushed up too early by the flood.

Esen was curled so tightly around Aisling, her entire being bent on protecting her. She had lost her parents, her faerie…

He would never, never be able to make up for what he had done.

But he could do this one thing.

He would stay. He wouldn't let her lose Aisling too.

Shouldering the sack, he trudged forward, ducking beneath the branches. Neither Esen nor her sister stirred as he approached. Their faces were tight, eyes squeezed shut.

Fafnir dropped the sack and worked to heave the snow off the stone firepit. It was like moving mountains. His internal body temperature soon heated, while his fingers quickly went numb.

A large brown hand swept past him and pushed away the rest of the snow. Esen looked up from where she lay. Emotion ravaged her eyes, her brows pressed together. A tightness seized his chest. It was the same look his mother had given him the day his father left.

Fafnir dragged the sack closer to him and knelt, arranging the wood. Largest pieces on the bottom, smaller ones threaded through them with enough room for the fire to breathe, and pieces of dead leaves to flare the spark.

He struck at the flint, counting each failed attempt until the sparks finally flew. A flame licked along the edge of a leaf and leaped forward, devouring the leaves and catching hold of the wood.

He caught her gaze through the flames, watching him.

"Did you…" It was a morbid thing to ask, but he didn't know what else to say. "Did you bury him? Ian, I mean?"

Esen bowed her head as tears spilled from her eyes. "Yes."

Fafnir stiffened. He'd scarcely spoken to Ian this past moon. Now he was buried beneath cubits of snow.

He looked over at Aisling. "How is she?"

Esen followed his gaze, her lips quivering. "Not well. But a Walker is coming to Root for her. I am just hoping, praying—" Esen's voice broke. "Th-that she will survive until then."

Oh. His ears drooped. He'd forgotten how critical the Root Tie was for the health of Rootlings.

He gripped an extra stick and moved a few elements of the fire, perfecting it. "I will rebuild the shelter and make sure the fire does not go out."

"We need it now more than ever. Thank you." A pause, and then, "But how will you sleep?"

Fafnir frowned at the fire. It was a good question.

He slipped a hand in the pouch on his hip and pulled out his journal and a wooden pencil, flipping to where he'd bookmarked a page with a crease of the corner. He added a new tick mark in the chart. There were eighty-six suns left before the second week of the Seed Moon, when the first thaw usually came. Assuming it took longer to thaw this year, there were about ninety-two suns left of the thick of winter to survive.

Going without sleep that long would kill him.

He chewed his lower lip and tapped the charcoal point of the pencil on his chin.

The fire was almost certainly safe from spreading. The walls of the stone pit rose seven spans above the flames. When he rebuilt the shelter, the flaps at the top would allow smoke to filter out. But there was still the chance of smoke overaccumulation, and the fire had to be regularly fueled with new wood—approximately every three hours—to keep it warm enough for Aisling.

He could not sleep for longer than three hours, then. That would be impossible without an external stimulant to wake him. When the body is weary, it pulls the mind down with it. He needed something like his timekeeper, but it would take too long to make one. The inner mechanism alone required thirty-two parts, and each had to be carved perfectly to make the whole sing…

But he could do a rudimentary version.

Flipping to a fresh page, he began to scratch down ideas. He needed something to transfer energy over a period of three hours and wake him with force at the precise time. If he created a funnel of sorts, which allowed a tiny but steady stream of snow to fall on a spring-loaded platform… his pencil flew, marking up a diagram. He could time it so at precisely the right time, the platform would descend to the bottom, transferring the energy into one gear, and then another, triggering the release of the lid to a second container that he could attach to the first. If he filled the second container—

Then he'd be greeted back to consciousness with a face full of snow.

Hideous. It would do the job.

He glanced back up at Esen. Her face was lowered, her eyes roaming over the snow as though she were looking for something.

"I thought of a way," he said. "I'll create a device that will enable me to wake every three hours to keep the fire going so you can sleep without fear."

Esen tilted her head. "How?"

"If you wake again, you'll see," he said. "It won't be pleasant. But that's my problem, not yours."

"Be careful." Her voice shivered with emotion. "And please, look after Niamh."

His chest tightened. He had forgotten to factor Niamh in. "I will."

An uncomfortable silence followed. "We will get through this," he added. His words were useless though. Time would tell.

Esen nodded, her branches creaking like old bones. "Thank you."

163

A rattle flared up in his throat, and he coughed, puffing white clouds. He turned and strode down the hill. He couldn't stop seeing Esen's eyes... like looking into the depths of the ocean with layers of sorrow rather than water.

He put his hands to his temples, and his fingertips shivered against his skin.

The invention, the invention... how would he design it? Well, he could dangle the device from a wooden post composed of two beams. The funnel must be dome-shaped, which would be quickest formed on Ian's pottery wheel. He could make the container of snow out of clay too, and affix them together through wooden chain links and a rod. The lids would be of wood, and the spring of spider silk, of course. All quite simple; he could finish it in just a few suns after the shelter.

Fafnir opened the door and ducked inside, shaking the snow from his cloak and hat. He turned to see Niamh sitting up in her bed, staring at him.

"Where is my father?" she asked, her voice quick, anxious.

Wringing his hands, he looked away from her. "He's dead. The cold was too much for Esen's parents. I will be taking care of you in his place."

A strangled cry tore from Niamh. Fafnir looked up, his hands twitching at his sides, as fabric spilled onto the floor. Niamh was rising, shoving off her blankets. Her face was flushed, contorted. "Where is he? I want to see him."

He stiffened. "Esen has buried him already."

She went white and sank to the floor, sobs of heart-wrenching grief bursting from her.

He turned, rubbing his temples again. Her sobs scattered his thoughts like a storm of arrows. He had to do something for her. He hadn't eaten yet, and likely, she had not either. He walked to the larder and piled two bowls of dried, salted meats. She was still crying when he came back.

"I'm sorry." Crouching, he extended a bowl toward her. She stared at it, her gaze distant. "Please... eat."

Niamh had been everything to Ian. It had radiated from every look he gave her, every gesture he did for her. Wherever Ian was now—lost with the death of his mind, or floating in some eternal place—he knew his only concern would be for her.

The bowl lifted from his hands. Niamh put a few pieces in her mouth and chewed slowly, then sniffled. "I am afraid for my daughter."

Fafnir nodded. "How are you feeling?"

She looked at him, her brow lowered.

He scratched his head. "Physically, I mean. Do you think you could go to her now?"

"I don't know." Niamh looked faint. Barely there, like a flame clinging to the wick of a candle. She fell to weeping again.

He helped her to lie back down and left the bowl by her, then ran his hands through his snow-crusted hair, slowing his breathing.

He would survive this. It would be over before he knew it.

He began to poke around the house, gathering materials for a new shelter and his invention. The snow-eater. That name fit it well.

He lost himself in the work.

SNOW PUMMELED FAFNIR'S FACE. Gasping, he shot up. A dark world wobbled and solidified before him. His head pounded. Too soon…It felt as though he had only just fallen asleep.

The wooden lid to the now empty chamber above him hung open. He slammed it shut, wiping the snow off his neck and shoulders.

He had only been using the snow-eater for three suns. It was torturous already.

He left the shelter and went to Ian's to gather fresh fuel for the fire. As he returned, a Walker stepped out from the darkness of the Rooted Ones. Her branches grew in opposing directions and bore the distinctive large dark-red buds of an elder dryad. Her silver bark was grooved in a flowing pattern that resembled a river, but it had yet to take on the crisscrossed ridges that signify an elder of advanced years. Fairly young, then.

Oh, yes. This must be the Walker who had agreed to Root for Aisling. She was likely younger than the usual appointed age for dryads to join the Root Web...

The elder Walker crouched before him, her brow furrowed, her moss-green eyes shining with a steadiness that surprised him. "Who are you?" she asked.

Fafnir shifted his shoulders, acutely aware of his youthful skin and lack of wings. "I am here to help Esen and her sister."

She stared at him a moment longer and smiled. "That is good of you," she finally said.

She rose once more, lumbered over to Esen, and knelt down. She shook her gently. When Esen woke, she embraced her. "I am so sorry," she said, while Esen wept.

Fafnir drew back the squirrel skin framing the entrance to Aisling's shelter and stepped inside. Bent over the fire, he arranged the sticks and rolled strips of light birchwood in his palms, scattering the pieces over the top. He struck at his flint until a spark caught, licking at the bark.

Esen's weeping sounded muffled through the skins. His skin crawled. He rubbed his arms.

"Aisling, dear?" Large silver fingertips drew back the squirrel-skin curtain. The elder dryad's face filled the doorway. "My name is Fiona. I am going to Root, to join with the earth and sustain you."

Aisling, awake behind him, tilted her head up at Fiona. Her mouth gaped open.

Fiona hung the skin up over the tip of the structure. The cold leeched in, sucking the warmth from the space, but it was temporary, of course.

Fafnir slipped out and stood beside Esen. She was kneeling in the snow, silent now, a pained smile flickering on her face.

Tears trickled down Aisling's cheeks. "Is it your time to Root?"

Fiona shook her head. "That does not matter, little Rootling. I have walked among the mountains, tasted the clear running water, and woven many nests for birds of all colors. My hands are restless now, longing to serve, to do more." She grew quiet, looking up toward the cold, gray clouds. "I want to reach my spirit to the sky and rest knowing I have given all I can."

Aisling stared at her with wide eyes. "That is beautiful."

As Fiona rose, Esen stepped toward her. "Fiona, how is the rest of the forest?" she whispered. "Have many fallen?"

A shadow passed over Fiona's face. "Too many, but let us not think of that. We are here to help one live."

Fafnir flinched.

Fiona squared her shoulders and positioned herself north of Aisling. She slowly lifted her arms toward the sky, like a bird testing the air for flight. Her eyes were fixed above, her mouth a straight line.

It was the dead of winter. This Walker should be sleeping right now, storing her energy. Rooting took an incredible amount of strength. It was dangerous to do it now. But despite that, Fiona was here, about to risk everything she had to try to save one little dryad.

"Oh Mother," murmured Esen. She bowed her head and closed her eyes. "We bear witness to the ancient rite of Rooting. Please bless and honor Fiona in this sacred symbol of the Trinity of Unity—Aoradh, the union of the soul with you alone—and please watch over Aisling. May she grow strong and healthy, and Walk soon upon your green earth. *Aeonida*."

"*Aeonida*," Fiona echoed. A tremble broke over her body. She lifted her arms higher, straining with all her might, her face tight with concentration.

The snow shuddered beneath him. A long, dark blade of grass shot out, just missing him. Another poked out at his feet. He dodged it as it sprung toward the sky, long blades twisting along a green stem before splaying out. A bulb formed at the top and opened to reveal the yellow-golden petals of a daffodil. More sprouted behind him, in front of him, all around him, until he was standing at the bottom of a sea of swaying daffodils.

What was happening? Was this normal?

He climbed onto a rock and peered up through the nodding golden petals.

Fiona still stood with her arms raised, a wide smile on her face. Behind her, Esen had her hand over her mouth, her eyes wide with wonder. Aisling was utterly still, her gaze fixed on Fiona. The daffodils surrounded them in a perfect circle, stretching seven martens back.

There were hundreds of them.

Fiona tilted her head back and closed her eyes. She was like a storm cloud, shivering with potential energy, until all at once, she erupted. Fibrous green sinews burst from her fingers and the ends of her branches as she shot up toward the sky. They looked remarkably similar to his own muscles. They were more alike in inner composition than he'd realized.

Her face sprung up from her neck, the body she once had vanishing in the interweaving, thickening forms. Fearless roots sprung from her feet, cracking the frozen earth to dive deep within. Thick gray bark formed over the green sinews as the last of her branches formed so high above him he had to bend his back to see.

So that was how they did it. It was wondrous. A true metamorphosis.

"I can feel your roots, Fiona!" Aisling cried. She squirmed with delight, reaching her little hands toward the lowest of Fiona's branches as they draped down toward her.

A dry clatter sounded as Fiona stirred her branches. Wind-Speak, no doubt.

Esen embraced Aisling. "You are safe," she said breathlessly. "You are safe, Aisling. Sleep well. Spring will be here soon."

A soft wind rustled through the daffodils, nodding their heads together. Esen swept a hand over them. "You are all so kind," she said. "Bless you all."

She caught Fafnir's gaze and smiled at him.

"I did not know…" Words fled him, until finally, he said, "…that flowers accompany your ceremonies."

Tears pooled in her eyes. She shook her head. "I have never seen this before. I think they were grieved that there were so few here to witness, so they came to bear witness themselves." She wiped at her eyes. "Like Aisling, they came up too soon."

THE WINTER WORE ON. White skies signified day, and gray skies the night. If not for the chart in his journal, Fafnir would have lost all sense of the passing of time.

Thirty-seven days left… Twenty-eight… Twenty-two… Days were nothing but a number to him. He experienced time as a continual bracing for the next rude awakening. In units of snow to the face.

He was often sleeping, but it never felt enough. The cold would keep him awake, lying there, glaring at the chambers dangling over him. He would just be sinking down at last to the depths of sleep, blinking out from the world, when the snow would slap him awake again.

Once, as he trudged toward Aisling with a bundle of firewood, his consciousness crystallized with a strange severity. Every gnash of his teeth in the cold reverberated through his skull like it was a singular astounding incident. Wind hurled sharp snowflakes that stung his face like daggers as it moaned shrilly. The world was a white smear.

The outline of a faerie-sized figure formed amid the haze. Something in the hunch of the shoulders, the jerky, staggering gait reminded him of—

Fafnir dropped the wood with a clatter.

No. It couldn't be him. Not here, not—

His father's dark, grayed face emerged from the fog. The lines of old age cut his features. But it was the same sharp nose; his pale lips drawn tight, the memory of a smile long forgotten from them; and those black, penetrating eyes, shadowed by his brow.

His father sat beside him in the snow, withered, skeletal wings hanging limp from his back. Leaning forward, his father's gnarled hands worked to tighten the laces of one of his boots. They were falling apart at the seams, stained with mud.

His eyes never left Fafnir. They probed him, digging under his skin…

Fafnir wet his lips, his breath ragged. For one thousand and eighty-seven years he had run from him. How had he ever thought he could get away?

No; it was a trick of the mind. His father would be over one thousand two hundred years old. He was most likely dead. He had gone mad; that was why. He was seeing things that weren't there, *hearing* things that weren't there. He bent over, rattling his head until he felt faint.

Make it go away. Make it go away.

"Have you found it?" The voice, low and cutting, cleanly sliced through all the years Fafnir had built between them and laid them aside. He was a child again. Vulnerable.

"Found what?" Fafnir rasped.

"Your serenity."

A tumult of emotion writhed in his father's face. Fafnir dropped his gaze. He knew the answer. But the words clashed together in his brain, tangled and confused.

When he lifted his head, his father was gone. The wind swept over perfectly smooth snow, no sign of footprints or his father's weight beside him.

Fafnir leaped to his feet. The world swirled around him, his head spinning. Sleep. He needed to sleep.

A sound like the cracking of a spine split the frozen air. An oak crashed to the earth some distance away, tearing down a smaller alder in its wake.

A tremor walked cold fingers down the back of his neck. The Rooted Ones shivered in a gust of wind, their trunks creaking with shrill sounds like shrieks.

He needed to keep Aisling alive. He needed to keep her alive...

He staggered toward the snow-eater. The two ceramic pieces hung still, bound to the wooden post. He filled the top of the funnel with snow, and the second compartment, before dropping onto the squirrel skin beneath it. He folded his cloak around him, shivering.

His bones were blue. Hollowed out, jammed with ice. The fire flickered near, but its warmth only ghosted him, teasing. In the funnel, the snow pooled in a thin stream, counting down to the hour of his next torturous wakening.

Nineteen more days...

Nineteen more days...

The daffodils had died the day after they bloomed.

Spiral of the Moon

We have created The Spiral of
the Moon, situated just outside of the
Rath Siaori, to keep track of the
seasons.

It consists of eight pits dug in the
ground, corresponding in size and
placement to the waning and
waxing of the moon in its cycle. A
fire is burned in the appropiate pit
at each new phase of the cycle,
and so we go in and out of the
spiral, twelve or thirteen times a
year. Then, when the watcher sees
the sun rise between the twin peaks
of the eastern mountains (as seen
at the top of the Rath Siaori), we
know the Winter Solstice has
arrived. The cycle is reset at the
appropiate moon phase, and
continued until the next solstice. In
this way, the witness of the Winter
Solstice corrects for lunar drift.

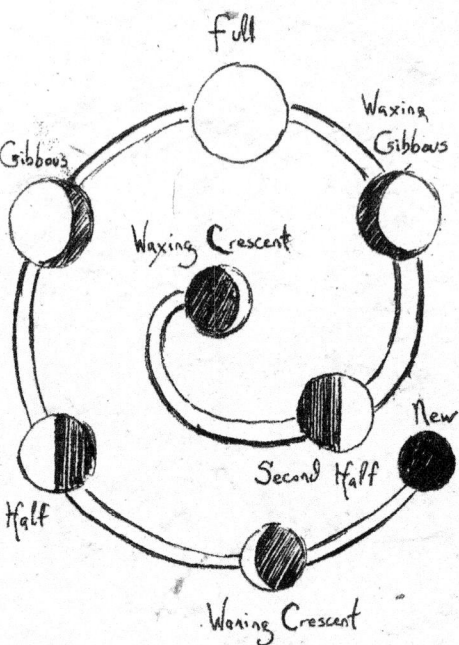

Full

Waxing Gibbous

Waning Gibbous

Waxing Crescent

New

Second Half

First Half

Waning Crescent

Rath Siaori

Spiral of the Moon

A wooden post is tallied with
a mark every time a
moon cycle is completed.
After the Winter Solstice, it is
taken down and a new one
put in its place.

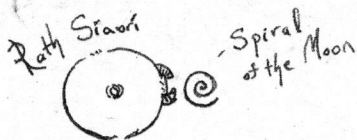

Time

CHAPTER 21: SETTING FORTH

Red sunlight glittered in Esen's eyes as she woke. She started up in wonder. A chill lingered in the air, but its bite was gone. The green leaves of buttercups dotted the hillside, their yellow heads just beginning to rise. A sweetness colored the air.

Spring.

A thrill surged within her.

Spring was here at last.

Esen rose and found her limbs lighter, free of the deathly grip of frost. Twirling, she lifted her arms high, gazing into the yellow sun.

"Thank you, Mother," she whispered.

A gentle, cool wind caressed her. Though Fiona's branches were bare, white buds dotted the tips. The mighty roots of her parents stretched toward the sky, their trunk pointed away. Dragans swarmed through their bark, as little green shoots nodded about below.

Esen bit her lip. Grief beckoned to her with icy fingers. If she let it in, she would not be able to stand, let alone do what she knew she must.

A few white petals had fallen onto Aisling's shelter. Esen drew back the skins, peering inside at Aisling's face and the peaceful quietness that graced her features. The fire flickered, its flames low. Beneath his strange contraption, Fafnir lay on a pelt, his brow pinched in sleep.

He had done it. He had kept the fire going.

Stooping, Esen reached an arm into the shelter. She placed a finger over the lid of his contraption to hold it shut, then pulled the wooden pole out of the hard earth. She laid the thing gently on the ground outside.

It had served its purpose. Now, he needed to sleep.

She pulled the skins off the framework of the shelter and knelt by Aisling, a smile breaking over her face. Bright white buds were growing on her branches, their tips tinged with a flush of pink. Soon, they would blossom into beautiful flowers.

"Aisling," she said, gently shaking her shoulders.

Aisling stirred, blinking open her blue eyes. "Esen," she said. Her eyes opened wider, her jaw dropping. "Esen! Spring is here."

Esen wrapped her arms around her, pressing her close. "You made it, dear sister."

Aisling laughed. Warmth blossomed in Esen. She had nearly forgotten how Aisling's laughter sounded—like little heather bells singing in the wind.

When Esen pulled back, a somber look had filled Aisling's eyes. "Will you be leaving today?" Aisling asked.

Esen stiffened. They had just endured the cruelest winter she'd ever known. The pillars of her childhood—her dear parents and Ian—had been torn from her life, and now the final hurdle to her journey lay in her path.

She had to leave her sister behind.

"Not today," Esen said, wiping at her face. "But soon."

Esen tarried with her sister for two days. She sang songs with her, and played games, like before. But Aisling was quiet, a cloudiness in her eyes. Several Walkers who lived near came and helped her move the trunk of her parents to where Aisling couldn't see them. Fafnir mostly slept.

When he first woke, she asked him about Niamh.

"As soon as she was able to stand, she found a marten and went to the river-fae village to be with her child," he said. "That was eleven suns ago. She gave me directions and promised to help us when we arrive."

"That is good," Esen said.

At last, on the morning of the third day, Esen knelt by Aisling and enveloped her small green hands in her own. Her hands were so small… just a little larger than a faerie's.

"Aisling," she said. "Our lives will not be as they once were. But I will do everything I can to better the world for you, so that when you rise up from the earth, we will Walk together, dance in the sunlight, and know all will be well."

With her thumb, she traced Aisling's fingers. "I will miss you terribly. But to make the world better for you, I must be away in it. I am sorry. Fiona will be here to support you while I am gone."

As she spoke, Fiona's branches wordlessly clattered above them. Aisling's gaze trailed down to the flowers at her roots. When she lifted her head, tears clung to her eyes. "Okay."

"Aisling," Esen breathed. She embraced her once more.

But Aisling soon pushed her gently away. "You must go," she said.

Esen wiped at her eyes. "I will be back before next winter, okay? I promise."

Aisling nodded, a quiet look of determination filling her face. Her eyes had dried. She was so strong.

Esen turned to Fafnir. He was sitting up, rubbing the golden petal of a buttercup growing beside him. His eyes were heavy with sleeplessness. "Are you ready to go?" he asked her.

She nodded.

Her parents' last words echoed in her mind. Whoever Fafnir was, he had single-handedly ensured her sister's survival for the past few moons, at the expense of his own health.

She put her arm out toward him and flowered open her fingers. "Thank you, Fafnir. For what you did for us. Please let me carry you there. You still need to rest."

Fafnir's eyes flitted toward her hand, then back up to her face. "One moment," he said. Whirling round with sudden force, he pounced on the pole lying on the ground and, seizing it with both hands, swung it in midair and hurled it to the forest floor. The ceramic chambers shattered open, snow pouring out from them.

"I've been looking forward to that," he said. He pulled off his bark hat and wiped at his red-brown hair.

A giggle erupted from Aisling. "I want to help!"

Lifting his brow, Fafnir placed a piece of the ceramic in Aisling's hands. She threw it on the ground, laughing as it cracked. Esen found herself laughing too.

Fafnir's lips curved in a smile.

He turned and slowly approached Esen's open hand. For a moment, he hesitated. Something like grief, or perhaps regret, flashed in his face. At last, he stepped forward, gripping her thumb with both hands as he stepped within. She flexed her wrist to steady her palm as his legs pushed against her. He rose to his full height; he was light. Light as a bird. He looked at her with his mouth parted, a pinch in his brow.

It occurred to her that he would be most comfortable lying down to sleep. But his feet would dangle off her if he lay on her shoulder, and he would have to curl up to sleep in her hands. And in both scenarios, though she would keep a very careful eye, there was always the chance he could fall.

Her heart chamber would be the most ideal place...

"I can rest on your shoulder, if that is all right," he said. He was bent over, pulling a thick cord out of a bag on his hip.

"Of course," she said. Fafnir gripped tight to her thumb as she brought her hand to her right shoulder. He stepped off and seated himself on the moss growing over her wood. With his back against a thick branch growing from her clavicle, he wrapped the cord around the branch and himself, and tied it tight.

Ah. Resourceful.

He gave her a nod. "I'll be fine like this."

"You are sure?" she said. It did not look very comfortable.

He nodded again.

Esen straightened up, her branches rattling with her movement. Golden catkins dangled from her, her own sign of spring.

Aisling looked up at her, her eyes wide with wonder. Esen saw herself suddenly through Aisling's eyes. Only a few seasons ago, Esen had been a little Rootling. Now she stood tall, about to embark on a perilous adventure with a faerie on her shoulder.

She felt as though she stood on the brow of a hill, just approaching the top, knowing she was about to finally see past it to the great rolling world beyond.

They would succeed, in some way. They had to. But she somehow knew, however it went, she would not return the same.

She gave her final parting to dear Aisling and Fiona, then let Fafnir direct her toward the village river fae.

WINTER NEVER HAD the last word. Somehow, the forest always sprung back to life with sweet perfumes, and tender green leaves grasping toward the warming sun.

Even this year. As Esen wove through the Rooted Ones, the last of the snow soon melted, unveiling the leaves of the buttercups and daffodils. Through the bitter, bitter winter, they had waited, drawing up their energy, pushing up through the soil and waiting for the day when they would break free and bloom beneath the sun.

Like the daffodils that had come up to honor Fiona's Rooting...

She pressed her lips. It had meant the world to her. But she also wished they had stayed beneath the soil. The winter had made quick work of them.

For the first several days, Fafnir mostly slept. Esen soon realized with a pang how deeply the winter had affected him. Every three hours, he would jolt awake, blinking his eyes wide, as though he still expected a blast of snow in his face. At last, he would frown and slump his head down once more.

On the fifth day, she approached the bank of the River Ifrati. The silver waters flowed before her, slower than she remembered, but she had been here soon after the flood. Squinting her eyes to gaze into the distance, she glimpsed the blocky form of the dam, stifling the flow of the water.

Frowning, she turned and walked down the length of the river. She felt movement on her shoulder; Fafnir had woken. He lifted a pouch shaped like an animal's bladder off his belt and tilted it over his mouth, swallowing. She had seen Ian carry water in a similar way. The thought twisted her middle. Ian was no more... This was a very different faerie.

"How are you feeling?" she asked him.

"Better," he said. He looked better too. The dark circles under his eyes had mostly gone away. The sweet smell of grasses and flowers drifted on the wind, and Fafnir looked to the bright blue sky as an osprey circled overhead. "How are you doing? I'm sorry I haven't been present."

"I am all right," she said. As well as she could be. "How far downriver is the village?"

"About two hundred twenty-four dryadic leagues," Fafnir said. "We will be there in fourteen suns."

Esen nodded. "Do you have a plan?"

"I will explain to them the cause of their flooding; I suspect they don't know it. And you can speak for your people."

What would that look like? Would the fae stand before her, youthful and unwinged like Fafnir, and give her their attention? What would she say if they did? Or would they refuse to listen to her?

There were hundreds of thousands of her kind, all of them suffering. How could she speak for every dryad in the forest?

Fafnir dug through his pouch with a furrowed brow. "I will need to gather food today. I will be quick."

"We could do that now," Esen offered.

Fafnir pulled a ceramic vessel out and shook its contents into his hand. Some kind of dried meat. "This will hold me over for the morning."

Esen walked on. An orange butterfly flitted past her and rested on a bluebell, gently flapping its wings. Suckling sounds surrounded her as the last of the snow melted into the earth. Green moss and blue lichen carpeted the trunks of the Rooted Ones and the ground beneath her feet. A song pulled at her memory. She lifted her flute from the cord around her neck and began to play.

Memories of Tristan swept over her—the promise she made as she had carved her flute with him, and his dark, sinister plans later. A ripple of unease came over her. She hoped he was not thinking of such things now.

"That was beautiful," Fafnir said.

She realized she had stopped playing. "Oh. Thank you."

Fafnir was leaning back against her branch, gazing at her with an expression that was unusually soft. He still had that leather case strapped to his back, shaped like a stringed instrument. He had brought that with him wherever he had come from, so it was clearly important to him.

"What kind of instrument is that?" she asked.

He swallowed a mouthful of meat. "A violin... with personal modifications."

Violin. A distant word her parents had taught her as a Rootling as they spoke of Fae culture. She had not seen any fae with one at Athas. Excitement fluttered over her. "What does it sound like? Would you play for me? If you don't mind..."

He looked at her a moment longer before dropping his gaze. With a single fluid movement, he unstrapped the case and swung it in front of him, then took the violin out to rest in his lap. With his left hand, he procured a long, thin piece of maple wood tapered to a point at the tip, like the triangle of a bird's beak, with a string of braided ligaments affixed to the length.

"One moment," he said. "I haven't used it in a bit."

Fafnir ran a small block of amber sap back and forth along the ligaments with a precise, measured movement. At last, he positioned the body of the instrument beneath his chin and hovered the thin piece of wood over the strings.

Sound shivered through Esen as his bow glided up and down. It wove with the melody of the birds, swayed with the new leaves of the Rooted Ones, and murmured with the river. It was as though he were taking the sounds of the forest and embodying them in music. There was something very private in the sound; like it was a part of him released into the air that would soon be bottled up again.

How strange that the bodies of her kind could be crafted into a new form and laced with strings, to sing so beautifully beneath a faerie's hands.

Fafnir stilled his violin, an open curiosity in his face. "Why do you love music, Esen? What does it do for you?"

Her hand drifted to her flute, feeling the smooth, cold bone. "I've never thought about it. I think..." She paused, listening to the song of the birds. "Music is like breathing to me. It is simply a part of life. I felt

179

that, with your music. You put into sound the feeling of the forest. It felt familiar to me, like I'd lived and breathed the vibrations all my life."

He flushed slightly and looked away. "It is like that for me too. It is as though music gives us a fleeting glimpse of the vibrant colors we cannot see with our eyes alone."

The sunlight glittered in Esen's eyes. The tones of his music echoed in her mind amid the birdsong. "Yes. That's a wonderful way to put it."

Losgann Bank

Key

🐸 Diviner home
🌱 Gourd fields
🐸 Frog den
🐸🍐 Homes

CHAPTER 22: THE RIVER FAERIES

Brightly colored gourd houses rose from among the mossy rocks ahead. Fafnir straightened, unraveling the rope that held him. When he had come here with Niamh in the night, he could distinguish the homes of the river fae only by their stark black outlines. Now, his brows lifted. Though they all had the bulbous body typical of a gourd, each home bore a distinctive shape and design. One had the bottom bowl of a gourd flipped and placed on top of the base. It looked like an acorn. On another, painted down from the drooping neck of the gourd was the body of a dragonfly, its wings painted on either side of the door.

He had never seen gourd houses painted like this before. These fae certainly valued visual appeal in their surroundings.

"That is their village," he said. He dug his fingers into the moss beneath him as Esen's shoulder moved. Her hand approached him.

"Are those their homes?" she asked, her voice lilted with wonder. "They look like dried fruits."

"Precisely," he said, as he stepped on her hand. "They're gourds—a type of fruit grown on vines. They grow farther south, but these fae must have brought the seeds up with them. And they have been cured, a careful process I am sure, to prevent rotting."

A woosh of air left Esen. A wistful smile lit up her face. "I love that."

Centering his weight in his legs, Fafnir managed to hold himself steady as she lowered him down. He stepped off onto the soft, springy ground, a stable foundation. The rush of the River Ifrati was a steady chatter, as the birds chirped their songs in tune. Voices, low and melodic like the river itself, broke through the din.

"Let's look at the river for a moment," Fafnir said. "I want to be certain of something."

He parted through the tall yellow reeds, mayflies buzzing in his ears, until he came out onto a crest above the riverbank. His eyes had not failed him in the dark when he'd been here with Niamh. The river was clearly overflooded here, even worse than downriver, where he lived. The water pressed against its new banks, brown with heavy sediments. Some grasses still holding onto their green color had been swallowed by the stream. Upriver, several of the river fae's brightly painted homes sat threateningly close to the waterline.

They would soon be swallowed too.

Farther down the bank he glimpsed the scattered remains of what had once been a massive stone structure. Stones as tall as two faeries lay strewn across the riverbank like they'd been hurled in a fit of rage. A channel dug out from the riverbed trickled through the circular foundation.

Interesting. The flood must have done that too.

"There is a story here," he said, turning. Esen stood in the river, staring at the water as it swirled around her feet.

"I wonder sometimes," Esen murmured. "How it would feel to live underwater like a fish. To be bathed in a sea of rushing sound and breathe water instead of air."

A lovely concept, but terribly ironic.

"Wait a few years," he muttered, staring at the swollen riverbank.

Esen's brow pinched, and then she frowned. "Oh, yes. I see."

They climbed back up the crest and approached the village. Esen's footsteps boomed behind him, the weight of her feet making a squelching sound in the sodden ground with each step. Their presence would be well known by now. It still felt strange to be traveling with a dryad… or anyone, for that matter.

Fafnir broke out from the undergrowth into a wide clearing framed by river rocks. Forty-four more gourd houses dominated the space, scattered about in uneven rows. A wide circle of open space was reserved in the center, and voices carried from farther down the bank.

He started forward and halted.

Four faeries carrying thin bows of elm stepped out from a home. Two of them had skin the soft white of river foam; another was warm brown, and the fourth a deep, verdant green. They were dressed in coarse cotton garments reflecting frequent use, and thick leather boots wrapped with an added layer of cured frog skin. A smart choice for waterproofing. Only the green faerie had wings. He looked young still. Wrinkles ghosted on his face, only just beginning to carve into the smooth skin.

All four faeries stared at him a moment before tilting their heads up and up to gaze at his tall companion.

"You must be Esen and Fafnir," the green fae said. His voice was thick, with a slowness that felt somehow like a river eddy in summer. Niamh had told him her lover, Rowan, would be there. This may be him.

"Yes," Fafnir said. "Are you Rowan?"

Nodding, Rowan turned to the faeries beside him. "Go on without me. These are my friends."

The faeries narrowed their eyes. "You have strange friends," one of the foam-white fae said. "Be back by late sun to help us butcher the catch."

They shouldered their bows and slunk off into the thicket.

"Let me take you to Niamh," Rowan said, gesturing.

He led them toward a green gourd home at the edges of the clearing. Flower designs had been painted stemming out from the natural white stripes of the gourd skin, adorning the green. Rowan opened the round white door, peeked his head inside, and came back out, frowning.

"I'm over here!"

Niamh walked through the central clearing cradling a ceramic jar of water in her arms. She was dressed in river faerie fashion, with marriage bands about her wrists matching Rowan's, and her baby strapped across her chest in a swaddle of cloth. Niamh's cheeks were flushed with color. Good. She was recovering well.

Rowan hurried over and took the jar from her. He walked alongside her toward their home, looking at her with devotion. He did it so thoughtlessly, so simply; a natural expression of his love.

What was it like, to give yourself to another like that? Did you get to keep any part of yourself to own? Or was the entire self offered to the other, colored, and molded into something new?

But he had seen his mother give herself to his father.

Only to have her heart torn out.

"How was your journey?" Niamh asked.

Fafnir started. Niamh and Rowan were standing before him, the jar gone, already placed inside the home. Niamh shifted her daughter around to her front, the infant's pale-green face peeking out from the cloth. She blinked at him with her wide, forest-green eyes.

The creaking of timber sounded behind Fafnir. Esen was kneeling by Niamh, smiling back at her. "It went well. You look so much better, Niamh. I am relieved. And forgive me, but I do not know your daughter's name."

Niamh's smile widened. "Her name is Iona."

Fafnir frowned. Iona was the name for the legendary land that may or may not exist across the sea.

"She is beautiful," Esen said. "How did she fare during the winter?"

"Better than I had feared." Niamh flushed redder. "Rowan cared for her while I was away. He fed her with fox milk."

Rowan folded his hand in Niamh's and pressed it.

Fafnir flattened his lips. "I saw that the river is encroaching on your homes, and that a large stone structure was destroyed. What was that used for? Did the flood destroy it?"

"That was our frog den," Rowan said. "We used to house and breed frogs in it. It was the flood, yes."

Judging from the size of the foundation of the stone, it must have held a hundred or more frogs. An impressive storage unit; likely very old, but a clever way to keep their prey in one place so they could slaughter them without having to spend time and energy hunting.

"We don't see fish in the river anymore either," Niamh added. "I don't—"

"Allow me to explain." A faerie with skin the rich gold of honey strode toward them, a stern confidence in her face. Her dark amber hair was gathered above her head and fell in thick plaits interspersed with colorful beads. She crossed her arms, jangling the loose bands on her arms made of shells and bones. Marked in white paint across her brow ridge and hugging the edges of her eyelids was a perfect circle—the dryadic symbol for *eternal*. She bore no wings.

"That is, if it's worth my time. I am Korey, Chieftain of the Losgann Bank Fae. Why are you both here?"

Niamh stepped back, a nervousness in her face.

It was up to him now.

"We have heard of your plight," Fafnir said. "We want to help you understand it so you can build actively toward a better future."

"We do understand. It was that rotting flood." Korey turned away. "I have a village to run."

"Think about it for a moment," Fafnir said quickly. "The flood did not happen by random chance. Before the past several hundred years, I assume your tribe has been more or less all right, unthreatened by natural activity. Is that correct?"

Korey faced him again, crossing her arms tighter. "Yes."

"Then what went wrong?" he asked. "Why have you been continually moving your houses back from the current? Why was that recent flood so devastating? Why was last winter the coldest winter we have experienced in our lifetimes?"

He could feel her weighing each question as he spoke it, stacking them on top of each other. Her brow lowered until her eyes almost disappeared into it.

"Do you know why this is happening?" he pressed.

Korey's lower jaw jutted out. "You tell me."

Adrenaline spiked through his veins. He'd broken through. "I will show you. Walk with me to the river."

"Very well," Korey said.

Fafnir nodded to Esen, who had risen to her feet. He strode forward, walking in step with Korey. They shouldered past the tall reeds. The river rushed before them, its brown waters flecked with foam. Faeries were laying stones the size of their heads in a circular pattern, like the foundation of the frog den that had been destroyed, but much smaller. This one would only fit seven frogs at a time, at most.

The stones from the original den had each been as tall as two faeries. Only a Walker could lift a stone that large. Now that they had forsaken the dryads, they had to do it themselves.

A badger lumbered onto the bank, towering over twice the height of the fae, a harness fastened around its chest. It pulled a wooden cart of stone behind it.

His gaze drifted, and he jolted. Isolde walked alongside the badger. Her white hair was hastily braided, tangled and stained with mud. A green cape sewed to look like a leaf fluttered about her shoulders.

She caught his gaze and stared hard, narrowing her eyes.

His stomach clenched. Why was she here, of all places?

He pulled in a deep breath to focus on the task at hand.

The river flowed before him, the wet sand cool beneath his feet. With a nod to Korey, he strode toward the place ahead where the vegetation began again along the river—higher up, on dry soil. Halting at the edge of the sand, he rolled his pant legs up to his knees, then stepped into the water.

"Look at this," he said, gesturing Korey over. Esen crouched at the edge of the bank, tilting her head.

Where the bank met the water, roots poked out from the soil. He pointed toward them. "The roots of this vegetation are binding the riverbank in place. They stabilize the soil and prevent it from washing down into the current. The roots of dryads do this, but on an even larger scale."

He swept his hand down the bank. "Do you see how, in areas of fewer vegetation, that is where the bank has folded in? This river has been losing vegetation for hundreds of years; I've observed it where I live, farther down. The recent changes in rainfall activity and extreme fluctuations of temperature have been actively eroding the topsoil. With the loss of topsoil, the nutritional quality is diminished. This weakens the grip of the roots of the vegetation like this along the bank. The banks collapse and become silt in the river, and the water levels rise. That is why you are always moving your homes, and why your frog den was destroyed by the flood. Are frogs your primary food source?"

"Yes."

"The frog population is dwindling rapidly."

Korey rubbed at her brow with two fingers, distorting the shape of the eternity symbol on her skin. "I get your point."

Excitement fluttered in his veins. "Then tell me what you're thinking."

"I'm thinking…" Frowning, she gazed down the river. "You say this is all due to the changing weather. Why is it especially worse of late?"

"Because this is happening all across the forest as the dryads die out. Their roots are the anchor for the soil. That is why the recent flood was so deadly. Their falling also opens up the forest floor to more sunlight, which warms the forest overall, resulting in erratic weather patterns and changes to the entire structure of the forest."

Korey stared at him, rolling her jaw. "The queen said we didn't need the dryads."

A smile spread over his face. She'd given him the perfect opportunity for the final blow.

"That same queen built a dam at the head of this river," he said.

"A what now?"

"A dam, to block the flow of the river. Have you seen many fish since then?"

"No," Korey growled.

"Precisely. She built the dam to try to mitigate the effects of further floods. It will help her in the short term. In the long term, it will only make things worse. It will lead to more erosion and nutrient loss in the water, and therefore the surrounding area. And no fish can travel past it."

Korey jerked her head back. The bones, shells, and other trinkets clinked together in a clash of sound. "All that because she's afraid of getting a little wet in her marble palace?"

"She doesn't care for you," Fafnir said. "She is protecting only her own interests."

Korey rubbed her brow again. All the fire fled from her limbs, like a milkweed pod that had lost its fluff and fallen to the ground.

"Why are you and your village not Uniting?" he asked, softening his tone.

"For reasons I am now unsure of," she muttered. She looked up at him, her gaze sharp. "I will gather the tribe. You may state your position to them as you did to me, and I will give them space to ask questions. Then, in fourteen suns, we will hold a consensus to decide how we will respond."

That was nearly half a moon.

"This is urgent," he said. "At any moment, another flood could put an end to your village."

Korey's face was a cold mask. "I have been alive for over a thousand years, thinking I would live forever. So have many of my people. You are asking us to make a decision concerning the eternity of our lives. We need some time to make it well."

Fourteen suns *was* hasty, when she put it that way. Waiting around would mean delaying the help the dryads needed, but they had no choice.

"Very well," he said finally.

Esen's voice lilted from behind him. "The Cycle of Giving is so entwined in our culture because it is true." She was standing in the river, her face far above them, her eyes fixed on Korey. He'd forgotten she was there. "We must obey it for the forest to live. For *us* to live."

Korey stared at Esen, rolling her teeth along her lower lip. "I had nearly forgotten the Cycle." She turned. "I must return to the sun's work. I will see you both at dusk. We will address the tribe then."

"Wait," Esen said. "I can help you rebuild the old stone den. It was Walkers that laid the original stones, was it not?"

Korey froze. Esen had gotten her. It was a smart move. They could talk with the river fae on an individual basis by staying to help them, and build a better name for themselves before the consensus.

"Yes," Korey said finally. She looked up at Esen, a warmth in her eyes. "That would be incredible."

"You also need to get your homes off the ground so they're safe from flooding," Fafnir added. "I'd recommend situating them up in the Rooted Ones. I can help you with that."

"We've thought of that," Korey said. "We could never figure out how to get them up there in the first place, let alone keeping them safely secured. A bad wind could rattle the house like it was built atop a tadpole."

"Well, Esen can lift them, and I can design a system of rods and platforms to hold them soundly in place, as well as enabling you all to ascend and descend safely."

Korey's brows shot up. "How? Tell me more."

He tilted his head back, squinting at an oak above them. A sturdy branch shot off from the trunk, forming a V. Perfect. "It would work best in the fork of a Rooted One. Like there, for instance. You could prop up a house on a platform that rests against the fork of the trunk and that branch splitting of it. The rods would go through the base of the house, and through the top toward the ceiling, and would have to be inserted into the Rooted Ones..."

He frowned. That was rather invasive. He could just use rope, but that might not be enough to hold it steady in a storm. He couldn't have a house crashing down because of him. "For best stability, we'd have to cut a hole a cubit deep horizontally—"

"Oh, you're a Rath faerie," Korey interrupted. "Explain what that is. We don't use those here."

Right. Standardized units of measurement were used mostly within the vicinity of the Rath Síoraí. Most fae farther from the Rath used either their own systems, or nothing at all, just eyeballing their measurements.

"This"—he traced the distance from his elbow back to the tip of his middle finger—"is a cubit. So that deep in, plus half a cubit in a vertical downward direction to lock it in place."

He turned to Esen. "Only if the Rooted Ones are okay with it. Esen, could you ask them? The river fae have fifty-four houses—"

"Fifty-seven," Korey corrected.

"Then we would need fifty-seven volunteers," Fafnir continued. "It shouldn't pierce more than the thick outer layer of bark on an older dryad. And that bark is dead, right? There is no feeling in it?"

Sweat pooled at the back of his neck. Maybe this was a terrible idea. He didn't want to hurt them.

"No," Esen said. "I forget how it came up, but Ian told me once that he felt no pain when the whites of his nails broke. Damage to our outer bark is like that for us. Although it does make us more vulnerable to the weather."

"The hole would be plugged up by the rod," he said, "and bark could grow back around it."

Esen nodded. "I will ask." She approached the oak he had indicated and laid a hand on his thick, fissured trunk. The oak stirred, leaves rustling in response. Korey stared with her mouth slightly parted.

Esen soon returned. "It's okay with them. They wish no harm to befall these fae. All are essential in the Cycle of Giving."

"Okay," Fafnir said, breathing even.

Korey looked between them with an odd expression on her face. "Thank them for us," she said, finally, then started to step out from the river. "Come. Have either of you eaten?"

Fafnir followed her. "No."

Korey frowned up at Esen. "How do you eat? I've always wondered."

"Don't worry about me," Esen said. "I am always eating, in a way. I draw up nutrients from the earth with my feet."

Korey rattled her head, her hair swishing in her face. A throaty laugh burst from her. "I wish we could do that. Then we wouldn't need to do all this work."

She glanced at Fafnir. "I've changed my mind. I'll get you some food, and then I'll summon the tribe right away."

Fafnir nodded. He stepped out from the water onto the bank, dripping wet from the knee down, and stole a quick glance toward the frog den. He stiffened. Isolde was looking at him, watching with a sharp, calculating air.

Wood creaked behind him, followed by the rustling of leaves. Esen had crouched with her face near him, her blue eyes wide with curiosity. "Do you know that faerie?"

"Yes," he said. He turned and followed Korey, wiping his sweaty palms on his pants.

Painting Gourds

1. Wipe down with clean water and soap
2. Paint first layer with frog skin binder
3. Apply paint! 1-3 coats recommended. Wait at least 2 sun phases in between coats
4. Varnish with linseed oil

Common Patterns

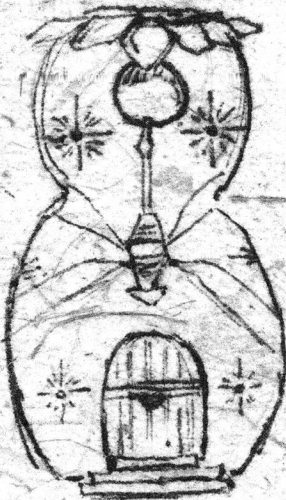

CHAPTER 23: CONSENSUS

When they returned to the village, Korey tossed Fafnir a cloth sack that he just managed to catch. As she went down to summon her fae, he peeked inside. The strong odor of garlic greeted him. Inside were chunks of lumpy dried meat: frog, by the look of it.

"You have a gift, Fafnir," Esen said. She knelt beside him, her leaves rustling with the movement. "Where did you learn to think like that, with your snow-eater and this rod system? It's unlike anything I've known before."

Fafnir shrugged. "I like to think of solutions."

A white butterfly flitted past and landed on Esen's shoulder, its wings casting a shadow over the green moss sprouting from her red-brown bark. She was a vastly different creature than him, with bark instead of skin, towering high above the undergrowth that made up his world. What was it like to live through her eyes? To have water, sap, and nutrients flowing through his veins instead of blood? To be born mortal?

"With their houses built into the branches of the Rooted Ones, these fae will be forced into a kind of intimacy with them," Esen murmured. "If nothing else convinces them, I hope this will."

He hadn't thought of that. How could they wake every morning supported by a creature they had denied and not feel any kind of guilt?

"Wind be with you," Esen said. "They are starting to come."

"Thank you. Please, speak where you see fit. I wish you luck as well."

He ate a few pieces of the frog meat as the fae began to arrive and sit in a circle in front of a large, oval-shaped house. Niamh and Rowan flapped down from the canopy, followed by several more faeries with brilliant green leaves like Rowan's. They must be his family. The youngest aside from Rowan looked to be his parents, the middle-aged one his grandfather, and the older two his second or third grandparents or something. The last one looked very, very old—likely she was his fourth or fifth grandmother.

It had been a long time since he had seen a generational family all together like this. Even still, there were too many gaps.

Hopefully, they hadn't lost anyone during the winter.

Rowan's family crowded a section of the circle. Niamh sat among them, bouncing her child on her lap. Korey appeared last. She stepped inside the home and reemerged carrying a dark staff made of yew. She seated herself on a straw mat in front of the house.

At the edge of the group, he glimpsed Isolde. Was she one of them now? But she was sitting apart from the others, like she didn't belong.

Korey beckoned to him and Esen. Esen walked carefully around the circle and seated herself just outside of it, the creaking of her joints echoing through the space. The faeries nearby edged back from her. Fafnir flattened his ears. He sat in the empty place beside Korey, on her left side.

A moment of perfect silence followed, broken only by the music of crickets as Korey gazed over the seated fae. She spoke at last. "Fae of Losgann Bank. The faerie Fafnir has come to us today with an explanation for the struggles we have endured for the past hundreds of years. He proposes that the root of our dilemmas trace back to the perishing of the dryads. Fafnir, you may speak."

She placed the staff in his hands. The wood felt cool to the touch, the surface gnarled with age. Whispers of dragans ghosted in the weaving cracks.

He repeated his argument in a concise summary. Some of the faeries grew looks of worry or went pale, but most of them simply stared at him, their faces betraying no emotion.

When he had finished, he gave the staff back to Korey.

"Those who have words, speak," she said, and held out the staff in her hands, resting it lightly in her fingertips.

For a long moment, the faeries murmured amongst themselves.

Eventually, a foam-white fae with sharp cheekbones lifted his hand and beckoned with his knobby fingers. Korey passed the staff to the faerie on her right, who passed it to the next faerie. Round the circle it went, until it reached the foam-white fae. He seized the staff with zeal and fixed his amber eyes on Fafnir. "The river system is always changing," he said. "Seven thousand years ago, an onslaught of storms, and then a drought the following year, wore down the banks so much that the river has been wider ever since. What is your proof that this time it has anything to do with the dryads?"

Still watching him with narrowed eyes, the faerie sent the staff back toward Fafnir. At last Korey deftly took hold of it, tilting her head. She gave it to Fafnir.

Interesting. It was like a long, patient dance where you were forced to form your words carefully, and hold on to them, before you could speak.

Fafnir leaned forward. "Good question. How wide did the river grow then?"

He passed the staff back.

The faerie rolled his eyes up, frowning. When he received the staff, he said, "about three and a half martens."

"And how much did the river widen from then to one thousand years ago? When the Ancient Law was revoked?"

"It fluctuated, as always," said the faerie, "but there was no significant change."

"And how much has it grown in the past thousand years?"

"Eight martens."

"That's over double the width, compared to the last change," Fafnir said, tapping the staff into his open palm. "How many major droughts and storms, lasting longer than one moon, have we had in that time?"

The faerie glared at him as the staff went round. "One," he huffed.

"Then something is happening that has never happened before, at least not to this degree," Fafnir said, holding the faerie's gaze. "What else could be causing it if not the dryads perishing?"

The faerie blew air out his mouth. He squirmed in his seat until the staff came toward him. He ripped it from the other faerie's hands and rose to his feet. "Who do you think you are? You think you can come here and tell us what's going on with this river that we've lived and breathed beside for over a hundred thousand years? Where are *your* wings, if you're so convinced?"

The faerie hurled the staff at the ground.

Fafnir stared at it. He sucked in a breath and exhaled slowly through his nostrils.

By the sound of clattering trinkets, he knew Korey had risen. "Wynn, communicate with respect if you wish to continue. Please be seated."

Wynn's gaze burned a hole in his skin. At last, a rustle of fabric sounded. The fae had seated himself.

0 and 1 is 1. 1 and 1 is 2.

Always and forever.

Lifting his chin, Fafnir looked to his right to see Korey offering the staff. He took hold of it. He couldn't leave the accusation unanswered. Every eye was trained on him. But to have to say his lie again, in front of Esen, and his sister…

His mouth felt dry, as though it was crusted with sand.

"I am enacting a plan for change," he said. "To spread the word among more faeries like all of you. I am refraining from Uniting until our mission is complete, to preserve my life at this time."

Wynn snarled. "He reveals himself. He's just a rotting coward."

Korey took the staff from Fafnir. "Wynn," she said, her voice tinged with pain. "You spoke without the staff. You are prohibited from speaking further in this meeting."

Wynn crossed his arms, glaring at the ground.

Murmurs sounded among the fae, but no one moved. At last, Rowan gestured for the staff. He held it lightly from his fingertips, as though he had already forgotten he was holding it.

"I don't know if this is relevant," he muttered, "but I once thought that all of you, except for me and my family, were like the stars." His eyes lifted toward the sky. "You lived for a thousand years before me, and would continue to live forever after me. I thought I was nothing but a blip in your existence. But I guess…" He dropped his head. "I guess I was wrong. Even Wynn could say nothing to disprove Fafnir's theory."

Niamh laid a hand on his shoulder. He leaned into her touch, the tension in his body easing.

How strange. To bear children, and grandchildren, and grow older and closer to the grave as your neighbors carried on around you, utterly unchanged—as timeless and distant as the stars.

As he longed to be.

A faerie with skin as green as moss spoke next. "How many dryads have perished?" she asked, her voice thick.

Fafnir hesitated. Too many. But as the staff came toward him, the moss-green fae shook her head, and pointed toward Esen behind him.

"You wish for the dryad to answer?" asked the faerie holding the staff.

The moss-green fae nodded.

Esen shifted, her leaves swaying softly. They looked even greener, fuller than when he had last noticed. She put out a palm as the staff was passed to her, and held it in her open hand. "I have only just begun to Walk, so I do not fully know. Tens of thousands, at least. Too many to count."

Tears welled in the faerie's eyes. "I am sorry," she said.

Silence reigned. Finally, the staff was returned to Korey. "The tribe has spoken. Consider what you have heard today and weigh it in your heart. Fourteen suns from now, we will hold a consensus to cast our vote. The decision will be thus: will we keep the New Law, preserving the freedom to choose whether you wish to Unite, or will we restore the Ancient Law among our tribe, calling all fae older than one hundred to Unite, like in the days of old?"

More silence. Korey rose to her feet. "Fafnir and the dryad Esen will be staying with us until we hold our consensus. Esen has offered to rebuild our den, and Fafnir to get our homes safely into the Rooted Ones. Meet me here at dawn, and I will designate who will help with each project. For tonight, continue as you were."

A rumble of voices broke out. Faeries rose and jostled about, gathering in groups to talk. Isolde had vanished.

Korey turned to face Fafnir. Although her face was animated, her eyes didn't quite meet his. His words had clearly affected her, but would it be enough to get her to change a pattern of thinking that she had worn for almost a thousand years?

"Let me show you where you can sleep," she said.

The next day, Korey assigned Fafnir eleven workers, including Rowan and his parents, and Rhiannon, whom he learned was Rowan's fifth grandmother. Just thinking of it made his mind spin. He tried to keep Rhiannon away from the labor at first, but she insisted on working as hard as the others. Although her skin sagged loosely like long-worn clothing, she was lean and muscled. She had a brightness to her eyes that reminded him of Ian.

For the first two days, they gathered dead wood and shaped it to the right sizes. Then he climbed up the oak—one of the Rooted Ones who had volunteered—and tied a rope to a branch above the fork. Rowan hovered near him, flapping his wings softly. This was the Rooted One he had United with, and his concern was evident.

Fafnir pulled hard on the knots, making sure they were secure, before connecting the end of the rope around to a harness at his hip. He turned around. The other non-United faeries were perched on the branch, while Rowan's family flapped beside them, watching.

"I'll watch the rope for you," said the moss-green faerie; Brighid was her name.

He nodded and walked along the edge of the branch before finally letting his feet fly out, dangling in the empty air. His breath escaped in a whoosh as he plummeted, and his stomach restricted as the rope reached the end of its slack. It took a moment for him to catch his breath. Wings would be rather handy right now. He jerked his weight back, and gravity swung him forward again. He grabbed hold of a strip of bark extending out from the dryads' trunk.

Carefully, he pulled out his knife and walked it around the diameter. He could hear Rowan beside him again. "I will be careful," he promised him.

He made the first insertion. Even after all the pain the faeries had caused the dryads, they were still willing to do this for them. The dryads were so kind, despite everything. Perhaps too kind.

When he'd cut a cubit in, he felt the bark at the back. Still within the outer bark layer. He wiggled his arm out and held it out to his audience.

"A cubit in," he said, indicating the distance, "is safe for this size Rooted One. It will not harm nor pain them."

Rowan's shoulders slumped with relief. As Brighid pulled Fafnir up and helped him back onto the branch, Rowan's father flew down to take his place, widening the hole. Rhiannon started on the other side. The other fae left to rest, except for Brighid.

Fafnir took a long draft of water and wrapped his arms around his knees. They pulsed with the memory of movement, stiff and sore. Brighid was staring up at the branches of the oak, her eyes distant.

She had been so compassionate in the meeting. He had to talk with her, understand why.

"How have you been feeling since the meeting?" he asked. A gentle prod, hopefully.

Brighid murmured, "I've been thinking… When I was a child, over a thousand and thirty years ago, I saw dryad children everywhere with their faerie families. I made friends with some of them. I brought my friends over and we played games together, Rootling and faerie, like there was no difference between us. That's such a rare sight now. And there was always a cluster of children in our village before, laughing, playing around, but now, they've all matured. It's only Rowan's family having kids, and they're by themselves."

She twisted her hair in a series of knots. "I don't know. I just miss that. And I keep thinking of all the dryad children that should have been born, but… weren't."

His stomach knotted. It had been one thousand and seven years since the Ancient Law was revoked. Hundreds of thousands of dryads should have been born, Walked the earth, and Rooted back to the soil already. They should be breathing the sweet spring air with them.

"I've thought of that too," he murmured.

The leaves rustled about them, but there was no wind. He tilted his chin up. The oak's green crown towered far above him, swaying softly.

Were there words in the oak's stirring? Or was she simply sighing, reflecting on Brighid's words?

He had forgotten she could hear them.

"Thank you for coming," Brighid said. "I feel so hideous that I scarcely thought of these things before. Now I can't think of anything else. The dryads have done so much for us, and this too. I've done nothing for them."

His hands tightened around his knees. "When the consensus comes, vote with your heart," he said. "If you do, you will be least likely to regret your decision later."

The next morning, they finished with the holes. Esen carved the openings in the gourds and fitted the rods through, then held them up as two winged faeries locked the rods into place. She pressed two fingers down on the gourd, but it didn't budge at all.

The faeries cheered. Fafnir couldn't help but smile.

They were just beginning on the sixth of the lowest-lying houses when the fourteen suns of deliberation were finally up. As the shadows stretched long on the day of the consensus, the faeries thanked him sincerely. A note of discomfort mingled with it.

They wouldn't be able to get the rest of the houses up without a Walker.

Fafnir turned to Rowan. "Do you know any Walkers?"

Rowan stiffened. He half-glanced toward the non-United fae among them. "Yes. But they don't come here very often."

Fafnir nodded. Likely they didn't feel welcome. He met the gaze of the non-United fae, but they averted his eyes.

"These Walkers are part of your family," he said gently.

"I've been trying to tell them that for centuries," Rhiannon growled under her breath.

The other fae were silent. Fafnir rubbed at the back of his head. This was a fight he would not win here. But the consensus could change this. It could change everything.

"Well, you know how to do it now. I hope it helps you."

He walked with them toward the village center. Faeries were coming up from the riverbank, muddy and wet but their faces beaming. He glanced past them to see the top of the den rising from the reeds, the stones fitted neatly together.

Esen had finished it for them.

A cricket leaped past him, landing on a swaying blade of grass several martens away. It rubbed its legs together noisily. Fireflies flitted in lanterns, glowing a dim green and lighting the way toward the center clearing.

The faeries took their seats in the circle; fifty-seven of them total. Fafnir sat beside Korey again, with Esen behind them. A basket of smooth white and black pebbles rested in Korey's lap. At her feet sat a painted bowl filled with water. Her face was unreadable.

Nervousness trailed tingly spider feet down his limbs. The past fourteen suns would mean little if they failed.

A gleam of red flashed in his eyes as the sun slipped below the horizon. Squinting, he glimpsed Korey raise her brown arms and trace a circle in the air over the sun. It was a gesture that reminded him of a Diviner. Under the Ancient Law, all chieftains had been Diviners as well as leaders.

Korey had spoken nothing of the Mother and performed no holy rituals in the past suns; likely she had given up that role.

At last, Korey spoke. "We gather tonight to determine the fate of our lives, our village, and perhaps the forest as a whole. I will pass the stones down the circle. If you wish to keep the New Law, take a white stone. If you wish to restore the Ancient Law among us, take a black stone. Hide the stone in your hand at once so you are not influenced by the decisions of your peers. Are we clear?"

All nodded. Korey passed the basket to the faerie on her other side. He stared hard, before finally reaching a hand in and pulling out his closed fist. He passed it on, his face grim. It went around the circle. Some considered for a long pause; others took their stone right away. Wynn grabbed his in a heartbeat. Not surprising. Niamh, Rowan, and Rowan's family chose theirs. That was eight black and one white he was sure of.

Iona was untangling one of Niamh's braids with a pinched brow as though it were terribly important. The last of the sunlight flushed the little points of her ears.

He thought of what Brighid had said. Iona's fate was being cast. Would she grow up in a community with other children—new faeries and Rootlings alike? Or would she grow up with the confusion of being the only young in her village?

Someone tapped his shoulder. The faerie on his left held the basket out to him, jerking her head toward Korey. He took it and passed it over.

Korey took it and grabbed her own stone. She placed the basket at her feet and laid the remaining stones in a circle in front of her.

There were fifteen white stones left.

And forty-two black.

"The vote has been cast," Korey said at last. "We keep the New Law."

Fafnir's ears drooped.

He had failed.

Wynn and several other fae leaped up and cheered.

"Prepare the bird," Korey said. "We will serve our guests one last time all the same."

"Wait." Rhiannon rose, tall and straight as a reed despite her age. Her coal-black eyes burned with fury. "You're telling me that after spending half the Seed Moon cutting holes into the dryads and taking help from a Walker to rebuild our den, we're going to reject them? Put our feet up on their branches and maybe hack up a nice spit on them while we're at it? That's rotting disgusting."

Korey's eyes widened, her mouth twitching.

Cradling Iona, Niamh rose and stood beside Rhiannon, her face hard. Rowan joined her, then his father, and finally, his whole family.

A thrill surged through Fafnir. He leaned forward.

Rhiannon continued. "Whether or not you believe what Fafnir said, the dryads will still die if we don't Unite with them. Those houses will come down, and it won't be pretty."

Wynn sprung to his feet, a crude snarl twisting his face. "The dryads are the disgusting ones, not us. They've demanded our deaths ever since the Mother made us. We want to live."

Rhiannon lunged forward. Rowan and his father caught her by the arms and held her back.

"You wicked young fae," Rhiannon howled. "If my mother were alive, she would slap that horrid mouth of yours—"

"Enough."

With a clatter of trinkets, Korey stood. Her face was red, emotion thick behind her still features. "We have chosen the New Law. As before, those who wish to Unite may, and those who don't wish it don't have to. This discussion is over."

A rumble of voices broke out. Wynn stalked off. The rest of the fae rose and gathered in groups to talk. Several disappeared inside the biggest house behind Korey and came back out carrying the body of a faerie-sized plucked bird on a wooden platform. They ran a pole through it and began to lift it to hang over the fire.

Fafnir lowered his gaze. His thumb pressed into the soft dirt, scarcely feeling the coolness against his skin.

Korey's words echoed in his ears. They had not won the tribe over to the dryads... but something had started here.

There were forty-two black stones left, so fifteen fae had voted black. Rowan's family and Niamh only made eight. So there had been another seven willing to restore the Ancient Law. Perhaps they would still Unite. It would be a small beginning, but immensely significant. Change had a way of growing exponentially.

But to effect that change, he'd divided an ancient tribe of fae that had dwelt here for over a hundred thousand years. A queasiness gripped his stomach.

He turned to Korey. She was sitting as still as a Rooted One, staring into the bowl of water at her feet. After slipping her hand within the water, she lifted it, put a dripping finger to her brow, and wiped the white symbol of eternity from her forehead.

Root Web

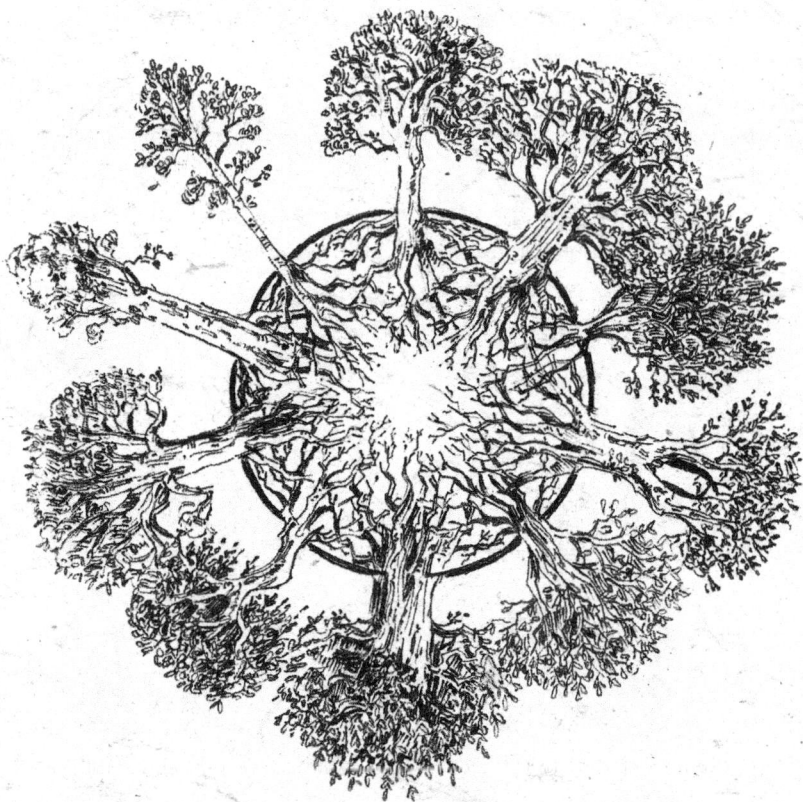

All the Rooted Ones are joined together by the Root Web. It is the term for the line of communication that is formed between them by their roots. Each Rooted One is entwined with the roots of their neighbors, and their neighbors' roots are entwined with their neighbors, so that messages can be passed through all of them, in a remarkably fast manner. Together, they act as one living organism.

CHAPTER 24: DECISIONS

A bruise-blue lake keeps a still surface in the winter, but when you draw near and listen close, you can hear the sound of the ice splintering and cracking within... or so Esen's mother had once told her. She had yet to see a lake in winter.

The river faeries bustled about, turning their bird on the spit above the fire until it became brown, running with juice. They gave out water in woven bowls of leaves and talked of the day's work, and the plans for their activities the following day. But beneath the surface, she could feel the moaning of the ice—the unresolved tension lingering in the twilight air.

Hearing Fafnir's voice amid the noise, she turned to see him speaking with Korey. "May I ask where you stand?" she heard him ask.

Korey swirled her finger in the bowl of water. At last, she looked up at Fafnir. "I know only that I am not truly immortal. You and Esen may stay this night and into the morning if you choose. Eat, and speak with my people as you will, but do not press them. Respect their right to choose."

Fafnir rose and bowed to her. "Thank you for hosting us."

"Thank you for helping us," Korey said, but her words were stiff. She rose with a clatter and walked away.

Esen fidgeted with her hands. How could Korey be so cold? She'd become almost like a friend to her as they'd worked on the den together. Korey had shared stories and jokes with her, and had even got Esen to open up about her childhood, her hopes and fears. Had that meant nothing?

The aroma of the meat filled the air. The faeries were gathered around the bird, pulling it apart into heaping bowls of its flesh. Esen dropped her gaze. It was a natural part of the Cycle of Giving, that lives were laid down to serve other lives, but she did not like to witness the act. Ian had always prepared his food well out of her sight.

"I am sorry." Fafnir sat beside her, his lips pressed tight. "I had hoped it would turn out differently. Although there are still seven, other than Rowan's family, who chose the black stones."

When she had seen so many black stones laid in the circle, she had only thought of how many had voted against her kind. After they had done so much for them, like Rhiannon said.

She looked carefully among the crowd. There. Six Wingless Ones sat separately from the others. Two of them she had worked with on the den. A few spoke quietly, but most of them were silent. The other faeries rioted and caroled around them, sharing jokes and stories.

"I think that is them," she said. Except for the seventh.

The ghost of a song murmured on the wind. A patch of daffodils grew near her knee, their yellow heads waving. Waiting for a song to revel in.

"I have an idea," she said.

She rose just as Niamh and Rowan approached her carrying bowls of meat. Iona smiled at her from the sash around Niamh's chest.

"Niamh," Esen said. "Has Iona heard a flower sing yet?"

A smile lit Niamh's face. "No. Let's go show her, away from the noise."

"Yes," Esen said. "I will invite the faeries who are sitting alone to join us. I think they are in need of cheer."

Esen approached the faeries and knelt in front of them. They looked up at her, their eyes clouded with heavy thought.

"Would you like to hear something beautiful?"

The moss-green faerie rose first. "Very much so." The others followed.

Esen gathered Fafnir, and Rowan's family too, and went deeper into

208

the forest. The fire flickered at their backs until it was only a dim glow. The dark wood enveloped them.

Esen glimpsed a cluster of daffodils gleaming in the moonlight. They were arranged in an almost perfect circle, with open green space within. Excitement blossomed within her. Circles were sacred spaces, thick with the Mother's spirit.

The moss-green fae ran to the edge of the circle. "I haven't seen a circle like this in years!" she cried.

"I swear I walked past here today," another faerie said, "but I didn't see this."

Esen walked to the circle. "Mother Wind," she whispered. "Breathe me inspiration."

A small wind ghosted by her ear. She stepped within the circle and closed her eyes. Though she felt no change, the honeyed fragrance of the flowers drifted to her, softening her senses. She called to her mind a song she had made as a Rootling.

"On a lonely winter day,
A fierce and fearless river flowed,
Upon the silver ice it hurled,
Its waters full and strong."

The daffodils bent their necks toward her, listening.

"On that lonely winter day,
Cracks and fissures there did grow
Until at last the ice gave way
And the river, she broke through.

"On a lone winter day —"
"A winter cold and gray."

There it was, the echo of the flowers. A little bell-like giggle sounded outside the circle. Iona perched in Niamh's lap, lifting her little hands toward the flowers as a smile filled her face.

"A cardinal flashed through the frost."

"So red against the gray."

"On a lonely winter day."
"Creeping out from her den."

Esen smiled. She flowed with the words the flowers added.

"A red fox and the cardinal."
"They came to see the river flow."
"She flashed and gleamed in the sun."

"Flowing free and true."

The last line echoed among the flowers, like they were passing it back and forth between them in excitement. Iona's eyes were huge. Niamh scooped her up and flew to hover by one of the daffodil's bulbs. Iona reached toward a yellow petal, running her fingers gently along its soft edge.

The faeries were silent, wide-eyed. The flowers' song slowly faded.

"Thank you for showing us," Rowan said. "You know, the flowers grow in the spring and die in the winter. New flowers take their place next spring." He scratched at his head. "I always thought there was something beautiful about that."

"Yes," Esen said. "I think so too."

Despite the stress it had caused Ian, Niamh had chosen a good faerie.

Esen beckoned to the rest of the faeries. "Come sing to them. They never tire of music." But the faeries held back.

"I have been hurting this forest by my negligence," said the moss faerie. "These flowers too. They had to bear that awful winter."

A soberness came over Esen. "What is your name?" she asked her.

"Brighid."

"You could Unite tonight," Esen said softly. She waited for someone to silence her. No one did. "You don't need the law to tell you to. You alone could create a life, or several lives, where there would be none. Do you know Wind-Speak?" Brighid shook her head. "Then I can communicate with the Rooted Ones for you. I can ask who is in most need of a faerie."

"Yes," Brighid said. A brightness broke over her face. "Please do that."

Warmth glowed in Esen. One change. Perhaps the other faeries would follow Brighid's lead.

Esen approached a nearby holly dryad, Brighid following close behind. Red berries winked among her shiny green leaves. Esen laid a hand on her trunk.

"*Aeonida*, holly," she said, looking up at her silver branches. "This faerie wishes to Unite. Who among here needs a fae most?"

The holly shivered her leaves. She was silent for a moment. Finally, the holly said, "*Aeonida, hazel. There is a yew by the river. She Rooted just a few years ago beside her partner. She is young and strong and will have many years to bear children.*"

"Thank you," Esen said. She turned to Brighid and relayed the message.

"I will Unite with her," Brighid said, "as I should have done, a long time ago."

"Bless you, Brighid."

Another faerie, this one with skin dark like soil, approached Esen. "I will Unite also," he said.

Her mouth opened. It took a moment for words to follow. "Thank you—" she began, but a third faerie stepped toward her, and then another, until all six stood at her feet.

"We here will all Unite," said the third faerie. She looked behind her at the other fae. "That is true?"

They nodded back at her. Every one of their faces looked young, though some of them might have lived for several hundred years; others, over a thousand. Perhaps a few were only a hundred or more, close to the traditional age of Uniting. How strange to not know for sure how long each of them had lived upon the earth. The hand of death had passed them over. But when they United, death would find them. It would carve lines into their faces, their bodies, until it took them from the land.

Though their faces were sober, a determination burned in their eyes. It fueled the fire in her own spirit. She was one step closer to saving the forest for Aisling.

"Thank you," Esen said, her voice thick. "Thank you all."

Footsteps crunched on the soft grass. Korey stepped out from the darkness of the Rooted Ones. Her face was heavy, as though she had fought a long and costly battle.

"I am ashamed," she muttered. "I fear that after rejecting the dryads for so long, they wouldn't want me now. I wouldn't."

A wordless murmur echoed among the Rooted Ones.

"You can always start again," Esen said, offering a smile. "Like spring."

Korey's face twitched. She wiped at her eyes. "I will try. My mother died four hundred and twenty-seven years ago—the last in my family to Unite. She was wiser than I."

Fabric swished, and Niamh fell into Korey, embracing her around the middle. "I was hoping you would join us."

Fafnir approached Korey and shook her hand. A smile flickered on his lips, brightening his face. It was a shame he scarcely smiled. It looked well on him.

"Thank you," he said to her. He swept his gaze to the others. "To all of you. You will help the forest more than you could know."

Drawing them in close, he shared the details of their plan. "We need your voices. Your story is not far from the story of many fae of the Rath. It will resonate with many and help bring more fae to our side. The more we convince, and sooner, the quicker the forest will heal. Will you vow to help us?"

The faeries turned their heads toward Korey.

"Of cou—" Korey started.

"Could you take out that rotted dam after this is over?" Rhiannon interrupted.

"Rhiannon," Rowan objected. "I don't think that's—"

Rhiannon put up her hand, silencing him.

Fafnir shifted his weight. "The queen wouldn't like that," he muttered.

"I don't care," Rhiannon said. "If your plan is successful, then we will be undermining her power already. Soon we can have her dethroned. We need that dam out if what you said about it is true."

Fafnir quirked his mouth. "Very well. I promise."

Korey's face held the glimmer of a cocky smile. "Rhiannon strikes a good deal. Either way, we will help you."

Niamh lifted her hands. "Let's celebrate!"

Esen glanced behind her. The fire lighting the rest of the river fae had blinked out.

Beneath the silver moon, the assembled group danced and sang within the flower ring. Esen swayed in its center, lifting one hand toward the sky as she played upon her flute with the other. Korey and many of the others leaped and twirled about her in wild reels, blowing on reed flutes as they danced, creating a shrill, ethereal sound. The Rooted Ones above swayed their branches, adding a steady thrum, thrum that churned behind the melodies. Rowan, Niamh, and others sat outside the circle and watched, swaying their heads to the melodies. At the edge of the ring, Fafnir stood, lost in his violin.

The music swelled, deepening. Esen closed her eyes, swaying to its rhythm. The sound was playful, quick, like a butterfly darting through the sky; so different from the deep, grounding tones of the music of the dryads.

A wind breathed from behind her, slipping by to stir the limbs of the Rooted Ones before rising to dance with the star-riddled sky.

At last, the fae grew weary. They spoke breathlessly to one another before parting to find their dryads. They would wake in the morning with wings upon their backs.

Only Fafnir remained with her. He was silent for a long moment, staring after the spaces the fae had left.

"You did it, Esen," he said at last. He returned the violin to its case on his back. "That was wondrous."

"We're a team," she said. "You gave them the facts, and I helped give them the faith… or something like that."

"I suppose it takes both," he said. He shuffled, fidgeting with one of the wooden rings on his ear before meeting her gaze. "Esen… may I ask the Rooted Ones a question through you?"

"Of course." She led him toward the holly.

"Place your hand on her," Esen said quietly. "It helps her connect with you. Ask your question, and I will interpret her answer."

Fafnir approached the holly's thin, silver trunk. It towered twice Esen's own height; she could scarcely imagine how tall the holly felt to Fafnir. With the sensitive deliberation of one searching their way in the dark, he put out a hand and brought it to rest on one of the holly's roots.

"My father, Fiachra Siegfried," he whispered. "Is he alive?"

A wind whipped through the holly's branches, moaning shrilly, then silence followed. Esen held her breath. The night crickets murmured. Still, the holly remained silent.

The question must be humming beneath them, traveling far across the land.

At long last, the holly stirred her leaves. *"There is mystery around Fiachra and his dryad, Eoghan. They passed over nine hundred years ago. They say it was Fiachra who fell first. His blood pooled into the roots of the dryads near, and a small stone knife clattered, vibrating the earth along with his fall."*

A chill crept up Esen's spine.

This was terrible. Terrible.

And all this time, Fafnir had not known.

What had happened? Could he have been... murdered? But murder was an immensely rare crime, punishable by death.

"Were there any other faeries near when it happened?" she asked, aware Fafnir was watching her, waiting.

"No," said the holly. *"That is the mystery. Most likely... I hesitate to say."*

"Please do," Esen said. "This was his father."

"A faerie came upon his body later. It is believed that his own soul had wished to be reunited with the Mother, and his own hand had made it so."

Esen's hand flew to her mouth. Then he had —

He had killed himself.

She turned to face Fafnir, swallowing hard.

"He is dead?" Fafnir asked, his face still as stone. Esen didn't want to be the one to shatter him.

"Yes," she said stiffly.

"There is more," he said. His hands twitched at his sides, the only sign betraying him.

"Yes." She sucked in her breath and looked away. With clenched teeth, she related what the holly had told her.

His face turned sheet white. He turned from her and took the strip of bark off his head to run his hands through his hair.

"I... I saw him," he whispered.

"What do you mean?"

He shook his head, putting a hand over his face. "Never mind. I need to go."

"Where are you going?" she asked, struggling to keep her voice calm. It couldn't be good to be alone after hearing such news.

"I don't know," he said. He began to walk toward the darkness of the Rooted Ones.

"Wait." She took a long stride and caught up with him. "Do you have family you can talk to?"

"No." His voice was rough, almost like a growl, but he did cease walking.

"Do you have family left alive?" she pressed. Surely, he must.

He hesitated, rolling his jaw. "Yes."

Hope surged in her, then her brow pinched as his answers connected. "Who are they? Why can you not talk to them?"

He rubbed at his face. "Can you please leave me be?"

She drew back. She tried to think of what to say, but he was already retreating. Soon, he disappeared amid the thick grass.

Esen swayed, her branches creaking. She remembered his startled expression when he had glimpsed the ebony faerie. He had said he knew her. Was she his family?

She hoped he would be okay…

The air felt colder suddenly. Energy slipped from her frame. She had already stayed awake long into the night.

She curled down into the grass and let herself drift toward sleep. As her mind softened, she sent her thoughts out to Fafnir, wherever he was, wishing him protection from the night.

THE
Hole Dreamland

bad
world

I older → To Fafnir

New
World

CHAPTER 25: OLD WOUNDS

Fafnir pushed through the long grass, walking mechanically. His hands shook, his stomach writhing. The moon hung yellow in the black sky, sharp as a sickle.

His father's face flashed in his mind, deathly pale. *"Have you found your serenity?"* he had whispered.

Fafnir halted in his tracks, jamming his hat back on his head. He muttered the numerical sequences to himself until the image melted away.

This wouldn't do. He needed to sleep, but adrenaline was shooting through his veins, his limbs jittery. If he lay down now, he'd never sleep. He'd only think.

And that was dangerous.

They were going to the mountains in the south next. He could plan out the route, predict where they might hope to find faeries. But with the thought came the memory of the wild, whipping wind, his cheeks smarting with its blasts as he stood beside his mother and sister, looking out at the entire land stretched out beneath them…

No. He couldn't do that now.

Turning on his heel, he strode back toward the river-fae village. They had just begun to till their fields. He could do it for them. Rot it, he'd till all four of their fields in one night. Frenzied work was the best cure when the hands ruled the body and fought against time.

The first field was lit only by the pale moon. It was about a wolf long and wide, the edges marked by wooden posts dug into the ground where the Rooted Ones took back over the space. He pushed up his sleeves, picked up a hoe from a pile of tools, and attacked the soil. All was muscle and motion; earth and crickets. His body bent to his will, forgetting its shakiness.

He could bury this too. Just like he had buried —

"What are you doing?"

Fafnir nearly jumped out of his skin. Isolde stood before him, frowning. Her white hair was disheveled, pushed back into a loose bun. She wore that leaf cape again, with a wooden butterfly brooch.

He dropped the hoe, stumbling back. Sweat pooled at his collar.

"I couldn't sleep," he muttered.

He risked a glance at her face. She looked older, somehow, than when he had last seen her. He couldn't name where he felt it... The same slight wrinkles marked her cheeks and brow. Maybe it was the heaviness in her golden eyes, as though a thought had been pressing hard upon her, weighing her down.

"Why are you still awake?" he asked.

"Same reason." Isolde squatted by the row next to him and began to work the dirt with her hands. He bit down on his lower lip. The silence palpable, he picked up the hoe and resumed his work.

"Why are you here?" he asked finally.

He hadn't seen her since the day he arrived. Especially, though, why was she *here*, beside him? Doing this stupid work that the river fae could easily finish the next day?

"I am here to help the forest," Isolde said curtly. She kept her head bent over her work. "In my own way."

He nodded. She had carried a significant load of stone on her badger for the river fae. She must be taking a practical approach, helping where her skills are most needed.

He finished one row and pulled briefly on his collar to air his skin before starting on the next.

A breath of wind gusted the Rooted Ones. The scent of woodsmoke lingered in the air. The faint moonlight illuminated the white paint on

Isolde's hands in a soft warm glow. The only sounds were the night noises of the forest and of stone scraping dirt.

The earth gave way beneath him, soft and yielding. In another lifetime, he and his sister had worked in the dirt like this, with shovels instead of a hoe. On nights just like this, by the light of the full moon, in case their parents caught them.

His lips pulled in a half smile.

They'd called their mission the Dreamland, or "dream" for short, if they might be listened in on. He doubted his parents would have cared much if they had caught wind of it. They had been determined to keep it a secret all the same. Like vapor in a bottle, they feared that if it was released to outside ears, it would look like nothing.

To them, it had been everything.

It all began on the first formations of his theory that the land, together with the sea, was like a piece of cloth stretched over a sphere, floating in an abyss of sky. For if there was sky above it, then there must be sky below it too. That meant that if they dug a hole all the way through the earth's crust, they would pop out the bottom and fall into the sky. And if there was one world, why not another just below it? They would drift down on a cloudy day, Isolde had insisted, so they could land on clouds on the way. He didn't know what he knew now about water vapor to contradict her. He modeled a design after mayapple plants for them to float down with, making mushroom-like shoots of flexible wood and cloth.

They would drift down onto an entirely new world beneath them.

They had spent so many late nights shoveling and exchanging excited whispers about what the world would be like. Maybe it was exactly like this world; or maybe it was always summer there, so they would never fear the cold again. Maybe it was a world dazzled with clouds of butterflies that flocked like birds. Or maybe the sky was inverted, and they would fall back where they had come from and into a backward world, where all that had been broken was now whole.

Where their parents loved each other.

It was a remarkable idea, but a childish one, of course. The earth's crust was far too thick to be penetrated much deeper than forty cubits.

But he still wondered sometimes about those other worlds. They had dug an impressive twelve and a half cubits down. But then he had fled home and never returned. Likely, the hole had long ago been swallowed by the land.

He glanced at Isolde. Her mouth was thin-lined, her brows furrowed in thought.

He had never wanted to leave her. Or Mother...

"Isolde," he said. Her name slipped out from him. There was so much to say. A thousand years of unspoken words, of hurt sharpened to a deadly point.

She looked up at him, pushing back a tangled braid from her face. The guarded expression she wore twinged a knot in his middle. What had he meant to say? The image of Father in the snow flashed before him.

"I learned something about Father today," he blurted.

Her eyes narrowed to slits. "What?"

Did she know? Her expression remained as hard as ice. If she didn't know, he didn't want to be the one to tell her. "That he, um... well, the Rooted Ones implied—"

"That he ended his life?" Isolde finished.

He flinched. "Yes."

Isolde turned back to her work. Then she'd known for nearly a millennium, and had borne it alone.

"I never meant to hurt you," he said. "Or Mother."

Isolde's chin lifted. Her golden eyes pierced his, as though looking for the proof somewhere. He forced himself to hold her gaze.

"I know," she said finally. She spoke with an old weariness, as though she had waged a long battle and spoken with the last of the breath in her lungs.

"You know?" he repeated stupidly.

His jaw still ached sometimes where she had punched him.

"I know," Isolde said. "But it didn't make your absence any less painful. For me, or Mother."

He dropped his gaze. The moonlight gleamed on each speck of dirt that he'd overturned with his hoe.

"I know you've been wondering why I am even speaking with you," Isolde continued. "It's because I see you working real change. You've befriended a dryad and got several of these fae to Unite. And yes, I lingered around to see how it would turn out. Listen, I'm still angry. But I miss you, Fafnir. Do you have a stump for brains? Why have you avoided me for over a thousand years as though I were some kind of disease?"

His jaw was hanging open. He shut it. "I'm sorry."

His words rang hollow. He'd had no choice but to leave. But maybe... maybe it wasn't necessary to have cut her off entirely the way he did. Maybe he could have found some kind of middle ground.

A way he could have stayed in the lives of his sister and mother, and lessen the hurt he caused.

Would that have eased his mother's grief enough...

That she might still be alive?

With the flat of her hand, Isolde brushed the rest of the hair from her face. Her lips were pursed, like she had tasted his words and found them sour.

"Do you want to talk about it?" she asked.

He stared at her. "Talk about what?"

"Father."

He winced. He had forgotten he'd revealed that. He started to work again. "What is there to talk about?"

"Plenty, clearly, since you're here tilling someone else's fields in the middle of the night, and messing it up too."

Fafnir started. He looked down at the earth beneath him. It looked fine. "What did I do?" he demanded hotly.

"You're digging way too deep," Isolde said. "Have you ever planted anything? Aside from that mugwort you grew once?"

Fafnir grimaced. A curiosity with vivid dreams led him to experiment with mugwort as a child. The nightmares quickly changed his mind. "I take what I find in the wild," he said.

"I can tell." She held out both palms with about a cubit's distance between them. "You only need to dig this deep, then you push the seed in and cover it back up."

He pressed his face into his hand. His head throbbed. "Why didn't you tell me?"

"I thought it was funny." A smile teased on her face. It had been a thousand years since he had seen her smile. He had forgotten how her eyes crinkled with it.

He crouched and knocked at the top edges of the row, packing the dirt that fell back into the bottom up to a cubit's length. Isolde joined him.

"It's only one row," she said. "It's easy to fix."

His hands suddenly felt sore, stiff with dirt. He kept working anyway. He didn't want to irritate the river fae in the morning.

"You're distressed about Father."

The name flashed the snowy visions back in his mind. Isolde looked at him intently.

"I'm sleep-deprived," he corrected her. "I'll be better in the morning."

"On the surface, maybe. But you will have buried it, pushed him into the recesses of your memory, like you did with Mother and me."

A knot tensed in his shoulders. He forced it out with a breath.

Isolde pressed on. "When you shove the pain away, it doesn't vanish. It lives in your bones, eating the marrow. It will break you, in time."

He stared at the dirt, rolling her words in his mind. If he were rational, fully rested, and fed, he knew he could draw up a well-fortified argument against her. But his mind was hot and hazy with sleeplessness. He had nothing to defend himself with.

"I didn't know Father felt that way," he muttered, poking the tip of his hoe at a dirt clump. "I thought him like the pond scum he reeked of — disintegrating everything he touched and caring nothing for it."

"We all have a heart," Isolde said.

Everyone but Father. Fafnir kept working.

"Do you remember when I first got obsessed with carving?" Isolde asked. "I pulled you into it, and we made little boats and animals, and you started making your lovely plates."

"Yes," he said hesitantly.

"I learned to carve from Father," Isolde said. "For a year or so, when I was six years old, he would take me aside occasionally to some secret place. He would build these little butterflies in front of me, beautifully carved, with light pine wood. When he launched it from his hand, it would spin in the air like it had real wings. He strictly forbade me to tell anyone, so I didn't. All of a sudden, he stopped. I tried desperately to get him to show me again, but he never did. I asked Mother about it once, not long before she died. She cried a little and said she never knew about his butterflies." Isolde shook the dirt from her hand and slipped it in a leaf-shaped leather pouch on her waist. "Here, look. I learned how to make them. I always have one on me."

She flowered open her hand. A little device sat in her palm. Thin vines twisted together made up the bones of the body, connected to a cord of spider silk at the center. It was a simple mechanism utilizing the power of potential energy. Glued to the vine structure was a beautifully carved wooden body and face, complete with curled antennae. Paper wings extended from the thorax, dyed a bright yellow with painted black and white spots. Isolde's personal touch, no doubt.

Isolde twisted the front wings, tightening the silk, and pressed the device to the tip of her fingertips beneath both palms. She released it, and it shot out from her hands, twirling up into the starry night sky. The wings glowed a pale gold in the moonlight.

Suddenly, it tipped down and plummeted. Isolde walked after it.

Where the butterfly had just been, stars gleamed, small white dots against the night. He lifted a hand into the moonlight. Scars ghosted his fingers and palms where his carving knife had slipped over a millennium of the craft. He had thought his inventions were wholly his own, that his father's hands had been useless.

When Isolde returned, he asked, "Why do you think Father showed you, if he was so secretive about it?"

"I don't know," Isolde said. "I think he just wanted to share it with some other soul. Mother would have been too moved for his comfort. And you... you, I'm not sure."

She trailed off, her brow furrowing. The butterfly stood poised in her palm, as though eager to fly again. He tried to picture his father bent over it, fixing a wing to the thorax, but the image wouldn't form in his mind.

"I thought he hated us," Fafnir muttered.

Isolde frowned at him. "I think he hated himself."

Images of his father assailed him. How sometimes he would disappear for a moon or more with no explanation, and other times lie on the bed for days on end, staring at the cracks in the ceiling like they held a secret. How he would sit in the corner of the room, running his blade over a block of wood until it became nothing, how his dark eyes would flick between his mother, him, and Isolde, as though he hated them, wanted them gone.

And that one day, when Fafnir was very young, he had come in alone from the garden for a cup of water, and glimpsed his father, through a crack in the bedroom door, sobbing...

"I never wanted this," he had heard his father say.

Fafnir dropped the cup with a clatter, the water chilling his feet. Footsteps pounded toward him — and the door slammed shut.

He was just a leech to his father, draining him of his life.

His freedom.

Sweat beaded at Fafnir's collar, his chest tight as a knot. He forced himself to breathe, running the numerical sequence through his mind.

Isolde straightened. He blinked, realized they had finished some time ago. He dropped his hoe.

"Are you okay?" she asked, shifting her weight to peer at him.

Fafnir rubbed at the back of his neck. He was breathing even now, though his head was hot and heavy. "I'm tired."

Isolde stared at him for a moment longer before continuing. "Listen, I saw your boat when you visited me. It's brilliant. You took what Father had, without even realizing it, and made it your own. Father let his talent rot. But it is finding new life in you and me. Don't be like him. Don't run from this pain. You must sift through it, let it teach you what it will. It is the only way to heal."

The vision of a river flowed in his mind. Particles spiraled through the water until they washed up on the banks. There were millions and millions of particles. How was he supposed to sift them? To discern one grain from another? The vision melted at the edges into a dull haze. "Thank you," he murmured.

Isolde offered a smile. "Tell me more about your mission."

He explained the details to her, and she nodded along. She made no comment on the parts he had already told her on that very different night when he had stood by her door.

"So how did you meet Esen?" she asked as he finished.

Fafnir rolled his jaw. He had departed from Esen rather forcefully. He hoped she was well and not worrying for him.

"I was looking for King Ian, to aid in my mission. Esen is the child of his dryads, so I met her through him. But his dryads perished in the winter… as did he."

A shadow passed over Isolde's face. "I am sorry. He was a good faerie. So now you are journeying with just Esen?"

"Yes."

"She is a brave dryad to go out and seek change after losing so much."

He would never forget the sight of Esen hunched over her sister—a frail, shivering shape amid the broken wreckage of her parents, protecting the smallest Rootling he had ever seen.

Everything she had ever known had been torn out from her. To rise in the spring and carry on, despite that…

She was very brave indeed.

And now she was working alongside him, the one who caused all her grief. He put two fingers to his burning temple.

"I heard your excuse about Uniting."

He looked up, not quite meeting Isolde's gaze.

"Do you think those river faeries sleeping within their dryads tonight are any less important than you?" Isolde asked. "What makes you so special that you should be exempt from the Ancient Law?"

He bit at the inside of his mouth. With her words, she completely swept his loathsome lie aside. He had nothing left but the truth. But he couldn't tell her that.

"Unite," Isolde said. "Put your feet where your mouth is and faeries will listen to you better. You are asking them to bind themselves to the dryads, who are more closely tethered to death than they have ever been, without taking that risk with them. You saw how it discredited your position today."

He rubbed at his arms. "I can't."

"I'm trying to be nice," Isolde said, a growl in her voice. "Make it easier for me."

He couldn't handle this now.

"It's hard for me to talk," he muttered. "It's been a long night."

Isolde narrowed her eyes. At last, she drew in a breath and let her shoulders fall. "All right. I'll let you wiggle out of it this moment, but I won't let this go. Sleep. Find me in the morning in the house closest to the river, with the painting of a snail. I want in on your plan."

225

Fafnir nodded. "Isolde…" He trailed off, trying to form the words. "Thank you."

A small smile flickered on Isolde's face. She grabbed his arm, opened his hand, and placed the butterfly device on his palm.

"Keep it," she said. "I have others."

Dragans

Although dragans have been a part of the land since
its creation, there is still little that is known about
them. It is widely believed that they are the visual
manifestation of the Mother taking her spirit back
from her creation. For they appear
mostly in the dying bodies of faeries and
dryads, who received the largest
portions of her spirit. Faint glimpses of
dragans can be seen in the other life
forms of animals, insects, and plants.

eel-like

Different shapes and sizes

Their faces and form are reminiscient of
serpents, and they are always in motion,
weaving through the form of the body. They
are made of the same material of the body
they consume. The faces of the dragans
reflect the last emotion the being felt before
they died. They disappear when the body has
been fully decomposed.

The Land of the Mother Wind

13

CHAPTER 26: JOURNEY TO THE MOUNTAINS

Esen blinked, lifting herself up from the soft, springy grass. A river murmured nearby. Bright sunlight glittered in her eyes, the long shadows of the morning already past.

Fafnir lay an arm's length from her, his face still in sleep. His legs were drawn up to his chest, his hair messed like he'd been in a windstorm. He looked even smaller, somehow, drawn into himself like that. Like he was a child.

Esen sat up in a seat, fingering a blade of grass.

It is believed that his own soul had wished to be reunited with the Mother, and his own hand had made it so," the holly had said.

Esen had tasted loss. It lingered in her frame, a kind of grieving that would never truly let her go.

But to lose your own father, in that way… she couldn't imagine how confusing that would be. She hoped he hadn't been gone long. That he had come back and slept there, not long after she fell asleep.

An osprey called in the distance. Lifting her gaze, she looked out into the depths of the Rooted Ones. She couldn't see the mountains now, but she felt their vastness calling to her. They would be headed there this very day now that their mission with the river fae had concluded.

Wonder sparked in her as she remembered the faeries who had

United in the night. A smile lit her face. They would have wings curling from their backs now, green and shiny with newness.

A quiet rustling sounded beside her. Fafnir had risen to a seat. He rubbed at his eyes, his shoulders stiff.

"How are you?" she asked.

He looked up at her, as though just realizing she was there. "Well enough." There was a steadiness in his eyes that surprised her. "The faerie you asked me about earlier is my sister. We spoke last night. It... it helped. She wants to join us in our mission."

Esen's eyes widened. He had a sister too.

"I am glad," she said. "I would like to meet her."

Fafnir stood, shouldering his violin. "Let's go into the village. I imagine she is awake by now."

The sunlight illuminated the vibrant colors of the gourd houses. A few faeries mingled about. One sat spinning cloth outside her home with alder leaves folded behind her back. Her nimble hands worked expertly at the cloth, following the same motions she had done for over a thousand years, perhaps, but now, the immortal spirit was gone from her blood. Her face was gentle, content in her work, as though she had done her duty to the forest and was carrying on as before, ready to face whatever came with quiet strength.

Most of the other fae were clustered on patches of black soil between the trunks of the Rooted Ones. They were digging nimbly and pushing white conical seeds the size of their hands into the soil. The Winged Ones clustered on their own section of the soil, while Wingless Ones worked the rest.

The tension from the night before remained, then.

Fafnir guided her toward a house at the edge of the village. It was round and squat, like a cloud that had drifted down to land. The painting of a snail adorned the hard golden exterior. Its large spiral shell wrapped around the shape of the house, with its spiny head poking out to face the propped-open door.

The interior was flushed with a golden glow, as vivid as the petals of a dandelion. After checking there were no dwellings in her path, Esen folded herself flat on the ground, leveling the house to her eyes. The ebony faerie squatted within, her skin a beautiful honey brown in the glow. Her alder leaves were stretched out loosely behind her, gently rising and falling with her breath. She was bent over a piece of parchment adhered to the wall, scribbling lines on it with a tapered stick of charcoal. Underneath her arm, Esen glimpsed jagged lines resembling mountains and a dotted path trailing through them.

The space within was small. A wooden bed was propped up against the other wall, beside a table heaped with papers and herbs and ash. Another wooden box rested at the foot of the bed. The only space left over was a narrow walking space, where the faerie crouched.

The faerie turned and smiled at Esen. She looked nothing like Fafnir. There was something vaguely reminiscent of him in her smile, though she couldn't put her finger on what it was.

"*Aeonida*, Esen," the faerie said. "It's good to meet you properly. My name is Isolde."

"*Aeonida*," Esen said. She found she didn't know what to say. Fafnir had said that they had bonded the night before. But when they had looked at each other that first day, as Isolde stood with her badger, the distance between them had felt a yawning canyon.

Isolde beckoned to Fafnir. As he stepped inside, his skin flushed golden as though he had swallowed the sun. Isolde straightened and stepped back from her map to stand beside him.

"Do either of you know of any fae in the mountains already?" Isolde asked.

"I was hoping to find a village by looking for the valleys on the westward side of the peaks, where the rain falls," Fafnir said.

"That's smart. Let me save you some time though. There aren't many faeries in the mountains, and it will take forever to find them without knowing where they are."

Turning back to her map, Isolde walked her dotted line further into the drawing of a high peak. She drew an oval shape and circled it. "There is a village right there, in the Éigniú Valley. You're welcome."

Fafnir's eyebrows raised. "Thank you," he said. "Have you visited the mountains since..." He hesitated before adding, "Since we went there with Mother?"

"Yes," Isolde said, her face sobering. "I found this village by accident. I was flying down from a high peak when I glimpsed a sliver of green amid the cliffs. I would have never seen it if I hadn't been flying. The faerie folk there greeted me kindly and hosted me for a time. I wonder how they are doing now, with the changes in the land. I am sure they have a story to tell."

Her words painted vivid imagery in Esen's mind. She could feel the wind on her bark already, the wild taste of the air. What kind of dryads grew there, in such conditions?

"Their voice will be valuable," Fafnir said.

"Do you plan to come with us?" Esen asked Isolde. "We would be glad to have you."

Isolde folded her arms, tapping her chin. The thin, spiraled shells dangling from her ears clattered faintly. "We need as many fae on our side as possible," Isolde said. "Both of you will be gathering faeries from different regions. I want to lead my own recruiting band and focus on the families who are scattered about the land, living on their own. I imagine they will be more free-thinking than those within groups."

Fafnir nodded. "And you will meet with us at the market?"

"Yes, with whomever I have brought to our cause."

Fafnir's brow pinched slightly. "That will be a great help."

Isolde shoved his shoulder. "I'll miss you too."

Fafnir looked away from her as though he did not hear. "Be careful of the queen. She is very hurt after Niamh's betrayal. If she catches wind of our mission, I am certain she will be quick to try to stop us."

"I will be careful," Isolde promised.

"Only speak of the meeting place and time to those you trust," Fafnir said.

"Of course. Stop being so grim. We will deal with the trials as they come. There's nothing more we can do now to prepare for them."

Fafnir stared at the floor, frowning.

"If something happens," Isolde continued, "we can use the Rooted Ones to communicate between us." Isolde winked at Esen. "I know Wind-Speak."

Isolde pulled her map off the wall, rolled it, wrapped it with a bit of string, and handed it to Fafnir. Fafnir filled her in on his studies of the land. She listened carefully, nodding often. When he got to the animals, she stopped him and shared her own knowledge. He took notes in his journal as she spoke. A fiery energy burned between them. They were both so impassioned to save the forest.

At last, they finished. Esen pushed herself to her feet as they stepped out, her limbs stiff. The sun beamed high in the sky, leaning toward the west.

Niamh walked toward them, holding Iona against her chest. "You're leaving?" she asked.

"Yes," Esen said.

Niamh's face was bright and serene. She looked so natural here, as though all the years Esen had known Niamh, she had been a shadow of herself. It was good that she had this place. Without Ian, home would be cold to her. A pang seized Esen at the thought. It would be cold to Esen too, when she finally returned. But she still had Aisling, and Fiona.

"I will be staying here," Niamh said. "Iona needs me. I will stand with you at the market with Rowan's family and Brighid."

"You don't have to," Fafnir said. "I don't want something to happen to you."

Niamh lifted her chin. There was no trace of the child Esen had known in her. "I know it is dangerous. I will be there. I want to make a difference."

Fafnir nodded, his lips pressed tight.

Isolde stepped forward and laid a hand on Niamh's shoulder. "You are very brave, Niamh." There was a familiarity between them. They must have spoken before.

Iona's face flushed red. She wailed, kicking her small legs, and tangled her hands in Niamh's hair. Niamh gently freed her fingers one by one.

"I have to feed her," Niamh said. She smiled at them. "May the Wind be with you. I will see you all again at the market."

She turned from them, rocking Iona, and disappeared inside a green-striped gourd home. Esen played with a leaf growing near her ear. Niamh had blessed them so warmly, in the Mother's name. She had never expressed a care for the Mother before.

It stirred a feeling of promise in Esen. All would be well, in the end.

Somehow.

They found Korey among the frog-den workers and wished her farewell. She stepped up to Fafnir, her new oak wings bobbing with her movement. She pushed her dark amber plaits from her eyes. "Thank you," she said quietly. "We will see you soon."

At last, they started off. Isolde shoved handfuls of dried meat and squash into Fafnir's bag until it was near to bursting, then he pushed her hand away. Esen helped Fafnir back onto her shoulder. He began to tie himself to her branch again.

"That looks really uncomfortable."

Esen started at the voice. Isolde was flapping by her shoulder, holding herself steady in the air with her arms crossed.

"Let me know of a better solution and I'll do it," Fafnir said, pulling the rope tight around his middle.

Isolde cocked her eyebrows at him. "I do know of a better solution."

As though she'd struck him, Fafnir flinched and looked away. Something had passed between them that Esen couldn't know.

Isolde turned to face Esen. "Fafnir told me of your loss. I am sorry, Esen. When this is all over, I want to get to know you better. You would be welcome to my home anytime. It's big enough to house all creatures; even young Walkers like you."

Esen clasped her hands against her chest. Her home must be a palace like the Rath Síoraí—huge and beautiful. "I would love that."

Isolde smiled, though a heaviness lingered in her eyes. "I will see you both again at the World Market."

She waved to Esen and Fafnir, then flew off.

ESEN STEPPED FORWARD, weaving through the trunks of the Rooted Ones. Between her fingers she curled a leaf growing from a branch near her head. Her shiny green leaves were fuller, filling out her branches fast, swishing with every step she took. Where the sun glinted off her leaves, she could feel energy flowing from them, through her veins, and filling her body with strength. Winter was a distant nightmare.

She'd be home with Aisling before next winter. Aisling's leaves would be fuller now, a little crown shadowing her head. The thought filled her with warmth.

"Fafnir?" she said. He was frowning at Isolde's map, tilting it toward the right.

"Hmm?" he murmured, eyes fixed on the map.

"How far is it to the mountains?"

"One moment," he said. He took out his wooden pencil and made a few light markings on the map. At last, he looked up at her. "Will you need to sleep during the night?"

Esen tilted her head, her leaves swaying in tune. "It is still cold most nights, so at first, yes. But come summer, on hot, humid nights, I have no need of sleep; my limbs are restless."

Fafnir nodded, tapping his pencil on his chin. He wrote for another few moments before responding. "It will take us approximately thirty-seven suns to reach the foothills of the mountains. It will be midsummer then, but it is cold in the mountains; you will need your sleep. We could scale the peak in about three suns. If it is the one I am thinking of, then it may take even longer. The valley is on the other side."

Esen widened her eyes. "That is a long journey."

"We are crossing two-thirds of the entire land," Fafnir said. "The mountains lie at the southern tip, just above the cliffs of the sea. We will look for sea fae there next."

A broken branch pressed on the limbs of a young ash. Esen disentangled it and tossed it aside on the grass. The distant silhouettes of mountains filled her mind.

"Please take frequent breaks," Esen said. "You will need to move sometimes."

"I will let you know," he said.

Flipping the map around, he drew a mass of land representing the whole of the land, perhaps. He circled a mark in the center and drew a dotted line skirting it in a wide berth.

"We'll need to go well around the Rath Síoraí, which will delay us, unfortunately. Start heading east. We need to get away from the river; it runs right by the Rath."

Esen turned, leaving the steady hum of the river behind. The chatter of birds and the swaying of her branches filled the air in its stead. Dappled light gleamed amid the blue shadows.

Fafnir sat with his legs stretched out in front of him, staring at the trunks of the Rooted Ones as they flitted by. His hands fidgeted in his lap.

"Is your sister one of the river fae?" Esen found herself asking.

Fafnir looked up at her, as though remembering where he was. "No. She was just there to help them."

"That is kind of her." It seemed Isolde had already been carrying out a plan of her own. "I am glad we have her aid. Between her efforts and those of the Winged river fae, I hope we may have a good number on our side."

"Do you know how your sister is doing?" Fafnir asked.

A spark surged in her at the thought. "I have been meaning to ask the Rooted Ones. I will check."

She paused before an old oak and an ash wound tightly together. She asked her question and waited. A warm wind fluttered by.

The two dryads stirred in unison. *"Fiona says Aisling is well. She has made several new songs and sings them to the flowers every day. Her roots are healthy and strong."*

The sun glowed inside Esen. "She will be a better singer than I am when I return," she said, wiping her eyes. "Tell me of her leaves. Are they green? No trace of brown or wilting?"

"She has a little less leaves than usual for her age, but they are all green."

Esen's smile faltered. It hit her as though she had been at fault, but they had done all they could for her. At least she was well. "Thank you," she said. Putting a hand to prevent Fafnir from falling, she tipped her shoulders forward in a bow.

"May the Wind guide your path," the oak stirred. *"We Rooted Ones are all holding our breath. We are hopeful because of you."*

Esen's breath quickened. The whole forest was watching her, hoping. She couldn't fail them.

She bowed again. A sharp intake of air escaped Fafnir as his shoulder fell against her hand.

"I'm sorry," she said to Fafnir. She straightened, leveling her shoulders. Fafnir adjusted the rope that held him. "I will be more careful. And Aisling is well; thank you for asking."

"I am glad," Fafnir said, with a small smile.

"Thank you deeply for your blessings," she said to the oak. Further words escaped her. She turned and walked on.

She passed mighty oaks, slender hawthorns, dark, thick yews, and moved around broken trunks on the ground, devoured by moss and lichen. Weeping dragans spiraled through the decaying bark.

All of the dryads were waiting, depending on her. She had to succeed so they could have faeries by the winter, and the strength to carry on.

Too many had died already.

Storykeepers

The keepers of dryadic history. Instead of recording their history on paper like us, they mark the bodies of select dryads named Storykeepers with the stories of their kind.

Three Storykeepers are appointed at one time. They wander the land and share of their stories to all those who would hear. It is also tradition for a Storykeeper to visit each new Rootling in their first year of life.

Their written language consists of artistic symbols grouped together to form something like our written word.

A few Dryadic Symbols

Grá

Stór

Aoradh

Mother Wind

Life-Sacred

One-with-Mother

Everlasting

Bird

Dryad

Faerie

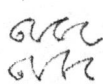

Great-forest   Water-that-runs   The Land of the Mother Wind

17

CHAPTER 27: FLAME

"Ah, you have chosen the Trinity of Unity," said Cillian. "It's a fundamental system that runs beneath the workings of the forest, like the Cycle of Giving. There are three points to it. Let me show you…"

Tristan shifted his legs, propping up the beginnings of his bird's nest on his uninjured knee. Pricks of pain still jolted from his other leg, where that rotting queen had burned him. He had it stretched out stiffly.

Her rangers had shot at him like he was a pesky fly. She hadn't even deigned to look at him. He was nothing to her; to all the fae of the Rath. Just an unfortunate stain that would soon be wiped out.

He crunched a pine cone in his hand until it splintered.

Cillian looked up with concern, before turning back to face the ash Rootling, who was busy writing with a bone knife on a stone tablet. The Rootling—Brann was his name—watched with wide eyes as Cillian instructed him, like the world was still new and exciting and not on the brink of collapse. A whole slew of Winged Ones sat watching too. The faerie of Brann's parents—slim, with skin the color of birch bark—sat beside his wife, their parents and siblings, a few grandparents, and their three children, who were rolling around like woodlice.

It was a little bubble of the Ancient Days; the way things were supposed to be. This Rootling would grow up well, until he started Walking and saw how terrible it was outside his bubble.

Like Esen...

Tristan grabbed a fistful of rootlets from water avens and began to weave them around the twigs. It might've been her that got the Rooted Ones to breathe down his neck. Either way, he'd been given two options: let a Walker come to keep an eye on him at his home, or travel with Cillian and help greet the newborn Rootlings. He'd chosen the latter, naturally. He wasn't a child. And he and Cillian had been good friends once, before he'd made Cillian nervous with his talk about forcing a change.

They treated him as if he were a wolf gone mad. He'd only acted in Niamh's defense. Why was he the one in the wrong? They were content to stand by and twiddle their thumbs while Esen went about on her little plan of peace with that faerie who hadn't even United yet. She might bring a few faeries to her side, but it wouldn't be enough to make any difference. She would come home for the winter with all the spirit knocked out of her, and she'd show the dryads herself that peace didn't work.

Then they would have to listen to him.

The Rootling and his faerie family kept asking Cillian more questions. He went on and on with the patience of the Mother herself. Finally, as the sun began to set, they finished. Tristan rose with a grunt, leaning heavily on his good knee to lift himself. He approached Brann and held out his nest in one hand, and a raven-down feather in the other.

"Here," he said. "You put in the last feather."

Brann took the feather and laid it gently in the nest, pressing it down against the other feathers and moss lining the bottom. He looked back up at Tristan with bright, gray eyes.

Emotion burned in Tristan's chest. All the dryads were endangering this Rootling by not taking action now. He had to be protected. Him, Aisling, and all the little ones like him.

Tristan held up the nest and placed it in the lowermost crook of the branches of Brann's parents.

"Stay strong, Brann," he said.

That night, he crept away from Cillian as he slept. The river was frigid. He slipped an arm in its stream, wincing at the shock, and pulled it out. The water streamed off, his arm glistening.

That might do it. He'd have to see.

He started a tiny fire on the riverbank. He put his arm back in the water, shook it until it only dripped a little, then held it over the fire, just above the flames. He gritted his teeth. It felt like a sharp rock was being pressed into his bark. But he didn't catch fire.

His mouth stretched in a grin. He pulled his arm away and cooled it in the river.

Fire was the only weapon of the fae.

Before launching an attack, the dryads could coat themselves in water.

Then the fae would be utterly defenseless.

Rubbing of "Mother Rock"

CHAPTER 28: WONDERS

Esen would have lost track of the days if not for Fafnir's careful tally. She spent each day in deep thought, thinking of her carefree days as a Rootling, the journey she'd had so far, and the adventures ahead of them.

She couldn't think long of the winter.

Fafnir was very quiet. Occasionally he would correct her course or ask to be brought down for a moment. Sometimes he would walk for a length of time. At his size, his strides were long, but she had to walk very slowly to not overtake him.

She did not mind his silence. There were no expectations in it. Whenever she spoke, he would listen attentively. When they did not speak, it felt almost as though he were not there; as though she only had herself to mind.

The first time Fafnir stepped down from her, he came back to her with a flat piece of wood from an ash. Since then, he'd been using it as a flat surface across his lap to play a fascinating game. She would glance at him to see him maneuvering neat rows of circular wooden chips spread across the board, each chip with different markings on it.

One day, she asked, "What is this game?"

"Patience," he said.

Esen frowned, and waited. He must be holding a thought.

Fafnir picked up a whole row of chips and moved them onto another row. He stared at the chips, tapping a finger on his chin. How long was he going to make her wait? It was a simple question.

"Feel free to let me know when you're able," Esen said.

Fafnir looked up at her, puzzlement in his face. "Let you know what?"

"The name of the game," Esen said.

"Oh." A smile broke across Fafnir's face, and he laughed. It was a warm, open sound, with nothing of his usual stiffness in it. "It's called patience. Which you clearly have."

Esen laughed, covering her mouth with her hand. "My apologies. I should have guessed that."

Fafnir lifted his eyebrows, then turned back to his game. He shuffled a handful of extra chips and placed one in the empty space. There was some kind of order to it, like he was starting with a blank slate of possibilities and moving toward a single organized outcome.

"It looks fun," Esen said.

Fafnir pushed up his lower lip, nodding. "I would offer to let you ride on my shoulder so you could play, but I'm not really in the position to do that."

A laugh sputtered from her. "No, I don't think so."

After fifteen days, or so Fafnir told her, the river surged before her once more. "We are well downstream of the Rath now," he said.

Something felt familiar about the space, in the way the brown waters flowed against the bank, the shape of the mossy rocks... All at once, the memory came to her. The small body of a faerie flailing before slipping below the water. The breath hitching in her throat as she threw herself into the swollen river, searching desperately. It was a miracle she had found him.

"You almost drowned here," she said.

"Yes," Fafnir said, his face sober. "Once again, I thank you."

"Of course. I could not let anyone die like that."

But her words felt flat. She couldn't let *him* die, especially. For his own sake. And if he had never come into her life, she had no idea where she would be now. Hopeless, and lost in grief, perhaps...

For several more days, she walked alongside the river. The softly undulating hills they had traveled across so far transitioned into a low-level plateau. At last, she turned south and left the river behind.

"It flows out into the sea to the west," Fafnir explained. "Our journey is southward."

Her spirit flooded with excitement. She had never been this far from home before. Through the gaps in the Rooted Ones, she glimpsed the blue slopes of the mountains ahead, calling to her.

The landscape began to shift. Though no rain had fallen, the ground grew wet beneath her feet. The deciduous dryads thinned out. In their place grew strange pine dryads. Their branches were pointed down rather than up, the wood hidden within a blanket of blue-green needles. The solid underbrush she had always known had vanished beneath her. Instead, she squished through layers of soggy moss and water. The moss clung to her legs as she passed, cold and viscous against her bark. With each step, the moss ahead of her rippled as though it was murmuring, pondering her. Squirrels rustled in the pines, and she once glimpsed the red flash of a cardinal.

Several tiny yellow flowers jutted out from the water ahead of her. With a little noise of wonder, she pushed her way toward them. Underneath the water, the plant's yellow roots were suspended in an intricate network, swaying gently. Little fish and invertebrates floated among the roots. She fought the urge to lean over. She wanted to plunge her face in the water, feel the roots swaying against her bark. It was like a whole other world below—vast and mysterious.

An insect brushed against a leaflike shape extending from one of the roots. The shape opened, and the insect vanished.

Esen gasped. "It swallowed it."

"Some plants are carnivorous," Fafnir remarked.

"I never knew."

She was glad she hadn't put her face in.

At last, the ground flattened, and she came out of the soggy moss. Tall grass whispered against her knees. New Rooted Ones surrounded her, their trunks shooting up straight as arrows. Their bark was sheet white, pierced by the occasional black mark resembling the shape of an eye. Their leaves were almost perfect circles. A gentle sigh shivered in the wind, as though all the dryads were whispering a lullaby to her, the words inaudible.

"*Aeonida*. What is your name?" she asked, laying a hand on one of them.

"*We are aspen*," the dryad whispered.

"Aspen," she murmured, drawing out the *s* sound. "Your voices are beautiful."

She walked on beneath their foliage, her head swimming with their sounds.

"Fafnir," she murmured. "We haven't even got to the mountains yet, and I am so stricken with the beauty of the land."

Fafnir looked up from his journal and smiled at her. "Just wait until you see the mountains. It is less common in the southern mountains, where we are going, but up north, there are seas of golden gorse dotting the foothills."

A whoosh of air escaped her. "I would love to see that," she breathed.

"I could show you sometime," Fafnir said. A strange shadow cast over his face the next moment. He looked away from her.

The singing of a river reached her ears. Ahead of her, a blue line of water spilled out into a shimmering lake. She traced the river all the way to the mountains in the distance. She could make out individual slopes among them now, in the patterns of sunlight cutting against the blue shadows.

Esen walked quicker, an eagerness in her step, following the line of the river. The grass was crisp and springy beneath her. The white trunks of the aspen flitted by her, and sometimes, a dark spruce grew, stark against the aspen. Toward dusk, the aspen thinned out, replaced by familiar oaks, cedars, and pine.

At the edge of their ghost-white forest, she paused. "*Aeonida*," she whispered to them.

"*Aeonida*," whispered the aspen near, in their shivering tones.

Throughout the next five days, Esen scarcely tore her eyes from the mountains. They had always been something unattainable to her; a far-off dream from her childhood years. But with each passing step, they were drawing closer. They did it sneakily. She would stare at the mountains for hours, and they scarcely seemed to move an inch. Then suddenly, she would start as she realized how close they had become, as though in a blink of an eye they had taken a giant leap forward and grinned down at her.

At last, as morning dawned, bathing the peaks of the mountains in red-gold light, she found herself standing at their feet. The ground sloped dramatically ahead of her, dark pine forming a dense blanket. She tilted her head back. The peaks towered above in gentle undulations, except for the tallest peak, which was sharpened to several points, like the beaks of birds. A white mist veiled the peaks, shrouding their details in mystery.

"We are finally here, at the feet of the mountains!" she cried.

"Yes," Fafnir said. Though his voice was even, a wonder ringed within it. "Allow me a moment to get water."

"Of course."

Esen put a hand to her shoulder and laid him gently on the heather. With a nod to her, he walked toward a trickling stream stemming from the main river.

Esen hummed in her throat, breathing in the rich scent of pine and peat. She half turned, and started. The thickest Rooted One she had ever seen, apart from the Sage, surged up from the earth before her.

She had never truly considered the term "Rooted" before. She had seen Fiona Root to the earth, and it was beautiful. Somehow, with no words, this dryad made her truly understand. Her trunk was as thick and hard as a boulder, and just as immovable. Her branches surged out, cutting horizontally above the ground before sweeping back up to seek the stars. She towered only five times Esen's height, maybe—shorter than the average Rooted One—but she had built herself into the ground with feet of stone. It felt as though she had never walked, but rather had pushed herself out from the soil just like this, a tooth of the earth's own mouth. As timeless as the sun. She and the earth were one, wedded together.

Esen stepped toward her. By the oval tips of her leaves, she knew her to be sessile oak.

"Oh, oak," Esen whispered. The oak's bark spiraled within itself, forming countless weaving patterns. "How long have you been alive?"

The oak stood silent. A wind fluttered by, stirring her leaves. No speech uttered from her.

Esen traced the bark with her fingers. It was incredibly thick, and intricately layered. If she spread herself out on the ground, this oak was as thick as she was tall, branches and all.

It would take at least a few thousand years to form a trunk like that.

"Oak," she said again. "Can you hear me?"

She heard only the wind murmuring through the meadow grass. Was she asleep? But the air was warm, breathing soft and sweet on her bark. Few dryads would sleep in such weather. Had the long march of years stolen her voice? Or perhaps…

Perhaps she no longer had need of it.

The lyric of a lullaby her mother and father had sung to her when she was a Rootling came to her.

"Passing through the hand of time,
With roots in earth, hands in sky,
The earth was she, and she the earth.
Her true voice she found at last,
Wind and water, water and wind,
All other words mere sound and shadow."

She pressed her forehead against the coarse bark. "Bless you," she whispered. "When I Root, I want to be like you."

She wondered if the oak had a faerie. She must, if she had lived for as long as she thought. Coming out of that cold winter, she feared still that dryads could die at any moment; that they were fragile, and quick to snap, like twigs. But this oak was strong. A thick canopy of leaves grew from her. She would live for perhaps another thousand years yet.

During the Ancient Law, before the forest was harmed, faeries lived an average of a thousand or two thousand years with their dryads. Or longer, as this oak proved. Was not a thousand years already like an infinity? Why did the faeries hunger for more? How did they bear it?

This oak would fall in time, back into the earth from whence she grew. But it is this knowledge that she bore like a crown upon her head. It gave her beauty and grace. Without words, she sings, *I am alive*, with the joyous delight of one who knows their end is near and treasures their last drops of the nectar of life to the fullest.

Turning, she glimpsed Fafnir standing in the heather beside her. His head was tilted up toward the oak. His brow furrowed with the weight of his thoughts. "She is beautiful," he murmured.

"Yes," Esen said.

His words about delaying Uniting pricked her suddenly. They were surrounded by dryads, most of them in need of fae. They looked healthy and strong, like they would survive not just the next winter, but for hundreds of seasons to come.

Here Fafnir was—a Wingless One, asking other faeries to Unite. Some of the river fae had already United. Why couldn't he do it too?

"I found Mother Rock," Fafnir said. "I had forgotten it was here."

"Huh?"

The name turned a leaf in Esen's memory. It was an ancient marker her parents had told her of. "Oh, I want to see it."

At the foot of the mountain, half hidden by goldenrods, a small, worn stone poked out. Esen held back the goldenrods with one hand and crouched. Carved into the coarse gray stone were countless tiny divots. At first, she saw only a stone. But as she stared, two concentrations of the divots seemed to form themselves into the resemblance of eyes. They felt neither dryad nor faerie; they were the very essence of eyes, beyond such categories. And then she saw how, farther down, a sharp nose was suggested, and beneath that, an open mouth. Then the curve of something like a cheek, and all the other lines about it flowing, wild strands of hair.

A strange sort of shame flooded through her for looking upon such a holy face. But at the same time, she could not tear her eyes away. It was so beautiful.

"Do you see it?" Fafnir asked.

"Yes," she breathed. "If ever the Mother Wind had a face, this would be it. Shapeless, yet suggesting a shape. Here, yet not here. I didn't see it at first, but now that I see it, I cannot see anything but it."

"Would you call that a miracle?" Fafnir said.

"Of course. It must be the Mother herself who formed it, as a sign for us to remember her." She reached down and helped Fafnir back onto her shoulder. She gazed at the stone for a moment longer, wonder filling her, before following a grassy trail winding up through the cliffside, resuming their ascent into the mountains.

Suddenly, Fafnir's question struck Esen as strange. "Is it not a miracle to you as well?" she asked.

He took a long pull of his water before responding. "It is a natural wonder—an alignment of chance over a long period of time that produces something beautiful. It is very windy here. The wind carved that over time by blowing particles of sand into the face of the rock."

"What of the image of the Mother Wind? Is that itself not a miracle?"

Fafnir furrowed his brow. "I don't know, honestly. It could be explained as rare chance. Beauty can be created that way."

Esen stared at him. "Are you denying the existence of the Mother?"

Fafnir's fingers tapped on his waterskin. "Perhaps."

Esen's breath caught in her throat. She thought of the river fae. They had not mentioned the Mother. "Is that common now among the fae, to not believe? I had not thought such a thing could happen."

"I can speak best for the faeries of the Rath. They believe in her still, but they are actively disobeying her, and they know it. So it is easier on their conscience to forget her. The queen's active removal of the Mother from the festivals is not helping. More and more, she is slipping from their minds. Soon, perhaps, they will forget her altogether." He rested a hand under his chin, his eyes far away. "As for the other fae scattered throughout the land, I don't know."

Esen rubbed at the back of her hand. "That makes sense, but it is distressing. Without faith in the Mother, they will have no care for the land and the creatures beyond them. The two go hand in hand."

"The queen is well aware of that," Fafnir muttered.

The wind picked up, blasting her face. She screwed her eyes against it. The distant bleat of a sheep sounded in the distance, the grass crackling in the wind.

"Why are you unsure of her yourself?" she asked.

Fafnir held up the ash wood he'd used for his game to act as a wall between him and the wind. "Let me ask you this first," he said, looking at her intently. "Why are you certain of her?"

Esen hummed a noise deep in the back of her throat. She pushed on through the grass as the way became steeper.

It was a good question, one she had never considered before.

"I have simply always known," she said. "Deep down, at the core of me. It is like asking if I am certain of the stars."

"You can see the stars," Fafnir said. "But have you seen her?"

Esen's brow creased. "Neither of us have really seen the stars. Not up close, I mean. I assume, right? It seems like you've been everywhere else."

Fafnir's eyebrows rose. "I would love to, but no."

Esen continued. "We see only distant suggestions of them—mere shadows, perhaps, of what they actually are. It is like that with the Mother. To me, anyway. I have felt her breath upon me... Once, I even heard her voice. I know it was her, because it came to me like a dream, singing in tones far beyond what my ear could ever imagine and words far beyond my comprehension."

Cillian's voice, from a summer that felt like long ago, rang in her mind. *"The truest truths are beyond our understanding."*

Fafnir nodded slowly. "That is beautiful, but it does not prove her existence. Only your perception of her existence."

Esen shook her head, her leaves swishing. "But you also cannot prove that she does not exist."

"That is true," Fafnir said. Hunching down, he propped up the wood between his shoulder and her branch and tucked his knees into his chest. His gaze wandered among the mountain peaks, growing ever closer.

"I understand well why she is believed to exist," he said. "Wind is the force that stirs your leaves and carries the scent of the flowers to us faeries below. Without the wind, the forest is still; lifeless. The clouds would not glide through the sky, water would not pass from the rivers into the sea, and rain would not be gathered to fall upon the soil. All of life depends on the wind. It is the breath, the lifeblood of the land. Therefore, it is reasonable for us to worship such a force."

He paused for a moment, as though his thoughts lay curled among the mountain tops and he was working to call them down. "Although it is reasonable, it is not necessarily true. That is... interesting, to me, that you have felt her. Few have claimed such a thing. As I myself have never felt nor seen her, I am simply not sure. I cannot prove it either way."

A fog curled in ahead of her, weaving a whiteness over the landscape. She could still make out colors and shapes, but everything became soft, with one foot in the mist. A shiver coursed through her. It felt like the flurries of snow in winter.

"I can understand that," she said.

The wind battered the hazy forms of the birch dryads about her.

If all wind was the strands of the Mother's hair, as she had always been told, then why did it sometimes blow so harshly? Did she not know what the hair at the back of her head was doing? Or did she know of every hair and do nothing to stop the strands that hurled like knives upon her creation?

"It is hard to have faith in these times," Esen murmured. "To believe that the Mother is with us when all my kind are dying."

Fafnir's gaze softened. "Yes. And that is why I admire your faith very much."

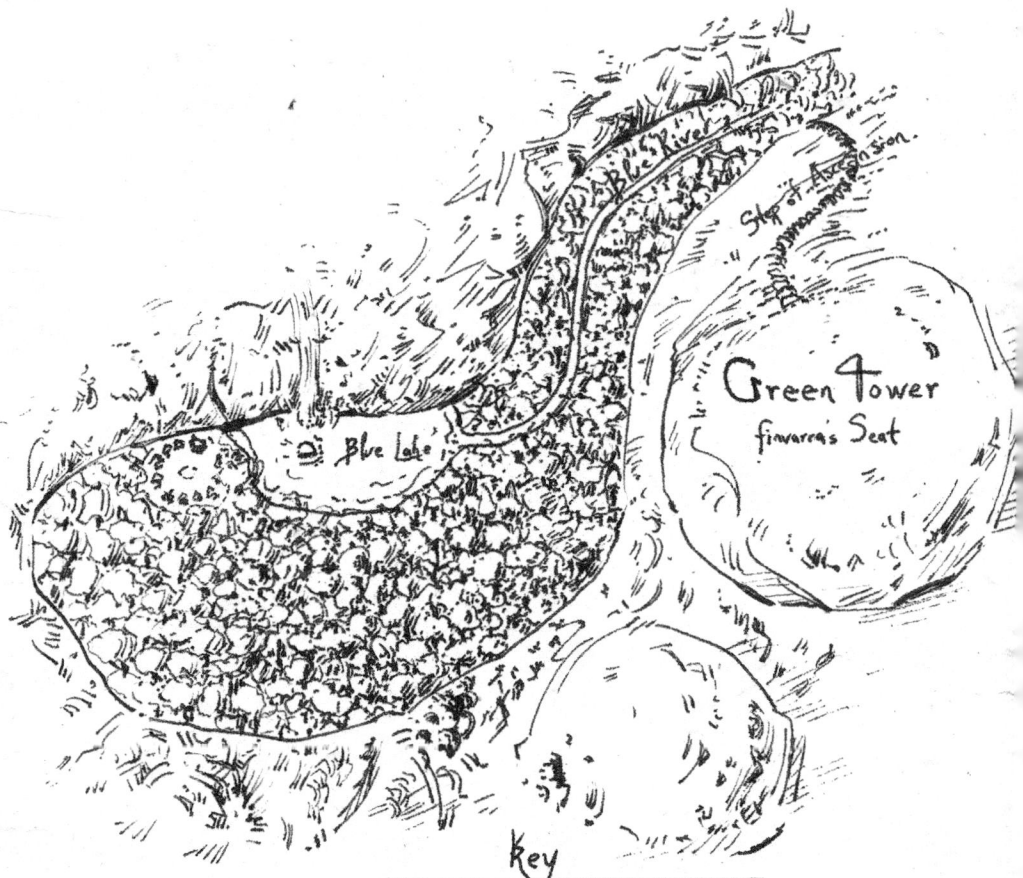

Éigniú Valley

Blue Shives

Step of Ascension

Blue Lake

Green Tower
finvarra's Seat

Key

Diviner

Home

Blue Seat

fin

CHAPTER 29: SOMETHING IS WRONG

The air grew colder as they ascended, lending strength to the wind that bit at them. Fafnir wrapped his arms together under his cloak, sitting curled up, with his head resting against the board of ash. It rattled against his skull. His ears popped as they accumulated to the rising air pressure.

Fortunately, the ground was a steady slope upward, for now. Esen's shoulders swayed with her movement like his boat upon the river. Though he was well used to it by now, it was still strange, when he isolated the thought. It felt oddly personal to be this close to her face for such a long time.

The white trunks of the birch were scarcely distinguishable from the mist. He could mark the edges of each dryad only by the black marks that dotted their trunks. Their leaves were already splitting from their branches and fluttering down like ghosts.

When Esen noticed, she said, "It is midsummer. Autumn is a long way off."

"It is colder up here," Fafnir said. "Autumn begins sooner for them."

Esen hummed a note of wonder. She was full of those hums these past few days. He was continually reminded of how young she was. She was like a child, discovering the earth for the first time. It was inspiring to watch her — how her eyes gleamed with excitement at every marvel she discovered. He felt almost like a child again himself with her.

But he wasn't a child. He was far removed from that small, naive version of him that had scaled these heights with his mother and sister.

Who he was now instead… he wasn't sure.

When they lay down to sleep that night, his cloak felt like paper, even though he had let Esen shelter him within the wall of her folded arm. He lay for a long time, listening to the wind howl.

It was too like that night when the raving of the wind drove him from his home and he nearly drowned in the flood.

Unease had been growing in him during the long journey. What if they came all this way only to be rejected? Time made the difference between lives lost and saved. He had known it would take time when he first formed the plan, but it was easier to throw away time in theory than to live it out himself. It could not be a waste though. The insights and aid they received from these mountain faeries could be the deciding factor.

And already, something about the journey felt significant. Like just by being here, they had won something.

The stars were innumerable.

They started forward in the early dawn. Though the fog had thinned, it still hazed their view. Soon a grove of apple dryads caught Esen's attention. She surged forward.

"*Aeonida*, dryads! May we taste of your fruit?"

They must have consented in their rustling, as Esen reached an arm forward and plucked a rose-red apple from a swaying branch. She sniffed it and sighed.

"It smells like the sunrise, if sunrise had a smell." A high compliment for an apple. She brought it near him. "Would you like one?"

Fafnir cocked an eyebrow. It was almost three-quarters of his height and twice his girth. He studied the dryads around him until he eyed one with smaller fruits. "I'll take a crabapple over there."

Esen tilted her head. "Crabapple? There are different kinds?"

The excitement was so plain in her voice over such a simple thing that he couldn't help but smile. "Yes. Those are smaller. The size of my head, instead of three-quarters of my body."

Esen looked at the apple, then back at him. "Oh, yes," she said. "That makes sense."

256

Holding her apple in one hand, she walked to the crabapple dryad. After gaining the dryad's permission, she plucked down a fruit and handed it to him. He balanced it in his lap.

"Thank you."

It was good timing. He had been storing the last of the food Isolde gave him in case of emergency, and he had just eaten the last of his beetle from the prior day.

He pulled out his knife and began to slice carefully into the apple. He pulled out a triangle of the flesh, then sheathed his knife. A sharp crack sounded to his right, jolting him. Apple juice ran down Esen's fingers. She bent into a crouch, careful to keep her shoulders straight as she sprinkled the apple bits and juice onto her feet. A smile lit up her face.

Right. She ate with her feet.

He could feel himself smiling with her. "Does it taste like a sunrise too?"

"Yes," she breathed.

He took a bite into his triangle of apple. It tasted light as a cloud, but with a wildness to it, like the winds of the mountains. The sweetness lingered in his mouth.

He could see how she could draw that association.

Esen was looking away from him. He followed her gaze and started. A massive deerlike creature stood at the opposite end of the grove. Mist curled at its hooves as it bowed its head slowly, tilting its massive antlers, each one nearly as thick as its own head. Black, beady eyes regarded them.

The creature brought its head back up and lifted one hoof. For a moment, it stood like that, poised mid-action, before turning and leaping back up the cliffside and vanishing behind the rocks.

"Elk," Fafnir said, as the name returned to him suddenly. In all the years he had been alive, he had never seen one before. "That was an elk."

Esen hummed deep in her throat.

By midday, pine dryads replaced the white birch. They towered high and silent, like sentinels, their leaves reserved near the very tops of their trunks. Esen's leaves shook with every step, her breath quick as the ascent grew steeper.

A twinge of shame pricked him. He was sitting here on her shoulder, his legs stiff from lack of use, while she toiled beneath him. He wished he could help her. Instead, he was just another weight for her to carry.

"Please rest as you need to," he said.

Esen shook her head. "I want to reach the top today."

Soon they reached the edge of the forest line. Only low-lying grasses and heath grew ahead of them, aside from a few hunched Rooted Ones. Before them towered jagged rock cliffs veiled in mist, a gray cloud hovering below.

They were going above a layer of clouds.

Wind hurled itself upon him. He tried to reposition the board of ash, but the wind tore it from his hands. *Rot.*

"The valley is on the other side of that cliff," he shouted above the wind.

Esen bowed her head in a firm nod. She started forward. By one of the Rooted Ones, she halted and crouched. It had grown twisted horizontally along the ground like a snake, using a rock as a partial wind barrier. Several tiny shoots sprouted out of the pale bark with quivering blue-green needles.

"What is your name?" Esen asked, inclining her ear. She rested a hand on the dryad's bark. Though the needles shivered together quicker than before, her face remained puzzled.

"He speaks," she said finally, "but it is a tongue unknown to me. His voice is all breath; wild and cold."

Fafnir stared at the dryad. His trunk bent with the wind, flowing like water to adapt and survive. Why had he Rooted up here, alone, in the hard wind? Why not among his brethren behind them?

Esen rose slowly and bent her head to the dryad. "*Aeonida,*" she whispered.

A dry rustle murmured from the dryad's needles.

Esen walked on. She waded through a river, though it was likely bitterly cold. At last, Fafnir glimpsed a pathway of loose stones cutting through the wall of the cliff. He took out Isolde's map and confirmed. Yes, this was the way she meant for them to go. He frowned at it. It was awfully steep, even close to vertical at times.

"That is the best path up to the peak," he explained.

Esen looked at the pathway and drew in a deep breath. "Okay."

Isolde's words struck him anew.

Esen was very brave.

"I am sorry I cannot help you," he said. "At least, don't worry about steadying me. I will manage myself."

He turned himself around to face the branch he'd tied himself to. He pulled on the rope to hug his middle tight. It was hard to breathe but better than falling off.

"It is okay," Esen said. Her voice was a steadiness in the whipping wind. "I can do this."

She started up the steep path. She put out her hands to steady herself on the edges of the rocks and pushed up bit by bit. Her torso bent forward and straightened again and again. He clung to her branch to keep gravity from pulling at him. Her breathing filled his ears.

The rocks were, to her, mere minor obstacles. The difficulty lay in climbing all of them at once, and at such an angle. But to him, each rock was a giant, most of them half the height of that elk. He could have never made it up this path without Esen. The mountain fae must have reached this valley by flight, though how they managed in this wind, he didn't know.

At last, Esen reached the top. "We made it!" she cried, breathless. Rows and rows of pale slopes wreathed in fog stretched before him. Beneath them curled swaths of clouds. The wind blasted his face, smarting his cheeks, just like it had when he had stood here all those years ago.

He began to reach for the map to check their course but started at the sight of Esen's hand moving toward him.

"Come on," she said, beaming. "Let me lift you up."

"Lift me?" he asked, but Esen's smile was so radiant, he forgot why he questioned her.

"So you can see the view better." Her palm flowered open, inviting him.

There was no reason to deny her. He undid the rope binding him, breathing easier as he freed himself. He stepped carefully on her palm, bending his legs to ground himself. As she lifted her hand, her face and the rock on which she stood grew smaller. The sky surged before him, the clouds rolling swiftly like birds.

Thin golden light pierced through the wall of fog, then it lifted. Fields upon fields of green yawned before him, slashed by lines of golden light and dark blue shadows. Blue hills rose in the distant horizon—the hills of Esen's homeland, where their journey had begun.

The wind stung Fafnir's face, and a circling raptor shrilled above them.

He could still see how his mother had stood beside him, her pale face ruddy with life. Her hair had sprang free of its tight bun, billowing out from her face as she unfolded her long green wings from her back. She looked like a bird perched to soar. Isolde had been another bird beside her, her arms outstretched, a wild glint in her eyes.

He had never felt so small, and at the same time, so free.

The world was infinite. Full of wonders and magic, ripe for the reaping.

That day, as he had stood with his mother and sister, a glint of shining black had caught his eye. He stooped and picked it up, twirling the thing in his hands. He discovered later that it was obsidian glass. With it, he made his first invention—the buoyant temperature indicator.

He had been very young then, eight perhaps. The years had tried to prove him wrong. His home life grew darker, harder. Or perhaps he had grown old enough to know how dark it had always been. Either way, he had continued to dream of escape.

And he had escaped. That life was far beyond him now. But he had fallen into a second, even deadlier vice—that of bearing the weight of the entire forest upon his back…

But when this was all over, he would be free. He could wander every crevice of the land, answer only to his own will.

At long last, he would know peace.

He half turned his face to glimpse Esen still beneath him, holding him high. Her expression was like the sun, warm and radiant.

Soon, he would leave her forever, and not Unite with a dryad as he had promised.

And Isolde… He squeezed his eyes shut. He was already walking on thin ice with her. But what did it matter? If Esen and Isolde learned that all this destruction was his fault… they would hate him.

It would likely be better that way. It is easier to let go of those you hate.

He thought of his father and bit his lip.

Esen's palm began to move beneath him. He sunk into a crouch, suddenly dizzy as the mountains blurred below.

Esen's face filled his vision, her brows pinched with worry. "Are you all right?" she asked.

Why was there such care in her eyes? He hadn't meant to grow close to her. Or to Isolde, again.

He had to keep himself distant. To lessen the hurt when he left.

"It is beautiful," he muttered.

The fog had closed in again. He could only see as far as the next peak, the rest lost in gray.

Esen's brow pinched tighter. "Do you want to return to my shoulder?"

He nodded, and she guided him back. He stepped off and tied himself to the branch. His lower back stiffened in protest, but their journey was nearly over.

Clouds blocked out the light overhead. Thunder boomed, and the wind picked up, howling as it tore through Esen's leaves. A sudden slap of rain struck his face. He pulled out the map and squinted through the wind, comparing it to the veiled slopes, but he could hardly see in the sudden downpour.

He should've looked when the sun was shining. Idiot.

The dip in the rock on which they stood caught his eye. It cut away in regular intervals, stair-stepping down the cliff. A hand had carved that rock. The steps were small enough for a faerie, but wide enough for a Walker to share the path.

"There," he said, pointing. Esen stepped toward it.

The steps wound down across the jagged face of the cliff and vanished beneath the fog. "Follow that path," he said. "It must be the entry to the valley."

Esen cast one last glance about her before beginning her descent down the stairs. The fog soon curled thick about them; all was white and wet. Fafnir kept his eyes on the hazy outline of the edge of the path. Esen managed to stay clear of it.

It was eerily silent. The wind had died down, and no birds called in the sky. Just the sound of Esen's footfalls and the pebbles scattering. The peak on which they had stood rose up before them, frowning down. They followed the line of the cliff as though they were traversing the spiral staircases of the Rath Síoraí, curling round toward a center point. At last, the fog began to lift as they descended below it. When Esen stepped off the last of the steps and onto soft, springy heather, no trace of it remained.

On either side of them, the huge walls of the mountains towered, hemming them in. The only way ahead was a narrow path. But a massive heap of stones and loosened dirt had spilled down from the cliffside, blocking it, as though the mountain had wretched up its insides and left them lying there. A slight stream of water trickled out from beneath the rocks.

Fafnir's ears flattened.

A landslide.

"What happened?" Esen cried.

"These rocks eroded off the side of the cliff," he explained. "Something must have dislodged them."

He tilted up his head. The heap of rocks towered almost twice Esen's height. It would be a risky climb. At any moment, a stone could loose suddenly under her... or from above.

"Hold on," Esen said, starting forward. Her face was shadowed with emotion. "I am going to climb over."

"Look carefully before you step anywhere," he said. Turning around to face Esen's branch again, he gripped it tightly.

"I will." She started to climb up the first few layers of rocks. "I am worried for the mountain fae. I hope this is not their only path out of their valley."

Fafnir pressed his lips together. It was a genuine concern.

Esen tested a rock ahead of her with a shove of her hand. She dodged just in time as it dislodged and came tumbling down. A cloud of dirt sprayed Fafnir's face. He pressed his forehead against her branch, his hands clammy.

Esen remained still for a moment, breathing quick, before reaching out to test another rock. This one held firm, and she climbed it.

Again, shame pricked at Fafnir. Esen was enduring so much, while he did nothing.

At last, she scrabbled to the top and let out a startled gasp.

Strewn across brown, scorched grass lay several blackened bodies of dryads. Dragans spiraled over the wood, their mouths and eyes wide open in silent terror.

Fafnir's stomach clenched.

The valley stretched out before them, hemmed in by the steep walls of the mountainsides. A vast lake gleamed ahead, white with the reflection of the fog. A thin stream trickling down from the cliffs above fed into the lake, where a river snaked out toward them, pooling at the base of the landslide. That explained the trickling water they had seen on the other side.

Although some shrubs and patches of green grass grew by the lake, the rest of the valley was charred. Almost a hundred dryads lay broken about. Some still stood, black and leaning, with thin, scraggly branches like ribs. Others had torn at the lower trunk, leaving their base sticking up like a jagged tooth.

Esen's shoulders shook beneath him. He glanced at her to see tears wetting her eyes. He quickly looked away.

How had this happened? The fire must be connected to the landslide…

Esen started forward, stumbling down the rocks. She was moving quickly, her grief making her clumsy.

"Please be careful," he said.

Esen kept her gaze fixed below her, her face wet. Just as she was reaching the bottom, she pitched forward suddenly, crying out. Fafnir's legs flew out from under him. He wrapped himself around her branch, breathing ragged, as she ran beneath him—slipping and sliding downhill, rocks tumbling everywhere.

With a final frantic leap, she rolled onto the dry grass. She collapsed to her knees, heaving.

"I… lost… control," she gasped between breaths. "I'm sorry."

Blood pounded in Fafnir's veins. The rope bit into his middle.

He would have died without it.

Shaking his head, he forced his trembling hands to untie the rope. As though sensing his wish, Esen drifted a hand toward him. She brought him to the grass. His legs wobbled beneath him, his head swimming.

"Are you okay?" he managed to ask.

Esen lifted her head. One of her branches had splintered, the end piece hanging off like a hangnail. He winced.

Gazing around with teary eyes, she whispered, "What happened here?"

He stared around them, trying to think. His brain felt like it was made of gelatin.

Voices echoed in the distance. Fafnir turned to see a dozen faeries running toward them. They ran as one flock, with a desperate wildness, as though all their lives depended on their running.

As they came closer, he saw that most of them were children. One was perhaps no older than two, carried by an older child of eight or nine years. They were dressed in wool cloaks and furs that billowed out behind them. The faerie at the back wore all black wool, with bones and trinkets dangling from him. A bird's skull covered his face.

They were all without wings.

Fafnir's stomach sank. Wildfire. It had killed all their dryads, and their Winged Ones with them.

Leaving only the children.

Diviner Traditions

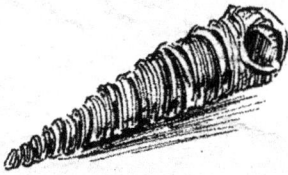

Diviner practice is centered on the breath of the Mother. Diviners will sit on top of a sacred spot above the village, and listen for the Mother's voice in the wind. Often they will use a concial shell to cover one ear, blocking off the channel of the self. With the other ear, they listen to the wind.

Pray in motion.

If a fae seeks healing in their arm, a Diviner might make a model of their arm, and offer it to the Mother with something precious, like fruit or honey.

Keen watchers of the stars.

Diviners direct seasonal performances that serve as a reminder of the Mother Wind's story. Diviners play the roles of the Mother and the Wind of Worlds, as that role is too holy for any other to take on.
Fall : The Mother circles with her Father, considering the world. Her departure is imminent.
Winter : The Mother leaves the Father to tether herself to the land. All is barren and she grieves her Father.
Spring : The Mother creates life on the land.
Summer : The life flourishes. All is in full bloom.

CHAPTER 30: THE MOUNTAIN FAERIES

The faeries skidded to a stop before them like a flock of birds landing. The faerie wearing the bird skull stepped out from their ranks. He put both hands to the skull and lifted it from his head. A thin, somber face with skin the deep blue of a mountain lake looked back at Esen. His eyes were fog white.

He looked young… likely no older than twenty. But something in his eyes suggested a wisdom far beyond his years.

"*Aeonida*. Are either of you hurt?" the faerie asked, breathless. He hung the skull across his chest with a cord. "We saw you fall."

Esen bowed her head to the faerie. "*Aeonida*. We are okay. But please, tell us of you. Something terrible has happened."

"Fire!" said a tiny faerie, no bigger than an acorn. An older faerie child held her. Both of their faces were thin. Esen swept her gaze across the fae.

They were all thin. Their bones jutted out against their skin, their eyes hollow. A pang struck her. With the valley scorched, there must be little for them to eat, if anything.

"It killed our dryads, and our parents," said the fae holding the acorn child.

"And then the rockslide happened," said a third, "and we were trapped."

267

The blue faerie swayed, his head lowered.

"I am so sorry," Esen said. It was as though nature itself were against them. "Are there no dryads left in the valley?"

The faeries shook their heads.

"How did the fire happen?" Esen asked.

The blue faerie lifted his head. Bones hanging from his ears clinked together. "It began with the drought. Over the last two hundred years especially, the air has been warmer here. This past summer, it was especially bad; the soil was hard as rocks. So, when the valley flooded, the water ran right over the soil, killing some of our dryads." His lips trembled. He put out a flat palm and circled his other hand over it, opening his fingers in the shape of a sun—Saol, the gesture of peace. "We recovered. Things were okay, for a time. Then the hard winter killed more of our vegetation and our dryads. It didn't rain for a moon and a half... so when the lightning struck, the fire held. It burned everything. We couldn't stop it."

They were so small. What could they do to stop a raging fire?

Esen put the back of her hand to her mouth. She could imagine the heat of the fire against her, her heart knocking against her ribs as she watched the dryads splinter and fall, shrieking; as her mother, her father, all the elders she knew and loved fell around her, their bones burning like their dryads—from the inside out.

Tears spilled from her eyes. "I am so sorry," she sputtered, but she had said that already.

She remembered Fafnir's words about the temperatures rising as the dryads died. Anger flared inside her. If the Ancient Law had never been revoked, this wouldn't have happened to the mountain fae.

Her parents and Ian would still be alive too...

She pushed herself to her feet. "I will get help at once. I'll ask the Rooted Ones to bring you Walkers to Root here again. We will bring seeds too, and plant new things here. We will make this your home again."

A wetness gathered in the blue faerie's eyes. "Aoradh. The Mother has answered us."

He lifted his hands and gestured three points in the air—the Trinity of Unity. The faeries behind him mirrored his gesture. "Aoradh!" they cried.

A slight wind shivered by Esen. Her mouth pulled in a quivering smile. They still believed, even though the land had battered them.

"What dryads were here before?" Esen asked.

"Apples," said the blue fae. "Their fruit gave us most of our strength. As well as oak and rowan."

If she had just thought to bring apples with her. Instead, she'd taken them for herself.

"I will look for them especially," she said. "And please, what is your name? All your names?"

"I am Elouan, son of Angus and Adair, the revered Diviners before me. May the Mother bless their souls."

Elouan made another gesture of peace, then pointed to a little faerie standing stiffly by him. They had the same lake-blue skin. But the little faerie had white hair, while Elouan's was the dark blue of a summer night. "This is Lugh, my brother."

A slight smile flickered in Lugh's face. Esen smiled back.

Elouan gestured to the acorn faerie. "This is dear little Owen, with Senan." Senan waved Owen's little hand at Esen.

"I'm Finley!" cried another fae.

"And I'm Reagan," said the one beside her.

"There's also Seán, Naoise, and Shaw," Elouan continued. "All siblings. Shannon and Ciara, also siblings; and Quinn, Tierney, and Brendan, unrelated."

The last three fae Elouan introduced looked to be nearly of Uniting age.

"Daffodils!" Owen piped up.

"He likes to sing to them especially," Senan explained, his eyes creasing. "If you could bring some bulbs, they can grow back next spring."

"Of course," Esen said. She thought of Aisling swaying and laughing as they sang together while the flowers filled the forest with music.

"And what are your names?" Elouan asked.

"Oh, yes. I am Esen, and this is Fafnir. *Aeonida*. I will be right back." She faced the heap of rocks and swallowed. Her branch was still splintered. She peeled off the piece of bark still hanging off her branch, wincing, and tossed it aside.

269

"Esen," said Fafnir. His voice was thick with concern. His throat bobbed as though he meant to say more, but he only looked at her.

"Stay with them, Fafnir. Help them until I get back. I know you can."

Fafnir's brow was still furrowed, but he nodded.

Esen set her jaw and began to climb back over the rocks. Her limbs ached, her fingertips splintering. Somehow, she made it safely to the top and back down the other side.

With enough Walkers, they could clear the rocks together. It would free the river too. She could see the gulley where it had once flowed before the landslide had cut off its stream.

A cliffside rose steep above her. The only way back to the dryads was the way she had come. She started back up the narrow steps, going as swift as she dared. She found herself holding her shoulders straight, although Fafnir was no longer with her. It was strange, to look to her left and only see the yellow-green moss growing over her wood. She had come such a long way with him there.

Fog curled thick above her like a cloud. She plunged within it.

"Oh Mother," she murmured. "Let there be enough Walkers to help them. Bring them swiftly to their aid."

She inclined an ear to the wind that whistled by her. She heard no words in it.

Dusk settled like a bat, swift and silent. The mountains shrunk beneath her, until eventually, she came out onto the peak once more. Her branches clattered as a wind whipped through them. The pale glow of the moon pierced through the fog, the stars winking as the full moon lit her way.

She hurried back down, sliding on stones but thankful this was a path with firm ground beneath her. Although the cold slipped its fingers along her spine, she ignored its sleepy call. At last, she reached the bottom, where the path leveled out. Tall, dry grass whispered at her feet.

A twisted Rooted One grew close along the ground, like the one she had seen before against the rock. She hadn't understood the other one, but maybe she would hear this time. She hurried toward her. "*Aeonida.* Can you hear me?"

The dryad's needles quivered in the wind. As before, it sounded like one long, drawn-out breath, with rising inflections and falling murmurs. The notes of words flowed in them, but she could discern nothing. "I apologize," she said. "I cannot understand you. If you can understand me, please send Walkers here swiftly. We need at least two dozen. Apples, oak, and rowan."

She ran on. In case the dryad hadn't understood her either, she had to speak with the forest. The cold pressed on her limbs, weighing them down. She fought to keep her eyelids from closing.

The dark shapes of the pines finally surged before her. She fell upon the nearest dryad, letting her forehead fall with a thud on his coarse bark.

The pine stirred. "*Aeonida, Esen Hazel. Onora Pine has shared your request. We are calling out to all Walkers near. Three apples and a rowan are already on their way.*"

Esen sank to her knees. "*Aeonida,*" she murmured. "Thank you. Thank you."

"*Rest now. I will have them wake you when they arrive.*"

Esen curled into herself. The heaviness coated her weary limbs like a blanket. As sleep folded over her, she saw in her mind Fafnir looking at her again, as she held him above her head over the mountaintop.

A grief had colored his eyes…

Yet he hadn't told her why.

FAFNIR WATCHED as Esen began the ascent over the landslide again, a pit of worry in his stomach, before turning to face the mountain faeries.

He wasn't sure what he had expected, but not this. Not a dozen children staring back at him, their cheekbones ghosting behind their skin; starved and grief-stricken, their homeland decimated by the work of his hands.

He had never meant for this to happen. So many dryads had fallen…

among them Esen's parents, King Ian, and here—all the parents of these children, and their dryads.

He rubbed his fingers together. They were stained with secret blood.

He had to fix this. As soon as possible. So he could at least prevent more harm.

Elouan was looking at him, his head cocked. Not with scrutiny, but with a sort of frank curiosity.

"Take me to your village," Fafnir said to him. "I will see how I can help you."

Elouan nodded. Tucking the bird skull under one arm, he gestured to the rest of the fae. They leaped into motion. Some walked alongside Elouan, while some of the little ones skittered ahead in undulating motions like fish. Fafnir fell into step at the back.

Elouan slowed his pace and walked beside Fafnir, his black cloak swishing at his heels. Up close, he could see that the bones dangling from his ears and throat were tiny rib and knuckle bones, interlaced with beads made from hickory nuts. The faint smell of burnt heather followed him.

It was the traditional garb of the Diviner to wear black and bones as a remembrance of death. The bird skull, its hollow eyes staring from its crook in Elouan's arm, was an addition he'd rarely heard of. The queen had cast all Diviners from the Rath Síoraí when the Ancient Law had been abolished. With time, the role had been largely abandoned among the perimeters of the Rath.

He had not encountered a Diviner in the past few hundred years.

"What objective brought you here?" Elouan asked. "Are you mountain travelers?"

"We were looking for you and your people, actually," Fafnir said, before hesitating. This is where he would tell them how their calamities befell them while omitting his own fault in it.

He cleared his throat. "We—Esen and I, I mean—are on a mission to bring the faeries back to the dryads. We wanted to gather voices of fae from different regions to share their unique stories. You have more of a story than we imagined. Do you know… how this happened to you?"

While he spoke, a glimmer flickered in Elouan's milk-white eyes. "Firstly, these are not my people. They are the Mother's. I only shepherd them. Or I am trying to, anyway. My training ended early—" His voice choked with emotion. "As you know."

Fafnir quirked his mouth. He did not have to say more.

Elouan squeezed his eyes shut before opening them again. "Secondly, that is wonderful. I wish to help however I can. And lastly..." He trailed off, staring at the withered grass they crunched underfoot. "I have been thinking of how all of this must be related to the dryads. My father told me many dryads have died, and that was from a journey over twenty years ago. I don't understand how that could lead to a drought."

"You are correct. It is related to the dryads," Fafnir said. Elouan's ears perked up. He looked like a squirrel that had been hunting for acorns all morning and finally found one. "There are many factors at play. One of the largest is the gap in the canopy the dryads leave when they fall. Sun heats the ground where there was once shade and contributes to an overall higher temperature. This feeds the clouds, which in turn give us rain. Then, since the soil is dry as a rock, the water runs off it in floods."

"I see," Elouan said, his voice higher. "Which harms the soil further and leads to more droughts, like what happened to us?"

"Yes," Fafnir said. "And droughts lead to fires."

Elouan nodded, his eyes clouding. "And the landslide..."

"When the soil is degraded, it can't hold itself together as well. It can slip, and... well... fall."

Elouan's eyes grew wide as moons. He breathed a string of words with a lot of wind in them, like the language of those twisted snake-like dryads.

"I see!" he cried, slipping back into the common tongue. "I've been thinking and thinking, and now I finally understand. It wasn't some meaningless cluster of catastrophes. It was all linked in a pattern. Thank you, Fafnir. I am so glad you and Esen have come. The Mother is with us yet. Although, I..." He lowered his gaze. "I still struggle. It felt like the Mother herself hurled that lightning bolt; it struck so suddenly and so terribly. And though she has the power to tear down the thickest and sturdiest of dryads with one thrust of her arm, she did not breathe on the fire to put it out."

There was a jerkiness in Elouan's step, as though he bore a burden on his back and stumbled with the weight of it. Fafnir frowned. A steady flame of stability still burned in his eyes. How was it that his faith gave him assurance when the being he devoted himself to may or may not have lent a hand in the destruction of his people?

Despite everything, there was a serenity to Elouan the likes of which Fafnir had never found in all his thousand years of searching.

Fafnir's skin crawled. He shot a glance behind to catch two children creeping alongside him, ogling. They fled like startled birds when they caught his gaze.

Fafnir scratched at the back of his neck, frowning.

"I think they're still wondering if you're a spirit," Elouan said. "We were praying for help when Esen appeared like a great bird upon the rocks. We didn't believe she was really there until the valley rang with the sound of the rocks scattering beneath her. Even still, we could scarcely believe it."

If he had suffered the same, he would not have believed it either, not until he touched the bark of his savior.

"How long has it been since the fire?" he found himself asking.

"Three and a half moons," Elouan said, bowing his head.

The lake shone white in the distance. Beside the stream that trickled down from the cliff face, he glimpsed a cluster of clay houses—more than the number of children. Most bore black scorch marks. Green reeds grew alongside the river they walked by and clustered along the edges of the lake. He had not seen a single animal or insect, just dry grass and the broken husks of dryads.

"What food do you have left available?" Fafnir asked.

"We've eaten all the food we can find," Elouan said. "We are living off the leaves and bulbs from the plants leftover. They are a thin sustenance."

Fafnir bit his lip. It showed in their bodies. "Are there no more fish in the lake or river?"

"No. They used to leap up the mountainside like gleeful children into our river. The landslide has blocked their way."

A simple but sturdy boat rested by the shore of the lake. Tall green reeds rustled in the wind. The reeds by the bank would have roots in the water, which would naturally attract insects and other invertebrates that ate off their roots...

Fafnir looked back at Elouan. If he adhered a cloth like his cloak to the back of the boat and sailed along the edge of the lake, it could serve as a kind of makeshift net to catch the insects.

He glanced at his shoulders. Oh, yes; he was wearing a cloak too. He'd use that, then. It would give them something. Something that could hold them over until Esen returned.

"Let me borrow that boat," Fafnir said, "and I will get you food."

Elouan's mouth parted. He looked younger suddenly. Younger even than a few of the other faeries that walked with them. His words about his short training stung Fafnir anew. He had taken on this role far too soon.

"The boat is yours," Elouan said.

Land of Ice

The land of the
Mother Wind

Wet front

The sand

N
NNW   NNE
NW   NE
WNW   ENE
W   E
WSW   ESE
SW   SE
SSW   SSE
S

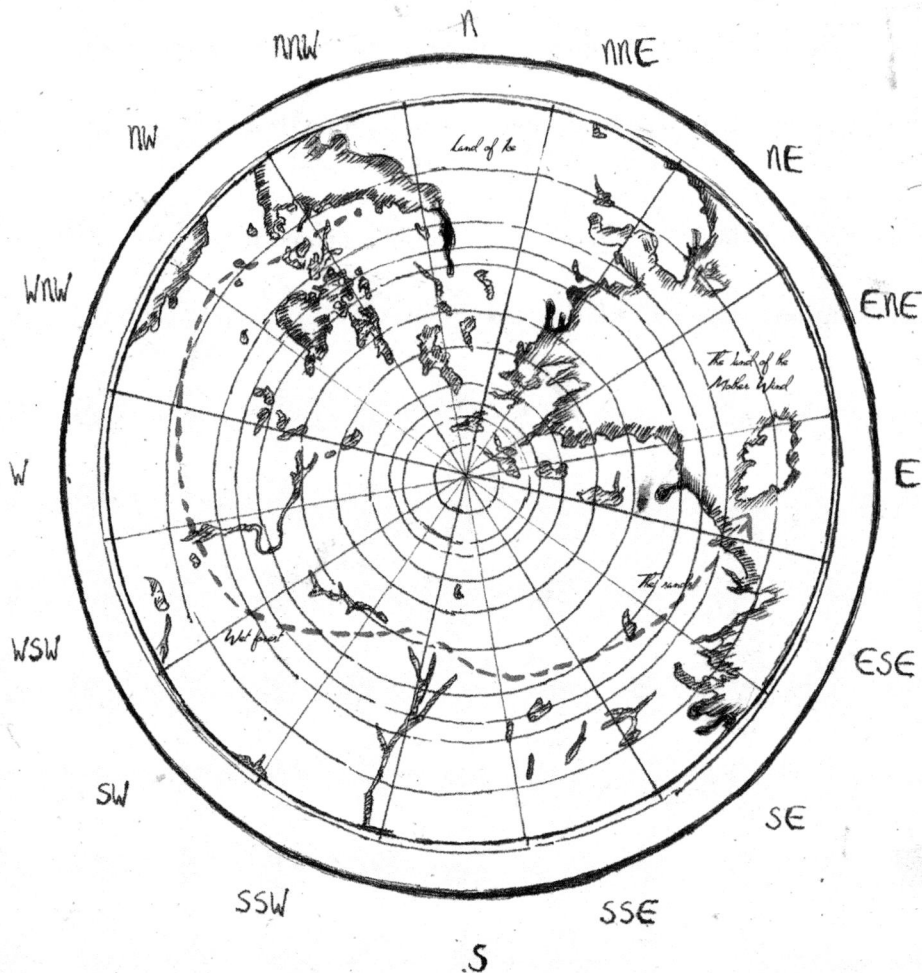

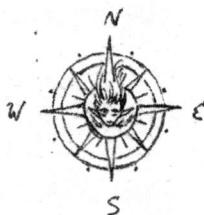

As witnessed by Downy son of Angus and Adair
received in holy vision from the Great Mother Goddess

CHAPTER 31: WORMS AND LARVAE

Children circled around them, staring, as Elouan and Fafnir drew up to the village. Fafnir kept walking toward the boat, his neck stiff. The children parted before him in one fluid motion. "How old are you?"

Fafnir whipped his head round. One of the smaller children walked at his heels, fixing him with white eyes like Elouan's. The child wore a small brown cloak pinned at his shoulders, and swung around a short staff like it was a blade. It must be Elouan's brother. What was his name again? Either way, he knew where this was going.

"Older than you," Fafnir replied.

The child—Lugh, that was his name—screwed his face up in a pout. "I knew that."

Biting back a retort, Fafnir shouldered into the thick of the reeds. They pressed against him, chilly and damp. The child fluttered beside him, flitting through the reeds with ease, uncomfortably close.

"Are you old enough to Unite?" Lugh asked, whacking at a reed with his staff.

Fafnir pressed a hand to his face, breathing deep. How many times would he have to repeat this awful lie? He could pretend he hadn't heard, but the other children crowded in a line behind him, their faces attentive.

"I could die," he said flatly. The child's eyes widened even more, if that were possible. "I will Unite later."

Lugh's mouth pulled in a frown. He walked with his gaze on the ground before saying, "You'll Unite with Esen, right?"

Fafnir rubbed the skin at his temple. Reaching the boat, he pulled the rope from his bag and bent down. As he tied it to the rear of the boat, a thud startled him. Lugh popped his head out of the boat in front of him. "You will, won't you?" he asked.

With a slice of his knife, Fafnir severed the rest of the rope free. He used the second piece to tie it on the adjacent side. He'd deal with needing a new rope later.

Lugh was still staring. He couldn't give him what he wanted to hear.

"I don't know," Fafnir said finally.

Fafnir winced as another thud shook the boat. A second child sat beside Lugh. "I like her," she said.

Soon all the young children flocked around him. The older fae stood aloft with their arms folded, watching. Trying to breathe even, Fafnir swung the cloak from his shoulders and tied the corners to the rope. Without the wool to shield him, he found himself shivering.

"I'll need to push the boat out now," he said.

As if he'd cast a spell, the children all leaped out of the boat and pushed at it until it rocked above the water. Fafnir stepped in. He looked around, frowning. This wasn't Serenity, his motorboat. He would need an oar.

Pattering feet raced toward him. A child rushed up to him holding a two-sided oar with a paddle on each end.

"Thank you," Fafnir said.

Children were strange creatures.

His cloak floated above the water, the edges beginning to sink. He pressed on it with the oar. Water pooled in the center, until eventually, it grew well saturated and fell to the floor of the lake amid the yellow-green rocks. Seating himself on a plank of wood in the center of the boat, he began to paddle forward. The reeds brushed the edge of the boat. The ghosting of their leaves on the wood sounded almost like whispering. He thought of the way the flowers had sung back to Esen. Did all the plants of the land have voices?

Glancing behind him, he glimpsed the mountain fae standing where he had left them, staring after him. Frozen with anticipation.

He hoped this would work. A tightly woven net would've done the job much better than his cloak, and a better designed rope system. He'd been rather sloppy for the sake of time.

After rowing a little farther, he dug one end of the oar into the rocks, halting the boat. Laying the oar across the plank, he went to the back of the boat and pulled on both ropes. He strained, the cloak heavier than he'd expected, before it came out of the water, green with algae and dripping. He pulled it toward him, grasped a corner, and hauled it onto the boat.

He lay it flat and smiled with relief. A hundred or more brown worms, each the size of his pinky finger, wriggled about the cloth. Even better, a few stonefly larvae hopped about on skinny black legs. He pinned one down and ran the edge of his dagger along its back. It stilled beneath him.

Feet pounded through the rushes. A storm of children rushed toward him. He sheathed the knife, stumbling back as they fell upon the wriggling insects. One child struck a stonefly larva dead with a stone. She gave it to a younger child, who bit down into its back, the juices flowing down his chin. Other children snatched at the worms, snapping them in their teeth.

Soon the cloak was bare.

Lugh's tiny hand pulled at Fafnir's pant leg. "Do it again!"

Elouan and the other older fae stood on the bank, smiling. They had let the youngest have the first pickings.

He'd do it again, then.

Fafnir crouched and pulled at his cloak, but several children were still standing on it.

"I need this back," he said. They jumped off it and gathered into the rushes, watching as he fixed the cloak back to the boat and picked up the oar once more.

As he pushed off and rowed farther down, the children ran along the bank beside him. They were leaping and laughing now; pushing each other, lifting each other back up, and chattering like songbirds.

Aside from Aisling and Iona, he had scarcely seen children in the past several hundred years. For so long, he'd kept mostly to the land around the Rath Síoraí, where all the children had grown up. All were immortal there, so no more were being born.

How could they laugh and play like that after losing so much? There was a lightness to them, like they had one foot in the air. He felt hollow looking at them. Like he'd lost something he couldn't name, couldn't even begin to try to find.

He had been like them, once. Laughing and playing with Isolde.

Light as a bird.

His second haul brought in a hundred and fifty worms. No larvae though. As the children leaped on the worms, giggling, Elouan and the other fae appeared carrying earthen jars. They filled the jars with water and placed the extra worms inside while munching on a few themselves.

Fafnir did a third round to help them fill their jars. The sky darkened. The cold grew sharper, raising goose bumps on his exposed skin. As he folded up his cloak to cast it back into the water, Elouan lay a hand on his shoulder.

"That is enough for today," he said. "We thank you."

Elouan wrapped a thickly woven cloak over Fafnir's shoulders. Fafnir rubbed at the cloth. Hare wool. It was very well made.

"Thank you," Fafnir said. "But please, take this back if any of you are in want of it."

Elouan shook his head gently. "It was my father's cloak. It is an extra."

Fafnir stiffened. He felt suddenly cold again, like the cloak was made of snow.

"You have taken nothing for yourself," Elouan said. "Come rest and eat with us."

Fafnir hung his own cloak over the edge of the boat. It was slimy with algae and insect juice; too far gone to use as a cloak again.

"I'll leave that attached so you can use it yourself," he said.

"Thank you." Elouan's eyes glimmered. "It was a brilliant idea."

As they walked toward the village, Fafnir cast a glance back at the landslide in the distance. Esen was out there somewhere. He hoped she had made it safely down the mountain and would be able to swiftly find aid.

It felt odd not to have her near. He frowned. That thought itself was odd. He had been alone for so long and been content in it.

"As one and one and one and one they flew,
All across the twilight sky."

His ears swiveled toward the sound. The children were gathered, some sitting, some leaping in circles as they chanted a light, airy tune that floated along the wind.

"Each one a rare and pretty bird,
On their way to the sea."

The children that were sitting were yanked to their feet. They twirled along in a circle, each with their hands out, flapping them like wings.

"They flashed and twirled across the sky,
Dazzling the passerby.
As one and one and one they flew,
Together a great serpent cloud."

With a final "Aieeeee!" they fell to the ground, laughing and clutching at their stomachs.

A great serpent cloud... Were they singing of starlings? In the twilight sky, especially on spring nights, he had seen starlings fly in migration as one entity. They indeed looked like a serpent coiled in the sky, turning its head from one direction to the next. They must have beautiful views of the starlings' flight here in the mountains.

"Here." Elouan held out a bowl of the tiny worms. Fafnir's stomach growled. He had not eaten since the previous day. He was hungry, but he was not starving.

"No," Fafnir said. "Those are for you and your people."

Elouan pressed the bowl into his hands. "You have taught us how to do it," he said. "We will get more for ourselves tomorrow."

Fafnir gripped the bowl. He couldn't eat in front of them, not when he had done this to them.

The strike of a flint caught his ear. One of the older fae had lit a fire. She breathed on the embers until they licked onto the sticks and dried reeds. The children flocked to it like moths to the light. They seated themselves in a circle, the older fae joining them.

Elouan gestured Fafnir over, and they sat within the circle. After gathering a handful of dirt, Elouan whispered to it in the wind language, then tossed it into the fire.

"Tell us a story!" a child's voice cried.

Fafnir grimaced. Lugh sat beside him, pawing at his knee. "Please?"

Fafnir shirked away, resisting the urge to flee. He had seen and done many, many things. Mostly a lot of the same things—perfecting his carving and music over the depths of time.

But none of it could be told as a *story*. Stories always concluded. His story was still going, being written day by day... hopefully with the ending he longed for.

"I would prefer not," he said finally.

The child pulled away from him, thank the Mother, and pouted. Elouan rose and bent toward Lugh, but the child leaped up and began to examine the dirt several arm-lengths away, as though it bore a sudden mystery. Elouan dropped his hand, his ears flattened. He swayed a moment before sitting back in his spot.

"I apologize," Elouan said, turning to Fafnir. "We often spend our evenings immersed in stories. Today has been a story of its own. They are simply curious to know more about you."

Fafnir shifted the bowl in his lap. A few of the worms had begun to escape. He gathered them in his hand and placed them back in.

"I can tell the story of our mission," Fafnir said. "Of how all of you can help to preserve your land and save the forest."

The children *ooh*ed and leaned in.

Elouan leaned forward too. "Please do. That is a story we must hear."

Fafnir related the plan, trusting them with the whole of the details. These were honest folk. When he came to the subject of gathering for the World Market, he hesitated. It would be asking a lot of them to leave their homeland after just beginning to rebuild it, and they were all weakened, not to mention below Uniting age.

"We came here to see if you could join us to make a stand against the queen," he said. "We will be amassing together at the World Market. We did not know of your situation though. It is a long journey for you, and you have been through much."

Elouan spoke with the older fae among them. Two of them looked on the cusp of adulthood, likely around thirteen to fourteen. The other five ranged from twenty-one or so, as Elouan looked, to close to one hundred.

"Sean, Quinn, Tierney, Brendan, Naoise, and I will Unite with the dryads Esen brings," Elouan said at last, indicating the five oldest fae. "We will have wings then. We will fly down from the mountain and stand with you. The children will remain behind. Shannon and Ciara will look after them."

Fafnir stiffened his jaw. It had taken so long for Niamh to recover after giving her energy. While these fae were older than Niamh had been when she United, they were still too young.

"Some of us have had to Unite before age one hundred before, in hard times," Elouan said quickly, as though reading Fafnir's thoughts. "As long as it is done after the body has matured, it is safe."

Fafnir shoved more of the worms back in the bowl. Curse the worms; he should have refused them. Elouan and these other fae had not even known a century of years, and yet they were willing to tether themselves to a dryad that could perish this very winter, if it was as brutal as the last one.

While he was gorged on centuries...

"Very well," he said. "Thank you. Your aid will be invaluable."

The fae fell to talking amongst themselves—of their excitement when Esen came, the weather, and light jokes and games. Fafnir fidgeted with the worms.

Elouan remained silent, bent over with his chin rested on his hand. Soon he rose and bowed to the fae. "I will retire for the night. *Aeonida*."

"*Aeonida*," they rang back to him.

Elouan lifted his gaze to the sky, his eyes half-lidded. He murmured a river of wind words, forming shapes and gestures with his hands. At last, he opened his eyes and gestured to Fafnir. "Are you going to eat that?"

"No," Fafnir said. "Please put it back in your reserves." He felt weak, but not so weak that it would affect him in any significant way.

Elouan frowned at him. He went and got one of the jars, and Fafnir dumped the worms back in.

"I will show you where you can sleep," Elouan said.

N
NNW · NNE
NW · NE
WNW · ENE
W · E
WSW · ESE
SW · SE
SSW · SSE
S

Land of Ice

The land of the
Malice Wind

The islands

Wet forest

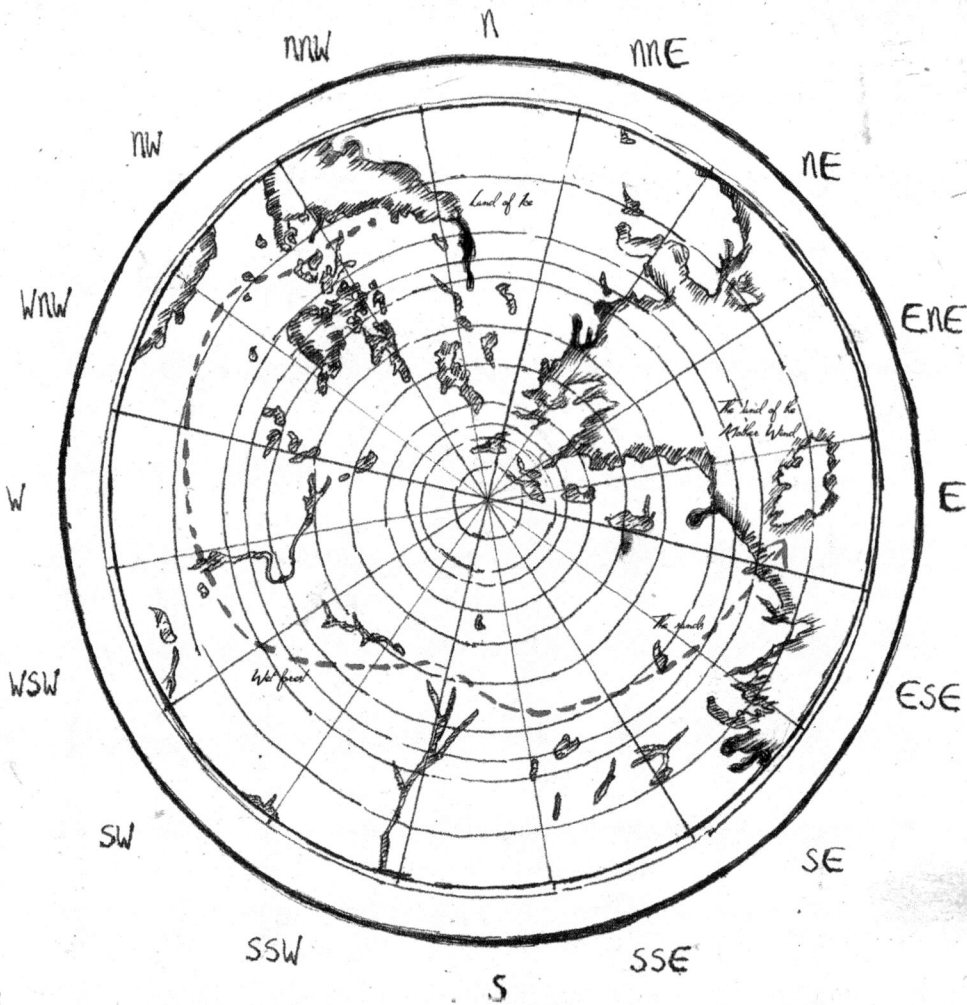

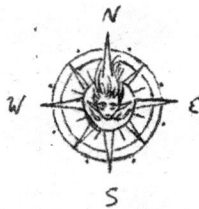

As witnessed by Douany son of Angus and Adair,
received in holy vision from the Great Mother Goddess.

CHAPTER 32: THE VISION

Elouan led Fafnir toward a clay home built into the cliffside, beside the stream where the water flowed into the lake from the cliffs. Carved stone stairs led up to the entrance. A bird skull hung above the doorway, casting a sharp shadow below. Fafnir studied it. A starling skull, with the symbol for *Aeonida* carved on its front plane. Inside the shadow, he glimpsed the skin of a hare fluttering, the only divider between the outside world and the interior.

It must be the Diviner home.

The shadow engulfed Elouan as he stepped within it, coloring him like the night sky. He held the hare skin back to allow Fafnir to pass through.

A silver stream of moonlight illuminated a cluttered interior as the smell of sage wafted over Fafnir. Skins and herbs hung from the ceiling, draping over a bed of moss in the corner. The center of the room had a circular space cleared. Every other space was packed with bones, trinkets, sculptures, and other strange things. He glimpsed several reed flutes, finely made.

"The fire spared this place," Fafnir observed.

"Yes." Elouan stepped within. He pulled off the bird skull that hung across his chest, which was also a starling. "You can sleep here tonight. I will be out."

Fafnir glanced again at the bed. It was big enough for two. Elouan's mother and father must have slept there together, and now Elouan slept there, alone.

Fafnir's skin crawled. "I can sleep outside. I do not mind."

"Please, do not pity us. Let us give to you as you have given to us."

Fafnir pulled at his ear. A greater gift would've been letting him sleep outside; he could handle the cold. But Elouan's words pierced him. He *had* been pitying them. "Very well," he said.

Elouan placed the skull over his head. White bone replaced his face, dark hollows where his eyes had been. It was startling how it changed him. It made him like the younger children, with one foot in another realm.

Elouan turned to go, passing a desk Fafnir had not noticed before. Scattered papers and bound journals were strewn across it, the pages marked with dried herbs. An interesting array of charts, diagrams, and hasty scrawls filled the pages. It reminded him of his own studies before he had tried appealing to the queen.

One chart held his attention. It depicted a circle divided by the cardinal wind directions...no. It was more than that. It was a map. But it looked nothing like the shape of the land. There were numerous land masses broken into distinct groups, separated by stretches of ocean... his jaw gaped. It was a map of other lands.

Lands beyond their own.

Fabric fluttered past Fafnir. Elouan gathered up the papers, placing them underneath a block of hazel wood. "Don't mind that," he said.

A spidery tingling sensation raced through Fafnir's veins. He couldn't unsee what he had seen. "Is that your work?" he asked Elouan, trying to keep his voice even.

The skull dipped in reply.

A breath escaped Fafnir. In the early days of written history, faeries had tried many times to set sail upon the sea to seek new lands. Each time, either the remains of their ship soon washed ashore, or they disappeared entirely, without a trace. Since then, so few faeries still considered the notion of other lands, and even fewer to the depth which the map suggested.

"Tell me more, please," Fafnir said, leaning forward. "You have indicated such specific locations for lands beyond our own. What did you study to reach such ideas?"

"A lot." Elouan turned his face away from Fafnir. "But mostly... it came from one source."

"What is this source?" Fafnir asked.

"It comes from a time of my life I am ashamed of... which is all of my life before this moon."

Fafnir furrowed his brow. "What has brought you to study our world like this?"

The words issued quietly from the skull. "Like I said, it is hard to have faith."

His words were almost a perfect echo of Esen's. What did faith have to do with studying the prospect of other lands? Was he looking for a place to flee to? But he had been trapped in this valley...

Maybe he was studying the world to see if it aligned with the myths; to see if there truly were a goddess to hope in.

"I'll be going now," Elouan said. He turned toward the door.

"Wait," Fafnir said, starting forward. "Were you questioning the Mother Wind?"

Elouan jolted as though he'd been struck with lightning. He turned slowly. "Yes. I-I know it is sacrilege for my role."

Aside from the queen, he had never known another to question the Mother before. He had thought he was alone.

"I have questioned her too," Fafnir said.

Elouan stood still a moment. At last, he put both hands to the skull and lifted it off. His face was bright as a firefly.

"Really?" he breathed. He fidgeted with the skull in his hands as though he didn't know what to do with himself. "Why have you questioned her?"

"I think all things should be subject to questioning," Fafnir said. "That is how growth occurs."

"Yes, yes," Elouan said. "I was always a skeptic myself. I was the destined-to-be-Diviner who didn't believe. I can't just take things at face value. I have to think of all angles, find the clearest truth." Elouan started to pace, radiating energy like a moth in an enclosed space. "What parts have you questioned?" he asked, speaking faster. "How the stars suggest the presence of a greater world, and therefore room for other lands upon this globe? How temperature and pressure creates the force we know as wind? Why we call the wind Mother and find comfort in her? Why when the wind shakes the Rooted Ones, the forest comes to life with words when it was silent before? And why the hairs on our arms and neck stand up in some sort of salute to a majestic wonder far beyond our own comprehension?"

Fafnir's eyebrows nearly climbed out of his face. "Some of that, yes."

"And what did you conclude?" Elouan asked.

"It is not for me."

"The Mother Wind, you mean?"

"Yes."

"What process did you follow to come to that conclusion?"

"I determined that I can't know whether she really exists or not," Fafnir said. "We are speaking of air here, literally and figuratively. The truth is of no consequence. Whether she exists or no, she does nothing for me, so I stay in my corner."

Elouan's brow pinched. "But isn't it of infinite consequence? If it is true—if there is a higher being directing us, guiding us—then our laws are above the individual. They come from a noble, objective source."

Fafnir shrugged. "Why are you assuming the Mother is objective? Is she not still an individual like us, acting by her own will?"

A shrill breath broke from Elouan, like the cry of a raptor. "You are right! I spoke in haste. The Mother is one of many of her kind. And she herself is unsure, although it is a well-placed bet; far better than we could make from our own tiny perspective."

One of many? Apart from the Mother, he had only ever heard of the Wind of Worlds. And what bet was Elouan speaking of?

"How do you know this?" Fafnir asked.

Elouan's face grew somber. "I... I had a vision."

Fafnir stared at him.

"You won't believe me," Elouan said. He started to strap the skull back on his chest, then folded it back under his arm. "Sometimes I don't believe me. Well, it wasn't me. You get the idea."

"I would like to hear it," Fafnir said. "If you are comfortable sharing."

Elouan hesitated. At last, he shrugged on the skull and sat down on the moss rug. He fidgeted with his thumbs. Fafnir sat beside him.

"So... I never saw my mother," Elouan said. "After the fire, I mean. She was out getting water. She became just another pile of ash when it was all over. But my father... I was with him when his dryad died. His screams were terrible. I hear them sometimes still. He fell into my arms... and as I held him, little Lugh—" His voice quivered, and a redness came over his face. "I-I'm sorry," he mumbled, wiping at his eyes.

"Take your time," Fafnir said. The wool of the cloak Elouan had given him scratched against his neck. He felt dizzy suddenly. He put out a hand to steady himself.

When he had recovered somewhat, Elouan said, "All that to say I grew black with anger. I wanted to prove the Mother wasn't real so I could disown my inherited role as the Diviner rather than give my people false hope."

Fafnir nodded. "I can understand that."

Elouan brightened slightly before his face darkened once more. "So I locked myself in this room. I vowed I wouldn't come out until I had learned the truth. I scoured all the books that had ever been written by our generation of Diviners and picked apart everything I knew. But I just kept hitting more questions; the concept kept expanding rather than condensing. On the eve of the third moon, I found a little forget-me-not flower on top of my open book. It could've only been from Lugh. It was a secret exchange we had."

Squeezing his eyes shut, Elouan pressed a hand to his forehead. "I'd forgotten my own little brother, and all the fae of the village. I was supposed to be their beacon of hope. Instead, here I was, trying to destroy the very source of that hope. But I still had to know... I couldn't come out and pretend to interpret omens from a goddess who didn't exist. So I went to the mountaintop and prayed for a day and a half. At noon on the second day, I fell into a light sleep. It was then I had my vision."

Elouan leaned forward and traced circles in the moss as he spoke. His eyes fogged over.

"The wind whipped through my hair. I flew alongside hundreds of thousands of wind gods and goddesses. I cannot begin to describe what they looked like—we do not have sufficient comparison. They had the bodies of faeries, but were the size of Walkers, with strands like hair, but also nothing like hair, that flowed from their heads and kissed the clouds. I understood, looking at them, why we revere the starling as holy, for these wind beings flowed in the sky like the starlings in their murmurations, losing their form and then gaining it anew in a startling new shape. They were amorphous; no one shape could define them."

The shapes flowed in Fafnir's mind. That explained the song, and the skull...

"They all flowed, like water round a vortex, around the Wind of Worlds. I knew in my bones he was the father of them all. He was bigger than all of them put together, yet nimble enough to stir just one petal of a dandelion if he wished it. I flew among them, gazing as though my eyes were upon their backs. We wove through the world, circling it like the ant climbs an acorn. Vast and wonderful lands stretched beneath us— mountains and forests unlike any I've ever seen, lands of great red sand, and an island of silver ice floating upon the sea. Strangest of all, though, was that I saw no Walkers; only Rooted Ones and many faeries, dwelling in thick concentrations throughout, behind high walls of stone. No wings grew on their backs. The old and the young lived among them. In one dry, stony land, the faeries clashed in great masses and slew each other, their blood staining the earth."

Fafnir leaned closer, his mouth parted. Due to the law of Aon Mharú, blood had scarcely been shed in cold murder. Of course, the dryads dying could qualify as breaking this law, but they were not killed openly by any hand. To think of thousands upon thousands breaking open skin, bodies falling on the ground, bleeding out... it was horrific.

Elouan continued. "We came to a lone, desolate island, adrift far, far out at sea. Only cracked grass and thin, shriveled Rooted Ones grew there. All else was bare rock and sand. One face held still in the flowing mass of the wind gods and goddesses, gazing on the lone land. I knew her, in the same way I knew the Wind of Worlds. The Mother Wind. But then, she bore another name I cannot know. Tears stood in her eyes.

"Suddenly, I was beside her, her thoughts flowing through me as though they were my own. She had blown across the world for many, many years. She had seen faeries band together and fracture again. She had seen carnage like the one I glimpsed, time and time again. Needless pain repeated; an endless cycle. Here, there was a chance to begin something new. She flew to the Wind of Worlds and begged him to let her take the land as her own. He permitted her. As she severed her tie to her father, my heart burned with her pain. She wreathed herself about the land like a cloud of mist and gathered her breath. She blew such a powerful gust at the land that it drifted away into the depths of the sea... I woke, then, looking out on the mist above the peaks of the mountains. A warm breath lingered in my ear before fading."

Elouan lifted his head, his gaze hovering above the floor. "I believed in her, though there was no rational reason to. I was starved and sleep deprived, but I could not explain how I had come upon such sights in my mind. How could I conjure up such a vision, when half the things in it I had never seen the likes of before? And the warmth in that lingering breath... I couldn't explain that either. The rest of the wind was bitterly cold. I realized... I had forgotten the truth. Or maybe I had never even known it.

"The world was not chaotic and meaningless. The Mother Wind had designed the laws of her land to prevent as much meaningless pain as possible. She made a map of peace, and the three-hundred- thousand years of history we have has proven her law works. No carnage has ever occurred here. Our culture has remained unified. It is only now that her law has been revoked, that we are seeing mass pain and divide among us. So I knew the fire, too, must have happened as a result of the law being broken. Thank you for confirming that."

Fafnir nodded. He could find no words to say. He felt as though he were beneath that ancient, massive oak again at the foothills of the mountains, shadowed by things far beyond him.

Elouan's final words made sense. If a people as a whole were structured in such a way as to promote love and care beyond themselves, then things like massive fights and cultural fracturing were significantly less likely to occur.

That was... interesting. So the law was meant to promote selflessness. To strengthen peace and community. But what of the individuals like himself, those who did not fit into the mold?

Quietly, Elouan said, "I still don't understand why the Mother didn't spare my village."

His words drew Fafnir back to the space about him. He had no answer for such a question.

"Thank you," Fafnir said, "for sharing that with me."

291

He recalled Elouan's map in his mind. From the brief glance he'd had, he hadn't been able to discern the placement of their own land.

"Can you show me your map again?" he asked.

Elouan rose and handed it to him. Fafnir traced the land masses with his finger, searching...

He realized Elouan was speaking, and swiveled an ear toward him. "...I didn't see everything. In the path by which the gods and goddesses led me, we flew over the edges of some lands that stretched on farther than my eye could see. I believe I was only given a small glimpse of all that there is. And some details I only remembered faintly, so I attempted their depiction as best as I could."

There it was—floating amid an open stretch of sea, was the outline of their land as recorded by the scribes.

Elouan was still talking. "And I put our land where I had first seen it, before the Mother Wind blew it further east. I don't know where she blew it to. She must have done that to protect us."

The page swam, the lines blurring together in Fafnir's brain.

According to this map, their land was a mere ant compared to the hugeness of the world.

"Do you believe me?"

Fafnir started. Elouan was looking at him with the sharp eyes of a hawk.

"In the reality of your vision, you mean?" Fafnir asked.

"Yes."

Fafnir quirked his mouth. He lifted his hand from the map, leaning back. He had gotten swept up, like a child over a new fable. Naturally, if this land existed, there must be at least a few other lands out there. But it was impossible to know how far away they were. Likely too far to ever be able to sail to, since no fae had achieved it before. Elouan had only dreamt up his map. As he had said himself, he had been delusional with hunger and sleeplessness. Just as Fafnir had been when he had conjured up his father in the snow.

Although, was that a hallucination? Couldn't that also have been a kind of a spiritual vision?

Or worse... a ghost?

"Answer honestly, please."

Finally, Fafnir said, "The mind does strange things when the brain is

292

ill cared for. Although I understand that this affected you deeply, you cannot prove the truth of this vision, just as you cannot prove the Mother's existence."

Elouan winced as though Fafnir had struck him. He rose to his feet and turned from him.

Fafnir rose too, and held out the map. "I apologize. I am a hard audience. Please share your vision with us at the market. I think it will help draw the fae back to the Mother Wind, and in turn, to Uniting."

A breath heaved through Elouan. He faced Fafnir, and took the map. "Sorry," he said. "I have not shared my vision with anyone else before you. I am afraid it makes me look like a lunatic. I would have thought it to be fake too if I heard someone else say it to me. But you weren't there."

"No. I wasn't there," Fafnir said. For a brief moment, he let himself imagine if such a vision had come to him. How it would have felt, soaring above wild, strange lands, among the amorphous forms of gods and goddesses…

Would he have perceived a truth within it?

"Thank you for listening," Elouan said. A pinch formed in his brow. "Why are you doing this?"

"Hmm?"

"We used to receive news of the goings in the Rath from our dryads. I have never heard of another fae rising up as you are and making an active campaign to restore the Ancient Law. Why are you doing it if you do not know the Mother?"

Fafnir scratched at the back of his head. "We will all die if things continue as they are. I saw that. So I had to stop it."

Elouan nodded. "You are doing a good thing. Esen too."

Elouan slipped off his starling skull and placed it over his head. "Rest well," he said. With the dry clatter of bones, he flurried out of the room and shut the door behind him.

Fafnir rubbed his face. He took off his bark hat and placed it on a strangely shaped chair. He glanced at the bed and grimaced. Pacing, he looked at everything and nothing at the same time. The walls seemed to close in around him; the strange, beautiful things staring, questioning him.

Elouan's final words echoed in his ear. It was the right thing. But what Elouan didn't know was that he was cleaning up a mess that he had caused in the first place.

At last, Fafnir stretched himself out on the floor. The moss carpet cushioned his back. He closed his eyes, sleep trickling along the edges of his mind. He could almost hear the waves of the ocean crashing below, feel the wind stinging his face, as he soared through the sky like a bird.

As strange and wonderful lands folded out beneath him.

Dedicating a day to the study of
Spiorads, whom I have always admired.
This one sketched below — his name is
Arvid — I found leaning over the ledge
by the ninth step of the Stairs of
Ascension.

Some Spiorads
shoot straight up,
and bear
branches only on
their lee side. I
call these the
"praying hands"
variety

His roots shoot out with a ferocity that
startled me at first sight, clinging to the
rocky soil. He's a pine dryad of the
blue-green needle variety, and in very
good health considering the circumstances.
A limestone wall on the dryad's windward
side protects him from the hard freezing
winds. All Spiorads I have found Root
near some kind of sheltering force like
his. It is what keeps them alive.
I am learning to speak with Arvid, and
his fellow Spiorads. His language is like
wind and water in one. It is the closest
speech I have ever heard to what I
imagine the Mother Wind's speech to be.
He tells me that on some nights, when the
wind is a knife to his bark, and all is
so, so cold, he fears he may lose his life.
But even then, the fear is a quiet thing.
Because he has loved his life, and already
given it up in his spirit. Each new day
is an unexpected gift to him.
I long to live like that, too... —E.

CHAPTER 33: PARTING GIFTS

Esen did not appear the next day, nor the day after. Fafnir sewed a more suitable net to attach to the boat from tightly woven strands of rushes, with rocks attached to the bottom for weights. Still, the mountain fae were careful not to take too much. They dug up the roots and bulbs of the reeds and the few other growing plants by the lake and ate them boiled with as many worms as they dared to portion.

He didn't know what to do with himself otherwise. There was little work to be done. The older fae sat weaving baskets, cleaning, mending their clothes, or joining in on the children's games. They ran about pretending they were birds or elks, played a guessing game with bones behind their backs, or told ancient stories.

Elouan was very quiet. He spent the mornings with his people, and often disappeared for the rest of the day, either holed up in his home or wandering the edges of the valley.

Fafnir spent much of his time pacing, looking up toward the peaks, hoping Esen would come soon. Time was sliding away.

On the fifth day, Fafnir woke in the middle of the night to the sound of crumbling stones. He rushed out of the Diviner home to see rocks tumbling down the heap blocking the path into the mountains.

Esen had come at last, and with enough Walkers to tear through the stones.

Elouan flurried beside him. "Praise!" he cried. "Help has come at last."

He ran and woke the village. The stones continued to crumble with crashes that shuddered the earth. The mountain fae streamed forward as one mass toward the landslide. Fafnir hurried forward with them. They were running toward the mass of rocks, just as he had met them when he and Esen first arrived.

A flock of birds dove over the rocks, swooping into the valley. Falcons and magpies and thrushes, and several glossy-winged starlings. They cawed and chirped, filling the barren space with sound. Up ahead, a path had been torn through the rocks. Walkers strode through, their faces bright and determined, thirteen in all. Eight apples, three oak, and two rowan. Each of them held a woven basket over one arm. Hares leaped out at their heels, followed by several foxes, squirrels, and sheep.

The children leaped and shouted with delight.

At last, Esen appeared, looking out over the valley with concern. She carried a basket too. From this distance, she looked so tall... almost like she was a piece of the cliffside that had dislodged itself to roam the earth.

As they drew near, her face fixed on him, and her features relaxed into relief. A strange sensation fluttered through him—that such a creature not only thought of him, but cared for him.

The Walkers halted and crouched down. The children ran to meet them, flocking at their heels. Lugh ran straight up to Esen.

"What's in your basket?" he asked.

Esen tilted it so he could see. It was filled with bird's nests, tightly woven with twigs, heather, and down feathers.

"We come bearing gifts," she said. The other Walkers showed their baskets too. Three carried fish flopping in water, and another's was full of insects—grasshoppers, salamanders, frogs, beetles. There were animal hides, freshly picked apples, berries, green plants just uprooted, seeds, and raw, black fertilizer.

Soon the valley would thrive again.

Elouan bowed deeply before them. "We thank you for your gifts, and for yourselves—the greatest gift of all."

WARMTH GLOWED in Esen as she saw the joy in the mountain fae's faces. They looked ruddier, with more energy than when she had first seen them. Fafnir stood among them as though he were one of them. He must have found them food before she arrived.

She had known he could do it.

She turned to Elouan. "I have brought thirteen Walkers to restore the land. I know all of you are below the age to Unite, so please do not feel pressured to do so."

Elouan nodded. "We have decided already. Six of us, including myself, will Unite this night. We will join you in your mission. The youngest will stay behind."

Esen hesitated. Was that safe?

Fafnir drew up to her. "They are much older than Niamh was," he said to her. "They are assured of their safety."

"That is kind of you," Esen said, bowing to Elouan. "May the Mother bless and keep you all."

She bid the Walkers farewell, handing one her basket. Some of them had come down from the heights of the mountains, others from the neighboring forests on all sides. All of them came with a beautiful spirit of giving. Like Fiona, it was not yet their time to Root, yet they knew of the mountain fae and grieved their loss. These dryads were willing to sacrifice the rest of their Walk for them.

When at last they were successful and brought the fae back to the dryads, Walkers would roam the forest in the thousands once more, like in the ancient days. She longed for that day. There were too few of them now. There would be even fewer this night.

It was for the best.

She watched the Walkers stride among the fae. The children hitched rides on their hands and shoulders, giggling. A tear trickled down from her eye. She wiped it with the back of her hand.

"I am sorry we took so long," she said, turning to Fafnir. He was wearing a new cloak; a soft, brown one made of hare fur. He pulled at the fabric by his neck, his eyes fixed on the mountain fae. "How did it go with them?" she asked.

"It went well," he said. He looked at the ground, as though looking for words in the dry grass. "I helped them find food in the lake."

"But there were no fish, were there?"

"No. We found worms. Larvae and the like."

"Ah."

"That was amazing... what you did for them," Fafnir said.

"You helped them too." Esen smiled. "We are a team."

"Yes," he said, though he did not return her smile.

Elouan invited them to stay the evening. Esen sat beside Fafnir round their fire, surrounded by the Walkers and the children, the flames burning bright against the dark-purple sky. Elouan gave a starling skull to each of the fae who would Unite, then donned his own skull. With their faces shrouded, they danced round the fire, their shadows fluttering in strange shapes on the ground. Songs flowed from their throats that tasted somehow of the sharp pine of red cedars and fluttered high above like a raptor. The children leaned forward, their eyes gleaming, waiting for the day it would be their turn.

At last, at some late hour in the black night, they ceased their dancing. Elouan gathered dirt in his hands and let it spill onto the fire, the flames hissing until they gave in and sputtered out. Elouan went to each of the fae who were to Unite and made the symbol of Aoradh, union with the Mother, with his fingers in the air before their hearts, then repeated the gesture over his own heart, and bowed.

The fae bowed back.

He blessed the Walkers too, before they chose their places, and Rooted into the earth.

The next dawn, Elouan and the others stepped out of their dryads' heart chambers, still shrouded by the starling skulls. Green wings budded from their backs, unfurling like open palms toward the sun. At the edge of the lake, they dug together at the earth with their hands and knees in the soil. They laid their skulls in a pile together and laid earth back over the top.

"Why did you bury them?" Esen asked Elouan when they had finished.

"We are fused with our dryads now," he replied. "Death lives within us. We bury the skulls to reflect the day when we, too, will be buried."

"Oh," Esen breathed.

They had United so quietly, yet with a full awareness of the good and pain alike that came with it.

She thought of the dryads bent by the wind on the mountaintop. How they, too, did their duty quietly. Bending with the pain, holding fast to where they had Rooted.

"Elouan," she said. "Is there a name for the dryads who grow on the high places?"

"Yes," he said. "We call them *Spiorads*, meaning *those who bend and do not break*."

At high sun, they said their farewells. Lugh held Elouan's hand, and the two of them waved, beaming. The newly Rooted Ones swayed their branches in a great rustle. The rest of the children ran up to Esen and embraced her ankles. She knelt down and let them climb on and off her hand, laughing.

She would hold this memory in her spirit forever.

Fafnir resumed his place on Esen's shoulder. They started up the spiraling path along the cliffside, cutting through the thick fog, climbing back up the mountaintop. The fog thinned as they came up, the wind shrill and beating upon her face. The land rolled out before her eyes, hill upon sloping hill.

The blue sea beckoned beyond.

A crinkling of paper exploded in her ear. Fafnir was holding Isolde's map in his hands, trying in vain to hold it steady as the wind tore against it. He quickly put it back in his bag.

"The closest shoreline is southwest," he shouted above the wind, pointing far below where a dark pine forest bled out into hard layers of limestone. She glimpsed in one area a thin sliver of sand between the rock and the sea. "Go down the way you came, and then we'll cut west."

Esen started down the rocky path.

Songs for Young Fae
Ballad of the Faerie and the Frog

"Hello, my darling," said the wee yellow frog.

"Hello, my love," cried the fae. Come onto me, and I'll set you free. Come dance with me in the night." One twirl round, and he had wings of gold. Two times round twirled she. Three times round, and she'd lifted him high. And they danced so free in the night. "My darling, pray tell me," said the wee yellow frog, "Pray tell me, why you so seldom come? For I have been longing to see you, my love, I've been waiting for you for moons." "My darling, my true love, what a silly thing to ask, what silly sounds you make!" And she twirled him round by the first light of dawn. When he fell, he could see her no more. "O mouse, o mouse," said the wee yellow frog. "O mouse, pray tell me this. What must I do to become a faerie prince? For my lover, she cares for me not." "O frog, o frog, o flee your love. Do not lose yourself to her!

Yet if you cannot flee, go bid the snake, To bite off your head, and make you fae." "O cricket, o cricket, you sing an elegant song. Pray tell me, how might I become a faerie? For I have given my heart to another. Lo, I am nothing without her." "O frog, o frog, I pity you so. It is true she may love you in part. But whether fae or frog, she will love you not. For her heart is of the wavering winds." So the frog he wept, and went to the snake. For who could he be without her? "O snake, o snake," said the wee yellow frog. "I bid you to bite off my head." "O frog, o frog, I see you are in love. You say you are blind without her. Yet I say to you, you must love yourself true. Truer than any other can." So the frog, the frog, he went back to her. He waited till she stood before him. "Oh, I do love you, my own true love, Yet never must I see you again."

CHAPTER 34: SAVE THE FAERIES

Queen Maeve tangled the bedsheets into twisted spirals. Tears dripped from her eyes, staining the cloth with dark splotches. The little plush mouse with its shabby crown was draped on its side by the pillows, its head strewn back like it had been stricken.

The room was empty, empty, empty; like it had been for over a thousand years as she'd waited for her. Like her daughter had never come home.

But she had. She'd returned to her for a single moon, only to leave her again.

Forever...

Her daughter hated her.

But what had she done wrong? Niamh had come to her so happily, gladly forsaking her father.

Maeve had given her everything. All the comforts of the palace; fair food, games, music, beautiful jewelry and clothing, and all her love and attention—everything to make her happy. But the more Maeve gave her, the more she shrank back from her.

Niamh hadn't wanted happiness. She wanted pain.

She had too much of her birth mother in her.

And then she chose the dryads over her own mother. The *dryads*. The ones who had killed her birth mother, who had been stealing the lives of faeries since the dawn of creation under their hideous law. Now her daughter hated her. *She*, who had saved her from death, and fawned over her, giving her everything, everything—

A scream erupted from her throat. Maeve tore at the sheets, scratching long lines through the soft cotton. She seized a pillow and tore it in half, feathers flying. She kicked at the stupid bed until it splintered. She tore down the curtains, fabric streaming in a frenzy, tore open King Squeaks, and knocked a firefly lantern to the floor. Half the fireflies within blinked out, their lights forever extinguished.

Her chest heaved up and down, her ears ringing. The blood boiled in her veins.

At last, she straightened her spine, adjusting her crown.

The room looked hideous. Good.

She would have an honorary tear the rest of it down and turn it into a dressing room.

Her daughter was gone, farther than death could ever take her. But she still had her people.

With a sweep of her cloak, she began to pace.

She had left Niamh with Fafnir. The two of them were likely working up some plan behind her back to undermine her; to bring back the Ancient Law. To bring back death and pain.

Maeve clenched her fists. To her dying breath, she would fight to protect her people.

She would have her rangers search the land for any sign of Niamh and Fafnir.

If they were seeking to undermine her, she would do whatever was necessary to end them.

No matter the cost.

No *matter* the cost.

Summer - Sun XII

I can't stop thinking about the numerical sequence of life. I remember that moment when it all first came together — when I was standing in Mother's garden, and seeing, really seeing, how the seeds of the dandelions, and the precise order they followed, was the same pattern I'd observed in a dragonfly's wing, and the spiral of a spiderweb too, and the pine cone, and the veins of leaves, and the shell of a snail...my brain buzzed like I'd been set on fire. I'd always wanted there to be a meaning to this life. A reason that I woke again every morning, and went about underneath the leaves of this forest, pulling air into my lungs, and out again, and why...why I was alive to witness my mother's pain. I found it, then. Meaning was embedded into the veins of every living thing, down to the smallest of components. The smallest of gears churned the one beside it, which turned the next, and the next, to create the system as a whole. To live without meaning would be to ignore the nature of life, the innerworkings of existence. I was born at this time, in this body, under this roof...for a reason I suppose. I am still discovering what that reason is; what the tiny mechanisms of my body were orchestrated to perform. I feel it has something to do with music. When I play, all the world fades away, and time marches in a straight, predictable line to the rhythms of my violin. I am fully, more fully than I am anywhere else, and I am also not. Not existing, I mean. I am more me and not me at all. Can't think of a better way to phrase that. This life seems ugly when I look at its surface. It's made of hard stone, and when I beat my fists on it, I bleed. But when I look past the surface, the stone disappears, and I see those numbers flowing in a dance, everywhere I look. They speak of order, reason, stability.

Serenity...

But I can only see it for glimpses at a time. In a matter of mere heartbeats, my thoughts go somewhere else — I am thinking of the day before, when Isolde's eyes looked like a frightened hare, or a word I shouldn't have spoken, or a word I should have spoken, or the way my father's mouth twisted in a frown. And the stone wall has reappeared. It seems impossible that I ever saw something beyond it.

I don't know. I sometimes wish I had the courage to leave this place. If I left...I could leave these distractions behind. And I could seek those numbers...and live among their dance. Isolde's calling — something about toad riding. I'll stop here.

CHAPTER 35: QUESTIONS

R ain began to fall as the pine forest transitioned to red cedar, their trunks dark and tall, coated with green moss. Red pine needles crunched under Esen's feet. Among the cedars were familiar oaks, ash, hawthorns, and other hazels, only their leaves had a waxier look to them; perhaps to help them with the burn of the salt in the air. She could taste it in her mouth.

By the third day, the rain still had not let up. As twilight settled, Esen glimpsed the Rooted Ones thin ahead of her. The sea stretched ahead, the water pink from the reflected sunset.

She hurried forward, excitement in her veins. She broke out from the forest cover, the rain pattering on her bark. A pair of black-and-white birds with startling red eyes sprung into the air, squawking.

"I'm sorry," she called to them. They circled once around her, then flapped off down toward the shore.

She scrabbled down a narrow incline, white pebbles scattering, and stepped out onto the smooth sand. It shifted beneath her with every step she took, the tiny glimmering fragments settling around her feet—like a living thing.

Black and gray rocks jutted up around her. Yellow-green seaweed, looking as slimy as snails, clung to their lee sides. Waves broke against the sand, curled back into themselves, and then hurled upon the sand anew. The smell of salt filled her senses.

And far, far away, stretching seemingly forever, the edge of the sea kissed the horizon.

It was a different kind of beauty than the mountains. The murmuring of the waves was like the lullabies her mother had sung to her. The sea held a quieter joy. It did not shout; instead, it pulled gently at her spirit, drawing her toward it like the tide.

She could feel Fafnir sitting up. As he worked to untie himself from her branch, she put a hand toward him, and then helped him onto the sand.

As she stooped to lower him, she glimpsed countless white shells covering the backs of the rocks where the seaweed grew. She put a finger to one. It felt firm beneath her, like part of the rock itself.

"What are these?" she asked.

Fafnir drew up to the rock. Taking out his knife, he dug at one of the white shells until it fell off into his hand. An underbelly of soft flesh flashed up at Esen—a creature of some sort.

Fafnir tore out the flesh with his teeth and swallowed, then tossed the empty shell in the sand. "Food," he said to her. At her puzzled look, he added, "Barnacles, to be precise." He started digging at another one.

"Why do they cling to the rocks?" Esen asked.

"It's a stable place," Fafnir said. He bit into another barnacle. "When the tide comes in, they open up their shells and feed from the water."

"They are very patient." Each day was like a season to them—a winter of waiting, a summer of thriving.

Esen and Fafnir walked along the shore. The waves lapped cool against Esen's feet.

"You have been to the sea before?" she asked Fafnir.

"Yes, a few times," he said. "I like to look at the waves. They soothe me."

The waves murmured. *Sssh, sssh. Sssh, sssh.*

"What is it about them that soothes you?"

Quietly, Fafnir said, "There is a rhythm to their motion. A push and pull. What goes out always comes back in eventually. I suppose it reminds me of the order composing the framework of the world."

She felt the waves break against her feet. They pulled back as though

308

retreating before rushing upon her once more with fresh earnestness. It struck her that the waves and the barnacles were doing the same thing—striving forward, and falling back in surrender, again and again.

"I feel that too," she said.

As they drew near the cliffside, a wail pierced above the sound of the sea. It smote through her spirit like a knife. It was the raw cry of her own spirit.

Further down the shore, two dozen or so faeries walked in procession among the rocks toward the waterline. They bore the body of a pale fae upon a light raft of planks. His face was still as death, the faint shifting of dragans weaving over the surface of his skin. Another wail erupted from a storm-gray faerie at the back of the procession. Her kelp-green hair fell in drenched ribbons down her shoulders, hopelessly tangled. She held the hand of a little child whose skin was the light pink of a sunrise. With her other hand, the faerie beat on her breast, her face red with grief.

The other fae were strangely silent. Reaching the waterline, they continued beyond the breaking of the shore, until they were waist-deep and could lay the raft down upon calmer waters. There, they watched as the tide pulled back and sucked the raft in. Little by little, surrendering to the tide, it drifted out to sea.

The storm-gray faerie screeched. Releasing the fae child's hand, she fell to her knees in the sand and tore at her hair. The rest of the fae stood around her, shifting. One of them bent toward her, but she lashed out, driving them back.

A few faeries looked in Esen's direction, their faces hard and strained. This was not for her to see.

Esen walked hurriedly toward the cover of the Rooted Ones. She crouched by a cedar, wrapping her arms around her legs. Rain dripped from the needles above her onto her shoulders, cold. The screeching lingered in her ears.

Fafnir soon caught up with her. He looked at her, his brow pinched. "Are you all right?"

Esen gathered a handful of sand and let it fall in clumps through her fingers. She had been trying to not think of the pain of losing her family, but it came flooding over her, hollowing out her limbs. Once, when she had just begun to Walk, she lost a beautiful leaf in the river. She had watched it spin away from her, sinking below the foam, and realized she would never see it again.

Now, with Ian and her parents gone, it felt as though she had lost a piece of her own self in a river. That must be how that faerie was feeling too... She could not follow her loved one where he was going.

At last, she managed to say, "It is hard... to lose someone."

Fafnir sat by her, tracing a line in the sand.

"Yes," he said. A slight emotion tinged his voice.

Esen knew he had lost his father... Was his mother still alive? It felt strange she did not know this after all the time she had spent with him, and yet, it felt too personal to ask.

"This will be hard," Fafnir said. "Did you notice that the grieving fae was the only one with wings? She and the faerie on the raft."

Oh. She had not thought to look.

"They are losing their Winged Ones," she said. "Yes. They may be afraid to Unite."

Fafnir nodded. "Let's try all the same. Tomorrow, when the grief is not as fresh."

THEY DREW FURTHER into the forest until the line of the shore vanished from view. They stopped within a circle of cedars, the needles soft beneath her feet. She could feel the rain less here. She glanced down at where Fafnir stood beside her. He was just a little taller than her ankle. He seemed much bigger on her shoulder, with his face close to hers.

"I'm going to hunt something," Fafnir said. "I'll be back."

Esen nodded. He soon disappeared within the shroud of the Rooted Ones. She wandered along the circle of cedars. A broken dryad lay to her left, dragans weaving through the green moss and crusty blue lichen

310

coating the trunk. There was a beauty in the way the forest reclaimed its children.

But this dryad looked young. It had not been her time.

She felt lonely, all of a sudden. She walked up to a cedar. His branches curved upward, beginning horizontally toward his base, and then reaching higher and higher toward his crown. His needles grew far above her.

"*Aeonida*, cedar," she said. "What is your name?"

The cedar stirred. "*Aeonida. I am Graham Cedar.*" There was a coarseness in his voice, like salt rubbed against it. "*Are you Esen Hazel?*"

"Oh, yes," she said. She had forgotten she was known among the Rooted Ones.

"*Hail, Esen. May the Wind be with you. Your success with the mountain fae was wondrous.*"

"Oh." Esen bowed deeply. "I am doing what I can. How is my sister doing?"

Graham was silent for a moment. "*She says she is immensely proud of you. Fiona says her growth has been slow, though.*"

Esen pressed a hand to her chest. "How many leaves has she grown since winter?" she asked.

"*Three leaves.*"

"Only three?"

"*Yes. She is strong, Esen. She is just a little behind.*"

Esen rubbed at her forearm. "Okay. Thank you, Graham."

She walked away, shuffling through the needles. She longed to grow wings like a faerie and soar out to her sister. To hear her laugh, and sing with her, and spend the night beside her. Maybe she could get Fafnir to invent some kind of a device that would help Aisling—something to reflect more sun onto her, provide a steady flow of extra nutrients, or somehow keep her warm all through the winter without him having to wake up so often. And then maybe Aisling would catch up in the next few years. She would have thirty times as many leaves, without a trace of harm.

But what if, before next winter, it stormed long enough to cause another flood? And Aisling's roots were torn away while Esen was all the way out here and could do nothing to save her?

Esen wiped an arm across her face. It came away wet. She wanted to go home. But she was needed here. They would be preparing for the final stage of their plan, after meeting with these sea fae…

"Esen?"

Fafnir stood beneath her. He gripped a mottled brown insect by the legs. It was smaller than an acorn. He wore that look of worry again.

"I am okay," she said. "I think. I… I am afraid. For Aisling."

"Did you ask of her?" Fafnir asked. "Is she all right?"

"Yes," she said. "But it is late summer now. Autumn will be approaching soon, and she is not growing as I had hoped. I am afraid something could happen to her while I'm gone, and… I-I won't be there for her."

Fafnir nodded. He set down his insect on the needles and paced for a moment. "When I am… troubled," he said finally, "I've found it helps quiet my mind to focus only on my breath, and the sounds and sensations around me. Would you like to try that with me?"

Esen looked at Fafnir. "Okay."

Fafnir settled into a seat, crossing his legs. He laid a hand on each knee, his palms facing up. His fingers curled toward the sky. He looked so composed, like a rock in a storm. Immovable.

"I like to hold this position," Fafnir said. "But you can rest however you like. Sitting, standing, lying down. The breath is what matters."

Esen assumed his posture. She let her fingers fold comfortably.

"And… just… breathe." Fafnir lowered his voice, drawing out each word with a breath. "I have a rhythm… worked out. You can follow me. If you like."

Esen nodded, and Fafnir closed his eyes.

"In," he murmured.

Esen drew in a breath, watching Fafnir's chest swell with hers. Fresh tears started in her eyes.

She had to let this go…

Worrying for Aisling, all these leagues away, would do nothing.

"Out."

Fafnir breathed out with his mouth, his chest slowly sinking. She did the same, releasing the breath slowly.

Let it go…

Fiona is with her.

"In."

Drawing in her breath, Esen fixed her gaze on the red light of the setting sun glimmering on the trunks of the Rooted Ones. A slight wind breathed in her ear and slipped by her to stir the needles above. Rain spattered like notes of a song. The Mother was with her.

"Out."

Let it go...

She released her breath. The light drew out the rich details of trunks, highlighting intricate weaving patterns of bark, all flowing together like a river.

"In."

Lidding her eyes half-shut, she lost herself to the rhythm. Soon Fafnir grew quiet, and they breathed in sync with each other. Birds twittered overhead, and still, the wind stirred about her, breathing soft.

She imagined herself hollow as she let loose a breath, filled only with the birds and the breeze.

At last, she opened her eyes. Fafnir looked back at her, a softness in his face.

"Did that help?" he asked.

"Yes," she said. She found her mouth was curved in a smile. "Thank you."

"I am glad." Fafnir dropped his gaze. "Esen, if we are successful and the fae Unite with the dryads once more... how will you spend your time?"

The word *if* rang in her mind.

She couldn't let there be an *if*. They would succeed, somehow.

"I will dance beneath the green dappled light, with my sister by my side, in time. We will lift our hands toward the canopy of leaves above us, unbroken, and know in our spirits all is well."

Fafnir sifted a hand through the needles on the ground. "I want that for you very much."

"What about you?" she asked.

His hand froze. He kept his gaze turned from her. "I want that also— to dance and know that all is well."

Esen tilted her head. She didn't know what she had expected him to say, but his answer surprised her. "You could dance with us."

He looked at her, his brow furrowed. "Thank you."

It wasn't a yes. It wasn't a no. It was an acknowledgment. She frowned as she became painfully aware of his lack of wings. Like an echo from a long-distant past, her parents' last words came to her. *"Do not place your trust in that which may deceive you."*

He did express a genuine care for her, and for all the forest. He had almost killed himself keeping Aisling alive. She didn't understand.

"Fafnir," she said. She knew the question made him uncomfortable, but she had to ask. "Why is it that you haven't United yet? Really?"

Fafnir flinched. He rose to his feet. "You heard my answer already."

"I know," she said. But it didn't align with what he was asking of those around him. "Why didn't you do it before, when you were one hundred?"

He was stiff as a reed. "It took me time to see the danger the forest was in."

"So you were one of the fae who let their hundredth year go by without Uniting, because of the New Law?"

"Yes."

"And then it took you a thousand years to realize what had happened? We dryads were dying long before that."

A muscle clenched in his jaw. "Yes. I was a blind idiot."

Confusion spiraled within her. Then he had been like all the other fae of the Rath, willingly looking past the bodies of her kind for over a thousand years.

"When did you see it?" she asked, her voice low. "The danger?"

"When the flood hit," he said.

She bit back a retort. So he only noticed when his own life was in danger.

He was looking at her now, something akin to a plea in his eyes. "I will see this through with you, Esen. Please be assured of that."

"Do you care that we are dying?" she found herself asking.

"It hurts me," he said. She could hear it in his voice. "Like it hurts you."

Now she was even more confused. Was it fear that had kept him from Uniting when he was supposed to? But he couldn't have been afraid. The dryads were not dying then.

She thought again of his reasoning for not Uniting now. Did he think himself that important, that the mission could only be done through him? That if he died, no other could save the forest in his place?

314

"Okay," she said. She didn't know what else to say.

The sun had long since set below the horizon. Dusk reigned, darkness settling in. A chill was in the air. Fafnir twisted to pull a pelt off his back, and laid it on the ground some distance from her. He stretched himself out on it, staring at the sky.

Esen laid down, curling into herself. Her thoughts clogged in a tangle. She pictured Fafnir walking past the bodies of her kind, holding his immortality to himself.

As the wail of that sea faerie screeched in her mind.

WIND BATTERED FAFNIR'S FACE, stinging his eyes. He was flying over the sea, flapping mechanical wings affixed to his arms. He'd improved his childhood conception of floating with mayapple plants into fully functional wings of cloth and wood. The fierce wind should have battered him into the sea, but somehow, it did not touch him. He flew on.

Endless blue surged beneath him. Sea, sea, and more sea.

He looked up and started. Green land stretched just ahead.

He'd done it. He'd really found a new land.

He dove down, adrenaline racing through his veins. He flitted onto the grassy turf and folded in his wings. Rooted Ones surrounded him, their branches scraping the sky, a dry rustling in their leaves.

No. This wasn't a new land. He'd been here before, looked up at these exact dryads. He was back in the land of the Mother.

There were no other lands. Just this one, where it was demanded he give up his immortality.

He could never be free.

A ragged cry escaped him. He whipped out his dagger and stabbed at the trunks of the Rooted Ones, red in his eyes, gasping. Then a sickening squelch startled him. His father looked back at him, his eyes wide with

315

fear. Fafnir's white-knuckled hands gripped the dagger hilt, dripping with hot, sticky blood.

The blade was buried in his father's chest. No, not his father.

Himself.

He had pierced the blade into his own chest.

Pain radiated like fire, tearing through his veins. Fafnir fell to his knees, clutching at the ground. All around him, the Rooted Ones were bleeding where he'd stabbed them, dark-red blood pooling together with his own, staining the green grass. A hot breath prickled the back of his neck.

"Have you found your serenity?"

A strangled scream tore from Fafnir. He bolted upright, breathing heavy.

Silver moonlight dappled the trunks of cedar dryads. Crickets hummed a steady rhythm. To his right, Esen lay on pine needles, curled into herself.

Fafnir pressed a hand to his chest. No knife. No blood. Just his heart within, hammering like a drum. He groped for his belt strewn in the grass and felt the outline of his dagger, sheathed safely where it belonged.

It was just a dream.

He shot up and paced in a tight line. He needed to sleep. They were going to appeal to those sea fae tomorrow; he needed his full capacity of thought. Maybe if he kept walking, he could exhaust himself enough to sleep once more.

Why had he dreamt such a thing? Was it with a knife that his father had killed himself?

Why had the dream changed to reveal the knife in his own chest?

Fafnir rattled his head. Stop it, stop it. He sought for the sequence of life, but the numbers slipped away.

A wind shivered through the leaves of the Rooted Ones. Raindrops scattered about him. He tilted up his head. Their trunks scraped the sky far, far above.

Every one of them had once Walked the land like Esen. Now, they were all Rooted, waiting for a faerie. But they had waited most of their lives. If nothing changed, they would all die soon, with no faerie and no children; no legacy to leave beyond them.

And here he was, asking other fae to Unite with them.

Without lifting a finger to help them himself.

He dug his nails into his scalp. What was he doing? What was he *doing*?

Esen had every right to question him.

"Fafnir?"

He started. Esen's head lifted, concern in her eyes. His stomach pinched. She wasn't supposed to see him like this. She knew too much about him already. He racked his brain for a response, but nothing came to him.

"Can I help?" she asked.

He ran his hands through his hair, his eyes burning. "You can't," he said.

She shifted her hands beneath her chin. It would be... comforting, perhaps, to sleep curled in her hands. Safe from the rain, enshrouded in her kindness...

But how could he take of her kindness when he had caused her so much pain?

He stepped back from her. "I'm sorry. Please go back to sleep."

She drew toward him instead. "You are distressed."

It was the same thing Isolde had said to him. Did he wear his emotion that clearly? He was making too much of a scene. He had to diffuse her.

"I couldn't sleep," he said. "I will be okay."

She kept looking at him, too closely.

"I'm going to walk myself to sleep," he said. That was a stupid way to put it. "If I'm not back earlier—at night, I mean—I'll be back in the morning."

Without waiting for a reply, he spun and strode away.

Sáile Cove

Dock

Black Maw

Key

- Center hut
- Home
- Boat

CHAPTER 36: THE SEA FAERIES

Rain drummed into Esen's face, the sky a dull gray. She blinked rapidly, pushing herself up on one elbow. Fafnir lay on his pelt not far from her, his eyes closed, his chest slowly rising and falling.

The memory of the night before struck her as though it had been a dream. His vague, tense answers to her questions, his frantic sleeplessness... She looked for the insect he had killed, but she couldn't see it. Good. He must have eaten it.

She rose, trying to rustle her branches as lightly as possible. Fafnir opened his eyes and was on his feet in a moment. He strapped on his belt, rolled up his pelt, and hooked it on.

"Are you ready?" he asked.

Esen frowned. "Did you sleep?"

"No," he said. "I'll be fine."

Dark shadows bruised under his eyes. He didn't look fine. But he was already walking toward the shore, so she followed.

Soon they broke out from the shroud of the Rooted Ones. Esen squinted ahead, shielding her eyes from the rain with her hand. The sea was gray like the sky, mist rolling off the white foam.

She couldn't see any faeries.

"Let's look where we saw them," Fafnir said. She walked with him down the shore. The sand sank beneath her, squishing around her feet, the water cool and bitter against her bark.

A shallow cliff face surged ahead with more forest growing upon it. Gray and black rocks clustered where the sand met the edge of the cliff. She noticed a sandy path trailing up where the ground rose among the rocks. Fafnir must have seen it too—he headed toward it. As they followed the path, she heard voices above. They had a strange echoing quality to them, as if they came from beneath the ground.

At the top of the path, she halted. A little village was tucked into the side of the cliff. Stone huts with roofs of rush were built neatly in a circle following the cliff line. At the center of the clearing, a stone firepit was dug into the sand. A wooden framework was built over it; for putting things over the fire, most likely. Skins circled the firepit. She counted twenty-four in all.

Voices echoed behind her, and she turned. A massive cavern cut into the cliff gaped open before her. Rows of lamps along the ceiling illuminated the way in. Toward the back, she glimpsed a mass of faeries clustered around and beneath a massive boat carved from red cedar. Unlike the little riverboats she'd seen that could hold a few faeries at most, this one towered far above them. A crisscrossing pattern of wooden stakes supported the boat's belly. The highest point of the boat faced her, the boards tipped up like the curve of a bird's beak just shy of the cavern ceiling. A dragan-like face protruded out, an intimidating fierceness in its gaze.

"That's a massive boat," she whispered to Fafnir.

"The largest I've ever seen," he whispered back, wonder tinging his voice. "And very well crafted."

There was only one reason to build a boat like that. "Do you think they plan on journeying out to—"

She stopped. The faeries were looking up one by one, ceasing their work. The ones on the top of the boat swung off, while the ones beneath ducked out. They headed toward them. Their skin tones ranged from the differing blues of the sea, to foam white, to the pinks and blacks of the shells dotting the sand. They wore loose garments of kelp and woven cotton, with bones and shells about their ears and throats. Their faces were hard, crusted with sand.

One light-blue faerie strode ahead of the rest. He wore a skirt of kelp pinched at his waist by a band of black gleaming shells, and nothing else, save for a brown tooth dangling from his neck by a cord.

"Do you like ogling at funerals?" he said as he approached them.

"I apologize," Esen said. "We did not mean to intrude."

The faerie's eyes slid toward her, before looking back at Fafnir.

"As Esen said, we merely happened upon your funeral," Fafnir said. "That aside, we have come here with a message that concerns you greatly. Are you the leader of these fae?"

"We have no leaders here," the faerie said. "We have done away with such concepts. We are a humble gathering of sea fae by the Sáile Cove. But come, we have rudely skipped introductions. My name is Bedwyr. Yours?"

"I am Fafnir, and this is Esen."

Bedwyr did not look at her. There was an intentionality behind it that rubbed her like salt.

"Now tell us this concerning thing, Fafnir," Bedwyr said. "We will spare you a moment."

The rest of the fae gathered around them, their eyes narrowed. The strong odor of fish followed them.

"How has your fishing yield been the past few hundred years?" Fafnir asked. "Have you noticed a lack of any particular species, or a decline in available food overall?"

"I thought you had something important to say," said a faerie in the crowd.

Fafnir's ears twitched. "Then you have not experienced any lack?"

"What he means to say is that our time is rather valuable," Bedwyr said. "We would prefer you get to your point."

Esen grimaced. They were so coarse.

"Very well," Fafnir said stiffly. "I suspect you were affected by the flood that occurred last spring. Perhaps it damaged your homes, made the ocean wild and dangerous —"

"Ah," Bedwyr said. "Did you come to tell us we should be afraid because the forest will fall apart soon?"

Fafnir narrowed his eyes. "Yes."

"Then you've wasted your time and ours," Bedwyr said. "We know that already." Bedwyr crossed his arms, studying Fafnir. "Has the queen had a change of heart? Is she sending out messengers like you to tell us of our doom?"

"You know as well as I do she will never change," Fafnir said, a coldness in his voice. "Tell me what you know. This is a matter of life and death. It is worth your time."

A crooked smile twisted Bedwyr's face. Esen liked it no better than his words.

"If you insist. I find it interesting, Fafnir, that you are invested in this affair. Few of the land fae seem to know what's going on. By the Rath Síoraí, they like to talk of living forever here without the dryads, but that's a load of fish guts. That flood happened because too many dryads have died and taken their protective roots with them. Isn't that what you wanted to say to us?"

"Effectively, yes," said Fafnir.

Bedwyr's smile grew wider. He began to pace, gesturing with his hands. "We caught on to the danger in the past hundred years. Since then, we began work on the Sióg Síoraí. She is a beauty, isn't she? She is the result of the very best of our skills and ingenuity, sharpened over thousands of generations of the craft. And she is nearly finished. Soon we will set sail and leave this land behind, taking our immortality with us."

A rustling sound caught Esen's attention. The storm-gray faerie with kelp hair shuffled out of one of the huts carrying a basket of fish. Her little child twirled at her feet with the lightness of a summer gust. The faerie met her gaze. Her chin quivered, a shadow blackening her expression. Her skin was sagged with age. She looked separate; almost like a different creature than the other fae, with their smooth, toned skin.

The faerie dropped her basket with a thud in the sand, the fish scattering. She approached them with stunted, almost pained steps.

This faerie had just lost someone dear to her. But there was something deadly in her face as she looked at Esen. A strange rush of fear coursed through her.

"You are risking your lives on a fantasy," Fafnir was saying. "How do you know for sure—"

"Get out!"

Esen flinched. The storm-gray fae was looking up at her—speaking to her only.

"Get out, I said! We won't help you. We are sick of your kind."

Esen shuddered. She stepped back, her hand flying to her chest.

Fafnir rushed between her and the storm-gray faerie, throwing his arms wide.

Bedwyr strode over to the faerie and whispered in her ear, but she shoved him back. "I mean what I said," she growled. "Get her out. I can't stand to look at her."

Bedwyr beckoned to the other sea fae. A few of them ran over, hooked their elbows around the faerie's arms, and pulled her back toward the hut. She began to scream and wail, her words incoherent.

"Sorry about that," Bedwyr said, turning back to Fafnir. "Morgan's rather out of it. She lost her husband, Hedrick, as you saw. His dryad was eaten from the inside out by an infestation of bark beetles. The loss has been hard for her."

Morgan disappeared inside the hut. Her sobs, though quieter, reached her still. Esen fidgeted with a hazelnut ripening near her ear. Hurt and confusion writhed in her.

Fafnir glanced up at Esen, concern in his face, before stepping back toward the other fae. "As I was saying, you cannot know for sure that there are other lands out there. It is a deadly risk. This land still has time to heal. You will be far more assured of your life by staying here and Uniting, restoring the balance."

Bedwyr cocked an eyebrow. "Your lack of wings suggests otherwise."

Esen stiffened. Fafnir had walked himself into a trap. He had spoken the truth, but his own behavior suggested the opposite—that death was a close and terrifying threat if one United. It would only affirm the sea fae's beliefs.

Fafnir looked at the ground, rolling his jaw.

"Here, death is a guarantee," Bedwyr said, leaning toward him. "But upon the sea, there is a chance. We will brave that chance."

Fafnir wasn't responding. Esen curled her fingers into fists as anger boiled up from deep inside her, heating her veins.

She wouldn't stand by and take this.

If Fafnir couldn't, she would speak up for her people.

"What more do you hope to glean from life by living ten thousand years, a hundred thousand, forever?" she cried. "I met an oak in the mountains who had lived for thousands of years. She was utterly content within herself. She had done all she wished and knew death would come soon and fold her away. Tell me, what will you do with all those years if you reach another land? Dance, sing? Make more boats? Why isn't a thousand years of those things enough? And isn't the legacy you leave behind the most important of all? If my parents' faerie hadn't United, I wouldn't have been born. My sister wouldn't have been born. I am forever grateful for that. What will all your years be worth?"

The faeries stared at her, their faces as cold as the sea.

"Answer me," she demanded, "or do you not care for anyone but yourselves?"

Finally, Bedwyr said, "That's a nice sentiment, but you're missing the point. You will never get enough fae to Unite in time. This forest is doomed to die, probably within a few hundred years. Any children we might have would die with us. It is not a question of how many years we get to live; it is a question of living at all."

"It just so happens we get to live forever, too," said another fae, with a pointy grin.

Esen faltered, confused. Was that true? Would they get to live forever?

"It's been nice chatting," Bedwyr said, giving Fafnir a final look. There was something odd in the way he looked at him that she couldn't understand. Fafnir did not meet his gaze. At last, Bedwyr turned toward the cave. "But we have work to do."

The rest of the fae began to leave with him, but Esen hadn't finished. She curled her fists tighter.

"What about all the souls you are leaving behind?"

Bedwyr threw a look over his shoulder, utter disinterest coating his face. "You think we can build a boat big enough for everyone?"

They disappeared back inside the darkness of the cave. Esen stared after them, her chest heaving, before storming back down the path. The waves murmured quietly.

Fafnir walked up to her. "He is not wrong. But he is not right, either. It is both. We could all die very soon, or we could all live. We are simply playing riskier bets with chance the longer things continue as they are."

Esen twisted a leaf by her ear with her thumbs. "Then we must try to win as many to our cause as we can, as quickly as possible."

Fafnir nodded. He tilted his head up at her. "Esen, I am sorry. Are you all right?"

She shook her head, a sigh shuddering from her branches. She looked back up the path, digging her fingers into her palms.

"Do you want to leave?" he asked. He wore that look of concern again. It was still strange to her, to see emotion plain in his face.

Esen crouched down, wrapping her arms around her legs. She tried to place her emotions in a neat box and lay them aside, to evaluate what truly had happened, but her feelings lingered beneath her bark, burning through her.

Morgan's words echoed in her ears...

She lost her husband because of his bond to his dryad. In the rawness of her grief, she must have come to despise his dryad, and all dryads, in turn.

"It would be easy to leave," she murmured. She traced a pattern in the sand. "But then they will have won. I think... I want to try to talk with Morgan. And her child."

"She spoke horribly of you," Fafnir said.

"Yes, but I can tell she is deeply hurt, and the other fae are not comforting her."

"You don't have to do this. She is a porcupine; I fear she will only wound you more."

Esen curved the tip of the symbol in the sand. She straightened. "All the same, I want to try. And if I let this break me, how will I stand before thousands who shun me at the market?"

"That is strong of you," Fafnir said. "You are sure?"

Esen nodded firmly.

"Okay. I will work alongside them on their boat and see if any paths open up to me."

She smiled faintly. "Thank you, Fafnir."

Whoever he was, whatever his personal motivations were...

He was always kind to her.

"Let's regroup tonight at the circle of cedars," she said.

How to make a dryadic flute

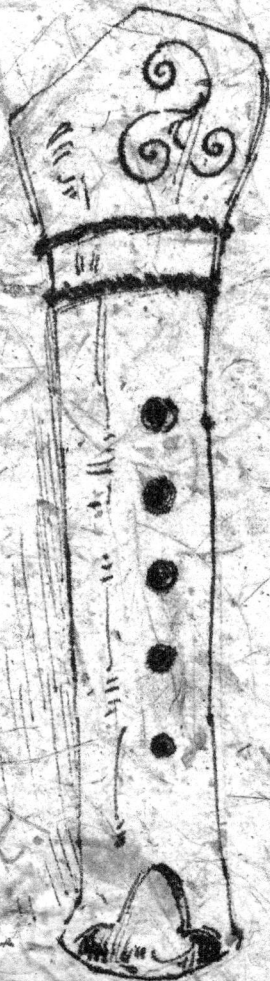

1. Boil the bone for one sun in a water and vinegar solution
2. Scrape clean
3. Smooth with sanding stone
4. Carve the blowing notch
5. Saw off the bottom in alignment with desired pitch
6. Feel out a comfortable place for holes and drill

In a traditional dryadic flute, there are five holes representing the five points of the Trinity of Unity.

Tools

1. Knife
2. Saw
3. Sanding stone
4. Drill
5. File

Recommended bones:

Mouse or vole femur - traditional sound

Chaffinch or woodcock ulna - light, airy sound

Bat tibia - best echo

Dryadic Traditions

CHAPTER 37: DIPLOMACY

With a nod to Esen, Fafnir walked back up the path. He hoped she would fare all right. Morgan's hatred had been venomous.

Something had grown in Esen in the mountains… or maybe it had been in her all along, and he had not realized it. She was childlike, but she was not a child. She had not only spoken back to the fae that despised her, but had somehow preserved a heart for them, if that were possible. If he had been itemized and rejected like that, he would have left. It wouldn't have been worth his time.

But it was important for her to keep trying.

She had too much heart. Or did he have too little?

He glanced at the village as he passed but did not see Morgan or her child. He approached the cave. The fae were back at work as though they had never been interrupted.

Keeping to the shadows just within the entrance, he studied the boat. A series of planks and posts held it off the ground. Once again, its sheer size impressed him. Its length could hold a little over a hundred fae if they lay from stern to bow.

Fafnir blew air out the side of his mouth. They *could* fit more on their boat. About seventy-six more, fairly comfortably.

There were only twenty-four of them; they must have built it bigger to better withstand the force of the waves, particularly the breakers just off the coast. That was where most ships sank—where the fae watching on the shore could either weep, or laugh in irony.

The boat was nearly complete. They would not take him on as merely another common worker.

He would need to make himself invaluable.

Through the dim light, he squinted beneath the boat. No keel. Just as he'd expected.

That was his way in.

Holding his spine straight, he strode within and shook his head of the rain. Bedwyr was lifting a plank from the ground and resting it across his broad shoulders. Fafnir approached him. A few other faeries looked up, their brows furrowed. Bedwyr followed their gaze and turned to look at him, a crooked smile growing on his lips.

Fafnir's ears drew back. He didn't like that smile.

"You have a long journey ahead of you," Fafnir said, before Bedwyr could speak. "You will want your boat to be as swift and true as she can be. I wish to help you."

Shifting the weight of the wood, Bedwyr brushed past Fafnir. Fafnir strode forward until he walked in step alongside him.

"You are a land fae," said Bedwyr, keeping his eyes fixed ahead. "You know nothing of our craft."

When they reached the boat, Bedwyr dropped the plank in the sand and began to arrange it alongside a stack of others. His back faced Fafnir, though his ears were turned toward him.

"You have a fairly vee-shaped hull," Fafnir began. "Which is good, but you can maximize stability by adding an adjustable keel that projects outward from the hull. In shallow waters, you can fold it in to cross, and unfold it again after."

Bedwyr straightened, his eyebrows raised.

He was reaching him.

"A water ballast will help too. I assume you will be tying rocks to the bottom to help hold down the weight in the water?"

"Naturally," Bedwyr said, crossing his arms.

"A water ballast will strengthen that support," Fafnir said. "Keep a tank in the hull. You can fill it when sailing in deep waters, and then empty it, as well as raise the keel, to sail through shallow waters. You will be more stable in deep waters, and have a smoother course in the shallows. You can use it to adjust your speed as well."

That smile crept back on Bedwyr's face, but there was warmth in it now. Before Fafnir could shirk away, Bedwyr clapped him roughly on the back. Fafnir grimaced. His skin tingled.

"That's good," Bedwyr said. "That's very good. Show me."

Fafnir pulled out his journal and pencil and thumbed through to a blank page. He began to sketch out the design.

"Are you *drawing* it?" Bedwyr asked.

Fafnir halted his pencil. "Yes. Don't you use illustrations to map out your designs?"

Bedwyr's face pinched with a squished smile, his eyes buried in his skin. "That's silly," he said. "Why would you do that?" Gesturing to him, Bedwyr stepped up to the boat. "Show me with your hands."

Fafnir twitched his ears. He put the journal away and approached the boat. The sea fae paused in their work, their expressions stern.

Watching.

Fafnir ducked beneath the boat. Its broad belly formed a ceiling. He frowned at the layering of the planks. Clinker style, with nails to hold them in place, they were laid with remarkable finesse and efficiency. He mapped the boat in his head. If he had the middle fourth of the boards taken out to make a chamber for the keel, and attached it with a series of gears so it could swing with ease...

Then he'd increase their efficiency by tenfold, and have it done before sunrise. He could return to Esen before the end of the day.

Fafnir explained his plan to them. "I'll need some spare planks and cutting tools, and I'll need to get up into the boat."

The sea faeries stared at him, unmoving.

At last, Bedwyr nodded to them. "It's a good idea. Let's see how he does it."

"We are not fools," said a tall, sand-colored fae. "You are doing this to gain our favor. It will not work."

Fafnir forced a smile. "I appreciate your honesty." He gestured toward the boat. "Let's get this done."

As he shouldered a plank from the pile, he glanced behind him. Past the cave opening, he could see Esen's silhouette by the shore.

What was she doing there?

329

He hoped she was well.

Frowning, he wiped the residual rain from his face with one hand and walked toward the boat.

Esen hummed deep in her throat as she walked along the shoreline. The rain bounced off her leaves, streaming from her branches. It provided a steady hum behind the push-pull murmurs of the waves. A mist curled over the horizon.

She would go to Morgan in a moment, but she just wanted a moment alone first, to still her thoughts and let the song of the ocean soothe her.

As the water pulled back, she crouched and put a hand in the sand, rubbing a little blue shell. Then the waves rushed over her hand, cool and salty. White foam bubbled and frothed with a quick, light sound like the rain.

"That's how I found my wind jelly."

Esen started. Morgan's little child stood beside her. Her golden hair was braided in thick knots, with pieces of little shells poking out wherever they could fit. A smile was on her face, but her eyes looked quiet and thoughtful. Though she was drenched, she seemed entirely unaware of it.

A pool of dazzling blue liquid oozed in the child's hands. Curling up from the blue was a thin, gelatinous material that folded at its triangular point like the ear of a pine marten.

She could see the ocean through it.

"I held out my hand like that," the child continued, "hoping something pretty would fall into it. Just when I was thinking of giving up, the sea left this wind jelly in my hand. I was so happy. Daddy said it was a gift from the Mother." Her coral-pink eyes grew red and swam with tears. "I miss him."

Esen offered her a hand at once, which she hugged, rubbing her face on her palm. She reminded her of Aisling. Innocent, and tinged with a sorrow that should have never befallen her.

"What is your name, child?" she asked.

The child looked up at her, her eyes still wet. "Róisín."

"I am sorry, Róisín." It wasn't enough. What else could she say?

Róisín rubbed at Esen's hand a little longer, messing up her braids. At last, she pulled back and wiped her arm over her face. She held out the wind jelly.

"I want you to have it."

Esen shook her head. "The Mother gave that to you."

Róisín began to extend Esen's fingers out. She placed the wind jelly in her palm. It felt cool and wet as the sea.

"Take it," she said, "as an apology from my people."

Esen's spirit fluttered. She closed her fingers gently on it. "Thank you."

Róisín smiled. She fluttered about, humming.

"How did you find me?" Esen asked.

A big, toothy grin spread over Róisín's face. "You're hard to miss. You're so tall."

Esen laughed. Róisín spun in a little circle.

"Róisín," Esen said. She drew in a deep breath and released it. In, out. "Could you take me to see your mother? I want to speak with her."

A sober look came over Róisín's face. She grew still. "Mother is not well right now. I don't think she would want to see you, although she should want to."

"I know," Esen said. "I want to speak with her all the same. I want to see if I can help her."

Róisín stared at her toes. "Were you scared of her earlier, when she said mean things to you?"

Esen thought of the venom of Morgan's fury. How she had never even met her before, yet she had already been denied and despised by her.

But it wasn't that she hated *her*, specifically.

She hated her kind as a whole.

"Yes," she said softly.

"My mother's not scary," said Róisín. "She's just very sad and confused." She twirled a strand of her hair, her brow creased.

"Will you take me to her?" Esen asked.

Róisín nodded. "Okay." She spun, the shells in her hair clattering, and skipped away up the path toward the village.

As Esen followed her, she remembered the wind jelly still in her palm.

"Wait a moment!" she called after Róisín.

Bending over in the sand, she found a conical shell sharpened to a fine point at one end. She used it to pierce a tiny hole through the ice-like flap at the top of the jelly. She undid the cord around her neck and strung the jelly through it. It clinked against her bone flute.

Róisín stood not far ahead of her, swaying on the balls of her feet as though gravity had no hold on her. "Play your flute for her. She'd like that."

Róisín skipped away again. As they drew near the village, Esen looked within the cave. A mass of faeries crowded around the boat, working in ways unknown to her, like they had been when she first arrived.

She glimpsed Fafnir among them. He knelt in the sand, carving a careful line into a plank of oak. Bedwyr and several other faeries stood round him, watching. His lips were pressed tight, his face streaked with sand. He had been her close companion for almost half a year. But now he looked almost indistinguishable from the sea fae, with the same calculating coldness in his face. His words from the night before flooded back to her.

He had lived for over a thousand years before he had met her. She only knew a surface of him. Beneath lay infinite depths... like the deep, deep ocean.

Did she even know him at all?

Róisín stopped outside the hut where Morgan had been before. As Esen approached, she heard the sound of muffled sobs within.

It seemed she was always weeping.

Closing her eyes, Esen put her flute to her lips. She found herself playing the melody that had moaned among the leaves of the Rooted Ones as she had wept over her parents. A tremor passed through her, and tears gathered in her eyes. To steady herself, she turned and kept her gaze on the sea.

Esen started as a figure stepped out from the darkness of the interior. She ceased her song. Morgan stood with one hand on the door. Her dull green hair was matted into thick knots, her eyes sunken.

"Keep playing," Morgan rasped.

Esen looked back out at the sea. She flowed through the song like a river, sometimes speeding parts, and sometimes pausing long, breathing slow and deep. At last, she reached what felt to her an end, and looked over to see Morgan leaning against the doorway, her face in her hands. The silence stretched on until she lowered her hands to reveal eyes red and raw.

"Let me see —" She broke into a rattling cough. Róisín hurried over to her with a little ceramic jug. Morgan tilted the jug to her mouth, her throat pulsing. She wiped the water with the back of her fist and handed it back to Róisín.

"Let me see that," she said again.

Esen untied the flute from its cord and laid it in the sand in front of her. Morgan stooped over it and ran her gnarled hands over its smooth surface. A quiet focus came over her face. Rising on shaky knees, she retreated into the darkness of her home. She returned carrying a small white flute, carved with five holes, in the dryadic fashion. She held it up for Esen to see.

"Hedrick learned to carve flutes from his dryad," said Morgan. "He was good, was he not?"

Esen crouched down to admire its craft. "Yes," she said. "Very."

"This is the last one of his I have." Morgan pressed the flute against her chest. When she looked up, a light gleamed in her sunken eyes. "Show me how to make them. I want my hands to work as his once did."

"I will gladly show you," said Esen. "Do you have a good-sized bone to work with?"

A crease formed on Morgan's brow. She shuffled back into her home. Róisín twirled and followed her in. Esen heard the dry clatter of bones and the two of them talking, until Morgan came back out holding a yellowed bird femur.

"This one," Morgan said, holding it out for her.

"Will it sound like a bird?" Róisín asked.

Smiling, Esen let her place the bone in her palm and held it up to study it. "In spirit," she said.

They found a stone-carving tool with a jagged edge, and Esen helped Morgan cut the ends of the bone. Then she guided her in shaping the surface of the bone with careful strokes of the knife. Morgan worked quietly, frequently pushing her matted hair away from her face, which was hard-lined and somber. Róisín lay on her stomach in the sand with her arms folded under her head, spellbound.

It was the perfect time to speak. But the silence lay so thick, as though the mist had curled inside the room.

"You do not have to answer," said Esen, forcing the words from her mouth, "but... do you feel alone, in your grief?"

Morgan cut short her stroke, just missing her hand. Coarse bandages covered her knuckles. She looked up at Esen, her eyes dark. "What do you think, dryad? Grief is loneliness. No other can ever understand it unless they've gone through it too."

Pushing back a lock of her hair, she went back to carving. "It's been over a hundred years since another one of us died. They don't know what to do with me. Already my body was decaying, and now my mind is too. I'm a reeking fish left out to rot."

Esen faltered, the words sinking deep in her spirit. "I am sorry," she said at last.

Morgan continued to carve, then paused and inspected the surface of the bone. She held it up for Esen to see.

"It is wonderful," said Esen. "You have a natural hand for it. Now we can add the holes. Five, if you would like the traditional dryadic arrangement. Feel with your hand where it would be comfortable to add them."

As Morgan felt the bone, Róisín piped up. "Why are there five holes?" she asked. "Why not six or eight, like our faerie flutes?"

"There is a hole for each Uniting pair of the Trinity of Unity," said Esen. "The first pair —"

Morgan tensed her shoulders like the hackles of a wild animal. Esen swallowed. She could say nothing more. Her culture was a thorn to Morgan.

Nodding, Róisín turned her focused gaze back on the flute.

They drilled the holes once Morgan had decided where she wanted them.

"Chipping the breathing notch is the hardest part," said Esen. "Relax into it, and try it out as you go to see how it's sounding. Just carve what comes most natural to you."

"I know you bear grief too, dryad." Morgan hunched over her bone, beginning to chip at the end piece. "I can see it in your eyes."

"Yes," Esen said, almost to herself.

Morgan stared hard at her before looking back at her work.

At last, Morgan laid down the knife and turned the flute slowly in her hands. She put it to her lips. Róisín rose and sat right by her, her eyes wide.

A light, airy melody soared. It sounded in part like the murmur of the waves, but coarse too, like salt. Tears streamed down Morgan's face, and the song faltered. Hunching over, Morgan clutched the flute to her chest and began to sob. Róisín wrapped her arms around her.

Esen looked away, twisting her fingers.

"It sounds just like one of Daddy's flutes," she heard Róisín whisper.

Morgan soon quieted, her hands still shaking. All at once, she flashed her head up and fixed Esen with sharp, penetrating eyes.

"I United along with my dear Hedrick because he told me it was the right thing to do," she rasped. "But if we had listened to the others…" She swallowed thickly. "He would still be alive now, and I wouldn't be living in terror that I will die soon too, leaving our only daughter alone in the world, without a parent to love her." Her chest raked for air. "The Mother has cursed you, dryad. You are born infected with death. When we Unite with you, we catch your disease. Our lives are shrunken to one desperate, gasping breath, and then we die and leave our loved ones tortured in grief. Without you, we could be happy. We could be free. Do you understand now?"

Esen stepped back, a tremor seizing her limbs.

"Do you understand?" Morgan's voice, raw and anguished, tore through her like a knife.

"Mother, don't make her sad," Róisín said, but her voice seemed to come from far away.

Esen's hand grasped at her heart chamber, where she had hoped one day a faerie would lie and be bonded with her. But she would kill her faerie in the process.

"Morgan," she said, lifting her chin. She blinked back the tears from her eyes. She tried to speak, to somehow express the tumult of feeling inside her, but her head was hot with shame.

"Get out," Morgan growled through clenched teeth.

Esen took a step back, and another, before spinning on her heels and darting away from the village.

Rain slashed against her as she crashed into the forest. Once within the circle of cedars, she crumpled to her knees, wringing her hands. The image of that carnivorous flower ran through her mind—how it waited for its victim to draw near before snatching it within its chamber and devouring it whole.

She rubbed at her arms, her nails scraping along the bark. The forest blurred, her vision fogging with tears. Like that flower, she needed to devour to live. When she was bonded with a faerie, her death could take a lover from his beloved, or a mother from her child.

When they could have lived forever without her.

But that oak in the mountains... what of her peace? Maybe she had no faerie who would die with her. Or if she did, what then? Was she heartless?

She glanced at her shoulder, where Fafnir had sat. Her mouth trembled, and she pressed the back of a fist to her lips.

Sometimes... she had hoped he would Unite with her.

But she would infect him.

In time, he might fall in love and have children, like Morgan. At any moment, a cruel winter or a flood could tear her up from her roots, and kill him in turn. Leaving his children without a father. Or, if both parents died, entirely alone. Like Aisling...

Her fist shook. She bit at it, suppressing a wail. She caught a glimpse of the trifold spiral of the *Aeonida* symbol on her wrist. She ran a finger over it, feeling the grooves.

The law had seemed clear as water then. Pure and simple, and beautiful.

The Mother willed it... why would it not be so?

She gripped at a piece of bark on her arm, bending it back until it hurt. She imagined all the Walkers of the land stripping at their bark, down to their very core, until they all stepped out as faeries. Small and light, they would all dance together as one, with no shadow of death or grief.

CHAPTER 38: THE STORM

Fafnir was bent beneath the hull, marking the slot where the keel would fold in with a stick of graphite, when he felt a rough tap on his shoulder. Jolting, he straightened up. Bedwyr stood beside him. "We don't work all day," he said. "Come and eat with us."

Without waiting for an answer, Bedwyr strode off, disappearing into the light outside the cave. The dull thud of stone on sand sounded all around him as the rest of the faeries dropped their tools and followed.

Fafnir tilted an ear toward the cave's ceiling. He couldn't hear the rain anymore. It must have stopped.

Now that he had ceased moving, a faintness came over him. He took a swig from his skein, drinking deep until he'd emptied it.

The work had felt good. Methodical; black and white. Though the way Bedwyr and the others hovered around his shoulder, watching his every move, irritated him.

Work buried talk, so he had said and observed little so far, but this gathering would be a vital opportunity.

He walked out of the cave, putting up a hand to shield his eyes from the blinding light. The sea fae were gathering around a pile of long sticks near the stone firepit. Each faerie bent and chose a stick as they laughed and joked with each other. Another faerie crouched by the firepit, striking a flint until a bright flame blazed, licking greedily at the pile of pine and cedar bark. They began to seat themselves on otter skins arranged in a circle around the fire.

He looked out over the huts and down at the shore, but he couldn't see Esen. Or Morgan and her daughter, either. Where could they have gone?

His skin crawled. He turned to see that every faerie was seated. And staring at him.

"We're not sharks," hollered Bedwyr, beckoning him over. "We don't bite."

A rough chuckle passed among the fae.

Fafnir stiffened his jaw. He snatched a stick and seated himself beside Bedwyr.

A faerie with skin the color of sand emerged from the hut carrying a ceramic vessel, his face strained with the effort. He wobbled forward and placed the vessel down at the ring. The faerie nearest him wrapped her feet around it and dragged it toward her. She opened it with a grin. From the top, she pulled out several sizable chunks of raw flounder. She speared them on her stick and passed the jar to the next faerie.

Bedwyr was chatting idly with the faerie on his right about installing the mast. Fafnir swiveled his ears, catching snippets of conversations around him. If they weren't talking about the boat, it was about the tide, or their fishing yield. Nothing unusual there.

Two faeries not far from him were speaking of the rain in hushed, worried tones.

"You see that sky?" whispered one of them. "It's going to come back. It might last for several more days."

Another faerie erupted in a loud, guttural laugh over some joke, drowning them out.

Fafnir frowned. The sky was gray; one flat haze. It looked like it would rain again soon.

If what they said was right, that was concerning.

Fafnir turned to Bedwyr. He waited for a lull in his conversation.

"Why do Morgan and Róisín not eat with you?" he asked.

Bedwyr's eyes slid toward him. "They're invited," he said, "but Morgan didn't want to come. Something about needing to be alone. We're doing what we can for her, but it's hard."

Fafnir nodded. "How was she like, before the... accident? Was she happier?"

Bedwyr picked at his teeth with a jagged nail. His eyes were ice cold. "Why do you want to know?"

He had hoped his question would slip by Bedwyr's guard. Evidently, it had not. He'd stabbed himself in the foot by revealing his motives already.

"I am simply curious," Fafnir said.

"As am I," Bedwyr replied, his gaze sharper than a hawk's.

Fafnir looked away from him, pretending to be interested in the conversation around him once more. One faerie was dominating everyone's attention with a story of how he'd once hauled a shark onto his boat.

"It was so big that my boat sank with him. I was lucky he didn't eat me."

"Oh rot, Llyr," said a fae on his right. She took her share from the jar and passed it on. "Last time you told us it was an angelfish, and it only weighed down your boat."

"I heard it was a bunch of crabs," said another faerie.

"Well, something made him come home drunk to me," said the fae beside the storyteller. They all laughed at this.

"Take some." Bedwyr held the jar out toward Fafnir.

Fafnir took it and laid in front of him. It was about half-empty now. Chunks of fish of all different colors, most with the skin still attached, were piled inside. He reached in, grabbed whatever piece came to his hand, and stuck it on his stick, then passed the jar to the next faerie.

Bedwyr tapped him on the shoulder. He held a flask out to him. Fafnir took it, his ears flattening. It reeked of strong liquor. He gave it back. "No thank you."

Bedwyr shrugged. "Your loss." He slugged a long draft, his throat pulsing, before pocketing the flask.

The fish vessel was put away once it had made its cycle. The faeries gave a unified cheer and leaned forward to hold their fish over the flames. The salty aroma of flesh mingled with the thick woodsmoke.

One faerie with shells smothering his throat and waist began to tap his feet in the sand. A song lifted from his throat. One by one, the faeries joined in the chorus. Their voices crashed and churned like the wild ocean.

"Burn, burn, flesh of the sea;
Crackle and pop! Blacken the bones,
To light the fire in our eyes,
Hey, ho! Hey, ho!"

They repeated the verse, growing louder each time as they spun their fish to burn them on all sides.

"Hey, Fafnir." Fafnir turned to see the faerie on his left grinning at him. The fire illuminated the jagged points of her teeth. Her skin was the dark green of the deep ocean, her irises pearly white. "I see you have a violin," she said. "Are you any good with it?"

Fafnir lifted his chin. "Would you like me to play?"

Grinning wider, the faerie laid her fish on the rack to burn, and had him do the same. She began to clap her hands to the beat of the chant, cocking her eyebrows. "Come on," she said.

Why not.

Fafnir took his violin out from its case and swung it in front of him. As he tuned it, her eyes studied every movement of his fingers. He rested the violin beneath his chin and closed his eyes. The world faded away.

Only sound reigned.

He listened carefully to the melody, memorizing its flow. At last, he struck his bow on the strings, weaving a playful jig that flowed in and out of their voices. It was as though he'd set them on fire. Their voices roared, feet slamming on sand and hands clapping in a frenzy. He slitted his eyes open to see several fae leaping about the edges of the circle, twirling in wild reels.

At last, their singing broke apart into cheers and laughter.

Fafnir lifted the bow, wiping the sweat from his forehead. He smiled in spite of himself, but shame pricked him at once.

He couldn't let his guard down.

A low hum rose above the laughter. The green faerie swayed her shoulders, her eyes closed. Her throat pulsed with a new melody. She began to sing, to herself at first, until it spread like wildfire around the circle and every mouth sang.

"The sky of gray, the sea of green;
The sand of grit, the rocks so black
'Twas our home forever on,
And loathe we are to leave.

But the tides they are a-changing now,
The black is gathering on the clouds.
A death wind moans within the trees
Counting to our demise.

So out upon the sea we go,
Mast unfurled, our eyes ablaze,
To seek new land upon its shores
Where we may laugh and sing more!"

Fafnir wove his violin among the melody, but when she came to the last verse, he faltered, slowing his notes.

He thought of Elouan's vision and frowned.

"Hey, ho. Hey, ho!" cried the rest of the fae. Cheers erupted all around, and they began to devour their blackened fish.

"You play so passionately, Fafnir." The sharp scent of kelp wafted over him. The green faerie was leaning toward him, her eyes gleaming. She sank her teeth into her trout and tore off the skin. "How did you get so good?"

Fafnir shirked back from her. "Practice."

"A lot, clearly. How old are you anyway?"

He twitched his mouth. She was certainly chattier than Bedwyr. He might learn something by playing along.

"How old are you?" he asked.

A smile crept over her. "I was just a year away from Uniting when the New Law was put in place. I've never looked back."

If he hadn't worked to change the law… then she could be dead now. *He* could be dead now.

"Your fish is black as coal," the green fae said. Fafnir started. He looked at the rack where he had left it, but he didn't see it there. She pulled it out from behind her back and shoved the stick in his hands with a wink. "Just kidding. I saved it for you."

Fafnir frowned. Was she… flirting with him?

This hadn't happened to him in over four hundred years, and the few times he'd feared something was happening, he'd quickly put an end to it. It was simply not an option. Not after all the pain he had seen his parents go through…

A hand waved over his face. He blinked, shrinking back.

"Hey, eat your fish," the green fae said.

He ate it to silence her. It tasted of hot embers and the salt spray of the sea.

"Now you have to answer about your age," she said.

He'd never made such an agreement. He took a breath, letting the air circle through him, cooling him. He had to remember the mission.

"Tell me," he said to her. "Do you really think you'll find something out there, upon the sea? Or do you think you're more likely to die trying?"

Her smile wavered. "Of course we'll find something."

"The evidence of hundreds of thousands of years weighs against you."

To his surprise, she leaned toward him rather than away. He had to bend his back to keep his face away from hers. An ice-like hardness was in her eyes; the same look Bedwyr had given him.

"Picture a fisher who has never caught any fish," she said, a low rattle in her breath. "He angles all his life. He has heard of fish, dreamt of fish, but he has never pulled one up upon his reel. Don't you think he would keep trying, until his dying breath, clinging to the hope that this time, of all times, he really will *finally* catch something?"

Her words spun in his brain. It was a foolish dream, born of pride and stubbornness.

But then hadn't he been seeking serenity all his life, only to have it constantly elude him?

"I have said my part," he said.

"And I have said mine," she hissed, finally drawing back from him.

He straightened his spine, breathing easier. He looked to the fae around him as their coarse laughter echoed off the cliffside. Their hands, sharp and calloused, tore into their fish, devouring even the little bones.

They were all like that fisher—stuck in their ways. His efforts were futile here. He'd stay until the sun set or when he finished installing the keel, whatever came sooner, and then he'd go back to Esen.

They could move on from here, on to the final stage of the plan…

Where the fate of the forest would be decided.

Soon all the faeries stood and threw their sticks in the fire. The flames leaped up and consumed them. A handful of fae lingered behind to tend to the fire and clean up, while the rest strode back to the cave. Fafnir followed them.

They resumed their work on installing the keel. Not long after, as though the Mother Wind had cleared the sky just for their meal, rain began to beat once again on the ceiling of the cave.

As the light filtering into the cave grew dim, they finished. Fafnir tightened the ropes tethering the keel to the pulley that would enable it to be pulled out and back in. He pulled on the ropes to demonstrate. "Out in deep waters to keep steady and power through; in when coasting through shallow waters, and to slow your pace in times of concern."

The sea fae stared at him, their expressions unreadable.

"The water ballast is easy," Fafnir added. "I've told you how to do it. That should only take a day or so to make."

Bedwyr walked up to him and clasped his shoulder, pulling him close. His hot breath prickled the skin of his neck.

"You don't plan on Uniting with that dryad, do you?" Bedwyr whispered.

Fafnir stiffened. The question rattled in his brain, confusing him. There had been so much care in Esen's face as she had looked at him the night before. Her entire being had been bent on trying to make sure he was okay.

He had always known the answer. Saying it aloud felt hideous, like retching up his insides for all to see. And he knew how much it would hurt her.

"No." The word escaped from him, scarcely audible.

Bedwyr made a strange noise in his throat that was half gurgle, half chuckle. "Thought so. Listen, Fafnir. We scarcely ever let in outsiders, but I think we could make an exception for you. We would have to hold a concession. I would vouch for you. If you are chosen, you could come with us, to a land of freedom."

A thrill rushed through Fafnir's veins. He ignored it, shrugging out from Bedwyr's grip and stepping back.

"Thank you," he said, "but I cannot."

Without looking back, he turned and left the cave. As soon as he stepped out, sheets of rain slammed into him. He put out an arm over his face and struggled down the path to the shore. He still couldn't see Esen anywhere. He could scarcely see anything with all the rain in his eyes.

He knew he would die if he went with them. Elouan's vision was a mere fantasy. They would embark toward the blue horizon and travel through sea, sea, and more sea, and then they would sink or starve, with no land in sight.

But wasn't it possible that some fae had found land out there and simply loved it too much to return to their homeland? Or loved their own lives too much to brave the journey once more? A wind howled, tossing the rain about wildly. He hunched against it, shivering. He couldn't think of that.

When he reached the cover of the pines, the rain lessened some. All was dark, as though the Rooted Ones had sucked the last of the light into themselves.

At last, he found Esen. She was lying stretched out on pine needles, staring up at the thin slivers of the sky.

Emotion knocked against his chest. She did not look well.

"Esen?" he said.

Her face turned toward him. Tears stood in her eyes.

"How did it go?" he asked, drawing toward her.

"We must leave first thing tomorrow," she said, her voice thick. "Unless it fared better with you?"

"No," Fafnir said. "We should move on."

Fafnir found his cloak where he had left it and threw it on his shoulders, drawing up the hood to shield his face from the rain. He crouched beside her. "Esen, how long have you waited here?"

She watched a worm inching through the mud. "I don't know."

He fidgeted with his fingers. "Morgan did not treat you well?"

"No."

"I am sorry."

Esen had rallied herself so bravely to try to help Morgan. Morgan didn't deserve her sympathy.

"We will still have the river and the mountain fae beside us," he said. "And Isolde will likely bring more fae with her."

Esen nodded. She turned her head back toward the sky. "Thank you," she murmured.

She grew still. Rain streamed from her branches, her eyes tightly closed. Her chest shuddered with her breath.

She had been hurt; more than he could know. She had lost the parents who raised her, her faerie, and so many of her kind. And now she had borne another's hatred of her very being.

A feeling pulled at his heart, urging him closer.

She needed comfort. She needed someone to assure her that her life mattered, that the lives of the dryads mattered, that Uniting was a good thing that helped create a culture of love and peace.

Why couldn't he do that for her?

Why couldn't he Unite?

He slipped a hand beneath his cloak, feeling his shoulder blade — where the wings would sprout. His other hand rested on his cheek. If he United today, and peered at his own reflection a hundred years later, how would he look?

There would be lines in his face, his eyes hollowed with the weight of time, with dry, withered hazel leaves extending from his back.

He would look just like his father.

A pressure seized his brain. His hands flew up to grip at his hair, his breath choked in his throat. His heart pounded, pounded.

He could *never* Unite.

When he found he could breathe again, he fumbled with the straps of the sleeping pelt and pulled it from his back, laying it some distance from Esen. But sleep refused to come. Adrenaline raced through his veins. He could still feel the stone nails in his fingers, the jolt in his arm as he swung the hammer. The ghost of the fire's heat, as though he still sat before it, with the green faerie smiling at him, her teeth gleaming as she tore the skin from her trout.

Bedwyr's breath on his neck as he whispered his offer.

Throwing back his blanket, Fafnir rose and paced. He rubbed furiously at his arms, but he could not get warm. The wind whipped about him, moaning.

347

The world flashed white, and black shadows snaked along the ground.

Lightning.

When his heart beat next, all was black again. A terrible boom shuddered the earth, like the sky was splitting open, tearing at the seams.

He quickly calculated. The rain had begun four days ago. It had been light for the first day, moderate for the next three, and now, a heavy storm.

If it continued like this for the next day and a half...

His breath hitched in his throat.

A flood was nearly certain.

He resumed his pacing, running a hand through his hair.

It had only been one year and two moons since the last flood, but so many dryads had died in the winter. If it flooded, it would be worse than the last one. Terribly worse.

He could still hear the sea in the distance...

He licked his lips. They were crusted with salt.

"FAFNIR... FAFNIR! WAKE UP!"

Noise. Chaos. Esen's face hovered above his, fear flashing in her eyes.

Starting up, Fafnir's head collided with hard wood. Gritting his teeth, he saw that he was encased within Esen's hands. Through the slits in her fingers, he glimpsed the rain tearing down in diagonal sheets. A crack of thunder sounded. Panic shot through him.

The storm was still raging.

"Fafnir, the sea faeries!" Esen cried. He could only just hear her above the wind. "They are putting their boat out to sea. We must stop them. Hold on."

She lunged forward, hurtling around the trunks of the Rooted Ones. He locked his arms around one of her fingers to keep himself from sliding. His heart pounded in his chest.

If they were willing to risk the ocean in such weather...

They must think the land's demise was threateningly near.

Through Esen's fingers, he soon saw them. Bedwyr and several other faeries were hauling up the mast of the boat as the rest scurried to throw supplies onto the deck. Frenzied shouts and commands rose above the din of the storm. Beside them, the waves heaved, flecked with white foam.

Like a mouth open to devour.

"Where is Morgan and her child?" a voice shouted.

"I don't know. There's no time!" cried another.

He gripped tighter as Esen lowered her hands. As soon as he leaped out, Esen darted toward the boat.

"Don't go!" she cried. "You will die!"

Fafnir ran after her as lightning flashed in the sky. The rain stung his face, his eyes. A cry of pain sounded ahead. Esen had slowed ahead, her face tight. One of her heavier branches had torn off, leaving a gnarled stub.

"Get back!" he cried, catching up to her. "I'll stop them."

He only caught a glimpse of her face, filled with worry through the pain, as he ran past. The wind nearly blew him off his feet like a sail. He fought it by digging his feet deep into the wet sand with every footfall.

Up ahead, the faeries were leaping in, beginning to push the boat off the sand.

"Stop!" he cried, but the wind stole his voice.

Bedwyr was still on the sand, standing by the ropes tethering the boat. He turned and narrowed his eyes in Fafnir's direction. He waved his hand like a beacon. His lips were moving. What was he saying?

"...on, Fafnir. Sail with us!"

His heart skipped a beat. The boat grew closer, closer.

He could leap in and sail with them. Leave behind all his fears, his pain.

He could finally be free.

But what of Esen? And Isolde? How could he abandon this land when he was the one who had cursed it in the first place?

He found himself faltering, skidding to a halt. Bedwyr stared at him, his face hard, before cutting the ropes. Bedwyr leaped in the boat, and it drifted out.

He had lost his chance.

The boat broke through the wild breakers, then steadied, a testament to its strength. As he watched, a terrible black wave reared its head behind them, sucking the waters into itself until it towered seven times the height of the boat.

It would kill them.

"No!" Esen's ragged cry tore through the terror of the wind. She hurtled forward, though many of her branches splintered and tore, scattering in the wind about her.

The wave crashed down. Several fae were swept overboard, screaming. The mast splintered as water pooled over the deck. He glimpsed flashes of limbs and heaving backs, fae working desperately to hurl the water overboard with buckets, but the boat continued to sink.

Esen reached the sea and threw herself in it, but the waves beat at her until she was pushed back onto the sand.

Screams split the air. The boat had vanished. Hands stretched toward the sky before disappearing into the sea.

A gust of rain slapped Fafnir's face. His stomach writhed.

Esen lay on the shore, struggling to rise. She looked so small, with so many of her branches broken...

He hurried toward her.

"Fafnir," she breathed as he neared her. Tears streamed down her face, mingling with the rainwater. She tried to speak more but choked on her words, burying her face in her hands. Her frame shook with sobs.

Foam frothed where the boat had sailed.

Black specks formed at the edge of his vision. His body convulsed until he hurled up a sticky mess on the sand—the remains of the fish.

He wiped at his mouth, the sand tilting toward him, everything tilting before his eyes.

"They are dead," he rasped.

He could have died too.

He toppled over into blackness.

ESEN CAUGHT Fafnir as he fell, cupping him in her hands. She pushed herself up, fighting through the pain, and turned to flee.

Morgan stood not far from her, her skin deathly pale. She clutched at Róisín's hand.

Esen's breath quickened. She had seen them, then, leaving without her, and dying...

Róisín buried her face in her mother's tattered skirt, her shoulders clenched. "Mommy, mommy," she cried. "The sea... I-it—"

Quick as an adder, Morgan tore her hand from her daughter's. Lunging forward, she seized a pebble with white knuckles and hurled it into the thrashing waves.

"May the sharks feast on your flesh!" she screamed into the wind. "All of you!"

She threw herself to the wet sand, tearing at her mangled hair, screeching and writhing. For a few terrible moments, Róisín tried to comfort her, but her mother ignored her. At last, Róisín sank to her knees, buried her face in her golden braids, and wept.

The sight rent through Esen's spirit. She approached cautiously, holding her hands steady. She could feel Fafnir breathing softly within. His chest pulsed against her bark.

She didn't know what she could say, but she knew that Morgan had lost everything. Everything except her daughter...

Róisín sprang up as Esen drew near and wrapped herself around her ankle, clutching tight.

"I'm so sorry, Róisín, dear," she whispered to her.

She approached Morgan.

"Morgan—"

"Leave me alone!" Morgan snarled, barring jagged teeth. Morgan's eyes flashed with fear as she looked at Róisín. She lurched to her feet and snatched Róisín's wrist.

"No!" Róisín screeched, fresh tears in her eyes. Morgan swept her off her feet and darted down the bank.

"Come back!" Esen cried after them, but they were already too far gone to hear.

Her chest heaved. Agony rent through her, her branches groaning and straining, as the wind grew fiercer. She hurried into the cover of the Rooted Ones. The wind lessened as she drew back from the sea. At last, she crashed through the forest. She threw herself on the lee side of two thick cedars wound together.

She sank to her knees, gasping. Fafnir was still unconscious. His eyes were closed, his brow pinched. It was safe from the wind here, but the rain still pounded into the ground. It had rained like this before, when the flood had happened.

Like a bolt of lightning, she thought of Aisling. A gasp caught in her throat.

She whipped around to the cedars. "Tell me of my sister, please," she choked. "Is she okay?"

"*We can feel a Walker wrapped around her,*" the cedars stirred in unison, "*shielding her from the wind and rain.*"

Esen's eyes widened. Was it Cillian? Or perhaps Tristan?

Either way, she was eternally grateful.

"But what of this storm?" she cried. "Is it going to kill us?"

"*Do not fear, Esen,*" said the oak. "*This is not the end of the forest. The Mother Wind will calm her rage soon. I feel it in the bones of the earth.*"

The world flashed white and black. Thunder boomed. Esen shook her head, stepping back.

If it continued like this, even that Walker couldn't save Aisling. The water would push up from beneath her like before, and... and—

She ran, holding her hands close to her chest to keep Fafnir steady. Her breath rattled in her throat. She kept seeing the boat sinking, sinking... hands reaching out from the waves as screams split the air.

As the sun reached its peak in the sky, the black clouds began to part overhead, revealing gaps of bright blue. The rain lessened until the fury died down at last. She approached a stream where the waters had swelled until they burst from the banks, but they only traveled a little farther from the stream. The wind moaned, weaving through the Rooted Ones, but the sound was soft now. Thoughtful.

Esen halted, her breath ragged. She listened to the murmur of the wind for a moment before bowing her head.

"Thank you, Oh Mother," she murmured. "Aisling is spared. She is spared..."

Feeling movement within her hands, Esen parted them.

Fafnir pushed himself up from his curled position, gazing at her. His eyes were heavy and feverish, his hair matted with white sand.

"Thank you." His voice shook as he spoke. He swallowed as though he meant to say more before looking away in silence.

Bedwyr had stayed on the sand, beckoning to him...

As though he were inviting him to join.

"The rain has stilled," Fafnir said at last.

"Yes," she said thickly. "It was only a passing storm. Fafnir, what happened? Did you speak with them?"

"No." He coughed, a rattle in his throat. "I couldn't reach them."

He hadn't said everything; she knew that somehow.

"You weren't thinking of leaving, were you?"

She regretted it as soon as it slipped out from her. She would rather have not known. But the way he looked at her, a tightness in his face, said it all.

Her hands trembled.

"Esen," he said. "It was stupid. I didn't—"

Her eyes swam with tears. "You promised you would stay. To see this through with me."

His throat bobbed. "I did stay."

She closed her eyes, struggling to slow her breath. At last, she brought Fafnir to her shoulder. When he had tied himself to her branch, she began to walk.

"What is the plan?" she asked, her voice quavering. She cleared her throat. "From here?"

But Fafnir was still gazing at her, his brows knitted. Finally, he looked away. "We will have time before the market. We can meet at Isolde's and execute our final steps from there."

Statute IX
Aon Mharú

IX. No faerie shall cause intentional harm to another faerie or dryad. Only exception is confirmed self-defense. In the classes of animals, insects, and plants, the harm must be conducted as either for self defense and/or for nourishment.

Statute X
Meas Muinín

X. No faerie shall harass another faerie or dryad or any other creature to the point that another is harmed by it.

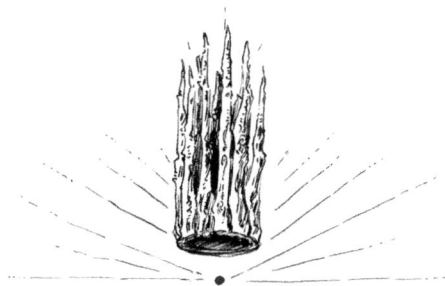

CHAPTER 39: VENGEANCE

Maeve leaned into the wind, her marten's quick breaths filling her ears. Her rangers rode behind her, thirteen-strong in all. Wynn rode on her left, leading the way. He wore a wild, toothy grin, his short green hair billowing about his ears like algae.

Just as she was growing mad with impatience, he had shown up in her palace with exactly the news she had feared. Fafnir *was* engaged in a very active mission to undermine her. And Niamh had helped him.

She had offered Wynn a year's supply of deer fat for his village as a reward, but he'd turned it down, asking to be one of her rangers instead.

She appreciated a fae who understood priorities. This mission would be the first of his training. She had no doubt he could make them bleed if she bid him to.

By the twilight, the smell of smoke thickened the air. Soon she heard voices, coupled with the warm aroma of cooked flesh.

Maeve nodded to her rangers and urged her marten through the undergrowth. A frog was turning on a pit above a bonfire. Over a dozen faeries were seated round it, laughing and joking, wings sprouted from their backs. She wrinkled her nose in disgust.

And there, bouncing a little child in her lap, sat Niamh. The firelight illuminated her, her skin a pale honey gold.

She was beautiful…

A faerie with deep-green skin and oak wings sat beside Niamh. The child was laughing, clapping her small hands into his outstretched palms. She scowled. That must be Rowan.

Gasps broke out as she rode into the light. The fae shot to their feet, rigid as reeds.

Wynn broke out beside her, glaring down at them. The rest of her rangers followed, forming a protective circle around her.

"Where is your leader?" Maeve demanded.

A well-built faerie stepped forward from the rest, adorned in bones and trinkets. "Good Queen Maeve," she said. "I am Korey, the chieftain. Forgive us; it is an unexpected meeting. Would you care to sit and share our meal? We could talk more comfortably that way."

"We can talk comfortably now," Maeve said. "I have heard you restored the Ancient Law among yourselves—that you will take away the choice of your kin. That is treason. The punishment for treason, as you well know, is death. But I would be willing to waive this punishment for you and your people, on one condition…"

Korey swallowed heavily. "And what is this condition?"

"Tell me everything you know about Fafnir and his mission."

Korey locked her jaw. A bead of sweat pooled on her forehead.

Niamh handed her child to Rowan, nodding to him, and stepped forward to stand beside Korey. She lifted her chin. "The New Law is about choice, isn't it? We have simply made one choice, and we will ask our kin to choose as we have. We are not a threat to you."

"Not a threat?" Maeve spat. Anger bubbled up inside her, seizing her bones. "Not a threat? You have restored a forbidden law. Did not Fafnir move on from here to try to get more faeries to join your death cult? You seek to take away my people's freedom."

The rest of the river fae stood and formed a bubble around Niamh and Korey—the same arrangement she had taken with her rangers. They were preparing to fight, then. At the edge of the Rooted Ones, she glimpsed Rowan trying to slip away with the child. She turned to her rangers, but Wynn had already darted forward. His marten lunged in Rowan's path, growling. He herded Rowan back to the others. Niamh glanced worriedly at the child in his arms.

"The forest is dying, Mother!" Niamh cried. "Can't you see that?"

She had spent such a long chasm of moons weeping, longing to hear that word from Niamh's lips.

Those days were over.

"I am not your mother," Maeve snarled. The words wrenched from her like knives. "I never was. You're a common brat with no royal blood. You may never call me that again."

Niamh flinched as though she'd been struck. Her lips flapped uselessly for a moment before she found her breath again. "Good Queen—"

She put a disgusting amount of emphasis on the "good." She *was* a good queen. So good that she'd give them no mercy, for the good of all fae.

Niamh continued. "Your people may be free, but they will die very soon. We want life. You are the one who is killing them by encouraging them to not Unite. You are enslaving them to certain death."

Maeve jerked her marten forward until her muzzle pressed against the front of Niamh's dress. Her hands spasmed, white-knuckled against the reins.

"Lies," she hissed. "You have swallowed Fafnir's lies hook, line, and sinker, all of you. I will not have you spread them like a disease."

She motioned to her rangers. "Kill them. Leave one alive for questioning."

Her rangers fitted their bows and fired. Arrows thudded into chests, bodies toppling. Deafening screams broke out. One faerie leaped into the air, flapping, but an arrow pierced through her wing. She fell to the ground in a heap.

Niamh was running. Maeve fired an arrow and pinned her dress to the base of a trunk. Before Niamh could pull the arrow out, Maeve leaped off her marten and seized her by the throat.

Niamh's eyes were wild with fear, a rabbit caught in the talons of a raptor.

She was her nightmare.

Hot tears obscured Maeve's vision. She swiped them off her face with her free hand and gripped Niamh's throat tighter, digging the points of her nails against her skin.

Niamh would be the most valuable one to question. She had conspired with Fafnir longer than all of them. She had lived in Maeve's house, eaten her bread, taken her love for granted, and tossed her for scraps when she was done with her.

Niamh deserved to hurt.

Her blade hissed as she drew it out. She pressed the tip of the blade against Niamh's torso, right between her ribs.

"You will speak," she growled, "or I will make you speak."

Niamh's lips quivered, her face ghost white. She had looked like this —pale, helpless, utterly vulnerable—when she had found her all those years ago, on her birth mother's deathbed.

Maeve's hands sweated, the blade suddenly heavy.

Could she do it?

Could she hurt her daughter?

But she had to save her people. She had to save —

A force cracked down on her head, and she tumbled to the ground.

Through a throbbing haze, she glimpsed Rowan wrench the arrow out of Niamh's dress with one arm, holding the child in the other. He took Niamh's hand and darted with her into the darkness of the Rooted Ones.

Arms lifted Maeve up. "Queen! Are you all right?"

"Unhand me," Maeve snapped. The arms slipped off her. She staggered, just catching her balance as the world reeled like a drunken dream.

A rock rested at her feet, the corner wet with blood. Her blade lay beside it.

He'd hit her with it. Because she had been about to drive a blade between his lover's ribs.

His face had been so soft with care as he'd looked at Niamh. Ian used to look at her like that, a long, long time ago...

Maeve squeezed her fist tight. Her brain pounded against her skull.

The village blurred into view. Bloodied bodies lay strewn across the grass, their green wings limp. Their leader lay among them, blood spilling from a gash in the side of her head.

Her rangers flocked around her. One held a Winged One by the shoulders. Good. They had kept one alive.

"Wynn, fetch my blade," she barked.

He stooped to grab it and handed it to her, his face grim as a moonless night.

358

Maeve turned to face the river faerie. She was a slight, short thing, with yellow-green skin like stale pond water. She reeked of fear.

Maeve twirled her blade. "Make this easy for me," she said to her.

The faerie trembled like a leaf and fell to her knees. "I beg on behalf of the Mother," she gasped. "We just want peace."

"So do I," Maeve hissed. "If you love death so much, then you will talk freely. I will kill you very, very slowly if you refuse me."

The faerie swallowed. "Okay," she whimpered.

She told the queen all.

Fafnir planned to lead a rally at the World Market. It was a simple plan; absurdly simple. It was bound to fail, even if she didn't lift a finger. But she would.

She would ruin him.

And in the past year, a strange
faerie with a violin has taken to
visiting her often, calling himself
her personal musician. They spend
long hours together, in a private
chamber, but I never hear music.
Just the murmurings of words.

The Uniting ceremony is
tomorrow. The day I will finally
Unite with her... But I can't
shake the feeling that something
will go terribly wrong...

CHAPTER 40: VILE VILLAIN

"*Esen! Esen!*"

Esen bolted awake. The forest was ringing with her name. She shot to her feet and went to the nearest oak.

"Yes?" she breathed.

"*The river fae; the ones who United. The queen slew them last night.*"

A startled cry escaped her.

"*Niamh, Rowan, and their daughter escaped. They are the only survivors.*"

"No," Esen gasped. She covered her mouth with her hands. Korey, Brighid, Rhiannon, and all the others…

Dead. And their dryads too.

They had only just United.

"But the law of Aon Mharú…" she stuttered.

The forest was drinking deep blood from fae that should have never been killed. Blood spilled in cold murder.

"*The queen called it justice. She judged them to have committed treason, the punishment death.*"

"That is not justice," Esen cried, shaking her head. "Where are Niamh and Rowan now? Are they okay? Is the queen after them?"

"*Isolde took them in. The queen has made no further pursuit, but we fear she has learned of your plan. Isolde and the rest of her company are headed to the base*" *of the mountain, where the mountain fae will join them. They will wait for you there."*

Esen slumped forward, pressing her forehead on the oak as shivers coursed through her. If she had never convinced them to Unite, they might still be alive.

"Thank you," she murmured.

She looked down to see Fafnir beneath her, his head craned up toward her.

"What has happened?" he asked.

When she told him, he turned pale as a ghost. He was silent for a long moment. Finally, he said, "We should go at once, if you are able."

She put out her hand to help him up. As she brought him up, she hesitated. "I am afraid of the queen. We don't know where she is or what she knows. I don't want you to be seen, just in case."

He nodded.

"I could carry you in my hands," she said, quickly, "but it's a tight fit, and I'd jostle you a lot. I want to move quickly. The safest place would be, well... my heart chamber."

"Your heart chamber?" he echoed, the slightest tremor in his voice.

"Yes," she said. Nothing would happen so long as they both stayed awake.

He nodded again, his face tight. "All right."

She brought him toward the opening. There was no time to think of what this meant. It meant nothing anyway. If he had wanted to Unite with her, he would have asked already, and never considered leaving her...

She felt the weight of his foot on the lip of the opening, and then he was within. She could hear the dead leaves crinkle as he settled down.

She couldn't see his face.

She didn't want to.

She began to run, her long legs striding, devouring the earth. Her breath filled her ears, quick and hot.

It felt like forever before the sun rose.

In four days, they reached the base of the mountain. Esen exhaled in wonder as she looked over the crowd assembled among the heather. Over two hundred faeries were gathered, with twenty-one Walkers crouched and talking amongst them. Their faces turned up as they approached.

Esen helped Fafnir down to the ground. Her spirit rose with relief at the sight of Niamh cradling Iona against her. Rowan stood beside her, one hand on her arm.

Carefully, Esen hurried up to them. "I am so sorry, Niamh."

Niamh stepped forward. Her shoulders shook. "Hi, Esen."

Isolde approached them. Her features relaxed as she saw Fafnir beside her. "I am glad you both made it safe."

A silence had gathered among the crowd. There was Elouan and the eldest of his tribe, and a few of the Walkers from Athas, but Esen knew none of the rest.

They all looked at her attentively, as though she were a dryad elder come to lead them.

Maybe she was, in spirit. Whoever she had been when she first departed from her sister and walked down the green hill of her home, Esen was not her anymore.

Despite the fear that churned inside her, she felt determined.

They would succeed. They *had* to succeed.

"*Aeonida*," she said, bowing to them. "May the forest live again through our efforts."

"*Aeonida*," the crowd returned, bowing back at her in a flowing undulation like a wave of the sea.

"Do they all know who we are?" Fafnir murmured to Isolde.

"Yes. I've spoken about both of you, and the plan," Isolde whispered back. She faced the crowd, raising her voice. "Allow me to introduce all of you."

She walked into the crowd and stood in front of Elouan.

"Elouan and some of his fae are here from the Éigniú Valley," she said. She faced Elouan. "We are very grateful to you and your fae for coming despite the hardships you've been through."

Elouan nodded. "It is our duty."

Isolde moved to stand beside a dark-gray faerie clothed in a sweeping black cloak lined with white fur. "We have Farrell, Diviner of the Spéir Driofaires, here with his fae, also from the southern mountains. They are mountain wanderers, seekers of beauty and meaning, and friends of Elouan's."

Farrell nodded solemnly, the bones hanging from his ears clattering.

Isolde walked next toward a light-brown faerie dressed in a black tunic tied at the waist with a belt of reeds. "We have Caoimhe, Diviner of the Nóinín Grove, another River Ifrati tribe. Korey recruited them to our side before her death."

"Like Korey, we waited far too long," Caoimhe said, her voice smooth like water. "We will do everything we can now to help."

Esen dipped her head, rustling her branches. "Thank you."

"And then we have many individuals who I've recruited from across the land," Isolde continued. "All have their own story. Some have been Winged Ones since they turned one hundred, and others have only just United."

There were so many of them; perhaps a hundred or more.

Isolde had done incredible work in gathering these people.

"And there's me, Gavin." A lean, well-built faerie with dark-brown skin and sand-colored hair brushed back into a bun leaned into Isolde. "Isolde adopted me." She pushed him off her, grinning.

"Yes, now we all know your name," Isolde said.

"It is good to meet all of you," Fafnir said, stepping forward. He spoke with a rapid, confident tone, like he had when she first met him properly, as they formed their plan. "We come as strangers, but we will leave the best of friends. We are going to save the forest together. Here is the plan. Although the queen knows we are coming, we will come anyway. She has already committed violence; lifting her hand against us will only prove our point. We come to accuse her, so we will do it openly, shamelessly. It is a half-moon's journey at a dryad's pace, but we must time the last few suns so we arrive precisely at twilight, the high point of the World Market. Our numbers will demand attention. We will speak at once, before the queen can stop us."

The Rooted Ones murmured above in a quiet rumble, like the thunder before a storm.

Their pain would finally be voiced.

"I will ask the Rooted Ones to shake their crowns with the cry of the murders as we travel," Esen said, "so all who know Wind-Speak will know of it, and perhaps join us to challenge her."

Isolde added, "And our entrance must be memorable. We may not have much time to speak, but we can speak by our entrance. We could arrive holding fifteen candles to signify each of the river fae the queen killed."

"Let us do both of those," Fafnir said. He turned back toward the crowd. "Queen Maeve was supposed to have stepped down as ruler nine hundred and eight years ago. She has continued to selfishly hoard her throne and perpetuate the deaths of tens of thousands. We *will* bring her down. We *will* stand together and win the fae back to the dryads. We will all live to see the forest as it once was."

Cheers erupted, the deep, rumbling tones of the dryads mingling with the light voices of the fae.

Excitement fluttered in Esen's chest.

Aisling's little face, swaying with the brightest of smiles, flashed in her mind.

Soon, Esen would be home.

ESEN FELL into line as the gathered assembly started toward the Rath Síoraí. Assured by the safety of the group, Fafnir rode on Esen's shoulder once more. Neither of them spoke of how he had ridden in her chamber.

As they traveled beneath the Rooted Ones' shaking crowns, new faeries began to join them. Most of them had already been Winged Ones for hundreds of years, but some came who had not yet United. "The river fae the queen slew were our good friends," they said. "We are coming with you to make her answer."

A few of them United on the journey, but most of them hesitated. They rode on the shoulders of other Walkers. "We will hear her answer first," they said.

Walkers from all regions of the land joined them too. Soon, Cillian appeared, smiling. Esen embraced him.

"*Aeonida*, Cillian. I have missed you!" she said. "How have you been?"

"*Aeonida*. I am well because of you. I am so proud of you, Esen. You are doing what none of us had the courage to do."

Esen clasped Cillian's hand, her wrist with the *Aeonida* carving resting against his. "I am glad you are here."

Their numbers swelled to two hundred and fifty, then three hundred. She wondered if Tristan would come and how she would respond if he did. He was as predictable as the mountain weather.

He never appeared.

As they grew nearer to the Rath, Isolde and Fafnir led a group of faeries hunting in the evening. Two Walkers carried the deer they slew back into their camp. Overnight, the faeries butchered the deer, and roasted and dried the meat to portion out. The fat they separated and melted in pots over a fire as others chipped at blocks of wood. When the fat was cool, they poured it into round, wooden holders. In each one a piece of string poked out at the top.

The candles Isolde had spoken of.

Toward late sun on the day they were to arrive, a little song burst from Iona. She swayed in Niamh's arms. Niamh soon joined her, her voice like the river. Those around her began to sing too, until the air rang with their voices, low and thoughtful.

Somehow, both joy and sorrow flowed within the sound.

Not watching her feet, Esen stumbled over the limb of a fallen ash. Dragans wove over its form. Isolde had said the group's entrance would speak for them before they spoke a word. The candles would speak for the river fae who had died, but what of the dryads?

Esen stooped and gathered the limb of the ash in her arms. Half the outer bark had been eaten away by dragans, the inner bark rotted.

Every day, fae walked by the bodies of her kind, their eyes glazing past, refusing to truly see. She would bring the seeing before them.

Cillian watched her, his brow furrowed. He gathered another body in his arms.

She glanced behind her. All the Walkers were stooping, gathering. They rose with trailing limbs and pieces of shattered trunks, their faces somber.

Even still, the Walkers sang on, together with the fae.

Esen pressed her lips.

Her sister's fate, and the fate of all the forest, would be determined tonight.

THE SKY WAS PINK, bats flitting silently overhead. Voices saturated the air. Esen's voice hummed among them, beautiful and low in Fafnir's ear. The dead limbs in her arms scraped along the ground.

A shudder coursed through him. He could not join in their song. There was a determination within it, burning through the sorrow. A determination to change the world, whatever the cost.

He shifted his stiff legs, glancing down at the knot of wood that formed the top of the entrance to Esen's heart chamber.

He could still hear the dead leaves crunching as he had stepped inside, could still smell the age of the wood. The darkness had pressed in on him with the weight of the floodwaters, the wide world reduced to a mere glimpse of green past the slitted opening.

He would not share that cost.

His role in the change was nearly complete. He had only to speak well before the fae of the Rath and promote them toward change. Then he would slip away, never to be seen again.

But… there were so many faeries with them, and Walkers too. He would betray all of them. He'd have to creep among the cracks of the earth for a thousand or more years before he could be assured of not running into them and receiving their hatred.

He tugged at his collar.

0 and 1 is 1. 1 and 1 is 2.

He pulled out his journal and read through his notes on his speech.

Firefly lanterns glowed bright in the gloom, lighting the way, decorated with red market ribbons. Wind chimes made of light ash wood had been fixed to each one; they clattered faintly in the wind. At last, the Rath Síoraí loomed up from the cover of the Rooted Ones.

Esen was first to step out into the clearing. An ugly cacophony of voices broke out. Esen ceased her singing, drawing back. Tens of thousands of unwinged faeries packed the space, jammed like barnacles. They writhed as one, pointing and throwing jests at them like daggers.

The merchant stands were abandoned.

"Get out! You're disturbing the peace!" one cried.

"You're not wanted here."

"We won't be deceived!"

Up on the platform on the Rath, flanked by guards, stood the queen. She lifted her chin, her obsidian eyes gleaming.

She had rallied the fae against them.

Panic knocked against his chest. With white knuckles, he untied himself from Esen's branch and stood.

"They hate us," Esen whispered to him.

"They think we are their enemies," he whispered back. "We must prove them wrong."

Esen set her mouth in a firm line. She faced the crowd and stepped forward. The faeries leaped back from her footfalls mere moments before they would be crushed.

Their uproar was deafening.

All around the sides of the circular clearing, Walkers appeared, pressing inwards toward the steps of the Rath, each of them bearing their burdens. The Winged Ones flew close by them.

Partway through, Esen adjusted her grip on the bodies. Several limbs fell beneath her. Faeries sprung out of the way, their faces white.

The queen remained stiff as a reed, watching.

By the foot of the steps, Esen and the other Walkers threw down their bodies with a terrible clatter. The abandoned merchant stands splintered, disappearing in the wreckage. The terrible pile rose up to Esen's head. A loose piece with hollowed cavities like a skull rolled until it knocked into a faerie's stomach. He fell backward, staring up into the dark hollows.

A silence sliced through the crowd like a blade. Only the clatter of the wind chimes could be heard.

The queen's mouth twitched.

Isolde, Elouan, and several others fluttered down to stand in front of the pile, facing the queen. They lit their candles and held them out.

"We carry a light for each of the fifteen river fae slain by the queen," Isolde cried.

"And we bring the bodies of our loved ones," Esen added, her voice thick, "whom all of you have killed by refusing to Unite with us."

The queen called out over the crowd. "Do you see how extreme these traitors are? Tell them to—"

"Queen of Faerie," Fafnir called over her, his hands cupped to his mouth. From where he stood on Esen's shoulder, he towered over the queen. "Your hands are stained with blood and sap. We have come to demand justice. You have broken the law of Aon Mharú, a law you did not revoke. You have slashed the throats of fifteen river fae and shed their blood into the earth because you did not agree with their beliefs. They had been weaponless, sharing an evening in peace. Every day, you watch dryads fall to the ground and ignore them. You are a murderer and should be sentenced to death as the law calls."

"The dryads are the murderers!" a faerie cried.

A roar ripped through the crowd. Faces twisted with rage shouted at them once more. But there, in the back, a good number of faeries shuffled in silence, their eyes fixed on the dryad remains.

The queen's face grew as cool as marble. "You murdered us first, when your Ancient Law demanded we die to satisfy the dryad's parasitic existence. If you were to pile the bodies of all the fae killed by the dryads since the beginning of this land, it would touch the sky."

The roars intensified, terrible, boring into his temples.

"You don't understand," Esen cried. Past him, her words were swallowed up.

Fafnir's ears drooped. They had to regain control.

"We are not immortal," Fafnir cried. "Not truly." A rush of shouts assailed him even louder. He sucked in his chest, yelling from the top of his lungs. "The dryads are the pillars of the forest. When they fall, we will all fall with them. We may die tomorrow, or a thousand years from now—"

He broke off, drawing for air. None of them were even listening.

The crowd was dictating who could speak, and they favored the queen.

A wicked grin spread over her face. "Ah. He says we will die with the dryads. But that is a lie. He is mad with guilt, faerie folk. Do you see any wings on his back?"

Sweat pooled at Fafnir's collar. *Rot.*

"No!" the crowd shouted.

"Before he founded this death cult, he was the founder of something else. Tell them, Fafnir Fiachra."

"That has nothing to do with our point," Fafnir cried. "Faeries, listen. If you don't Unite, you will all die. You must—"

"Stop lying!" the queen snarled. "It's quite revolting. Tell them the truth."

The blood pounded in his ears. The crowd began to chant in a low thrumming tone like a drum. "Tell us! Tell us!"

His breath raked from his lungs, feverish.

They would all hate him.

Even Esen...

Esen's face turned toward him, her blue eyes clouded with confusion. "Fafnir?"

She brought a hand to her shoulder. He hesitated before stepping carefully onto her palm. The world blurred until she was holding him out in front of her, both hands cupped around him.

Worry filled her eyes—an expression she had worn often when she was concerned for him over the moons they had journeyed together.

She would never look that way at him again.

"What does she mean?" Esen whispered.

He couldn't say it like this, not with her face so close to him.

"Can you lower me down?" he asked, his voice shaking.

Her brows furrowed, but she nodded. Wind ruffled his hair as her palm lowered, her branches creaking, then he stepped off her hand and onto the dry dirt of the clearing in front of the dryad bodies.

Down on the ground, the chant beat against him even louder. "Tell us! Tell us!"

Isolde, Elouan, and several other Winged Ones surrounded him. They stared at him, silent and unmoving. "This does not change the validity of my research," he stammered. The crowd quieted. "But I did... I–I–back then, I—"

He dug his nails into his scalp. His head pounded, pounded...

"Go on," the queen said.

"It was I who tore down the Ancient Law," Fafnir said through gritted teeth. "I instigated the idea. I wrote the speech. The queen only performed it."

Gasps burst from around him.

"That can't be true." There was a desperation in Esen's voice, like she was drowning, only her face held above water. "Tell me it isn't true."

He kept his gaze on the ground. "It is."

A choked gasp erupted from Esen. Feet shuffled back all around him, voices whispering low, Isolde's voice among them.

His chest shuddered. A ringing burned in his ears as a laugh broke from the queen.

"Haven't you wondered why he hasn't offered to Unite with you, dryad?"

Fafnir flinched. A clamor broke out in the crowd. He bent over, his breath ragged.

O and—no. O and... and...

The queen was speaking still with that smile plastered on her face, her gestures grand. What was she saying?

"...see how the coward has flipped his tongue? He comes to us with feverish fantasies of the world ending to get us to save the lives he is killing—"

No. He jammed his hands over his ears. They had made progress, perhaps really moved the faeries. Now she was dragging his guilt across the stage like a bloodied corpse to stain their mission with his hypocrisy.

371

A sob broke above him. Esen.

The ground shook as her feet pounded upon it. She was running away.

No. No, no, no…

"Esen!" he cried, his voice hoarse.

She didn't stop. He ran after her.

The queen was shouting something. He dodged through the thick mass of bodies, their faces unfamiliar.

A force slammed into him, and he stumbled, colliding with another fae. A flash of jeering teeth, and then he was jerked up above the crowd. Hands gripped at his back, his arms, his legs, shoving him over their heads. His head flopped like a fish, the crowns of the Rooted Ones spiraling in his vision. Then he was hurled through the air. Bracken cracked beneath him, scraping his arms.

The crowd had vanished. The shadows of the Rooted Ones enveloped him. He stumbled to his feet. Thin trails of red ran down his arms. Blood. His violin case lay where he had fallen, the flap smashed in.

A restless murmur shuddered through the leaves of the Rooted Ones.

They knew his secret too. The whole forest was ringing with it.

He darted forward. He had to find Esen.

Brambles stung his hands, his face. He ran on, his breath in his throat, until he broke out from a cluster of reeds and saw her. Esen knelt against a willow, her body trembling.

"Es-en," he said breathlessly.

She turned her face. A trail of tears gleamed down her cheeks, fury burning in her eyes. He had never seen such hatred in her before.

"Why are you here?" she demanded. Her voice thundered in his ears, fierce as the wave that had nearly killed him. He stared dumbly at her. "*You* killed my family," Esen snarled.

Fafnir flinched. "I-I never meant… I didn't—I didn't think this would happen."

"Then what did you think?"

His breath rattled in his throat. His old excuses withered away before her. They had never been forgivable. "I had thought… only a few wouldn't Unite."

She stared at him with the intensity of her entire being. Fresh tears fell from her eyes.

"I'm sorry," he choked.

The air was thick, suffocating. His brain kicked against his skull. When he squeezed his eyes shut, he was crouching beneath the table again, Isolde's hand pressed in his, her face stained with tears as his mother hurled a jar just past his father's head.

Terror clawed at his chest.

"Don't 'sorry' me." Esen's jaw jerked in harsh angles, her eyes cold as flint. Her face was horrible, monstrous; like the face of his mother in her rages. "Do you think you're the only soul in the world? The only one that matters?"

The words shot through his stomach like a blade.

"Why did you do it? For what reason did you kill my family, the entire forest, cause a wildfire to ravage an entire village, and then lie to me about it, again and again?"

The desire he'd treasured for over a thousand years shimmered before him like a golden flag, but it was dripping, drenched in dark-red blood.

"To be free," he whispered.

"Go, then." Her words twisted the cold blade in his stomach. She lifted her chin. "You might get a few years of freedom before we all die."

She rose, towering high, and left him.

CHAPTER 41: ALL IS LOST

A cold wind blew, chilling Esen. Her breath rattled as she blundered, branches raking against her.

All this time, the killer had been right beside her. She had let him into her heart chamber.

She rattled her head, brown leaves falling to the ground.

She was a fool. An utter, childish fool.

"Esen!" Isolde flew toward her, and behind Isolde flew all the other fae who had joined them. The Walkers followed behind. Isolde hovered by her. "Are you okay?"

Esen shook her head. "What happened?"

"She got them to think the death of the forest is a fable—a delusion Fafnir made up to get us to rally behind him so he could save the dryads and be free of his guilt. Some of the faeries left, and some turned to the queen's liquor table."

Esen's mouth twitched. The queen was half right. He had only been doing this for himself.

"Then we have failed," she said flatly.

Tears welled in her eyes. Winter was coming, and she had little hope to bring to Aisling. Cillian walked up to her, concern in his face. He offered her his hand, but she didn't take it.

"We could try again in the spring," Cillian said, with the faint attempt of a smile.

Esen's leaves drooped. "I want to go home."

The Rooted Ones creaked their branches in unison. There was a dry, scraping moan in their voices, echoing her name. She walked up to one of them.

A hawthorn stirred. *"We did not tell you, Esen, because we knew it would pain you…"*

"What is it?" she cried.

"Aisling did not make it."

"What?" Her throat constricted. "Do you mean she's—she's—"

"She died four days ago. We didn't think —"

She turned to run when an arm hooked her by the elbow.

"Esen, it's a moon's journey to your home," Cillian said. "Come with us —"

Esen flung him off her. She ran and ran, her spirit hammering in her chest. She didn't know herself until she was stumbling up the hill to her home, her branches torn, her body heavy as a Rooted One. At the top of the hill, Fiona towered, skeletal leaves rattling from her branches, and beneath her… beneath her…

Esen threw herself down in front of Aisling, but the spirit had long fled from her. A withered, sunken body hunched in her sister's place. Weeping dragans, with a glimmer of childish innocence in their black eyes, swirled over her, devouring her.

Fiona's dry branches scraped together. *"Esen, I am so sorry. I couldn't save her."*

Esen leaned forward and trailed a finger along Aisling's face. The ghost of a frown lingered on her lips, her brows pinched tight with pain, her eyes closed.

She had seen death in many forms. Her parents roots torn up from the ground. Ian, his white face stained with scarlet. Morgan's husband. Countless dryads in all stages of decay.

It usually took a full moon cycle for dragans to grow this much. Every bit of Aisling had been swallowed by them. Her body teemed with movement.

"F-Fiona," she whispered. "How long has she been dead?"

"Thirteen days," Fiona stirred, a shiver in her voice.

Esen dropped her hand, clenching her fist. She had come here in just nine days then. The dragans must have formed fast. Aisling would never sing again, nor Walk with her under the golden light...

A sob wrenched from her throat, and another. She hunched over, clutching at her middle, weeping...

"*Esen,*" Fiona stirred.

Esen threw up her head. "Why didn't you tell me? I could have run to her and held her hand. Maybe I could have saved her."

"*It was so quick. She was fine, and then with the first cold wind, she started coughing, and she didn't stop. You couldn't have gotten here in time.*"

Thirteen days ago, she had been walking to the Rath with hope in her spirit, believing the suffering of the forest was soon to be relieved; that she would come home and fold Aisling's hands in hers, and laugh and sing...

Anger seized her limbs.

If Fafnir had never come to her, she would have stayed and spent Aisling's last year by her side. He had taken her from her little sister, and then killed her.

With a last glance at the thing that was no longer Aisling, Esen choked, then hurtled down the hill. Branches bent back from her, but they still scraped against her in her haste.

A root caught on her foot. She crashed to the ground, crying out in pain.

She could still see Aisling's face crinkled in laughter as she watched Fafnir destroy his snow machine. She remembered how Aisling had broken a piece of it herself, giggling.

As Fafnir smiled at her.

Esen wrung her hands, scraping at her bark.

All this time, he had wanted to be free...

Free of her. She was just a speck of dirt that he had been looking forward to sweeping off. No wonder he almost left her for the sea fae. She would die, and he would forget her. All the fae would forget her.

She was a disease, like Morgan had said. They would all be happier once she and her kind were dead.

The world blurred as tears smothered her eyes.

"Oh Mother," she whispered. "Where are you?"

Not a breath of wind stirred.

She picked herself up. "Show yourself!" she cried.

Only silence answered her. She fell back down, curling into herself, weeping…

She thought of the carnivorous flower devouring its prey. She had thought it was beautiful before she looked into the water. Was beauty a mirage? A shimmering reflection on the water… but when one plunged their hand within it, it faded, leaving a heaving surface of broken ripples.

Maybe that was all there was.

A SHADOW LOOMED OVER ESEN. She blinked and rolled up from the ground, her limbs sore.

To see Tristan looking back at her. She started back. A heavy intensity burned within his gray eyes. He was sitting oddly, one leg partially bent. The bark at his knee was black and charred. A glimmer of a dragan spiraled down from his knee, eating into the bark of his leg. The wound was spreading.

Esen's hands flew to her mouth. "You look ill."

"So do you," he said. He glanced at Aisling, his face tight, before leaning toward Esen. "Esen, did the Rooted Ones tell you?"

"Yes," Esen said. "It was just before our mission failed that she…that she passed."

Tristan snarled, his lip curling. He glared up at Fiona. "So you lied to her."

Fiona's branches rattled. "*Tristan, please. It's easier for her —*"

"You're just like the others," Tristan spat.

"Tristan?" Esen sputtered. "What's going on?"

He laid a hand on her shoulder, his eyes dark. "They lied to you — all the Rooted Ones. Aisling died over a moon ago."

"No," she gasped. "That can't be true. How do you know?"

"I watched her, Esen. Cillian was supposed to be my guardian or whatever they're calling it, but he left me behind without telling me where he went. So I came back here, and Aisling, she—"

He choked, his grip tightening. "She was so weak. And then she just *died*."

Tristan released her, his hands shaking. "I begged the Rooted Ones to take a message to you. They were silent. They've said nothing to me. Not even my own parents. I was about to go out and break my leg trying to scour the land for you. You needed to know."

Esen bent over, digging her hands into the hard dirt. She clenched her fingers, clawing down, down. Tears spilled from her eyes.

This whole time…

This *whole* time…

While she was traveling the land with *him* on her shoulder, getting rejected, slandered, and shamed, until it all crumbled in a hideous mess—

Aisling was dying.

She leaped to her feet and rushed at Fiona to beat her fists against her bark.

"How could you?" she screeched.

Distress saturated Fiona's stirrings. *"Esen, I'm sorry. We are all sorry. I did everything I could for her. You were on such an important mission…"*

Pain lanced through Esen's hands. She fell to her knees, shuddering.

A dragan writhed over Aisling's closed eyes and stole them away. A featureless face looked back at her.

Emotion swelled up from her stomach, pushing through her body. She screamed. She was Aisling when their parents had shattered in front of her—all open mouth and vibrating throat, nothing more.

When she knew herself next, dusk had veiled the sky. Arms were wrapped around her, clasping at her torso. She straightened, her limbs heavy like they were weighed down by mountains of snow. Tristan's breath fluttered the dry, shriveled leaves on her neck.

"I'm sorry," Tristan whispered. "I'm so sorry, Esen."

"Were you the one who took care of her, during the storm?" she rasped.

"Yes," he said softly.

Esen shuddered, a pressure pounding on her chest. He had likely saved Aisling's life then. But she had died soon after anyway. She fell against him and wept.

When she finally pulled herself up, she saw Tristan's hurt leg stretched out in front of her. "Your leg. It... It looks—" She swallowed, her throat tight. "It looks infected. Hasn't Cillian been taking care of you?"

"He's done everything he can," he said, his voice low.

"You won't be able to walk soon." She frowned. He had said he was on the verge of Rooting age last summer. She counted the seasons in her head.

"You should have Rooted already," she said.

"Do you think I can when this is happening?" He swallowed thickly.

He was breaking the Ancient Law, like the fae. But what did it matter? Did anything matter?

She ran her fingers through her browning leaves. One detached itself and fluttered to the ground.

"Did you hear?" she asked. "What... happened?"

"I heard the queen violated the law of Aon Mharú," Tristan said. He spat on the ground. "The Rooted Ones made a ruckus over it. But I heard nothing more."

She had asked the Rooted Ones to keep a guard on him after he'd nearly lost himself to violence. Did he know she'd done that to him?

"You came back alone," he said.

"Yes." She rubbed at her arm.

"Cillian said you traveled with that faerie—the Wingless One. Where is he?"

She flinched. "I don't want to talk about it."

Tristan frowned.

"We failed, okay?" Esen cried. "We made a stand against the queen —hundreds of us. We gave it everything we had, and they rejected us."

Tristan rose and began to pace. Intensity rolled off him like a storm cloud. She knew that look in him. He was scheming.

"Where are the others?" he asked, whipping round.

"I don't know," Esen said. "I left them all behind when I heard... about Aisling."

He pulled her into another embrace, but she shrugged out from him. Was he thinking of his plan again? To tear down the Rath Síoraí?

380

"We can still do something together," he said quietly.

Esen stepped back. "No. I want no part of your schemes. Leave me be."

"To do what?" He stepped forward, a fire in his eyes. "Grieve until you die too?"

"Leave me alone!" she cried, startling herself with the violence of her tone. Tristan drew back, his boughs creaking.

Esen looked away.

"I will go," Tristan said at last, his brows pinched with concern. "But please know I will be here for you. If you need anything."

For a moment, Esen watched Tristan leave, before curling herself around the withered husk of her sister. She wept long into the night.

"Esen?"

Cillian. He was calling to her. As Esen struggled up, her elbow collided with wood. A splintering crack shattered her ears. She gasped. She had broken one of the branches on Aisling's body. It hung by a thin strip of inner bark.

Aisling's face... or what had been Aisling's face... was scarcely recognizable now.

She clamped both hands over her mouth to keep herself from screaming. How long had she been lying here, wrapped around her?

Warm arms folded around Esen. "I'm sorry," Cillian murmured in her ear. "I'm here for you."

She turned round and hugged him back, shaking.

"We are here to bury her," Cillian said.

"We?" she breathed.

She glanced behind him. Dozens more Walkers swayed; she

recognized them from the march to the queen. Tristan stood among them.

"Oh." Esen looked back at Aisling's body through a veil of tears.

She stepped back. They dug a hole for her beneath Fiona's crown, between her roots. Though she knew there was nothing left of Aisling in that body, she still flinched as they pulled her up gently from the earth. She came away so easily, her roots tiny and shriveled.

A hymn murmured in their throats. Cillian cradled Aisling in his arms, her head against his hand. As he lay her in the earth, the other Walkers scattered dried rose petals.

They were all fighting to hold back tears, except for Tristan, who stared darkly.

She could almost believe it was a dream. That if she turned and looked under Fiona's branches, she would see little Aisling swaying, smiling at her. Aisling had never stood on a mountaintop, heard the whispers of the aspen, or held a wind jelly in her hands. She had never fallen in love, or found a faerie, or danced beneath the stars, finding her voice amid the breeze. Instead, she had lived for only three seasons, and died on the same spot she was born.

So many children had died like Aisling. So many little bodies laid into the earth.

Eaten by worms.

The Rooted Ones still swayed above her. Soon the last of the ones born in the days of the Ancient Law would die. That is, if they didn't all die tomorrow in some flood, or the coming winter. Soon the forest would be no more. It would just be grasses, and small clusters of Rooted Ones huddled together. And then, they too would die. While the faeries watched with faces of stone, Fafnir among them.

"O Mother," Cillian said, his voice shaking. "We thank you for Aisling's life. Please fold this spirit in your own and take her to the realm of peace."

He scattered the dirt back over her. Tears fell from his eyes.

Esen's eyes were dry. Heat burned in her veins, curling like a fist inside her middle.

She saw her future self, Rooted beside Aisling's grave. In her vision, Fiona had long since fallen and died… and Esen had almost no Rooted Ones left standing by her. She was crumbling apart. Her roots

382

weakening, tearing up from the soil, until she finally pitched forward and decayed, her bark and her sister's eaten by the same earth.

The violence of her breath filled her ears.

She would fight back. She would avenge her sister.

"Tristan," she said.

Tristan jolted. He looked at her, his brow furrowed.

"Tell us of your plan."

A smile spread over Tristan's face. It was like she had told him of rain after a long, hard drought. He faced the others. "Do you want to live?"

One by one, each dryad looked at him and nodded slowly.

"Then we have to do something different. If you keep doing what you already tried—convincing a few faeries here and there—it will take too long. There are hundreds of thousands of dryads, and winter is approaching. We need to make big change, *now*."

The Walkers stared at him.

"We know," Cillian said, shaking his head, "but what else can we do?"

"We demand the fae Unite," Tristan said. "And if they refuse, we punish them."

Gasps sounded among the Walkers. Cillian stumbled back as though he'd been struck. "But that is against the ways of the Mother Wi—"

"Let me finish," Tristan said. "We rally all the Walkers we can and walk up to the queen. We demand them all to Unite. If they refuse, we destroy the Rath Síoraí."

"But that's—" Cillian started.

"If they still refuse, we make more demands," Tristan interrupted. "We could take back everything they use that is made of wood. If their walls are made of wood, we wrench them out from the floor. If their bed is of wood, we snatch it from under their backs. Their tools, instruments, weapons, and their rotting dam. When we're dead and gone, they won't have wood to use anyway, right? So we help them get used to it. If they still refuse, we'll figure out another thing to take from them. You get the point. We'll show them how much they're dependent on us."

It was wild and bold, and would certainly catch their attention.

Fafnir's violin was made of wood…

Cillian's brows were knitted. Though he bore countless stories of the land carved upon him, she did not imagine he had ever heard anything like this.

"How will we teach them to follow the Ancient Law again if we break it?" Cillian asked.

"We don't," Tristan said. "Don't you understand? Esen tried getting them to come out of the kindness of their hearts, but they refused her. Their hearts are made of stone. We can only get them to move by force."

The Walkers swayed, their branches creaking.

"Listen," Tristan snapped. "You can die in your ideals, or you can live."

Cillian turned to Esen. "Do you support this?" he asked.

A gust of wind stirred the freshly turned dirt over Aisling's grave.

"Yes," Esen said, lifting her chin.

Cillian blinked, his eyes wide.

"I will do it," said one Walker.

"I am afraid they will try to burn us," another said.

"If they use fire, it could spread from us and destroy the underbrush of the forest," Tristan said. "Their homes and food sources would be destroyed too. I doubt they would use it. But if they do, I thought of an idea for that too. We can douse ourselves in water before we meet them."

The Walker tilted his head. "What do you mean?"

"You'll see."

One by one, they agreed, until just Cillian remained, hesitating. He traced a spiral carving along his wrist. "I can't ignore the horror that is pressing in on us." He lifted his gaze, meeting Esen's. Grief colored his eyes. "I will do it."

"Let's go," Tristan said, his voice booming. "Let us march on the Rath and save the forest."

The Walkers hummed, their branches rattling as one, their leaves stirring as they began to walk back down the hill. Esen glanced over her shoulder, to the space where her sister lay beneath the earth.

She searched for a hymn, or the right words to think, but her spirit was numb. So she faced ahead, toward the Rath, where she would bring justice for her kind.

They traveled for suns on end, until at last, the cold crept into their sap and forced them to rest. As Esen lay, curled into herself, she looked up at the skeleton limbs of the Rooted Ones above her, silhouetting the thin sliver of the moon suspended like a claw in the sky.

The cold bit into her bark. A memory swam before her—the sea of faeries, pale with fear. They had leaped out of the way like frightened deer when she dropped the limbs of her kind.

In her mind's eye, she held that image still. She walked up to each faerie, peering closely at their faces. Some looked sick. Some look grieved. Others showed no emotion. Still, none of them had United.

If so many faeries turned from Uniting when given the chance... then how many of them had really United out of the desire of their heart back during the Ancient Law? Or had they only done it because the law forced them to?

She lifted a creaking limb and traced the sliver of the moon as though it were the carvings in the rock wall she had seen so long ago. If that was true, then the Cycle of Giving was a lie. It was a cycle of obligation. Nothing more.

If the dryads forsook their side of the Ancient Law that called them to Root, how many dryads would walk until they rotted? Tristan was already testing that...

Was nothing beautiful and noble like she had thought it was?

She dropped her hand, gripping at the grass.

Nothing could be. Not after what had happened to Aisling.

Some faeries United with their hearts. Ian, Brighid, Korey, Elouan, and a few others had. But most did not. Would not. They were selfish creatures, hoarders of their immortality.

Tristan was right; they needed to be forced. They were the same size as her hand. She didn't need to ask. The dryads could shove them in there and force them to Unite.

If that was how it needed to be, then they would do it.

Whatever it took to get it done.

Feet crunched on dry leaves. She lifted her head to see Cillian approaching her, his eyes heavy with sorrow. The moonlight illuminated his pale bark silver.

"Esen, do you need anything?"

"No," she muttered.

He nodded and half turned before facing her again. "Could I hold you?" he asked a little quickly.

There was a sickly softness in his face. A thought struck her. Had he known about Aisling too? Had all the Walkers known and not told her? He could have come and told her while Aisling was still alive. She could have run to her, held her as she died, whispered lullabies in her ear.

"Did you… did you know?" she asked. "About Aisling?"

His brow pinched. "What do you mean?"

"Don't you speak with the Rooted Ones? Wouldn't they have told you?"

He shook his head. "I don't know what you mean." He couldn't have been feigning; he was too honest for that.

"They lied to me," she said thickly. "She died a whole moon before they told me."

Cillian's mouth gaped. "What? She was dead for that long? And they hid it from you?"

He'd had no idea. No idea.

She hated him, suddenly. Hated his innocence, his care for Aisling.

He had done nothing to save her.

"Go away," she snarled.

His mouth was still hanging open, but finally, he shut it, nodded, and left.

for my beloved son...

CHAPTER 42: VIOLENCE

Fafnir threw open the door to his home. He tore two bags off the wall and hurried toward his wood-carving station, stuffing one bag with tools.

He coughed, a rattle in his throat. He ran into the larder and filled the other bag with jars of food and water. Slinging both bags over his shoulders, he grabbed as many spare planks as he could carry, then darted to the door. He glanced back.

A thin beam of sunlight trickled in from the windows, a soft glow illuminating his violins on the wall. A layer of dust coated them.

Even then, he had never been free. He'd only deluded himself as the destruction he'd begun pressed in around him.

He turned away and bolted out the door.

He was done hiding and lying. He was going to take himself away, away from everyone he'd hurt so he couldn't cause them more harm. To try to find another land where he could wander without a name.

Even if he died trying.

He ran down to the riverbank, leaped into Serenity, and wound the shaft of the crown. Whirring to life, the boat churned downstream. He sat on the cold bench and stared down the river. The moon was waning toward a crescent. He hugged his free hand against his chest, his teeth chattering. He felt hollow as a reed.

Days passed. At last, a gust of wind slapped him out of a haze, tasting of salt. The red cedars thinned ahead revealing a black sea beyond, swallowed in the distance by black sky.

He let the river spit out his boat into the sea, then let the waves carry him to shore. He got out and dragged his boat onto the sand. There was a small cavern somewhere in the cliff... There. He hauled the boat toward it, sweating. He slipped, and a jagged rock smashed into the hull. Never mind, never mind. He'd fix it. At last, he'd gotten it inside.

His knees shook. He bent over, wheezing like there was a pin rattling in his lungs. He slugged some water and climbed back into the boat, grabbing his tools.

He had built it for the river, not the sea. In the sea, the waves by the breaker line would crash onto the deck and sink it instantly. But if he made it fully enclosed, it would float on like a fish, unharmed. The motor was likely to break off. He'd design a two-piece sail instead that he could steer from within, and he'd need a deeper keel...

Fafnir worked feverishly. The sun rose and set again five, maybe seven times. All he knew was his work and enough sustenance to ensure he'd wake one more day. At last, it was ready. The wind was blowing toward the sea, and a new moon hung in the sky, entirely veiled from view. Perfect. The tides would be lower.

He pushed the boat until it jutted against the edge of the water. Their waves were calm; nothing like the huge, rolling waves Bedwyr and his fae had sailed into.

He was fleeing this land, just like them.

What would become of Esen? Would her sister be all right? Would they Walk together, like Esen had dreamed of? Or would another flood come, or a terrible winter, and take her sister away from her, shattering all her hopes...

And what of his sister? He was leaving her, *again*.

He pushed the boat forward. A wave caught it and held it aloft, and it began to drift toward the sea, the wind pushing at the sail. Fafnir hoisted himself up by the ropes he'd rigged and opened the latch at the top. He climbed inside and shut the latch tight.

Crawling toward the wheel and feeling it in the dark, he seated himself with his legs stretched out. The darkness pressed against him, the smell of the cedar thick.

It reminded him of Esen's heart chamber... but there, the dark had been only half present, warmed by the light slanting within. Here, it was absolute. Suffocating.

His hands shook. He gripped the crown that would start the motor.

He would never be free. He was leaving behind a whole land of lives that he had cursed. He would bear this guilt for all eternity.

A series of splashes erupted outside. A weight slammed on top of the boat. The cabin jolted, his head knocking against the ceiling. Stars swam in his vision.

The boat stopped moving. The keel must have caught on sand.

The low rumbling growl of a marten vibrated the walls as feet thudded onto the wood above him. His heart raced. It must be one of the queen's rangers, sent to finish him off. He fumbled for his knife at his belt when the latch was torn from its hinges. A black arm with painted white spirals shot toward him.

Was that—

He was seized by the collar and wrenched up into the light.

Isolde's face filled his vision, right before her fist cracked into the side of his head. Pain exploded like a crackle of flames. The world spun upside down, his stomach lurching, and then he was falling... He crashed onto the sand, a ringing vibrating through his skull.

Isolde stood over him, her face contorted with agony. A marten crouched behind her.

"All you know how to do is to run away," she cried, her voice hoarse. "Do you ever stop to think how your actions hurt others?"

A tremor coursed through Fafnir.

The same agony had trembled in her face all those years ago, when he had stood with his hand on the door, looking back. At his sister sitting at the table with her head buried in her arms. She had lifted her head and met his gaze, her eyes red with grief as the sound of their mother's weeping came from behind the bedroom door.

He had turned away.

And left. Mere moments after his father had.

And now, he had turned his back on the whole forest.

On Esen, when she needed him the most.

Isolde's lower lip trembled. "Where is my brother? My brother who conjured fantastic stories with me in the dead of night, who cleaned my

391

cuts when I fell, and threw himself on Mother's arm to stop her from throwing that jar at Father? Who found me crying in Mother's garden and told me how every moment was interconnected in a web of meaning, and that beauty would always prevail?"

Isolde broke off, breathing heavily.

Fafnir's breath hitched, his heart in his throat.

"Where is *that* brother?" Isolde choked.

Something deep inside of him shattered. Sobs raked his chest, ugly and gasping, as though he had forgotten how to breathe.

He felt himself lifted up from the sand. He started as warm arms wrapped around him. Isolde's braids pressed into his shoulder. She trembled against him.

He let his head rest on her shoulder as tears spilled from his eyes.

"I am afraid," he sputtered. The words tumbled out of him, like water from a dam. "That I am Father's shadow. That if I let myself become attached to another, I would come to hate them."

"Fafnir." Isolde pulled her head back, tears in her eyes.

"Do you hate me?" she whispered.

Emotion pressed at his heart. She was crying—for him. For all the years they never got to share together, because he had left her.

But she still loved him. After everything.

"No," he choked. "Never."

Isolde smiled, the corners of her mouth quivering. A deep, throaty laugh burst from her, with a rumble almost like a purr.

A shaky smile pulled at his lips. He had nearly forgotten her laughter.

"There you go," she said. She pressed him tighter.

The salt from his tears gathered in his mouth. He felt himself unraveling...like he had been the tightly wound cord in that wooden butterfly. His chest shuddered, half with sobs, half with laughter.

He surrendered to the feeling.

When Isolde pulled back from him at last, the sky had lightened to a bruise blue. The marten was curled in a ball beside them, her flank gently rising.

Blood stained the white paint on Isolde's shoulder. Fafnir put a hand to his face and felt it trickling from his nose.

Isolde fished a cloth out from a bag on her hip and handed it to him.

It was a verdant green, with faint patterns of leaves. It was a similar pattern to the cloth his mother had wrapped the flute in when he first found it at his doorstep.

He could see his mother playing her flute in the chair in her garden, her brow heavy as she thought of all she had lost. Of how scared she must have been for Fafnir, hoping desperately that he was okay.

She just wanted to know her son. To be in his life.

Fafnir wiped off the blood and handed it back to Isolde. She shook her head. "You keep it."

He put it in his bag. "Isolde. Do you remember how Mother used to play the flute?"

"Yes."

"Did she still play after Father left?"

"Sometimes."

"I... I broke the flute Mother made for me," he said. "I never got to hear how it sounded."

"I still have one of her flutes," Isolde said. "I could play it for you sometime."

A glimmer of red light flickered over her face, illuminating the bags under her eyes, but they were bright, like the morning sun. Like she had finally woken from a long sleep.

"I would like that," he said.

Both starting to speak at the same time, they instead grew silent.

"Go ahead," Isolde said.

He swallowed, trying to pull the words up from deep inside him. To apologize for all the pain he had caused her.

"I missed you," he said finally.

Her brows pinched. She embraced him again. "I missed you too."

She pulled back from him.

"How did you find me?" he asked. "I'm in the middle of nowhere."

"You're predictable," Isolde said, hunching her shoulders. "I was flying home. To do what, I don't know. I passed by your house. I was going to leave you to rot, but I was so scared and hopeless, and... I was afraid the queen was going to try to kill you. So I circled back. When I found your house empty and the boat gone too, I put the pieces together."

He nodded and pushed himself to his feet. "Where is Esen? How is she? And how is Aisling?"

Isolde tensed, turning from him.

Nervousness seized him. "What happened?"

"Aisling died," Isolde said thickly.

His ears drooped. No. That couldn't be. "Esen said she was doing well not long ago," he sputtered.

"It was very sudden."

He gripped at his head. He could still see Esen crouched before Aisling, pressing her little green hand as she promised to return to her.

All Esen had wanted was to Walk with her sister. She had lost everything else, and now Aisling, too, was taken from her.

"Is there anything I can do?" he burst out. "She must be distraught, heartbroken."

Isolde shook her head, her face tight. "I don't know. She is terribly hurt and angry. The Rooted Ones say she is launching a movement with other Walkers to make the fae Unite by force. They want to destroy the Rath Síoraí, and from there... I don't know."

He nodded, biting at his lip. "The queen will retaliate with fire, most likely. I have to go and do anything I can to protect her."

Isolde looked at him for a moment before nodding. "I will come with you." She roused her marten and leaped on her back, then held out a hand toward Fafnir. "Her name is Saoirse. Hop on."

He took her hand and climbed up behind her.

Saoirse leaped off the rock and through the bracken, huffing. As they rode, Isolde twisted around to face him. Her eyebrows were tilted up, the corners of her mouth twitching. She reached toward him and tugged at his bark hat, but the straps held it in place.

"No fair," she said, scowling. "What do you wear that for, anyway?"

As he shifted it back in place, a walnut thudded to the ground not far from them. He tapped the bark. "So I don't get concussed by a dryad."

Isolde laughed. "They always sense the ground before they drop them. But that's fair. Take off your hat. I want to see your hair. Does it grow slower when you're immortal?"

"The same," he said. Just as he unhooked the straps from his ears and pulled it off, she dove forward and dug her fingers in his hair, gripping at his scalp like her hand was a barnacle.

Rot. He should've known she would do that.

"Got your brain, got your brain!" She giggled.

A laugh escaped from him. He slapped her hand off.

"I haven't gotten to do that to you in a thousand years," she said.

She was smiling at him, her hair blowing in the wind, untangling from her braids. She looked wild, full of life. Like she had when they had gone on adventures together as children.

"Thank you for not giving up on me," he said.

She pressed his hand. "You are my brother."

At last, the day arrived when they would reach the Rath Síoraí. The morning dawned biting cold. Esen woke and struggled to rise, a flame surging in her spirit.

She would avenge her sister.

She turned to see Tristan approaching her, the other Walkers rising from their sleep behind him and following.

"Today is the day," said Tristan. A gleam shone in his eyes. He waited as the others gathered round and ushered them in close. "Follow me. I'm going to show you what I mean with the ice. The River Ifrati is this way."

He took off, weaving through the Rooted Ones. Esen followed, the rest close behind. Soon she glimpsed the River Ifrati emerge before her. Its surface was frozen, cast in a red glimmer from the rising sun.

"If we douse ourselves quickly," Tristan said behind her. "It will not hurt us. It will only stiffen our outer bark."

"Have you tried it yourself?" Cillian asked, shivering.

"I've done my arm," Tristan said, "and it's fine."

Tristan stepped up to the edge of the white ice and crouched down, piercing the smooth surface with his hand. Gritting his teeth, he submerged his hand in the water below, then pulled it out, the water streaming off. Within moments, tiny white crystals began to appear along his bark, hardening the water into a glossy sheen.

Grinning, Tristan waved his hand to the others. "See? It stings a little, but it's fine."

Tristan began to step within the water, his grin shaking. "We'll have to submerge ourselves all the way, just in case. Be very quick, in and out."

As the others moved forward behind her, Esen approached the ice and drew a deep breath before piercing it with her foot. A jolt seized her at once, the cold tingling along her bark, but it wasn't as painful as she'd feared.

Water swirled round her foot. Esen took another step, and another, drawing toward the middle of the river until she stood up to her shoulders, shivering. Squeezing her eyes shut, she tensed her body, trying to still her breath, before lowering her knees to drop her head beneath the surface.

Her head was on fire. Needles pricked her brain, her mind all vapor, seething. She rose back up, gasping, blinking the water from her eyes…

…to glimpse Tristan grinning at her. Water rained from the branches above his head, already forming into tiny crystals. "Shocking, isn't it?"

Esen smiled weakly. She turned from him to gaze into the red haze of the sun as it crept above the horizon. A tremor coursed through her as she glimpsed the mound of the Rath rising from among the Rooted Ones, not far down the river. She could make out a few forms of faeries walking up the marble steps.

Heat flushed in her veins, beating back the cold. How could they walk about, going about their lives, when so many were dying around them? When she had placed a pile of the corpses of her kind before their very eyes? Did it mean nothing to them?

Did it mean nothing to Fafnir?

A hand gripped hers and pulled at her. "Esen, come on," said Tristan. "You need to get out."

She had forgotten the cold. She shook her head free of the thoughts and let him lead her out from the river. The other Walkers and faeries stood on the bank, worry in their eyes.

Tristan pressed her hand, smiling at her. "We will soon bring justice to our kind. This pain will end, Esen. We will live again."

"Thank you." She pressed his hand back, before pulling her hand out to see the tiny glistening crystals forming to coat her bark. "I hope this helps."

"It will," said Tristan. A fire burned in his eyes. "Let's go."

THE RATH SÍORAÍ loomed before them at last. It seemed larger than Esen remembered—nearly three times her height. The midday sun hung high in the sky. Faeries mingled about the clearing, walking to and from the Rath. Several merchant stands were set up near the entrance, each with a line of visitors. Many of them looked up at the sound of their approach, their brows furrowed in confusion.

Anger surged within her. Esen charged forward as the others sped beside her. Winding through the trunks of the Rooted Ones, they burst out into the clearing.

Esen kicked an empty merchant stand. It collapsed in a broken heap. The faeries jolted, paling.

"Bring us your queen," Esen cried. "We have come to make a demand."

Several faeries darted toward the Rath; the rest ran off into the Rooted Ones. Esen kicked another stand, sending fruits and jars flying. Tristan seized a boulder seven times the height of a faerie and swung it at the statues on the platform. They toppled down with a boom. The faeries on the steps scrambled out of the way, vanishing inside the Rath. Splintering sounded all around her as the other Walkers destroyed the rest of the stands until none were left.

The queen leaped out on a marten, its tail as bushy as a squirrel's.

She was flanked by thirteen rangers on martens, all wearing thick leather clothing and wooden masks over their faces.

"What is this?" the queen demanded, her face white.

"Restore the Ancient Law," Tristan said, "or evacuate. Your choice."

The queen's face twitched. "Destroy it, then. Destroy the standing symbol of the tradition you cherish. Let the act speak of your hatred and violence. But we will keep the New Law for all eternity."

Tristan glared at her. "Tell your faeries to get out."

The queen gestured to one of her rangers. He urged his marten inside the Rath. The queen gathered with her rangers on one end of the platform, where they remained motionless as pillars, staring Tristan down.

Faeries began to pour out in masses. Leather bags bulged on their persons, arms full of their possessions. They walked hurriedly, bumping into each other, knocking each other's things from their hands. Two faeries carried a large harp between them.

Most of them were frightened. Some glared up at Esen with black looks.

Esen glared back at them, baring her teeth. They had lived so comfortably while her sister died of cold.

The smell of smoke reached her. Two faeries came leaping out brandishing flaming torches. She glimpsed the queen point toward the two faeries, mouthing a command. Her rangers darted after them, but they were already halfway down the steps. They darted up to Tristan and thrust their torches at his feet.

The fire faltered, smoking Tristan. The ice protected him. He backed away, unharmed, but they wouldn't leave him alone.

Esen squeezed her fists. She wanted to rush at them, smack them to the ground. "Get away from him!"

The faeries thrust their torches higher. The flames flickered, licking up Tristan's injured knee. Tristan's face grew black with pain. He thrust out his foot and sent them sprawling.

One of them twitched where she fell.

The other was completely still, blood pooling from a gash in his head. He had killed him.

To say unto another,
"Aeonida", is to greet them,
wish them a good and fruitful
life, and ask the Mother Wind
to flit between their steps
and breathe her wisdom in
their ears. Essentially, it is
to say, "Life is Sacred."

CHAPTER 43: ÆONIDA

Screams broke the silence. Esen stepped back, rattling her branches.

No. That wasn't supposed to happen.

"Mervin!" one of the rangers cried. He pulled back his bow, dipped the arrow tip into a fiery lantern, and launched it at Tristan.

The other rangers began to fire at Tristan too. Blue smoke billowed off his knee, the blackened bark pierced by arrows. Agony consumed his face.

"Attack the Rath, now!" he said. "They're trying to kill us!"

His legs trembling, he seized another boulder and hurled it on the Rath. The air shook with a terrible boom, followed by screams and a splintering crack within. The faeries coming out dropped their possessions, scrambling and screeching.

Esen grabbed a large dagger-like stone. They couldn't stop now. She needed to avenge Aisling. With a guttural cry, she drove the stone into the mound. The mound where they had hidden away, feasting and making merry, as her kind died around them. She tore out a clump of ivy and dirt and struck again, and again... At last, she threw the stone aside and tore at the dirt with her hands, clawing through its thickness toward the center, where they denied her, hated her.

Her fist pounded into cold, hard marble. Through the opening she had formed, she glimpsed a cracked staircase collapsing into itself. Several faeries, panic in their faces, were fleeing down the steps, stumbling and screaming as the stairs shuddered beneath them. Just as the last faerie sprung off the steps, the stairs collapsed, a stone crashing into his ankle and sending him hurtling to the floor.

Her breath quickened. Cracks and booms sounded as the other Walkers tore upon the Rath about her.

"There are still faeries inside!" Cillian cried. He was standing behind them, wringing his hands. "You are killing them!"

Another round of arrows fired, splintering Tristan's knee. "They're all murderers!" he snarled. Falling to one knee, he hurled another rock, the dirt spraying in a cloud. The mound shuddered, crumbling to one side. Terrible screams echoed within.

She heard the queen shout amid the chaos, pointing at Tristan. "Kill that one first!"

All around them, faeries on the ground were striking torches, their faces tight with fear and anger.

The rangers fired again at Tristan. Flames leaped forth, trailing up his leg. Tristan struck a fatal blow on the palace, aiming low. A massive marble tree pierced through the green ivy at the top, hurtling toward the ground with a groan. The whole structure fell with it, dirt spraying in a cloud, marble crumbling everywhere. Bodies fell amid the rubble, screams ripping the air. The other Walkers stepped back, their faces tight with horror.

This wasn't right.

This couldn't be right.

Tristan lunged toward the rangers. Arrows struck his face, licking along his cheek, while faeries on the ground flocked around him and thrust their torches, catching his feet aflame.

He wouldn't survive this. He was horribly burned, the fire spreading like mad.

She raced toward him. "Tristan, stop! You're dying!"

If he heard her, he didn't listen. The queen was racing inside the ruined doorway to the Rath. With a flaming hand, Tristan snatched her off her marten.

All at once, he became a torch. Fire billowed out of his eyes, his mouth, as the bark crumbled off his face, revealing a skull-like form of green sinews, blackening rapidly.

As the queen screeched in agony, Tristan brought her flailing body to his flaming mouth, gripped her head between his teeth, and tore. A ghost-white body skidded across the ground below, covered in black burns, red blood oozing from the gaping neck.

No.

Crying out, Esen drew back. Tristan's knees broke beneath him, and he collapsed to the ground, the flames raging from him, licking up the grasses.

No. No. No…

Esen could scarcely breathe. She had to run, to get away, but her eyes were fixed on Tristan's blackened form, crumbling to pieces before her.

This was all a mistake; a terrible mistake. She had come here with violence in her spirit, and now she had wreaked violence in the world.

The forest was red with blood and fire.

She needed to find Cillian. He was only here because of her. She couldn't let him die. She jerked her head around, but all the Walkers had fled. Faeries were running through the Rooted Ones, lighting their roots on fire. Smoke billowed into the air.

She stumbled toward them. "Don't hurt them!"

She gasped. A sting like many needles pierced her right arm. Several arrows were lodged in her bark, a flame sparking, beginning to eat at her wood.

"No!"

She smacked her arm, but the flame continued to spread. Pain lanced up her arm, her breath hitching.

She glimpsed several rangers aiming at her once more.

Squeezing her eyes, she covered her face with her hands.

But the arrows never came.

She looked up to see a single black-feathered arrow flash in the sun and pierce through the arrow-tips of the first several rangers in the line. As they scrabbled in confusion, a marten sprang out from behind them.

A breath escaped her.

Fafnir rode atop the marten, swinging a long, slim hawthorn branch in his arms at the other end of the line of rangers. The branch crashed into their bows, knocking them from their hands, and sent the final faerie hurtling off her marten.

"Esen, run!" Fafnir cried, his voice hoarse.

She ran toward the Rooted Ones. Fafnir darted below her, holding the branch out to shield himself. Behind her, another black-feathered arrow split through a ranger's drawn bowstring, rendering the bow useless. The ranger beside her jolted and stared hard into the Rooted Ones, fitting an arrow.

Yellow eyes glimmered in the shadows. A flash of white paint on black skin, and an arrow sliding into a white sycamore bow.

Isolde.

The ranger fired.

Isolde's face drew back. Marten fur flashed in a frenzy of movement, then she was gone, the grass trembling violently in her wake.

Esen broke into the cover of the Rooted Ones and gasped. Isolde lurched on top of a marten, her hands clutched around the shaft of an arrow protruding from her chest. Sticky blood coated her hands, her eyes wild with pain. The marten scrabbled about, whimpering.

Fafnir threw himself off his marten, rolling into a pile of dead leaves, and raced toward Isolde. She tipped to one side and fell. He caught her in his arms.

Her lips shuddered. "F-Faf...nir..." she whispered, blood pooling from her mouth. Her head went limp.

"No. Isolde..." Fafnir choked. He pressed frantically around the base of the shaft, then put his ear to her chest.

When he lifted his head, the color had drained from his face.

She was dead. His sister was dead.

She hadn't wanted this. Not for Isolde.

Not even for him.

"Esen." Fafnir lifted his gaze. His pupils were dilated, unfocused. "You're burning. You need to go to the river."

A searing pain gnawed at her right arm. The fire was still flickering, creeping down toward her hand. She had forgotten.

Fafnir lay Isolde gently on the ground, his hands quivering, red with her blood. He draped her braids over her shoulders, closed her eyes, and placed her white bow in her hands. For a moment, he clasped her hand, his head bowed. Then he leaped on his marten and beckoned to Esen. She followed him.

Smoke curled where they had left Isolde, flames licking the dry underbrush.

The fire was spreading. Soon it would consume her body.

The river surged before them, the waters still clear. Esen plunged her arm in, gritting her teeth as the cold stung. The flames died with a final hiss, leaving behind a line of charred black bark. Convulsions came over her. Visions of Tristan, alight with flames, the bark crumbling off his form, flashed before her. She curled into a ball and shuddered, her chest heaving.

"Esen." Fafnir sat atop his marten, his brows knitted. *Him.* The one who had caused all of this.

Her voice came out choked. "Why are you here?"

There was a tenderness in his face that she had never seen in him before. "I want to be different. I won't ask you to forgive me; I just want to do what I can to help you now."

Fresh tears sprang to her eyes. His words clattered in her mind amid a tangle of emotions. She could only manage a nod. A Rooted One fell with a crash not far from them, the roots splitting with an awful tear. White tongues of flame leaped forward, the smoke thickening.

Her breath quickened. "The forest is dying."

Branches snapped behind her. Cillian hurried toward her, his hands clasped against his chest. He knelt on the riverbank and lowered his hands. Two Wingless Ones were curled on his palms, their clothing black and charred. Red burn wounds blistered where their skin was revealed. He laid them at the edge of the bank, their heads propped up on the sand and their bodies in the water.

Cillian faced her. Black soot charred his bark, a burn mark slashing through the carvings on his cheek. He looked so scared, like a rabbit caught in a thicket.

"Tristan's dead," she fumbled.

"I know," he said, his voice scarcely audible. "I saw." His arms twitched.

Esen embraced him. He wrapped his arms around her, trembling. Her spirit writhed in her chest.

In another world of sweet summer grass and Aisling's laughter, he had spoken of the Cycle of Giving. Of how beautiful the forest was when the cycle was aligned, all the parts giving in service to the whole.

It had been hanging on by a thread. And she had snapped it.

She clutched at Cillian tighter, shudders coursing up from her middle. She let herself sink into him, give in. She was a fern tightly curled into itself, unraveling.

"I'm sorry, Cillian," she whispered. "I'm so sorry."

He shook his head. "It's okay."

A rending crack startled her. Another Rooted One had dropped a limb.

"I have an idea." Fafnir was studying the river with a furrowed brow. "We could break open the queen's dam. The surge of water will flood out from the river. If we are quick, it could spread enough to put out the fire."

She pictured the water bursting from the dam. It could tear the Rooted Ones down, especially the ones nearest it.

"That could hurt the Rooted Ones," Esen said. "And wouldn't that flood the forest, like you were always afraid of?"

"It should only hurt this area, where the Rooted Ones are weakened by the fire," Fafnir said. "There are enough Rooted Ones elsewhere to drain the waters down."

Esen hesitated, wringing her hands. "I don't want to cause more harm."

"It's the only way," Fafnir said softly.

"Okay," Esen said. She stepped back from Cillian, nodding to him, and they followed Fafnir as he urged his marten up the riverbank.

All around them, the flames rose on both banks of the river, burning away at the Rooted Ones near until they fell with great crashes. The smoke gripped her by the throat, her eyes watering.

At last, the dam rose before them. It towered twice her height, constructed of tightly bound trunks of fallen dryads. Brown waters surged beneath it.

"Fafnir, keep back from the bank," said Esen. "I don't want you struck by the waters."

"I don't want you both to be either," he said, urging his marten back.

Esen threw herself on the dam. "I will do whatever it takes."

A young, thin rowan rested on the top of the dam. She pushed at it on one end as Cillian pushed on the other, until they sent it hurtling downstream. But the others were thick and packed tightly together. They pushed and strained, trying to find handholds. The fire roared, surging up the bank of the river.

Esen loosened her aching arms to cough into her hands. "We need more help," she gasped. "We're not strong enough. I'll have to ask a Rooted One to send help."

"There's no time," Fafnir said.

Through the foam in her eyes, she glimpsed his marten spring onto the top of the dam. Fafnir leaped off the marten's back and drove her away. He knelt between two logs, slipped his legs below —

And vanished within.

Esen's spirit knocked in her chest.

What was he doing? He would die in there.

"Fafnir!" she cried, starting forward. The waters surged against her middle, driving her back. She jolted as a small log flew out at the opposite end of the dam. The dryads on top tilted, loosening.

He was breaking the dam from the inside out.

To save the forest.

Tears started in her eyes. She hurled herself forward, pulling with all her might at the dryad on top of the dam. Cillian joined her.

"We have to get him out," she choked.

But as she pulled in vain, her arms straining, more logs flew out, away from them. The dryads on top tilted, loosening.

Cillian touched her arm. "We need to go."

She bit at her lip. She strained and strained, but the dryad was too heavy, and her arms too weak.

Another log flew out.

The dam sank with an awful groan. Water began to leak through.

It was no use.

She let Cillian pull her away. She fell onto the bank, gasping, as the last log flew out. The dam split open, waters crashing forth like a herd of leaping deer. Trunks hurtled down the bank. Throwing her arms over her head, Esen flinched as the waters struck her.

She lost herself in their fury.

FAFNIR THREW himself out from the dam. The river raged beneath him, as fierce as the sea in a storm. He squeezed his eyes shut, the wind tearing through his hair, his shirt.

Water slammed into him. All was sound, fury, chaos. He fought to draw gasps of air when his head was briefly above water. His body spun, his limbs torn in every direction, as he was forced down the current.

A wave crashed into the back of his head. He was shoved below the surface, his nose clogging, muck coating his throat. Bubbles streamed past him, splitting apart and surging toward the light shimmering above at the water's surface. He was sinking...

No.

He clawed at the water, straining. But the pressure was so intense, his limbs heavy.

He fell down, down, down. The light grew smaller, dimmer. The cold chilled his bones.

He had been here before. He should have died then. But Esen had appeared by the sheer grace of fortune, and saved him.

And how had he thanked her?

Pain flowed through him. The water warmed and thickened, like Isolde's blood. He could still feel the skin of her eyelids as he slid them shut forever. His chest shuddered.

He had ignored her for a thousand years. And then, despite everything, she had invited him back into her life.

Now she was gone, gone...

He wanted to live. Differently; like he should have all along. He wanted to explore all of the land with Esen and Isolde by his side. To see Isolde's home, learn her healing ways with animals. To see Esen Root, and meet her children. And dance with her, like she had offered...

The waters churned round his ears. There was a softness in it, as it folded about him. A caressing. His muscles strained, but still he could not lift himself.

At least he had done this for Esen.

He could rest...and maybe, wherever his sister was...he could join her.

At long last.

Distantly, he felt his calf collide with stone. The water bore down, pressing into him, but his calf was stuck. Lodged between two stones.

The next he knew, he was falling farther. Blood clogged the water, saturating his senses with copper. He felt nothing; only a warmth blossoming in his chest like a budding flower.

Something hard stopped his fall. The embrace of death...

He felt himself lifted, higher and higher.

As blackness folded over him.

GASPING, her spirit in her throat, Esen lifted Fafnir from the raging river. The waters streamed red from her hands. His left leg had been torn out at the knee. The white bone poked through, his flesh raw and red, blood oozing...

Cillian crouched by her, his eyes wide.

"Go get help for him!" Esen cried.

Cillian took off down the riverbank.

Esen laid Fafnir over a smooth stone, and fell to her hands and knees, water lapping up to her chin. She plunged her hands in the water and felt desperately along the bottom. Most of the underbrush had been burned away in the fire. Pulling out a handful of algae, she wrapped it around his open wound, but it kept bleeding, bleeding...

"E-Esen..." Fafnir's eyes blinked open, then he squeezed them shut, his head rolling back as sharp gasps burst from his clenched teeth.

The fires were gone. A layer of water covered everything.

He had saved the forest.

A wind breathed on her neck, scraping the limbs of the Rooted Ones above.

The Rooted Ones...

Green sinews had burst from Fiona's limbs as she had Rooted. Live, flexible fibers, like the inner muscles of his leg.

She closed her eyes, drawing in a deep breath.

Cillian hadn't returned. Fafnir would only have a few more moments to live. If she Rooted now, she might be able to close his wound, and save his life.

But then she would never Walk again. She had only seen a tiny fraction of the beauty of the land. She wanted to explore every mountain peak and valley, every cliff and crevice by the sea, and walk among the golden gorse of the northern mountains, where Fafnir had promised to take her.

If she Rooted, she would give up the very last thing she had.

When he had taken everything else.

The world swam through her tears. He was writhing, his chest heaving. Dying...

Aisling, and Ian, and her parents, and so many others—they would all be alive if not for him. It would be fitting for him to die.

She recoiled at the thought. It was a burning, angry thought, like a tangle of thorns. She had caused harm too by acting in rage, without thinking this through. He was here dying because of her. And his sister was dead...she shook her head, her chest tight.

From another lifetime ago, she remembered Cillian's story of Cerridwen. How she had molted everything ugly and black within herself and emerged like that brilliant butterfly, light and laughing.

This had all happened because the Cycle of Giving was broken.

Even if no other lived that way, even if the forest collapsed around her this very hour—

She would embody it.

"Fafnir," she said. "I'm going to Root to try to save you."

His hands twitched at his sides. "No. You would lose your Walk—"

"I know," she said. "I'm going to do it anyway."

A softness came over his face, his mouth parting, then his face screwed up again, tight with pain.

"Okay," he whispered.

She folded him gently in one hand as he looked at her, his eyes trusting. The sun beamed bright above. She fixed her spirit on its heat, lifting her free hand toward it.

The sun was so beautiful, a golden ball of dazzling light. She would remember it, and all the beauty she had seen, for the rest of her life.

She traced the sun's image in her mind. "Goodbye," she murmured.

She strained with all her might. But no shoots grew from her. How had Fiona done it?

Tears rolled down her eyes. Fafnir had grown still, his blood dripping from her palm.

"O Mother," she choked. "I need you. Please, show me how…"

The wind picked up, stirring about her, rattling her branches together. She felt a breath in her ear, whispering to her.

She was strong. She was mighty. She was one with the earth…

She would save him.

The bark on the tips of her fingers began to crumble apart.

Now.

Pressing her finger to his wound, she focused all her spirit there.

Careful, careful…

Soft green sinews shot forth from inside her fingertip, sewing into the skin and stanching the blood. Lowering her finger, she imagined the shape of his calf and let the sinews flow until something resembling a leg had formed beneath his knee. Craning her neck down, she bit at the end of the sinews, flinching with a stab of pain as she tore them from herself.

The hand holding Fafnir began to burst with green shoots. She felt her feet lengthen, the ends thickening, splitting open the earth beneath her to dive within. Lifting her chin, she raised the arm holding Fafnir as her body stretched upwards, her neck craning higher and higher.

She was earth. She was sky…

She was growing, thickening, lengthening on all ends. With the last of her control, she bent the hand holding Fafnir, weaving the last resemblance of her hand into a thick, sturdy branch, cradling his limp form.

Her roots dove deep below the cool earth, latching between stones, binding her still. The tips of her branches blossomed, splitting smaller and smaller, while the last features of her face dissolved into the bark. First her lips, then her nose…

The forest gleamed golden bright, then blackness overcame her as her eyes wove within her wood.

But she was not lost.

She could feel—truly feel—in a way she had never felt before. The way the sunlight tingled inside her bark. The fluids flowing within her. The black soil beneath her, nutrients seeping into her roots.

I am Rooted. One with the earth.

"Aeonida, dear Esen."

A voice, full and deep, trembled inside her core. But it was more than one voice. Thousands—no, tens of thousands of voices echoed within it, speaking as one whole.

"We are so proud of you."

Her spirit swelled with gladness.

Her Rooted brethren.

"Aeonida!" she cried to them. *"Please, share the news. Fafnir lies within my limbs. He needs help as soon as possible."*

A murmur of understanding flooded over her from her roots. She felt their attention turning from her, flowing outwards, as the message rippled through the forest.

WATER WET FAFNIR'S lips and slipped inside his throat. Niamh's pale face hovered over him, her brows tight with worry. Moonlight illuminated her hair a silver-gold. He choked, coughing up a thin stream of water. Iona's little head poked out of the cloth strapped over Niamh's chest, watching him. Rowan crouched behind Niamh, holding a ceramic jar.

"You're alive," Niamh breathed. She pocketed a waterskin as Rowan handed her the jar. Removing the lid, Niamh dipped a hand in and pulled out a piece of raw liver. The dark-red blood stained her fingertips. With a pair of scissors, she cut a piece off and placed it on his tongue.

"Wash it down with this," she said, and poured more water in his mouth. He swallowed, feeling the cold, clammy flesh slide down his throat. A slight tingle buzzed in his brain.

"W-where is…" He choked, then cleared the mucus in his throat. "Where is Esen? Is she okay?"

He tried to sit up, but Niamh pushed him down.

"Lie still," she said. "It's a miracle you are alive. You lost a lot of blood." Niamh cut another piece off the liver. "We're in her limbs," she added, smiling.

Fafnir started. He remembered Esen's branches swelling all around him, growing higher and higher as he soared with her, cradled in her palm.

She had Rooted. To save his life.

Because of his —

He looked down and jolted.

Smooth brown wood sprouted out from his knee, forming into a base at the end that somewhat resembled a foot. Gritting his teeth, he propped himself up, pulling back the tattered ends of his pants.

It was impossible. But somehow…

The bark was woven into his flesh, closing the wound. Where his skin met the dark wood, he scanned hard, but he could see no signs of infection.

A faintness came over him. He folded himself back down, the bark hard against his back.

Niamh leaned over him and slipped another piece of liver down his throat. "I didn't know it was possible either," she murmured.

Shame flooded over him. He let it pass over him like a cloud over the sky. "How is she?"

"She is worried for you," Niamh said, "but she is doing well. She has been communing with the other Rooted Ones, telling them all that has happened and asking for wisdom."

Fafnir nodded. He lay quietly, swallowing each piece of liver she fed him. At last, she tilted the jar over his mouth. The leftover blood oozed out, coating his throat. He gagged, choking.

"Why are you —"

"You are ghost-white," Niamh whispered. "You need blood."

He let her give him the last mouthful, cringing as the bitter taste filled his mouth. A quiet river of strength murmured down his veins.

Niamh dabbed the blood from his face with a brown linen cloth and slipped a soft pelt under his back. "Lie still for the next few days. You are in no state to get up yet. I will keep bringing you liver, and stronger food when you can take it. It's rabbit, if you're wondering."

She handed the vessel back to Rowan, who tucked it into a bag at his hip. She rose and put out a hand. A pine marten appeared, nuzzling Niamh. She looked like Saoirse. Niamh climbed onto the marten's back, Rowan climbing on behind her.

"Niamh, wait —" Fafnir called.

Niamh turned to face him. With the slight return of his strength, the fears came flooding over him all at once.

"Are all the fires put out? What happened to the other Walkers, and the faeries? Does the battle go on?"

Niamh's mouth twitched. "You stopped the fires, and only two Walkers perished. To your last question... we will see."

She made a clicking sound with her tongue, and her marten sprung off the branch, scrabbling down the trunk.

Fafnir lowered his head back down, staring up at the golden catkins swaying gently among Esen's branches. The full moon hung in the black sky. The stars shone brightly.

The sky had looked just like this as he'd watched the yellow wings of the butterfly device dance among the stars. Isolde had given it to him. Did he have it still?

He twisted his neck, fumbling through the bag at his hip. His journal, soggy and torn; crumpled pieces of cricket legs; sodden herbs...

His breath quickened as his fingers brushed wood. He folded his hand around it and pulled it out. The little yellow butterfly. One of the forewings had been torn, and both the antennae had snapped off, but it had survived.

He ran his thumb over the torn wing. Gently, gently.

Isolde's hands had held it just a few moons ago...

414

He twisted the silk, pressed it between his palms, and let go. It spiraled into the air, twirling among the stars, before falling.

Vanishing.

Like his sister.

Like his old life.

In a way, he was that butterfly. Wounded, with one more chance to live before death finally took him.

Shame flushed over him. He had chosen his immortality again, by allowing Esen to Root for him.

A gust of wind breathed through Esen's limbs, the catkins bowing with its flow.

But she had chosen to save him. His immorality was not his now, but a gift from her—and he wanted to give it back to her.

To live the life he always should have. The one Isolde had wanted for him.

But… would Esen even want him? He had wounded her beyond repair.

He clasped his arms over his chest, each breath slow, painful.

Esen's branches clattered softly in a melody. If there were words within it, he couldn't tell. He couldn't understand her.

"Esen," he said, knowing she could hear him. "I will learn Wind-Speak as soon as I can. And I thank you. For everything."

Her branches murmured in reply. He let the melody lull him to sleep.

FAFNIR FADED in and out of sleep. When he was awake, grief flowed through him like a river. He didn't know what to do except let it run, eroding him. Memories of his childhood burst up in him like flowers after a long winter. The silly games he played with Isolde, when the world to them was full of wonder and magic. The sticky taste of the honey cakes she used to make. The time she pressed his hand and held him steady, his anchor in the storm, as their parents fought.

All those years he spent alone… he would take them all back for just one more day with her.

When he finished eating on the morning of the fourth day, Niamh nodded at him. "I think you are ready. Saoirse can help you back down."

"Wait," he said. He fidgeted with his fingers. A part of him recoiled as he prepared to speak, but that part held no strength anymore. It was only fear.

He knew her, and she knew him. He did not have to be afraid.

"I… I want to Unite. With Esen."

A gentle smile broke over Niamh's face.

"Could I speak to her through you?" he asked.

"Of course."

Esen's limbs stirred above them. Niamh tilted her head, listening.

"Esen asked why," she said to him.

"Why I want to Unite with her?" he echoed.

"Yes."

He rubbed the pads of his fingers on his nails. He thought of Esen singing to the flowers, inspiring the river fae to dance. How she had labored for days to restore the mountain fae's homeland with gifts. How she had borne the sea fae's scorn with such strength, and still stayed to try to help them one more time.

How she had given up her Walk to save him, asking nothing in return.

"Because she lives with the doors to her heart open and blesses everyone she meets, despite the pain that it causes her, and I… I want to live like that. I want to work alongside her to help the forest."

For a long moment, Esen was still. Then her branches stirred with a rush, an emotion thick within the sound.

Niamh listened with her eyes closed, her brows upturned. "Esen said, 'Will you promise to the Mother you will live that way for every hour you have remaining, for as long as you find breath in your lungs?'"

A breeze fluttered against his face, stirring his hair. He put up a hand and let the wind course through his fingertips. He willed it to flow through him, empty him of himself so he was only wind, birdsong, and open hands.

"Yes," he said, his heart fluttering. "I promise to the Mother."

Esen stirred again.

"Okay," Niamh said. "She wants to Unite with you."

A breath escaped him.

Niamh helped lift him to his feet. He leaned heavily on her arm, breathing hard through his nose, and tested his left leg, feeling out the stability of the strangely shaped foot. The bottom was fortunately flat, with a hasty indication for a heel.

Still leaning on Niamh, he slowly brought his weight fully down on both legs, finding that only a dull throb of pain remained. The leg was surprisingly buoyant. He remembered the green sinews bursting from her hands. They must compose the interior structure.

How strange… They were already bonded. Her bark fused within his skin. Still no swelling had appeared at the joint, as though the elements that composed their bodies were largely the same, welding naturally together.

And yet there had been so much division between their kinds…

"Her heart chamber is a little ways down," said Niamh. "I'll have Saoirse take you there."

Niamh beckoned Saoirse over and helped him onto her back.

"*Aeonida*," said Niamh. She formed the sign of Saol over him with her fingers. Iona copied the gesture, smiling.

"*Aeonida*." He returned the symbol, and Saoirse leaped forward, gripping onto the trunk with her claws and scrabbling down. He held on tight.

Several branches below, Saoirse halted, huffing, before the familiar crescent-shaped crevice in the bark. Darkness loomed within. He stepped off Saoirse carefully, wobbling as his left leg touched the bark. Saoirse tucked herself behind him, steadying him.

"Thank you," he said to her, passing a hand through her fur before stepping within the chamber. He kept one hand on the wall to steady himself.

The darkness folded around him, a sleepy warmth greeting him. Along the inner wall, he traced the soft, red-brown wood, starting as his fingers touched the pale fur of a moth. With a flurry of wings, the moth flitted by him for a moment before slipping out into the dappled light of the forest.

Here, he would lay himself down, and wake mortal in the morning. With wings of hazel.

He glimpsed his hands trembling and drew them closer to his face.

There was that fear again.

But what could he have in an infinite number of years that he couldn't in a thousand years with Esen?

He breathed deep. The rich, musty fragrance of damp bark and earth filled his lungs.

There was a stillness within this space.

A serenity.

That was all he had ever wanted.

Dried leaves and chips of bark crunched under his feet as he folded himself down, curling into a fetal position. Placing his hands on his heart to steady them, he felt its rapid beat gradually slow to a quiet pulse.

He thought of Esen, and the trifold spirals of the *Aeonida* symbol she had borne on her wrist. His muscles relaxed. With one forefinger, he traced the spirals over his heart.

"*Aeonida*," he whispered. "Life is sacred."

A warmth spread over him, a tingling sensation whispering along his shoulder blades.

Where the wings would soon sprout.

He drifted to sleep.

EPILOGUE

Wind whistled through Fafnir's hair. The air tasted of salt. Countless disks of basalt surged before him, stacked and fitted together like the slots of a honeycomb. Moss grew between some of their seams. They extended far beyond him until the sea finally swallowed them.

If Esen were here with him, how would it feel to her? What would she do?

He glanced to his right. A massive rock sat on top of the others, shaped rather like a foot, with a flat base and a sloping curve up from it. He could see her in her Walking form, sitting on that rock like a queen on her throne, looking out over the sea as the sun glimmered on the waves.

A wind flipped the corner of his open journal page into his thumb. He smoothed it back and began to write hurriedly.

The sights, the smells, the sensations...

She would love this one.

Niamh flitted beside him, folding in her wings. She smiled. "I am glad you are doing that for her."

The sea sprayed on the rocks, hurling white foam.

"She wanted to see the world," he said quietly.

"Are you finished?" Niamh asked. He nodded. "Let's see if we find a family before the sun sets."

She leaped into the air, flapping, and waited for him.

He put his journal away and tested the toe-like structure he'd built into his left foot. It still bent fine. Putting as little weight on it as he could manage, he leaped into the air, flapping his hazel wings. When he was high enough, he caught a drift of wind and soared. Niamh flew alongside him.

After over a thousand years of living on his feet, he still hadn't quite gotten used to it.

The mountains of the north rolled beneath them. More of the honeycomb-like basalt was carved into the faces of the cliffs. An assemblage of lichen, moss, and short-cropped grass composed a flush of green against the rock. No dryads were Rooted here, not at this altitude. Two osprey catchers flew alongside them, cawing, before diving down toward the green sea.

They tipped down the face of the cliff into a small verdant valley. The scruffy crowns of birch rustled below. Spying a river, they swooped down and landed in the shade of the birch.

The rush of the water filled Fafnir's ears; a quiet, steady sound after the wind. They had scarcely walked more than a few wolves from the bank when he saw a thin trail of blue smoke billowing up from the reeds. Up ahead, they glimpsed an oaken door built into the incline of the ground. A trail of pink and white seashells led a path up to the door. Green moss grew above and below it, carpeting the entrance.

It was one of the nicer-looking homes they had seen in some time, but very small. Likely only one or two faeries lived here. Nodding to Niamh, he approached with her.

A small lantern flickered a slight yellow. He could hear the fireflies flitting against the ceramic, beginning to open their backs for the night.

Niamh knocked. A shuffling sounded within, then silence.

Niamh was just beginning to knock again when the door opened a crack. A pearl-white face looked back at them, her sea-green eyes narrowed. He could glimpse no wings behind her.

The door slammed shut. A typical response.

Niamh leaned toward the door. "We just want to talk with you. Why are you afraid?"

The door creaked open slightly. "You're their queen, aren't you?"

Niamh lifted her chin. "I am Queen of the Winged Ones, yes, ma'am. Let's discuss this over tea. We brought cakes we can eat."

As she spoke, Fafnir scanned the room through the crack in the door. It was neatly and prettily arrayed with a fastidious eye. A vast, intricate quilt spilled over from a couch onto the floor. She had much time on her hands, after all. By the window, a violin rested. He frowned at it.

The craftsmanship was rather lacking.

"I don't want your cakes," the faerie was saying. "Listen, I know where I stand. You won't—"

"Is that your violin?" Fafnir asked.

The faerie started. Her eyes swept down his face, then his body, and, as usual, widened at the sight of his left leg.

"Where did you get your measurements from?" he pressed.

She swallowed, her throat bobbing. "You're the Corrupted One."

Fafnir flicked an ear. The tale of what Esen had done for him had spread across the land like wildfire. None had known that a welding of bark and flesh was even possible before, and many scoffed at the idea until they met him face to face.

The Winged Ones called him the dryad friend. Those without wings called him corrupted.

To the Rooted Ones, he was simply Fafnir, with all his wrongs and strivings to atone stored like water in their roots. Remembered, and watched.

"Where did you get your measurements for your violin?" he asked again.

Her lips were pressed tight as a string. "From a good friend."

Some friend. "The artistry is very good. But the measurements are off. You won't get a full range of sound with the upper bout compressed like that. I can show how to make the classic model, with some modifications I've perfected. I could draw up a diagram with the right measurements. It'll just take a moment."

She stared at him. She was still hesitating on how to respond.

"Did you start making violins out of a love for the craft?" he asked. "Or so you could make just one beautiful violin that was born of your own sweat and blood to play?"

421

"To make one that will sing," she said. Then, hesitating, she added, "and this one doesn't."

She looked back at Niamh. "You said you had cakes?"

Niamh nodded. "Honey cakes. Fafnir's recipe. Well, his sister's. What's your name, ma'am?"

"Léan," the faerie said, her shoulders relaxing. "Come in, then, for just a moment."

Léan gathered up the ends of the quilt and folded it on the couch. The rich aroma of meat and spices wafted from a pot hung over the hearth fire. Beneath the window, he glimpsed a bed adorned with moss and woven blankets. It was big enough for two. She had a partner, then, most likely.

"Your quilt is beautiful," Niamh said.

"Thank you." The corners of Léan's mouth twitched, as though she was unsure if she would let herself smile.

Niamh laid a folded oak leaf on the table and unwrapped the edges to reveal a pile of spongy white cakes. The bottoms were slightly burned. While they had been baking in Isolde's large clay oven, Iona had pulled him and Rowan away to help her with a painting. It was a sophisticated piece for her age, and he'd gotten lost in analyzing the spatial relation of the black charcoal strokes with the emerald pigment until he'd caught a whiff of smoke in the air. He'd hurried to the clay oven with his heart racing. It was the first time he'd dared to attempt Isolde's recipe.

They were nowhere near as good as Isolde had made them.

Léan stood for a moment, watching Niamh unwrap the cakes, before turning to her larder. She pulled out a small kettle, filled it with water, and set it to boil beside the pot.

When she sat at the table, she gestured for them to do the same. At its center, two lit candles flickered on either side of a vase of flowers.

"You have a sharp eye, Fafnir," Léan said. "I'm going to have to give Madoc a good kick in the shins. I knew something was off with the one we made. It definitely is the upper bout."

Fafnir rested his elbows on the table. "What made you want to play?"

Her eyes tilted toward the ceiling, as though she were looking for the answer there. "It takes me out of myself. I like that."

He nodded. "That is why I play too."

Tearing out a loose sheet from his journal, he began to sketch a model for her, jotting down the measurements of each piece of the form, explaining as he went. Léan ate a cake while she watched. Niamh took one too.

The kettle began to screech. Léan rose and brought it to the larder. She filled two ceramic cups carved with lily designs and placed them on the table. She steeped a helping of lemongrass in each, then shoved the cups to him and Niamh.

The steam heated his face.

He kept drawing. He could tell she did not want to be thanked.

When he finished, he stood, stepping back from the table, and pulled out his own violin. "This is nearly the same model I've sketched out for you. See how it sounds."

Shrugging off the strap, he took his violin out from its case and handed it to Léan. She took it carefully and stepped back, folding it under her chin. She plucked at the strings with a sharp, delicate hand, before putting the bow to the strings. She played well. It was just the craftsmanship holding her back.

She gave it back to him. "It's very different. I like it."

He returned his violin to its case and strapped it back on. She was smiling openly now. Then her gaze flicked down to his leg.

"How... How is that possible?"

"We are more like the dryads than you might think," he said softly.

She kept staring, as though his leg was a puzzle piece she was trying to make fit in her mind.

"Why is it that you don't want to Unite?" he asked.

Her eyes darted around the room. At the long sweeping quilt. At the fire.

At his leg again.

She had lived such a comfortable life for likely over a thousand years, thinking she could live this way forever. But he could tell in her face.

She did not want the dryads to suffer.

Just as she moved to speak, a shadow cast over the room. A tall, lean faerie shuffled into the doorway, gripping a beetle by the legs over his shoulder. He dropped the beetle with a start, lowering his brow.

"Uniters," he snarled. "Get out of my house!"

He lunged forward and shoved Fafnir hard. The floor tilted. Fafnir stepped back with his left foot, trying to stop his fall, when the

423

wooden heel shattered. He toppled back, and arms caught him from behind.

"We need to go," Niamh whispered to him, steadying him. She turned toward the faerie, who stood with his shoulders hunched, his eyes dark.

"You may keep the cakes," Niamh said, lifting her chin.

The faerie ground his jaw. He whipped toward the table, seized the bundle of cakes, and hurled them at Niamh. She stepped lightly to the side. The cakes splattered onto the floor.

Behind the table, Léan stood with her back pressed against the wall. All the color had bled from her face. A flash of paper stuck out from her pocket.

His drawing.

Niamh helped Fafnir out the door. As soon as they stepped out, it slammed shut.

The last light of the sun cast golden streaks along the ground. Esen's leaves would be lit aglow right now, as though she wore a crown of golden fire.

"I'm sorry, Fafnir," Niamh said. She heaved a sigh, her face calming into the quiet strength he had come to know her for. "Are you all right?"

"I'm fine." He ran a hand through his hair. "I just have to fix my foot."

"Go home," Niamh said. "You've been away from Esen too long."

He gathered his breath. He hadn't seen her since spring. "Will you join another group? It is hard to do this alone."

"Elouan and a few of his tribe are farther down the plateau. I'll join with them."

He nodded. "Wind be with you."

He flapped his wings and soared above her. A wind found him and carried him away.

He flew out from the valley and down the slope of the mountains. There, the forest stretched out beneath him. There were still so many gaps in the canopy. As he neared Esen, the canopy thinned even more, revealing dryads that lay blackened and broken on the ground from more than three years ago, when the Great Battle happened, or so it was now called.

But there were more Rootlings than there had been in several hundred years. He glimpsed some as he flew, little brown bodies swaying beneath their mothers and fathers. And sometimes, he saw their faeries with them. Talking with them, dancing, or carving with them. Several waved as he passed.

Change was agonizingly slow, but it was happening.

The memory of Elouan's vision shimmered in his mind, alongside his and Isolde's game of other worlds.

There were worlds other than this one. Among them was a world where both dryads and fae lived together in harmony—a deeper harmony than the forest had ever known. Where fae United by choice instead of by law. And he needed to continue doing everything he could to help make it happen.

Even if he never got to see that world himself.

At last, he drew near the place where Esen grew. He flitted down, smiling at the sight of her green hazel crown. Cillian's bluer, softer leaves wove together with hers. Cillian had been visiting her the past two years and sharing stories with her, until she'd asked him to Root with her last summer.

Before that, he had carved the symbol of Esen's Walk into her trunk —a spiral rotating inwards that blossomed at the center into a butterfly's wing.

In the blue shadow of their leaves, there was a shimmer of movement. The breath escaped Fafnir. It was a little Rootling. He hurried down to flap beside her. She bore her own crown of spiked hazel leaves, uncurling before the sun. Her spring green eyes widened as she saw him. She waved shyly.

A single daffodil grew beside her, the golden petals stirring in the breeze.

"Fafnir!" Esen's voice swelled on the wind. "*She was born not long after you left. We didn't tell you, because we wanted it to be a surprise. Her name is Deidre.*"

A breath escaped him as emotion swelled in his chest.

Esen had another chance now. To watch a young Rootling grow and fill the forest with her laughter.

"*Aeonida*, Deidre," he said. "We are so glad you are here."

"*Aeonida*," she breathed.

He held up a hand to her. "One moment."

He flitted up to the deck he'd built around Esen's trunk, careful to hover just over the floor. He lowered himself in the doorway, leaning on the wooden beam of the doorframe. The faint smell of sage still lingered from the last time he'd burned incense in the spring. He grabbed a staff hanging in the entryway. That would support him until he repaired his foot.

Esen's branches stirred as he limped back out. The sound soothed him. He had missed the music of her voice.

"How are you?" she asked. *"How did it go?"*

"It was hard," he admitted. "But I am grateful to be back. I will tell you more later. I want to sing to Deidre first. I am so glad she has joined us."

"I am sorry," Esen murmured. *"But that would be wonderful. She would love that."*

He felt for his journal. Good; it had not been damaged. "And I filled a journal of places to share with you."

"Oh." Esen stirred. He could feel her smiling with delight. *"Thank you, Fafnir. I would love that. Deidre too."*

"I could share in just a moment," he said. "But first…"

He flitted onto her lowest branch and positioned his violin beneath his chin. He smiled at Deidre. "Would you like to hear a song?"

Deidre's eyes lit up like the sun. "Oh, yes! I've heard you play from beneath the dirt, but it was so muffled."

"Let's change that," he said, "and I'll help you make your first flute tomorrow, okay?"

"Okay!" she said.

Her delight was infectious.

Grinning, he put his bow to the strings and lost himself in the flowing melody of his song and the soft, melodic tones of Deidre's voice as she sang along. The steady thrum, thrum of Esen's and Cillian's branches joined, swaying in tune.

A butterfly flitted by, its wings gleaming golden in the sun.

TO BE CONTINUED...

Acknowledgments

In 2017, I sketched two interweaving trees in the forest I grew up in and felt them to be two lovers holding each other. I spent the rest of the summer roaming the woods — sketching, dreaming, and exploring Irish folklore. A world was forming inside me. It was the seed that would eventually become *The Rooted and the Winged*.

Firstly, I wish to thank all the trees of the earth that I have known. Even when I am at my lowest, just the act of stepping within the dappled light of the forest — and drinking in the sights and smells and sounds about me — has never failed to comfort me. I get so caught up in my head and my rattling thoughts, but trees challenge me with silence. With stillness. I have always wanted to be like them — rooted deep in the earth, and stretching higher and higher without end. Without words, they sing out *"I am alive!"* with the sheer delight of finding life in their limbs. They are beautiful, simply by being.

In 2021, the hurricane Ida, intensified from climate change, tore those two interweaving trees that I had drawn to splinters. When I returned next, I found only a withered husk remained.

A fire burned in my veins. I had meant to delay writing *The Rooted and the Winged* for several years. But I knew then that I had to write it as soon as possible. We must save the trees. Not only because they are the lungs of the earth, but also because they are beautiful. Without them, we would be lost.

My deepest gratitude goes out to my husband Derek. You were the signpost along my path, always guiding me back in the right direction when I got lost. I could never thank you enough for all the lengthy discussions, late night jokes, and your constant enthusiasm for my story and characters. You knew my story as well as I did. And often, frankly, you knew it better.

I was blessed to have *The Rooted and the Winged* pass through many hands during the drafting process. *Huge* thanks to every member of The Rogue Writers. My book would still be a poetic mess without you all! Thank you to Lottie Hayes-Clemens for being my dream developmental editor and providing such honest and encouraging feedback. Thank you to Tomorrow's Writers — Charles Barouch, Lara Frater, Robby Ferrell, and Joe Rackowski, for reading my book through not just once, but twice. And shoutout to Robby who read it *three* times! Thank you to my sister Amanda — you gave me the keys to the perfect ending when I was utterly at a loss. Aster Wylde, you get a special mention for supporting me in both writing and my art.

Thank you so much to my amazing beta readers — Holly Merry, Starr Green, and Mozy Adless, all authors themselves, as well as Louise, Kristin, Sarah, Danny, and Deborah.

Thank you to Rachelle from R.A. Wright Editing for cleaning up my book with your incredible line and copy-editing skills. And Cassie from Weaver Way Author Services for your expert formatting.

My book would not be the same without every one of you!

Thank you to Peter Elfman of Stereo Static for shouldering my audiobook as producer and so much more. I couldn't have done it without you. And to my best friend, Izzy, for bringing your passion for stories into my characters, and offering your talent for Niamh. And Stephanie Healy and Josef Boon, it was an absolute honor to have your talents bring Esen and Fafnir to life!

To Samuel Haines, you had a vision for my story, and you actualized it in a rich, wistful musical soundscape that I want to get lost in forever. Thank you so much for lending your talents to my story.

I want to close with a beautiful poem that D.E. Carlson, fellow fantasy author, wrote for me when I was trying to articulate the themes of my book. I am still in awe of it.

"Every choice ripples out to eternity,
Every life has meaning.
Every tree draws water from the earth,
Hope keeps us breathing."

— –D.E. CARLSON

ABOUT THE AUTHOR
SAMANTHA CURRAN

I am an author and illustrator with a focus on intricate wistful worlds. Within these worlds I utilize high fantasy elements to emphasize the beauty of nature and the human experience. In my free time, when I'm not creating stories, you may find me petting a cat or a plant. Both are equally likely.

I'd love to chat with you about books, art, faeries, you name it. Send me an email or direct message me on one of my socials.

Email: samantha@windweaverpress.com
Socials: https://linktr.ee/samanthacurran

Sincerely,
Samantha

GLOSSARY

RACES

Faeries/Fae: Created on the third day of creation by the Mother Wind. She wove the faeries from strands of her hair and imbued them with her immortality. She bid them to give up their immortality by Uniting with the dryads, and so give what was never theirs to begin with, so their hearts could grow in love.

Dryads: Created on the second day of creation by the Mother Wind. She breathed her spirit in the trees, and bid them to Walk for a time, before they would Root forever in the earth. Once Rooted, the dryads were called to hold up the earth as one family, bound together by their roots.

FAERIES

FAERIES WHO DWELL IN NON-DISTINCT REGIONS

Fafnir Fiachra (FAF-neer FEE-ah-kra): Wingless One. Brother of Isolde Fiachra. Son of Fiachra Siegfried.

Fiachra Siegfried (seeg-FREE-d) Winged One with alder leaves, United with Eoghan Alder. Father of Fafnir and Isolde Fiachra.

Gavin (GAH-vehn): Winged One with hawthorn leaves.

Ian Finvarra (EE-an Fin-VAR-a): Winged One with hazel leaves, United with Niall Holly and Rowena Hazel. Former King of the Fae. Former husband of Maeve Finvarra. Guardian of Niamh Finvarra.

Isolde Fiachra (es-OLD-uh FEE-ah-kra) Winged One with alder leaves. Sister of Fafnir Fiachra. Daughter of Fiachra Siegfried.

Léan (LEE-an): Wingless One.

Madoc (MAH-doc): Wingless One.

Niamh Finvarra (NEE-v Fin-VAR-a): Winged One with blackthorn leaves, United with Aoífe Blackthorn and Ruairí Blackthorn. Adopted daughter of Ian and Maeve Finvarra. Mother of Iona.

FAERIES OF THE RATH SÍORAÍ

Caden Walsh (KAY-den WahL-SH): Wingless One.

Maeve Finvarra (MAY-uhv Fin-VAR-a): Wingless One. Queen of the Fae. Former wife of Ian Finvarra. Guardian of Niamh.

Tiernan Alberich (TIER-nan AELB-erihk): Wingless One. Ranger to Maeve Finvarra.

RIVER FAERIES

Brighid (BREE-ghd): Wingless One.

Caoimhe (QUEE-va): Winged One with ash leaves. Diviner of the Nóinín Grove.

Iona (eye-OWN-ah): Wingless One. Daughter of Niamh Finvarra and Rowan.

Korey (CORE-ee): Wingless One. Chieftain of the Losgann Bank river fae.

Rhiannon (ree-AN-uhn): Winged One with elder leaves.

Rowan (ROW-an): Winged One with oak wings. Father of Iona.

Wynn (win): Wingless One.

Mountain Faeries

Adair (aa-DEHR): Winged One with rowan leaves. Former Diviner of Éigniú Valley. Mother of Elouan and Lugh.

Angus (ang-GUS): Winged One with apple leaves. Former Diviner of Éigniú Valley. Father of Elouan and Lugh.

Elouan (Eh-LOO-en): Wingless One. Diviner of Éigniú Valley. Son of Angus and Adair. Brother of Lugh.

Farrell (FAH-rel): Winged One with aspen leaves. Diviner of the Spéir Driofaires, a band of nomadic faeries who wander the southern mountains.

Lugh (loo): Wingless One. Son of Angus and Adair. Brother of Elouan.

Owen (oh-WEHN), Senan (SEN-an), Finley (FIN-lee), Reagan (RAY-guhn), Seán (sh-AW-uhn) Naoise (KNEE-sha), Shaw (SH-aw), Ciara (SEE-air-uh), Quinn (QUIN-n), Tierney (TIER-knee), Brendan (BREHN-duhn): Faeries of Éigniú Valley. All Wingless Ones.

Sea Faeries

Bedwyr (BED-wee-ir): Wingless One.

Hedrick (hEH-drih-k: Winged One with oak leaves. Deceased husband of Morgan. Father of Róisín.

Llyr (leer): Wingless One.

Morgan (MOOR-guhn): Winged One with cedar wings. Widow of Hedrick. Mother of Róisín.

Róisín (row-SHEEN): Wingless One. Daughter of Morgan and Hedrick.

DRYADS

Walkers

Cerridwen Willow (ker-id-WEHN): Willow dryad. A famous dryad of legend whose name is often recounted by Storykeepers.

Cillian Rowan (KILL-ee-an): Rowan dryad. Last of the Storykeepers.

Esen Hazel (eh-SIN): Hazel dryad. Daughter of Niall Holly and Rowena Hazel. Sister of Aisling Holly.

Fiona Elder (fee-OWN-ah): Elder dryad.

Tristan Blackthorn (TRIHS-tuhn): Blackthorn dryad. Son of Aoífe Blackthorn and Ruairí Blackthorn.

Rootlings

Aisling Holly (ASH-ling): Holly dryad. Daughter of Daughter of Niall and Rowena. Sister of Esen Hazel.

Brann Ash (BR-ahn): Ash dryad.

Deidre Hazel (dee-AIR-dra): Hazel dryad. Daughter of Esen Hazel and Cillian Rowan.

ROOTED ONES

Aoífe Blackthorn (EE-fah): Blackthorn dryad. United with Niamh Finvarra. Mother of Tristan Blackthorn.

Eoghan Alder (oh-WEHN): Alder dryad. United with Fiachra Siegfried.

Graham Cedar (GREY-am): Cedar dryad.

Niall Holly (NEE-ill): Holly dryad. United with Ian Finvarra. Father of Esen Hazel and Aisling Holly.

Onora Pine (oh-NOR-uh): Pine dryad.

Rowena Hazel (Row-WEHN-uh): Hazel dryad. United with Ian Finvarra. Mother of Esen Hazel and Aisling Holly.

Ruairí Blackthorn (RUE-ree): Blackthorn dryad. United with Niamh Finvarra. Father of Tristan Blackthorn.

PINE MARTENS

Saorise (SEAR-sha): Companion of Isolde Fiachra.

PLACES

Éigniú Valley (EHG-noo): A small valley among the southern mountains. Home of the mountain fae of Éigniú Valley.

Ifrati Falls (if-FRAUGH-tee): The largest waterfall along the River Ifrati.

Nóinín Grove (NO-nee): A tucked-away grove along the River Ifrati. Home of the river fae of Nóinín Grove.

Losgann Bank (LUH-s-guhn): A section of the riverbank of the River Ifrati. Home of the river fae of Losgann Bank.

Pool of Divination: A sacred pool located at the base of the Sage. Six dryad Elders grow in a circle formation around the pool.

Rath Síoraí (wrath SHEE-ree): The palace of the faeries. Built by dryads and faeries together not long after the Mother Wind first breathed life into the forest.

River Ifrati: The largest river of the land.

Sáile Cove (SAI-leh): A grotto cut into the rocks along the southwestern tip of the land. Home of the sea fae of Sáile Cove, and the building place of the Sióg Síaorí.

TERMS

Aeonida (ay-oh-one-EE-dah): A greeting and blessing of dryadic origin. It is used to both greet another and to wish them a good and fruitful life in the name of the **Mother Wind**.

Aon Mharú (ay-on-MAH-rue): A dryadic phrase meaning "no-kill".

Athas (AH-thus): A festival led by the dryads, held every late summer. The Walkers of the land gather to the Pool of Divination and spend three consecutive days and nights in song and dance. This is done to thank the **Mother Wind** for the warmth of summer and to pray for strength against the coming winter.

Aoradh (UAR-rug): The bond of the soul with the **Mother Wind**. It is considered to be the highest union of the **Trinity of Unity**.

Cnámha (KLAY-muhn): A guessing game common among both fae and dryads. One player hides two bones behind their back, one in each hand, while a second player tries to guess which hand contains the Aeonida bone, the bone marked with the symbol for **Aeonida**. At the same time, onlookers will play instruments, often for the purpose of distracting the focus of the guessing player. The game is often held in rounds, in which the players swap between the roles of hiding, guessing, and playing music. The winning team is the one who makes the most correct number of guesses.

Cycle of Giving: The wheel of sacrifice by which the forest survives. The faeries **Unite** with the dryads, the dryads **Root** to hold up the earth, and all the animals, insects, and plants give in their own ways. The idea is that if every creature gives in the way they are called to, the next creature down the line survives to be able to give too, and the next creature, and on and on. Thus, it is a cycle of giving and receiving, designed by the **Mother Wind** when she first breathed life in the forest.

Diviner: A faerie spiritual meditator, avowed with the duty of communing with the **Mother Wind**, sharing wisdom with the faeries, interpreting natural events, and healing the sick through medicinal practices and gifts requesting intercession from the **Mother Wind**.

Dragan (DRAE-guhn): Mysterious entities with a serpentlike form that appear on decaying bodies; especially the bodies of dryads and fae.

Grá (GRAH): The romantic love bond of the **Trinity of Unity.**

Mother Wind: The goddess of the land. She is believed to have breathed life into the land and called the **Cycle of Giving** into being. It is said that she has no physical form, but flies continually throughout the land. Her hair is so long that it is always brushing every crevice, creating wind as we know it. However, her face can only be in one place at any given time. Legend has it that you can tell if her face is near, if the wind is small and hot like a breath.

Nollaig (Nohl-EHG): The eighth of the festivals held exclusively by faeries on the grounds of the Rath Síoraí. It is held on the winter solstice and serves as a celebration of the new solar year.

Ranger: A Rath Síoraí faerie who serves as both the Faerie Queen and Kings' personal guard, as well as a scout of the land. They are trained to be highly skilled in archery.

Root/Rooted/Rooting: The act performed by a dryad when they tether themselves to the ground, becoming a **Rooted One**. It can only be performed once, and then the dryad can never move again. Before Rooting, a dryad is mobile with a body like that of a faerie, only made of wood, water, and sap, and about a dozen times taller. When a dryad Roots, they undergo a rapid transformation in which their mobile body disappears into the form of a tree.

Rooted One: The latest life stage of a dryad in which they are **Rooted** into the ground and can no longer move. They have lost the form of their mobile body, including facial features.

Rootling: The young life stage of a dryad where they are above the ground but still bound to the roots of their parents. They are stationary and dependent on the nutrients fed to them through their parents' roots to live.

Sage: The leader of the dryads. The Sage is composed of two sequoia dryads joined in the act of **Rooting**. Together they become the Sage. The Sage is meant to represent all three unions of the **Trinity of Unity**.

Spiorad (sp-EER-id): The term used for **Rooted One**s who dwell at high altitudes in alpine regions and grow in a twisted manner that is often horizontal rather than vertical. The word is dryadic in origin and means *"those who bend and do not break"*.

Sióg Síaorí (SHEE-ogh SHEE-re): The largest boat to have ever been built. Created by the sea faeries of Sáile Cove.

Stór (stor): The friendship bond of the **Trinity of Unity**. The term applies to friendships between dryads and friendships between faeries, but is most deeply represented by the act of **Uniting**.

Storykeeper: The keepers of dryadic history. These dryads are carved with symbols depicting the legends of their kind. Three Storykeepers are appointed at a time and are tasked to wander the land and share of their stories. It is also tradition for a Storykeeper to visit new **Rootlings** in their first year of life to teach them the ways of the land.

Taibhse (TIE-shuh): The seventh of the festivals held exclusively by faerie on the grounds of the Rath Síoraí. It honors the death of the season of light.

The Ancient Law: The commandment of the **Mother Wind** when she breathed life into the land, which was later carved into a stone tablet and erected on the front face of the Rath Síoraí. The Ancient Law reads as follows: "At age one hundred, a faerie shall **Unite** with a dryad and so give their immortality. At age three hundred, a dryad shall **Root** into the earth and so give their **Walk**. For the forest to survive, we must unite."

The New Law: The law created by Queen Maeve of the Fae. It revoked the commands of the **Ancient Law** and required that every faerie must be given the right to decide if they wish to **Unite**.

Trinity of Unity: A concept believed to have come from the **Mother Wind** herself. Every individual is divinely called to form each of the three relationships of the Trinity of Unity, and in doing so, they are considered to be a wholly realized and fulfilled individual. The three relationships are **Grá**, romantic love, **Stór**, friendship, and **Aoradh**, the love of the Mother. **Stór** and **Grá** form the foundation of the triangle of the trinity, as they are mirrors of the highest form of love, **Aoradh**. **Aoradh** rests at the tip of the triangle.

Unite/United/Uniting: A sacred, mysterious act in which a faerie gives their immortality to a dryad. The act is performed when a faerie enters a dryad's heart chamber, a small hollow inside their trunk. When both the faerie and the dryad fall asleep simultaneously, the immortality seeps out from the faerie and is absorbed by the dryad in a process that eludes understanding. Both become fertile in the process, and the dryad's lifespan is lengthened by a few hundred years. In return for their sacrifice, the faerie receives wings made of the leaves of their dryad. Now that the two are bonded, when one loses their life, so does the other.

Walk: Can be a noun or a verb. This defines the period of time in which a dryad is a **Walker**.

Walker: The mobile life stage of a dryad. They stand about a dozen times the height of a faerie, and their branches grow to be as large as twice the height of their bodies.

Winged One (wing-ED one): A faerie who has **United** with a dryad.

Wingless One (wing-LESS one): A faerie who has not **United** with a dryad.

CURSES

Swear words center on the concept of decay and joining the loam of the forest. The word "**rot**" is the basis for much of their cursing, and can be used on its own, but also paired with a variety of phrases including "**rot take you**" to wish condemnation on another, "**rot it all**" to announce exasperation, and "**rot-brained**" to imply another's lack of intelligence.

A NOTE ON FAERIE LAST NAMES

The regions within the border of the Rath Síoraí contain the densest concentration of faeries in the entire land. Therefore, these faeries give last names to their children. The last name of the child will either be the first name of the mother, or the first name of the father. Last names are not common outside of these regions.

Printed in Dunstable, United Kingdom